# Two Steps from Darkness

A Novel by
**Jack L. Bodden**

Two Steps from Darkness

Copyright 2022- Jack L. Bodden

All Rights reserved

## Dedication

I want to thank my wife Marie for her loving support and encouragement to continue writing. She has been both my helpful editor and gentle critic. I also wish to express my appreciation to my daughter, Beth Felker. She has also been a strong source of encouragement as well as a lover of the same genre of fiction as I enjoy. Thanks also to Marie Gray for her careful proofreading and helpful suggestions.

December 2022

Prologue

The teacher filled then lit his pipe with great care. A look of contentment on his face, he blew a single smoke ring into the air while a small audience settled in around him. He told a story of a child, sent out into a cold and uncaring world by his cruel father. The child clutched a nickel in his small hand as he ventured forth from his home. Soon the child was drawn by the bright lights, the color and excitement of a carnival he saw in the distance. As he approached the carnival's entrance, the child found that admission cost a dime. Try as he might the child could find no way to gain entrance to the carnival. Thus, it seemed that his dreams of adventure and fulfillment, all the things a child could wish for must remain beyond his reach, seeming to both tease and taunt him. Where could he go? There he stood, paralyzed, between an unattainable goal and an uncaring father. Finally, the child sank to his knees and cried out for help, but no one responded. At this point in his story, the teacher paused, and his audience waited eagerly for the story to continue, hoping for some resolution to the boy's dilemma, but none was offered. The teacher rose silently and slowly departed, leaving his audience frustrated and unfulfilled, their many questions left unanswered. How could this be? Was there no God, no mercy, no balm in Gilead? As the teacher walked away, his listeners who had gathered began to disperse with soft murmurs and sad countenances. Suddenly one among them stopped and called out to the others. "This is wrong. We can create a new ending to this story!" Her call was met with pessimism and despair, but the woman was not deterred. She stood straight and tall as she continued speaking. "Perhaps we cannot give the child all that he needs in order to enter the carnival, but we can give him love. We can stand beside him so that he knows he is not alone. This we can do and this we must do." Hope was still alive even in the midst of the darkness.

Yes, there are two paths you can go by, but in the long run there's still time to change the road you're on.

-Led Zeppelin

## Chapter One

I ain't got no home and no place to roam.

Clarence Henry

Nathan Richards pushed the chair back from his desk and gazed dreamily out the window. From the dim confines of his small third floor office in the Gray Building which housed the Duke University Divinity School, Nathan had a good view of the university Chapel. Its' neo-Gothic style architecture always drew admiring stares from Nathan and all who gazed upon it. Since it was early December and finals were over, the campus was nearly deserted with only a few straggling students wandering across its grounds. Typical of December in Durham, skies were overcast, and an occasional snowflake sailed lazily past Nathan's office window. The trees had all shed their leaves which only a couple of weeks earlier were ablaze in fall colors. Now the campus appeared to have settled in for winter, and Nathan could hardly believe that he was finishing his second fall semester at Duke. Watching the occasional snowflake drift by seemed to lull him into a near trance-like state, but his reverie was abruptly interrupted by a large crow which landed on the window ledge mere inches from his face. The crow shook itself vigorously as if to eliminate any snowflakes which might have landed on its shiny black feathers, and then it turned to look squarely at Nathan. The bird's sudden appearance and impertinent stare caused Dr. Richards to draw back reflexively from the window. The crow departed almost as suddenly as it appeared, but its brief presence awakened a powerful memory of the first time a crow appeared on his office window at Trinity United Methodist Church in Lubbock, Texas. That memory triggered a surge of anxiety through Nathan's body that felt like an electric charge. Over the next several minutes he relived the dramatic and terrifying events of the two years Nathan and his wife Alexis spent there. Nathan had been trained as a clinical psychologist, receiving his doctorate from Ohio State. After completing his degree, Nathan worked as a staff psychologist at a VA hospital in Chillicothe, Ohio for several years before deciding to enter the seminary at Southern Methodist University. After seminary, Nathan served as an associate minister at a church in the Dallas area before accepting an unusual assignment at a church in Lubbock. Because of his training and experience as a psychologist, Nathan was strongly encouraged by his bishop to take his first appointment as senior pastor at a large church in Lubbock. Controversy within the Methodist church hierarchy over issues regarding gay marriage and the ordination of gay ministers combined with the murder of Trinity Methodist Church's senior pastor had threatened to fragment the church. Because Trinity UMC was seen as a once strong but still influential church on the South Plains of Texas, it was viewed as vital to keep Trinity and its congregation together. After some initial hesitation and resistance, Nathan accepted this unusual appointment which was to last no more than two years. After moving to Lubbock, Nathan and his wife were confronted with a series strange and sinister experiences. Gradually he began to see his chief nemesis as a powerful figure in the community named Arte Mantus. After a time, Richards began to understand that Arte Mantus was more than just a rich and influential person; he might well have been either the devil or perhaps one of Satan's lieutenants. Nathan was convinced that Mantus had orchestrated the death of his predecessor at Trinity Church and somehow caused Nathan's pregnant wife, Alexis, to become infected with the Corona virus. These and other acts were apparently part of Mantus' strategy to force Nathan to recant his faith and abandon the church. As his mind reviewed the events of the time in Lubbock, Nathan could feel his anxiety increase until at last he literally had to wrench his thoughts away from the memory of his final terrifying confrontation with what he knew to be the ultimate evil. Although Nathan refused to let his mind fixate on the details of his showdown with the evil one, he sensed that it was not the end of the story. Nathan completed the two years in Lubbock and he was reasonably successful in holding the church together. His wife, Alexis recovered from the virus and delivered a healthy baby girl. Perhaps because of their experiences in Lubbock, Nathan ventured down a new career path, accepting an academic appointment at Duke University. Nathan always felt deep down that he was probably given the position at Duke because of the strong recommendation he received from one of his former professors, a Duke alumnus and because he had become somewhat of a folk hero in the Methodist church. After arriving at Duke, Nathan quickly found that the world of academia was quite different from the worlds of clinical psychology or the ministry. His appointment at Duke was a joint appointment, halftime in Psychology and halftime in the Divinity School. To his chagrin, Nathan soon realized that a joint appointment looked good on paper, but the reality was a bit more problematic. Each half of the appointment tended to treat him as though he was fulltime. Thus, he ended up with what amounted to two fulltime appointments rolled into one. Nathan's trip down memory lane seemed like a nightmare, from which he was more than happy to be "awakened". There was a moment of confusion as the chirping sound of his office phone brought him back to the present. The phone call was from the Divinity School Dean's secretary asking Nathan if he could stop by Dean Albritton's office before heading home. *I wonder what the Dean wants Maybe he's going to invite me to a Christmas party at his house.* Nathan chuckled to himself at the idea of being invited to the Dean's home for a Christmas party. Although he didn't know Dean Albritton well, he never seemed like the partying type to Nathan. He glanced at the clock and was surprised to see that it was already 4:45 pm. *Where had the afternoon gone?* Nathan peered out the windows and noticed that evening was beginning to assert itself. The sky looked much darker and the snow had begun to come down in earnest. Nathan put on his overcoat but left it unbuttoned as he closed his office behind him and headed for the stairs. The Dean's office suite was on the main floor of the building. Nathan descended the stairs and then headed down the hall towards the Dean's office. He smiled as he approached the door to the office; it was decorated with a large, jovial looking Santa Claus cutout. Somehow a smiling Santa Claus with a bag full of toys just didn't seem to fit Nathan's impression of Dean Albritton. After exchanging pleasantries and seasonal greetings with the dean's secretary, Nathan knocked and entered Dean Albritton's office. Thanks to widespread COVID 19 vaccinations, the requirements of wearing face masks and social distancing had been greatly relaxed, so neither man wore a mask and hand

shakes were back in vogue

"Good afternoon, Nathan", Albritton said as he rose from his chair to greet Nathan. "Thank you so much for stopping

by. Do you have a couple of minutes? "Nathan wondered about the purpose for which he had been "invited" to stop by the dean's office. Dean Albritton was one of the pillars of the Divinity School, and he looked like the epitome of a scholar, even down to his sport coat with its elbow patches. A world renown Old Testament scholar, this was Albritton's second stint as Dean. He had stepped down a few years ago, ostensibly so he could spend more time with family and devote more energy to his writing. He was brought back rather abruptly at the end of the previous spring semester following the removal of Dean Marsha Grant. Grant was asked to resign over her handling of some highly controversial issues primarily surrounding the rights and recognition of LGTBQ students. Also, during her tenure, student applications as well as funding had declined.

Dean, I have plenty of time. What can I do for you?" The dean invited Nathan to take a chair. Apparently not wanting his desk to be a barrier between them, Albritton rounded his desk and pulled up a chair alongside Nathan. Albritton had a reputation as someone who never seemed to be in a rush. Even his manner of speaking was measured and unhurried.

"Nathan, I am sorry I haven't made time to visit with you sooner. Things have been a bit hectic for me since returning to this office. It wasn't something I expected to be doing at this stage in my career. What with the holiday break looming, I just wanted to touch base with you and see how things were going since joining the faculty. Are you settling in and feeling at home?

"Somewhat relieved, Nathan smiled as he responded. "Thank you, Dean. Things are going pretty well. I have enjoyed my classes a lot although I have to admit the transition to academia has been more challenging than I expected. "Dean Albritton leaned forward in his chair as he inquired, "How so, Nathan? Is there something I can do to help?"

Nathan shook his head. "I think it is just me. I guess I need to better allocate my time and energy…set my priorities, but the joint appointment sometimes causes me to wonder which department is my real home or do I have a home? Even though my initial training and experience was as a psychologist, I somehow feel more at home here, in the Divinity School."

Dean Albritton gave a knowing smile before he spoke. "Nathan, when I was in high school back in Wisconsin, I had a close friend, probably my closest friend. He was bi-racial. His dad was Black and his mom was Asian. His parents met while his father was in the military and stationed in Korea. I remember he once told me that because of his mixed parentage, he never knew where he belonged. His mother maintained close ties with her family who remained in Seoul while his dad's family all lived in the deep south. So, you can imagine what some of his family gatherings were like. His name was Lee and he would sometimes say he didn't know if he was Black or Asian, American or Korean. Although he was rather successful both as a student and an athlete, deep down he never seemed happy or at peace with himself. I guess you could say that psychologically he had some real identity issues."

"Yeah. That pretty much captures the feelings I have," Nathan said with a sigh. "In many ways I probably think more like a psychologist, but my heart seems drawn towards spiritual matters. I know I need to get a research program going in Psych, but I can't seem to identify an area of real interest." Nathan could feel a growing desire to unburden himself of the frustration and tension he had been carrying almost since the day he arrived on campus, but he wondered how far he should go. "I, uh, I don't want to sound like I am complaining. Dr. Quinn in Psychology has been great. He hasn't pressured me at all…I…just know what I have to do."

"Nathan, you know that the Divinity School is considered by the university to be your primary appointment, so we make the final tenure and promotion decisions…with input from Psychology, of course".

"Yes, Dean, I know that, and I really appreciate your understanding…but, as I said…I am not complaining, I just need to sort things out and get going."

Dean Albritton glanced at his watch as he spoke. "Nathan, it is getting late and I know you are probably anxious to get home before the snow starts to pile up, but I'd like to make a suggestion if you don't mind."

Nathan's countenance brightened when he replied, "I would really appreciate that, Dean."

"Well," the Dean began, then paused. "It just occurred to me that there might be a way to kill two birds with one stone so to speak. I was thinking about the book you wrote about your experience in Lubbock…what was the title?"

Where Does Evil Live?", Nathan responded.

"Yes, yes, that's it. You might research and write about evil…from a psychological and spiritual perspective. Let me explain. In your book you never could really identify how you saw the Satanic figure. What was his name?"

"It was Mantus, Arte Mantus", Nathan replied.

The Dean nodded and continued. "You also expressed difficulty seeing evil as an entity, a figure like Satan as pictured by Dante."

Nathan's interest had been peaked and he listened intently, "Go on please, Dean."

Dean Albritton rose from his chair and walked over to the large book case where he pulled out an ancient appearing Bible which he held out towards Nathan. "Remember the stories in here?" Albritton then turned and laid the Bible on his desk. "You know how Jesus was pure and without sin and the many miracles he could perform. You also know that as his disciples grew in their faith, they could also perform some pretty impressive miracles as well, right?" Nathan nodded in agreement but remained silent. Albritton continued, his enthusiasm obvious. "The Catholic church has a set of requirements someone must meet before they can be declared a saint of the church, and one of those criteria is the performance of a miracle or miracles. Here's what I am thinking...what if a mortal human being were to become so committed to doing evil...so perfectly evil that he or she would then be able to perform some *miraculously evil* acts? Could that person become a *devil* instead of a *saint*? Certainly, as a psychologist I think you would agree that the more evil acts a person performs, the easier it becomes to do still greater evil in the future...a complete erosion of conscience. So, is it possible that the devil, as we have come to know him, is, in reality, a perfectly evil human being, someone beyond redemption?" Dean Albritton sat back in his chair and folded his hands in his lap while he looked intently at Nathan.

Several seconds passed before Nathan spoke. "Hmmm, what an interesting idea, Dean! I think you've got something. I really need to give it some thought! Thank you." On the drive home, Nathan was pretty much on autopilot, his mind playing with the idea suggested by his dean. As a result, he paid scant attention to the increasingly heavy snowfall or the evening traffic. Twice cars honked at him when the traffic signals turned green, but he hardly seemed to notice. Perhaps it was only the hand of God that kept him safe on his drive home.

Chapter Two

Staring at the fire for hours and hours while I listen to you…

-Crosby, Stills and Nash

It was dark by the time Nathan pulled into the driveway of the house he and Alexis had leased. It was a three-bedroom ranch style home built in the late 196's, and they both felt lucky to find such a comfortable place only about twenty minute drive south of the campus. The house was situated on a one-and-a-half-acre wooded lot which was great for their German Shepherd, Jacob, more commonly known as Jake. The snow was falling heavily now, creating an almost hypnotic effect as the countless flakes danced in the car's headlights. *It is almost like being inside a snow globe,* Nathan mused as he turned off the car's ignition and then hurried on the sidewalk around to the front door of the house. Pausing on the porch, Nathan stomped his feet on the door mat in an effort to shake the snow off his shoes. As he did, he could hear Jake start barking excitedly inside. *One nice thing about a dog, they're always glad to see you even if you are only gone for a few minutes.* The inviting interior of the house had been extensively remodeled a few years ago and it now had a remarkably modern, open-concept feel to it.

Alexis looked up from the cooktop in the kitchen, greeting Nathan with a smile. "You got home just in time. The snow is really coming down! Jake and I were starting to get worried about you. It looks like we could have a white Christmas."

"The Dean asked me to stop by his office before I left, and we ended up talking longer than I expected. Sorry I didn't think to call you." Nathan had to keep pushing Jake down in order to make his way to the kitchen where he could finally give Alexis a hug. "It's good to be home. Driving in the snow at night is a bit scary. Seeing the snowflakes in the headlight is kinda disorienting to me."

"What did Dean Albritton want to talk to you about?", Alexis said, a note of mild concern in her voice. "Nothing serious, I hope."

No, it was actually a useful visit. I think it was intended to be a gentle reminder that I need to be preparing for my first tenure review coming up next semester, but it turned out that he gave me a really good idea for a book I might write. I guess I have been worrying some about how to satisfy the university's requirements for tenure and promotion. I knew there would be pressure to publish here, but I just didn't know how to get going. Having two masters, one in Psychology and one in the Divinity School has seemed more than a bit daunting. I never could figure out how to satisfy both departments, but the Dean gave me an idea that just might work. If I can pull it off, it could make it so I don't have to develop two separate lines of research, or as the Dean put it…I could kill two birds with one stone."

"I am all ears. Tell me all about it," Alexis said with a smile. "It's good to hear an adult's voice. Jake is a good listener, but he doesn't talk much, and bless her heart, our little girl is just full of questions. She also just couldn't wait for you to come home and help her build a snowman."

"Ok, I will, but first I am going to get us each a glass of wine and then stand in front of the fireplace so I can get warm." Nathan poured Alexis and himself a glass of unoaked Chardonnay and then walked into the living area where he warmed himself in front of the crackling fire Alexis had started a couple of hours earlier. "Oh, man…the fire feels good," Nathan remarked as he felt the fire warm his back while the wine warmed his insides.

Daddy, Daddy, look what I drew for you! Elizabeth Richards, Nathan's three-year-old daughter whom they affectionately nicknamed Lizzy, emerged from her bedroom and came charging up to her dad who Gave her a big hug. "Look, Daddy; I drew a snowman! Can we go outside and build one? Please!"

In the morning, sweetie. It's dark now and very cold. Brrrrr! But that is a great picture, and we'll make one just like it tomorrow. Daddy doesn't have to go to work then so we'll have plenty of time and lots of snow to work with. Ok?"

Lizzy made a brief pouty face but then skipped into the kitchen to show her mother the drawing of the snowman.

Alexis carefully inspected Lizzy's drawing, then handed it back to her daughter. "Lizzy, that is so good, honey. I wonder if you could go back to your room and draw some Christmas pictures we can send to grandma and grandpa while Daddy and I talk?" Elizabeth seemed to like the suggestion of creating more art and she headed off to her room, followed on her heels by her close friend and canine guardian, Jake. After successfully distracting their daughter, Alexis joined Nathan by the fire. He then described for her the idea the Dean had suggested. Although still just a vague concept, Nathan explained that the book would explore the concept of evil and how, for some individuals, doing evil becomes a means by which they may be gradually transformed into something demonic. He went on to suggest that if some persons, by developing a strong faith and by living pure lives, might be able to perform saintly, miraculous events, perhaps the opposite could be true for persons whose lives were corrupted by evil living. "Consider Charles Manson for example. Perhaps a person like him might, over time, become a truly demonic figure."

"Do you think that was what you saw there at Hell's Gate in Lubbock? If I understand what you are proposing, Arte Mantus wasn't Satan *per se* but a demon-like human being? That's a pretty radical idea, isn't it? It is certainly a reversal of what you thought back then." Alexis was clearly interested in but somewhat taken aback by Nathan's hypothesis.

"Yeah. I think that is what I am suggesting. Maybe the devil, or Satan, or whatever name you like isn't a fallen angel, but a human being who chose to travel down the path of evil and corruption rather than moving on towards perfection or sanctification as John Wesley suggested. And there may be not one devil but many devils; you and I encountered one of them." Nathan finished his wine and seemed to drift off momentarily into an inner reality of thoughts and ideas. After a few moments he seemed to refocus. "The real beauty of such a research topic is that it could be something valued both by psychology and theology."

After dinner Lizzy played tug of war with Jake, a game Jake always won rather easily. Eventually she seemed to run out of gas and Alexis put her to bed. Finally, the house grew very still. Alexis and Nathan sat silently watching the fire slowly burn down to a bed of bright red embers. The only sound now was that of the wind swirling around the house and Jake's soft snoring as he slept at Nathan's feet. There was an almost tangible feeling of peace which had settled inside the Richard's house, while outside in the December darkness evil waited.

Chapter Three

The wolf that one hears is worse than the Orc that one fears.

-JRR Tolkien

Sometime during the night, the snow stopped falling, but by first light, there was a good four inches covering the ground, creating a scene worthy of a Hallmark Christmas card. Lizzy could hardly wait to get outside and start building her snowman. Nathan hurried to take a few sips of his coffee before allowing his daughter to drag him out into the cold.

"Lizzy, let me get your coat buttoned. It is really cold out here." Elizabeth held still for a couple of seconds while Nathan buttoned her coat before she started to gather up the snow in her hands. "Where are your gloves?", Nathan asked in an exasperated tone of voice.

Come on Daddy! Help me. I don't need my gloves," Lizzy hollered as she began to create a small mound of snow.

Kiddo, let's try to start rolling a ball of snow. As we roll it, it will get bigger. That will be the base, then we can make two smaller balls to be the rest of the body." Nathan demonstrated the snow ball rolling method which seemed to work in the relatively wet snow. It wasn't long before Nathan and Lizzy had built a six-foot-tall snowman in their side yard.

"Brrrr! Let's go inside and get some hot chocolate. You and Mom can decide what clothes to put on our snowman."

"Okay. I think I will call him Mr. Frosty!" Seemingly oblivious to the cold, Elizabeth, Lizzy danced around the snowman a few times beforefinally heading inside with her dad. Once inside, Lizzy recruited her mom and together they searched through a couple of closets in order to find appropriate attire for Mr. Frosty. Finally, Lizzy and Alexis came up with an old Texas Ranger's baseball cap belonging to Nathan and an ugly plaid scarf which Nathan's mother had given him some years back. Alexis secured a large carrot from the refrigerator to use as Mr. Frosty's nose.

Nathan took several charcoal briquettes out of a Kingsford charcoal bag in the garage which would serve as Frosty's eyes and mouth. Giving the charcoal to Alexis, Nathan headed for the fireplace to warm up "Could you do the honors with Lizzy? I need to thaw out."

Yeah, I guess so," Alexis said as she pulled on her overcoat. I can't believe how excited she is. I don't think Lizzy feels the cold at all.

Alexis called to their dog Jake as she and Elizabeth headed out the door. "Come on, Jake! You can help us with Mr. Frosty." Jake hopped up from his bed by the fireplace and headed out the door with Alexis and Lizzy. Several minutes passed before Alexis stuck her head back inside the house and called to Nathan in a very excited voice. "Nathan, come quick! I think there is a wolf out here!"

Nathan could hardly believe his ears as he raced to the door without bothering to put on his heavy coat. Alexis, Elizabeth, and Jake were all standing near Mr. Frosty looking towards the wooded perimeter of the property. Nathan scanned the edge of the woods but saw no wolf.

"Where is it?", Nathan asked, anxiety evident in his voice."

"He's gone!" He was right over there when I came in to get you, but now he's gone." She pointed toward a group of pine trees about 100 yards away.

"What did Jake do?", Nathan asked, looking down at his German Shepherd. Nathan noticed the hackles on Jake's back. "Did he charge at the wolf?"

"No. He took a couple of steps towards the wolf then stopped in his tracks. He growled softly but that's all. I think maybe he was afraid. See his tail is still between his legs."

Nathan knelt beside Jake and stroked his head and neck. "What's the matter, boy? Did the big bad wolf scare you?" Jake looked up at Nathan and his dark brown eyes seemed to reflect fear. "I have never known Jake to be afraid of another dog, have you?"

"No. I haven't. The wolf was pretty big, certainly bigger than a coyote. It was hard to be sure about its color, sorta grey I think, and it just stood there looking at us. Jake just stared back at him. It was scary. I don't think we can let Lizzy play outside unless one of us is with her. Did you know there were wolves in this area of North Carolina?"

"I did not. I'll call around the university, maybe somebody in the vet school or animal sciences department can tell me if there are wolves in this area. Our snowman looks great, but let's go inside and warm up. As he spoke Nathan took another long look at the edges of their property but saw nothing. Back inside, Nathan made several calls before connecting with a professor Dandridge in the Wildlife Management Department. After introducing himself, Nathan described what his wife had seen earlier in the day. "Are there any wolves in this part of the state?"

"Well, actually there are a few. The last estimate I saw indicated that there may be around twenty red wolves living in the wild in North Carolina. Most of them are located in the eastern part of the state, but one or two might find their way this far west. In the entire country there are only about 250 living in protected and managed areas. The red wolf is the most endangered species of wolf in the world. The grey wolf has been extinct in North Carolina for many years. What did this wolf look like?

"I am pretty sure that what my wife saw this morning was a wolf and not a coyote or dog. We have coyotes in Texas and know what they look like. She described it as slightly grey in color and definitely larger than a coyote. Are they dangerous? My wife was pretty concerned since we have a two-year-old daughter."

Well, what you have described sounds like a grey wolf. As far as I know there are no more grey wolves in North Carolina, and red wolves are just slightly bigger than a coyote. As to your question about dangerousness, any wild animal can be dangerous, but a single wolf, if that is what it was, would be very unlikely to attack a human…but a small child…possibly. Wolves are pack animals, and that is how they hunt. The one you saw could be like a scout, searching for an easy kill or maybe just a loner. I would definitely not let your daughter play outside unescorted."

"Thanks, Dr. Dandridge. I just have one other question. We have a seven-year-old German Shepherd who is a pretty good size dog. He is normally very protective, but my wife said that when he saw the wolf he just froze. He didn't charge the wolf or even bark. Would you say that was unusual?"

"Not really. German Shepherds are big, powerful dogs but they are really no match for a wolf, even a red wolf. If your dog was cornered by a wolf or if he thought the wolf was going to hurt you or your child, he would probably fight, but it would likely be a losing battle. I am a little surprised he didn't bark, but not surprised that he didn't charge the wolf. I wouldn't worry too much about the wolf, just be careful and don't let your daughter play outside unless you or her mother is with her. The wolf is probably a loner and will move on soon."

Nathan thanked Professor Dandridge and then relayed what he had learned to Alexis. "He did say that it was probably a lone wolf and likely to move on. There probably are no large wolf packs in the area."

"Well, I am glad you called him, but I have to admit, it shook me up. I would swear that wolf was studying us!" Alexis was clearly shaken by the appearance of the wolf, and she found little comfort in the information Nathan had gathered from Dr. Dandridge. "Do you think it would be a good idea to get a pistol for protection?"

"Lexi, you know I don't want another gun in our house, especially a pistol. We've got that old shotgun that belonged to my dad, and that is more than enough. We'll be okay." Despite his assertion that they'd be okay, several times during that day, Nathan found himself drawn to the window to look for the wolf. A couple of times he thought he saw some movement in the wooded area east of the house, but each time closer inspection revealed nothing. As evening drew nigh Nathan and Jake went outside under the guise of inspecting Mr. Frosty, but they saw only a few hardy birds moving about in the trees.

The day of Christmas eve arrived and the weather had warmed some. As a result, the snow cover had begun to melt and Mr. Frosty was now several inches shorter than the day before. Elizabeth was clearly disturbed by Mr. Frosty's condition. Not only was he shorter but also, he had begun to list to one side like a drunken sailor on shore leave. So, at Lizzy's insistence the family ventured out after breakfast to see if they could do something for Mr. Frosty, but due to the warmer weather and lack of snow, there was little they could do but replace one of his eyes and his nose. As the family worked, Nathan watched Jake do a great deal of sniffing around the door and edges of the house, when he suddenly realized that the canine footprints in the patches of snow were not all Jake's. Some of the prints were clearly larger than the ones made by Jake. Nathan started to mention this fact to Alexis but finally decided to keep it to himself, reasoning that it would only worry her unnecessarily. *Was it just a lone wolf wandering through the area or something more sinister? Was the crow that landed on my office window ledge a few days ago just a bird?*

Chapter Four

Deep in December it's nice to remember the fire of September…

-Harvey Schmidt and Tom Jones

Christmas day at the Richard's house was a joyful occasion with much laughter and good cheer. This was the first Christmas that Lizzy was old enough to get really involved, although at times she still seemed more interested in the boxes and wrappings than the gifts inside. Of course, Jake loved charging through the ribbons and wrapping paper, periodically stealing a cookie from Elizabeth's plate. Nathan and Alexis seemed to have temporarily forgotten about the wolf sighting and as a result were more relaxed and spontaneous. The only downer for the day was that neither of Nathan's parents bothered to call and wish him or his family a merry Christmas. While his parent's slight was not unexpected it still left a trace of sadness deep down in Nathan's psyche.

Christmas night brought a strong cold front and another round of light snow. As was their routine, Nathan took Jake outside to potty before everyone bedded down for the night. The strong north wind and snow flurries made their potty time unpleasantly cold, but Jake was in no hurry to do his business. In fact, he seemed unusually vigilant, often sniffing the air and looking around. "Come on, Jake. Potty! It is freezing out here." Because the flood light on the side of the house had burned out, Nathan took a flashlight with him, and he switched it on to see if he could determine what it was that had drawn Jake's attention. He moved the flashlight's beam in a wide arc across the side yard when he saw something that caused his heart to skip a beat. There, reflected in the light, were two red eyes burning like coals. That sight caused Nathan to instantly recall the terrifying moment at Hell's Gate in Lubbock when he felt sure he was face to face with Satan. Gripped by fear, Nathan yelled at Jake to come inside with him. Back in the house, Nathan could feel his heart pounding in his chest and his lungs gasping for breath. *Oh, my God! Is it happening again? Has Satan come back for me?*

Jake ran ahead to the master bedroom and climbed into his dog bed, expecting his good night treat. Alexis had already gotten into bed and turned on her electric blanket when Nathan walked slowly into the bedroom. He started to tell her what he had seen, but he found it difficult to get the words out he was so shaken. All he could manage was a tooth-chattering "It's really ca, ca, ca, cold out there."

Alexis looked up at Nathan from the warmth of their bed and smiled.

What took you so long? I was beginning to get concerned."

"Oh, uh, I couldn't get Jake to potty. You know how he can be. Sometimes he just wants to sniff around. By the way, I checked on Lizzy and she was already sound asleep, so I turned off the light in her room."

Sleep did not come easily for Nathan Richards that Christmas night. When it did overtake him, it was filled with terrifying dreams of death, and demons. Around two a.m. Nathan awoke with a start, convinced that he was burning in the fires of hell. He looked over to see that Alexis was still fast asleep, and then he quietly went into the bathroom and took an Ambien to help him go back to sleep. It was almost four a.m. before he drifted off to a dreamless slumber. Although still groggy from the effects of the Ambien and lack of good sleep, Nathan was none the less grateful to see the first rays of the sun slipping through the bedroom window blinds. *Thank goodness it's morning!* In his days as a minster, Nathan had preached about God's relentless love for us, and now he wondered if Satan's hatred was equally unrelenting. After his conversation with Dean Albritton, Nathan had almost succeeded in convincing himself that maybe there really wasn't a Satan or devil *per se.* But the experience of the previous night once again flooded him with uncertainty. Maybe evil was personified and he really had met that individual. Perhaps the devil had come for him once again and would not be denied this time. How he longed for the good times, the days of his youth when God was in his heaven and the devil was just a cartoon figure wearing a red suit, with a long tail, and a pitch fork. Now deep in December, it was hard to remember alright.

Chapter Five

It's been a long December and there's reason to believe

maybe this year will be better than the last.

-Counting Crows

Early January brought the "thaw" that the locals all seemed to expect. Daytime temperatures rose into the upper 50's and lower 60's with the nights dropping only into the 40's. All traces of December's snow were long gone and a few robins could be seen in the nearby woods. There were no more wolf sightings after Christmas, prompting Nathan and Alexis to hope that the wolf they had seen had moved on. For Nathan, the hope was also that what he had seen really was *just a wolf*. The start of the spring semester was only a few days away so Nathan spent an increasing amount of time in the spare bedroom which he used as his home office. He was preparing for a new course to be offered in the Divinity School. The course was an elective entitled *Faith and Doubt in the 21$^{st}$ Century*. As he envisioned it, the course would be a seminar in which students could discuss the difficult questions they had about their faith and also consider the relationship between faith and doubt. Nathan had observed that for many students the fact that they were in seminary and planning to become ministers made them feel that they must purge their faith of any lingering doubts. He had learned from hard experience that such an approach was not a good strategy for anyone, especially ministers. His psychology classes were both undergraduate courses: Abnormal Psychology and Introductory Psychology, both of which he had taught the previous semester, so they required relatively little attention.

During one of her walks with Lizzy, Alexis had made friends with the young woman in the next house down their street. Her name was Nancy Bradfield and like Alexis, she was a relatively new mother with a four-year-old son named Robert. Mr. Bradfield was an accountant for a group of tax accountants in Durham. Alexis and Nancy really seemed to be kindred spirits, but Nathan and Richard Bradfield, Nancy's husband, had little in common. Clearly Nathan was happy that Alexis had made such a good friend; it eased some of his guilty feelings about moving her so far from her parents and the place she thought of as home. The Richards' house was quiet now. Alexis and Lizzy were visiting with Nancy Bradfield and her son. Nathan went on line to the university's webpage where he could look over the group of students that had signed up for his seminar. The information on each student included such things as their hometown, local address, undergraduate college, and in most cases, a recent photograph. There were twelve students who had enrolled for his class, half were first year students. Seven were males and five were female. Two of the females were Black, but the remaining ten students were Caucasian. Nathan's attention was repeatedly drawn to the photograph of one of the women, Lurleen Montgomery, a freshman from Mississippi. There was something about her picture, just a feeling he couldn't quite identify, and then there was her name, Lurleen. He had never known anyone by that name. Later in the afternoon he found himself going back to the webpage and staring at the photo of Lurleen Montgomery. He tried rather unsuccessfully to tell himself it was just so he could become familiar with the students' names, but in truth there was only one student he was interested in. Nathan's preoccupation with Lurleen Montgomery was broken by the sound of Alexis and Lizzy returning home from the neighbor's house.

"Daddy, Daddy, I got to play with Robert's Legos. We made a house with them," Lizzy called out to her dad. "We had some cookies too."

"That is really cool. I am glad you had a good time at the Bradfield's. Come tell me about the house you built with Legos." Lizzy's enthusiasm seemed to pull Nathan back into the present moment, temporarily erasing his interest in Ms. Montgomery.

"Nathan, the Bradfields invited us for dinner Saturday night. Is that okay with you? Alexis asked. "I know that you don't enjoy Robert all that much."

Lexi, that's fine with me. Robert is okay. What time?"

On Saturday the weather returned to a more typical winter pattern with a bitterly cold north wind and cloudy skies that threatened pre' cipitation.

The Richards left Lizzy with a second year Divinity School student that Lizzy really liked and they walked down the road to the Bradfield's house. By the time they made it, sleet had begun to fall and they were glad to get indoors. The Bradfields greeted them warmly and ushered Nathan and Alexis into their living room where a cheery fire was crackling in the fireplace. Nancy Bradfield served up hot mulled cider which she claimed was made from an old family recipe. After a couple of mugs of the cider, the conversation became more spontaneous. Eventually the topic of the wolf surfaced when Nathan asked Robert if he had seen the wolf. Robert said he had seen it once but not since Christmas. Both men seemed to agree that it was probably a solitary wolf that had moved on. *Maybe this year really will be better*, Nathan thought to himself as he and Alexis walked home.

Chapter Six

When you ask, you must believe and not doubt, because the one who doubts is like a wave on the sea... That person should not expect anything from the Lord.

James, 1: 1-7

For a teacher the first day of a new semester can be a little like sitting down with a new book you've been wanting to read. After examining the cover and reading the information on its jacket, you finally turn to page one and begin. Walking into his class on *faith and doubt*, it really felt to Nathan like starting at page one of a new novel. Since there were only twelve students enrolled in the seminar, he had arranged the chairs in a circle in hopes that it would facilitate more discussion and interaction among the students. One by one the students trickled in, laughing and chatting as they removed their coats and gloves. Nathan scanned each of their faces but did not see the face he was really searching for. The class was scheduled to begin at one o'clock and was to run until two-thirty. The large round clock on the classroom wall said it was now five minutes after one. Quiet settled over the room and the eleven students looked at Nathan expectantly. It was time to start.

"Welcome to Faith and Doubt in the 21st Century", Nathan said with a smile. "My name is Nathan Richards and I am your instructor. My goal for today is to give you an overview of the course and explain the requirements. Also, I'd like to introduce myself since I am a relatively new faculty member. After that I want to get some feedback from each of you." Just as Nathan completed his introductory comments, he could hear the sound of laughter and talking in the hall outside the classroom door. Heads turned toward the door as it opened. In walked a tall coed with shoulder-length raven hair, green eyes, and a gorgeous figure. She made little effort to make her entry unobtrusive. She seemed to literally glide across the floor, and then pulled up the one empty desk and removed her coat. Looking straight into Nathan's eyes, Lurleen Montgomery asked, "Is this Faith and Doubt in the 21st Century?"

Nathan smiled as he replied, "It is, and you must be Miss Montgomery. Welcome to the class, but I should remind you that we start at 1:00 p.m. not 1:15."

"Oh, yes, I know but my morning was full of distractions

what with this being the first day of classes. I am so sorry to disrupt things." The tone of Lurleen's voice suggested to Nathan that she wasn't at all sorry about disrupting things but in fact enjoyed the attention it garnered her.

Feeling mildly irritated, Dr. Richards tried to refocus on the course and his expectations for it. "Miss Montgomery, if you could stay a few minutes when classs is over I will mention the things that you missed." Nathan then picked up a small stack of papers from his desk and began distributing them to the class. "I am passing out a question with an accompanying rating scale." Nathan held up a copy of the paper he was referring to. "The question is about how you see the relationship between faith and doubt. Using the rating scale, mark where you see the relationship. A rating of one means you view doubt as the strong enemy of faith. On the other extreme, a rating of ten means you see doubt as essential for faith growth and development." Nathan scanned the student's faces then continued, "After you mark your response let's talk about your answers and why you answered as you did." Looking at the student to his left in the circle, Nathan said, "Mr. Trudeau, tell us, if you will, how you answered and why."

"I marked my answer as a *four*. I guess I think doubt may not destroy your faith but it doesn't help...it sorta undermines faith." Justin Trudeau was originally from Montreal, Canada but his family moved to New York when he was quite young. On his information page he described himself and his family as belonging to the Anglican Church. Since moving to the U.S., he has attended the Episcopal Church. "I worry sometimes that my faith isn't as strong as it should be, and I guess...I guess I am afraid of doubt."

"Thank you, Justin. Let's hear from the rest of you," Nathan said as he turned to the next student in the circle, Trent Greene. "Trent, how did you respond and why

"I marked my answer as a *two* because I think doubt is definitely the enemy of faith. It is probably the work of the devil. I grew up Southern Baptist, and all my life I have been taught that we must never give in to doubt. We must constantly fight it like a cancer."

The discussion continued through eleven of the twelve students, with most rating doubt somewhere between a one and a five. One student, Schmidt, a Methodist, rated doubt as a *six* and another female student, Ronda Hazen, rated doubt as a seven. Finally, it was Lurleen Montgomery's turn. Lurleen smiled then brushed back a lock of hair that had fallen across her face "I marked my answer as a ten", Lurleen responded in a confident voice. There was some murmuring from the class following her answer. She looked around the room, seeming to enjoy her response's apparent shock value. "I actually believe doubt is warranted, and I don't think it is honest or healthy to deny our doubts. There are so many preachers, especially tv preachers who are such phonies, how could a thinking person not have doubts?"

Nathan felt somewhat surprised at Miss Montgomery's extreme answer or her confidence. "Could you tell the class why you feel as you do?"

Lurleen forged ahead but her facial expression became somber as she so. "My father was a preacher," she said scornfully. "Some people thought he was so godly, but he wasn't all he claimed to be. I had to make some compromises in my life that I'd rather not talk about here. I guess you could say that those experiences, those compromises made me a skeptic and a doubter."

"And yet here you are in seminary. Thank you, Miss. Montgomery for your honesty. Doubters and skeptic are welcome here." Nathan had not expected such a strong, almost bitter response from any of his students, and yet he felt he understood Lurleen Montgomery's skepticism and doubt. "Well, we certainly have a wide range of backgrounds and positions represented in our class which should make for some interesting discussions throughout the semester," Nathan said as he summarized the group's responses. "Are there any thoughts that any of you have about what you have heard?"

There was a lengthy silence before anyone spoke up. Finally, there were a couple of questions addressed to Lurleen essentially asking why she would enroll in seminary when she had such doubts and negative feelings about preachers. Nathan observed that Lurleen never really answered those questions directly; she either brushed them aside or answered the question with one of her own, often putting the other student on the defensive. Time seemed to fly by as Dr. Richards looked at his watch and noted that it was almost two-thirty. "Wow, we've had some very interesting discussion, but it's time to stop for today. Please refer to our course's webpage and look up the reading assignment. Try to complete it before our next class. Miss.Montgomery, could you stay for a moment? Class dismissed,"

Because another class was gathering at the door, Nathan asked Lurleen to walk with him into the hall. Once out into the hall, they walked away from the class room and paused. Nathan started to speak, but Lurleen put her hand on his arm, and asked, "Could we walk over to the Brodhead Center for Campus Life and have a cup of coffee?" The Brodhead Center was an attractive multistory building that gave the appearance of being made mostly of glass. Nathan had never been inside so he was agreeable to the brisk walk from the Gray Building. As they walked, Lurleen pumped Nathan with questions about his family and background. Her interest seemed more than conversational, and her manner seemed to stimulate Nathan's willingness to talk. In fact, as he reflected back on their conversation, he was surprised about how personal her questions were and how freely he had answered them. Once inside they found an open table in the food court and ordered two coffees. To his great surprise they talked for almost two hours before Lurleen indicated that she had to meet someone. She rose from the table and donned her coat while Nathan looked at his watch and realized he had told Alexis he would call right after class to tell her how the day had gone. Nathan felt almost as if he were in an altered state of consciousness as he walked to his car.

Alexis and Lizzy greeted Nathan with enthusiasm when he walked in the door. Lizzy bombarded him with requests to go for a walk, get ice cream, or play her Candy Land game. Jacob seemed to opt for the walk

"Hold on a minute, guys," Nathan pleaded. "Let me get my coat off at least."

"How was your day?", Alexis asked after Nathan hung up his heavy coat. "I thought you'd give me a call."

"Yeah. I am sorry. I got roped into talking with some of my students right after class was over. I think the class will be a good one. We had some interesting discussion for sure." Nathan paused then continued. "I have been thinking that we need to get a second car so you won't be stranded here at home. I might be delayed at school some days and you might have an emergency or just need to take Lizzy somewhere. What do you think?"

"Well, I do think it would be nice especially since we live a ways from the main part of town. Also, we might want to consider finding a good daycare program for Lizzy. Even if it was only for two or three mornings a week, having a second car would really help.

Chapter Seven

Lead us not into temptation, but deliver us from evil.

Matthew 6:13

The labyrinth proved to be a bewildering maze of tunnels from which there seemed to be no escape. Nathan felt himself on the brink of panic. He had no idea how he had gotten there and certainly no idea of how to get out. All he knew for sure was that he was moving steadily downward. At times the descent was so steep he could hardly maintain his balance. Nathan cursed the darkness after he lost his footing and fell to his knees. Rising painfully to his feet, he noticed that what had been near total darkness was gradually giving way to a dim reddish glow. Along with the gradual increase in light, it was getting warmer, much warmer. He rounded the next bend and was greeted with a terrifying sight. The tunnel walls which had been solid and quite dark now seemed to be brightly illuminated as if they were made of molten rock, orange and red and oh so hot. Gradually the narrow passage way opened out onto a broad expanse of fiery rock from floor to ceiling. *Was this hell or the heart of a volcano?* Nathan knew he would surely perish if he went forward, but he had no idea where to go if he turned around and re-entered the darkness behind him. It was as if he had entered Dante's inferno without the benefit of Virgil as his guide. Drenched in sweat, Nathan awoke with a jolt. He could feel his heart racing as he looked around the darkness of his bedroom. Alexis lay sleeping beside him, and his dog Jake was snoozing on the floor at the foot of the bed. Quietly, he eased from beneath the covers and walked through the dark house into the kitchen where he filled a glass of water at the sink. While he sipped the water, he became aware that his German Shepherd Jake had followed him. Reaching down to pat Jake's head, Nathan spoke quietly. "Hey, big fella. Did I wake you up? Everything is okay, I think. Just a dream, a really bad dream. Let's go back to bed." Nathan crept quietly back to bed, but he knew it could be a long time before he might actually go back to sleep. He listened to Alexis' breathing and knew she was still sleeping. He could also hear Jake settling down once again. In the darkness of the bedroom, he had the feeling that his dream might have been a warning, but a warning of what? Silently, he offered up a prayer. *Lord, what is it you want me to understand?* Almost immediately, Nathan thought about his student, Lurleen Montgomery. *Was my nightmare a warning about her? Dear God, do you still speak to people through dreams? How can I know?* After what seemed like hours, the first light of morning made its cautious appearance and Nathan could feel his wife beginning to stir. Alexis tended to be an early riser, so Nathan knew she'd be getting up soon. Actually, he was quite glad to leave the night and its frightening dreams behind.

Breakfast brought noise and activity to the Richards's home. Jake was eager for his breakfast and Lizzy brought her favorite teddy bear into the kitchen for his breakfast too. "The diner is open for business," Alexis announced with a smile.

"Teddy wants Cheerios," Lizzy proclaimed, holding her stuffed bear aloft.

"Okay, and what'll you have, Miss?" Alexis answered. "I'll be happy to serve it up right away, ma'am."

"I want Cheerios too…just like Teddy."

Nathan smiled as he watched his family go through their morning routine. *Maybe my experience from last night was just a bad dream and nothing more.* He glanced at his watch and poured a cup of coffee. Today was Wednesday and he would meet his psychology classes so all seemed pretty routine. There were no storm clouds on the horizon…yet.

By the time Nathan headed to his office at the university it was past the morning rush hour so traffic was light, which was a good thing because Nathan's thoughts were clearly not on the cars around him. Among other things, he reflected on how strange his life had been over the last four years. Sometimes it was exciting and fulfilling while at other times it seemed like he had been dropped into a horror movie. His memory of the two years in Lubbock often seemed like a frightening movie from his childhood like *The Creature from the Black Lagoon* or *The Thing*. Sometimes God seemed very real and close at hand, but at other times, God seemed distant and unreal. Nathan also wondered about his current situation. Teaching at Duke felt like a dream come true. He realized that deep down he was probably more of a teacher than a clinician or preacher, and yet he had the nagging feeling that he didn't belong at a university either. Maybe he really was merely a fraud, a great imposter. He remembered how he had felt at the commencement exercise when he was to receive his PhD from Ohio State. Right up until the moment the diploma was placed in his hands, he had felt certain that when he crossed the stage the university president would call out his name and say that he, Nathan, had been "found out" and would not graduate after all. Was he really a man of God or just someone who had learned how to act like one? Was evil just a way to describe certain actions or qualities of people or was it an entity, a personage? His question about evil was one he could never answer satisfactorily. Pulling into his parking space near the Gray Building, Nathan's thoughts came back to his present reality…but what was that reality? Today's lecture in his Introduction to Psychology class was on early child development. Since Nathan's training had been in clinical psychology and all his work experience had been with adults, this was not a lecture he felt totally comfortable giving. He realized he had learned more about child development from being a father than from anything he had gotten from books or lectures. Oh well, he felt pretty sure he knew more than most of his students. Looking around the classroom, it seemed like nearly every student took notes with a laptop instead of pen and paper. How much things had changed since he was a student, and did his students look ever so young!

Chapter Eight

When the cat is away, the mice will play.

-Author unknown

It was a Thursday in the first week of March and although spring was not too far away, winter was still holding fast. Nathan's classes seemed to be progressing reasonably well; his research ideas regarding evil had taken a back seat to his involvement in the seminar he was leading on faith and doubt. A few days earlier Alexis had received an email from an old friend from college who was living not far away in Chapel Hill. Her friend was a woman by the name of Sandra McAfee. As children, she and Alexis had lived just a few houses apart in Dallas and they had been best friends all the way through college. In fact, Sandra had been Alexis' maid of honor when Alexis and Nathan got married. The two had lost touch after Nathan and Alexis had moved to Ohio, but through the wonders of the internet and Google search, Sandra had located Alexis. Sandra had married and had one child, a daughter the same age as Elizabeth. She and her husband had divorced about a year ago. He was a professor at The University of North Carolina, and Sandra had begun working as an elementary school teacher. Once she had discovered that Alexis now lived fairly close by she had reached out and made contact. Alexis was overjoyed to hear from her old friend, and after some lengthy phone conversations, Alexis had accepted Sandra's invitation to bring Lizzy and spend a weekend with her there in Chapel Hill.

Since it was Thursday, it was time for Nathan's seminar to meet again and Nathan was looking forward to the day's class. The previous week he had given the students an assignment to write their answer to what he thought was an intriguing question: describe what they thought would have been Jesus' response to Satan's temptation included in Luke's gospel. After everyone had taken their seats, Nathan gave some opening comments before asking students for their answers. "The Bible tells us that Jesus was tempted in every way that we as human beings can be tempted, and that he never sinned as a result of being tempted. We are also told that the pre-resurrection Jesus, as described in the synoptic gospels, was fully human, not God dressed up like a man. If that is so, how might he have responded emotionally to Satan's temptations? All Luke tells us is what Jesus said and did, not how he felt. We know he countered Satan's temptation with scripture. Recall too that Jesus had spent many days in the Judean wilderness without food or water and the devil tempted him to turn stones into bread. Food to a starving man is a pretty strong motivation to do whatever is necessary to get the meal."

After delivering his brief introduction, Nathan asked students to state verbally what they had written in response to his question. There was a long pause before anyone answered. Jonathan Pence spoke first, and his answer was a fairly typical, mainline preacher-type answer. "I don't think Jesus felt much desire for the bread or the other offers. He just wanted to do God's will."

"So, you think it wasn't much of a problem for Jesus? He felt no real temptation because his faith protected him like a suit of armor?"

"Yeah, I guess that's right," Jonathan responded. His facial expression suggested that he felt he was being led into a trap but he forged ahead anyway. "Luke tells us that He didn't sin, right?"

"He does, and of course, he omits what Jesus might have felt. Mr. Pence, are you suggesting that if you were starving, with no other food available, and you were told you could steal some bread and wouldn't be caught that you wouldn't even think about taking it? "Knowing that he was in an indefensible position, Jonathan walked back his earlier statement. "Well, I guess I would think about it, maybe even want it, but hopefully I wouldn't give in."

"Okay, probably so. That would be pretty human." Nathan continued. "When the devil took Jesus up on the high place and said cast yourself down and God's angels will prevent you from hitting the ground, do you think there was any doubt, even for a moment that God would save him from death?"

Again, there was a pause before anyone answered. Finally, one of the women, Ronda Hazen, answered, "Well, I guess he might have had some second thoughts. When my brother went into the Army, he was in an airborne unit so he had to parachute from airplanes. He told me that the first several jumps caused him to have some strong doubts and a lot of fear before he jumped, wondering if his chute would open properly. So, yeah, Jesus might have had some momentary doubts."

Nathan smiled as he responded, "That's a great answer. I think jumping from a high place and trusting that something, God or a parachute, would keep you from smashing into the ground might bring up some momentary doubts. It is interesting that the Bible tells us that Jesus didn't jump, so he never really tested his faith in God, did he?"

Ronda responded promptly, "He didn't jump because he didn't want to *test God*. He had complete faith and felt it wrong to try to test God's faithfulness."

The class discussion continued in an animated fashion for the reminder of the time. All of the students, save for one, participated. Just before time to end the class, Nathan addressed the one student who had remained silent. "Miss Montgomery, I noticed that you had no comments. Did you complete the assignment?"

"Yes, Dr. Richards, I finished it but forgot to bring it with me…"

"Well, you can drop it by later, but I am interested in your thoughts about the questions we have looked at today."

Lurleen Montgomery gave a sly smile before answering.

"Maybe what the devil offered Jesus wasn't really a temptation. For example, if someone said I could steal some sardines and get away with it but I hate sardines, I would have no trouble resisting the offer. Also, I don't see how being asked to jump off a high place to see if God would not let him fall would be must of a temptation."

"Interesting, but we don't have any more time to discuss your answer. Maybe we can talk about it some other time. Class dismissed."

Nathan drove home as soon as his class was over since Alexis and Elizabeth would be leaving soon heading off to visit Alexis's friend Sandra in Chapel Hill. When he pulled in the driveway, Alexis was loading the last of her luggage and Lizzy's gear into her Toyota SUV. She looked up and waved when she saw Nathan's car.

"Looks like you are ready to roll," Nathan said as he hugged Alexis.

"Where is Lizzy?"

"She's in the house giving Jake some last-minute instructions."

Alexis had hardly spoken when Lizzy came bounding out of the house followed by their dog, Jake.

"Daddy, Daddy, we're going on a trip, but you and Jake have to stay home. Jake says he will take care of you so you won't be lonely."

"Thank you, Lizzy. Now give me a big hug." Nathan picked up his daughter and gave her a hug, tickling her as he put her back down. Elizabeth squealed with laughter and tried to tickle her father.

After securing Elizabeth in her car seat, Nathan turned to Alexis. "I hope you have a great time. Give me a call when you get to Sandra's house. I've got her address and phone number in my cell phone in case I need to contact you. Please be careful and know I love you." Nathan stood on the driveway and waved as Alexis drove out of sight.

No sooner had Nathan Richards return to the house and closed the door behind him, he heard a car pull into his driveway. Thinking it was Alexis returning home because she had forgotten something, he headed back outside with a big smile on his face. His welcoming smile vanished and changed to a look of puzzlement when he emerged from the house. Instead of Alexis's SUV, a red BMW three series coupe had pulled into his driveway. "I wonder who the heck that could be," Nathan spoke under his breath. His question was answered promptly when he saw his student, Lurleen Montgomery emerged from the BMW. He had to admit he felt a sudden jolt of excitement, perhaps even sexual arousal as he gazed at her. Lurleen looked very alluring wearing an extra-large Duke sweatshirt that hung down over one shoulder and a pair of very snug-fitting pants. There was a certain feline grace about her movements as she walked towards the house.

"Dr. Richards, I am so glad you are here. I wanted to drop off my paper that I forgot to bring to class. I didn't want you to count it as late."

Nathan was more than a little surprised to see Lurleen, but he had to admit she looked very exciting. "You didn't need to drive all the way out here just to drop off your paper. I wouldn't have counted it late."

After handing him her paper, Lurleen started to open her car door to leave, but she paused and looked back at Nathan. "Oh, uh, I was wondering if you have a few minutes I could talk to you about my answer to your question from class? I guess I was a little reluctant to mention what I was thinking in class, but I would really like to know what you think."

"Uh, yeah, I guess I have a few minutes. Let's go inside. It's a bit chilly our here and you don't have a coat on." Nathan gestured toward the house, and as he walked towards the house with Lurleen he could hear alarm bells go off in his head. *Something wicked this way cometh.*

Once inside Lurleen stopped and looked expectantly at Nathan. "Do you really not mind listening to my comments? I know you must be very busy."

"Oh, not at all. I am not terribly busy at the moment. Would you like a cup of coffee? It's fresh."

"That would be lovely. Maybe a little cream and sugar if you have it."

Nathan handed her a steaming mug of coffee and they retired to the living room where there was a fire burning brightly in the fireplace. Nathan motioned for her to have a seat in the big leather recliner and he sat on the adjacent sofa. "Well, what was it you wanted to discuss?"

"The reason I was reluctant to say anything during class is that my answers to your question were about sex." Lurleen smiled and seemed to wait for a response from Nathan. When he remained silent, she continued. "Jesus was never tempted by sex, or the Bible never mentioned it if he was. Sex is the most powerful temptation for a man, wouldn't you agree? You are a psychologist. " Lurleen continued, "I have read several books…fiction, of course. All of them are by female authors like Anne Rice or Sue Monk Kidd. In their books they write about Jesus having sexual interests toward Mary Magdalene…even marrying her. In the movie, *The Last Temptation of Christ,* directed by Martin Scorsese, it shows Jesus experiencing sexual temptations. If Jesus was really a man, isn't it likely he was tempted by sex?" Feeling somewhat uncomfortable,

Nathan struggled to come up with a safe, neutral response. "The Scorsese film was based on Kazantzakis' book which was and is quite controversial…"

Lurleen interrupted, "It was controversial and maybe the whole thing about Jesus having sexual feelings was too controversial for the Bible or the church. Maybe that's too bad. Maybe if the gospel writers had been more honest, Catholic priests wouldn't have to pretend to be celibate and the church wouldn't be having so much trouble with pedophiles." As she spoke, she moved to the sofa and sat very close to Nathan. Placing her hand on his leg, she continued, "I think it would have been very instructive if the Bible had mentioned Jesus being tempted by sex. It would have made him seem more human, more believable."

Nathan Richards felt as if he were on fire and his memory of the hellish dream burst back into consciousness. In his mind there were all sorts of alarm bells going off, and he knew he should get up and ask his student to leave, but he felt paralyzed, paralyzed by lust. Finally, he managed to stand up and ask if she wanted more coffee. Before he could step away, Lurleen stood up facing him, wrapping her arms around him and pressing her body against his. With her arms around him and the sofa behind him Nathan was unable to move away, causing him to feel a moment of panic. He was trapped, but part of him didn't care. After what seemed like an eternity, Lurleen released him and stepped back, a wicked smile on her face.

"It's getting late, and I know you must have things you need to do, so I should go," she whispered. Even though she no longer had her arms around him, Lurleen held him with her green eyes. Nathan had once read that when a woman dazzles a man with her green eyes, he won't notice that there is someone inside those eyes spying on him. Who or what was that someone?

"Mmm, uh, yeah, maybe so. I do have some grades I need to record. Uh, it's been interesting talking to you. You've brought up some interesting things, I mean some interesting points. I'll walk you to your car." Walking her out to her car, thoughts of inviting her to stay flashed through his mind. Watching her red BMW drive away, Nathan didn't know if he felt relieved or disappointed. His thoughts returned to Lurleen's comments about Jesus. How would Jesus have responded to such temptation? Would he have remained celibate or would he have given in? Would temptation have produced doubt for Jesus? If Jesus had yielded to the desire for sex, would that have been a sin as well? Nathan clearly felt shaken. Had his desire for one of his students caused him to doubt, doubt his ethical standards, doubt his faithfulness to Alexis? He had always thought of himself as a straight arrow guy. He obeyed the speed limits, paid his taxes, and generally followed the rules, but now this? He tried to console himself by thinking that *technically* he hadn't done anything wrong. Doubts. Temptation leading to doubts and even a sense of guilt. Just like Jimmy Carter once said, "I've looked on a lot of women with lust. I've committed adultery in my heart many times." Maybe Lurleen was right. *What kind of name was Lurleen anyway?* Perhaps it was just a distraction, but Nathan decided to go online and look up the name Lurleen. What he discovered shocked him. The name Lurleen was of German origin and meant *temptress*. Still reeling from his experience of the afternoon, Nathan walked slowly into the kitchen to see if there was any coffee left. The pot was empty but there on the kitchen island was one of Elizabeth's favorite books open to a very familiar nursery rhyme, Humpty Dumpty. *Humpty Dumpty had a great fall.*

*All the king's horses and all the king's men couldn't put Humpty back together again.* Nathan knew he was probably only a couple of steps away from utter darkness, the abyss.

Chapter Nine

I can see clearly now the rain is gone

-Song by Johnny Nash

Friday morning Nathan Richards woke up, made his breakfast, fed Jake, and called Alexis. She reported that all was well and that she and Elizabeth were having a grand time. She planned to head home after lunch on Saturday. After a hot shower, Nathan dressed and headed to his office at the university. He was determined that his Friday was going to be a normal day, free of temptation and doubt. MWF were his psychology days and thinking about the subject of today's lectures served to clear his mind of worry. He could see more clearly now. Maybe the "rain storm" from yesterday was gone. Maybe so, but the mere fact he had been sorely tempted continued to nag at his conscience. Sitting comfortably at his office desk, sipping a second cup of coffee, Nathan looked over his lecture notes and his Power Point slides. Today's lecture in Abnormal Psychology was on personality disorders. Just for the heck of it, he decided to scan the internet for information on personality disorders. As he browsed through the listing of topics that came up in this search, he noticed an article about a convicted serial murderer, Jeremiah Murdoc.

Murdoc was convicted a few years ago of committing eight murders across the state of North Carolina. Murdoc had kidnapped and tortured his victims before finally killing them. The media had described him as a sadistic serial killer while his lawyers had claimed that he was mentally ill. Nathan read further and found that prosecution and defense experts came to different conclusions about Murdoc's mental condition. Psychologists for the defense said Murdoc was schizophrenic, but mental health experts for the state said he was an antisocial or a narcissistic personality disorder. Whatever his correct diagnosis, Jeremiah Murdoc was clearly a truly evil man.

A light went off in Dr. Richards' mind. He thought to himself that he could use some of what he had just read in today's lecture, and then a truly exciting idea popped into his head. It occurred to him that he hadn't done anything with the research topic suggested by his dean. The article about Murdoc said he was incarcerated at Central Prison in Raleigh, NC. Perhaps, Nathan thought, he might be able to interview Murdoc as well as do an in-depth study of some of history's most evil men. That information would help him explore one facet of his study of evil. The idea suddenly triggered a burst of intellectual curiosity and excitement. If human beings could gradually evolve into a demonic figure like Murdoc, perhaps interviewing one such individual could shed some light on the subject and possibly support his theory that Satan or the devil was really a human being who had devoted himself to a life of pure evil. Interviewing Murdoc would give an exciting and real-world flavor to his book.

Nathan became so caught up in his new idea that he almost forgot his classes. Once his two lectures were over, he returned to his office and then made a list of some of history's most clearly evil men. The list included such characters as Hitler, Stalin, Vlade the Impaler, and the Marquis De Sade. To his list of evil men, he thought momentarily about including Donald Trump's name. He chuckled to himself at that idea but decided that compared to the other names on his list Trump was a piker. Now, he had to think of a way to be allowed to interview Murdoc in prison. He knew that would not be easy and he would need someone with some political clout to help him gain the necessary access. *Who might be able to help me? Maybe Dean Albritton might know whom I should contact.* To his surprise, he was quickly able to get Dean Albritton on the phone and the Dean did, in fact, know someone who might be able to help. Albritton mentioned the university's Center for Science and Justice, a part of the Duke Law Center. Albritton said that he knew the professor who headed up that program and that he would make some inquires for Nathan. Later that afternoon, Albritton called back and told Nathan that a Professor Roland Jones at the Law Center might be able to help, but it could take a few days to find out. In the meantime, Nathan knew he needed to do a lot of research on the names on his list. Of course, interviewing Murdoc would enable him to ask vital questions and possibly gain more insight than he could get from just reading about historical figures.

Once he got home, Nathan threw the ball a few times for Jake and then called Alexis. He felt really good, free of temptation and doubt. It was helpful to have something he could focus on besides Lurleen Montgomery. He was eager to begin his research on the evil individuals he had listed, so he fixed a quick dinner by heating up some leftovers and then settled in front of his computer. Beginning with Hitler, he scanned the highlights of some of the individuals on his list. Right away he noticed some commonalities including cruelty, brutality, and enjoying the suffering of others. What he couldn't tell was whether or not these individuals thought they were doing evil or whether they found a way to justify their actions, Was Socrates correct when he wrote that *no man knowingly does evil*? If he could interview Murdoc, he might be able to gain at least a partial answer to this question, a question that was of central importance to his theory. After a couple of hours on the computer Nathan decided to watch some tv before retiring. He settled on an old Robin Williams' movie, <u>What Dreams May Come</u>. The movie was about a man's undying love for his wife, and it reminded him of how much he loved Alexis and his daughter, Elizabeth. That night a dream did come, a dream that was both erotic and disturbing. In his dream Lurleen Montgomery was in bed with him and they were both naked. He was about to make love to her when he awoke. Feeling guilty, he thought of Alexis and reflexively touched her side of the bed which was cold and empty. *Maybe the rain hadn't gone after all.*

Saturday morning dawned cloudy and cool with light rain in the forecast. After breakfast, Nathan tidied up the house in anticipation of Alexis's return home. He told Jake that Alexis and Lizzy would be coming home soon and immediately, Jake ran to look out the window. For Jake, just like a child, there was no concept of future time, everything was immediate. If someone was coming home that meant they were coming home *now*. Nathan looked over at Jake and spoke softly, "They'll be home soon, big fella, soon, not now. "It was shortly after noon when Alexis and Lizzy returned home. Nathan and Jake went out to greet them. Jake barked enthusiastically and ran circles around their car as it pulled into the driveway. Alexis emerged from her Toyota SUV and embraced Nathan warmly. Together they helped Lizzy from her car seat and then had to hold her up to keep Jake from knocking her over. *There is nothing like a dog to give you a warm reception when you return home even if you've only been gone a few minutes.*

"*It's* really good to be home. Did you miss us?", Alexis inquired of Nathan. "We had such a nice time. Elizabeth loved playing with Judith, Sandra's daughter. I think it was good for her. How did you get along?"

"I missed you too. My classes went well, and I actually made some headway with the research idea I told you about. You know, the one Dean Albritton suggested?"

Yeah, I remember. What did you do?"

Nathan gave Alexis a quick explanation before being pulled away by Lizzy who was eager to tell him about all the things she did at Judith's house. For Nathan it felt great to have has family all together once again. After dinner they all gathered in the living room with the fireplace ablaze. They watched tv for a while then all three played a rousing game of Candy Land. Jake watched for a while until he became completely bored and fell asleep. Lizzy wanted to read from her nursery rhyme book so Nathan did the honors. When he came to Humpty Dumpty, he felt a twinge of guilt, especially when Lizzy asked why they couldn't put Humpty back together again."They couldn't put him back together because he broke into too many pieces and they didn't know how to glue him back. Remember when that Christmas ornament fell off the tree and broke? It was glass and broke into too many little pieces to try to glue back together." Nathan couldn't think of a better explanation and Lizzy seemed satisfied since she wanted to go on to the next story.

After Lizzy had gotten into bed, Alexis and Nathan read her a few stories, then they both headed for their bedroom. Remembering his dream from the night before, Nathan felt strangely uneasy as he and Alexis climbed into their bed. In the quiet darkness of the room, Nathan held Alexis close until he could tell from her breathing that she was asleep. It was then he gradually relaxed enough to fall asleep too.

Chapter Ten

The ability to read people well is both a blessing and a curse

-Author unknown

Lurleen Montgomery and Myra Napier, both first year Divinity School students, became roommates through the university's roommate matching system. Lurleen was from a small town in Mississippi and Myra hailed from a suburb of Nashville, Tennessee. Although the two women were quite different in both appearance and personality, they quickly became friends. Both students were enrolled in Dr. Richards' seminar which they found to be engrossing. The coming week was spring break and the majority of students in their apartment complex had already headed home for the break. Neither Lurleen nor Myra had any such plans. Their Friday night looked to be a very quiet one. Come on, Myra. Let's do something fun tonight; this place is like a ghost town," Lurleen pleaded with her roommate. "You've got all next week to study, so don't give me that old excuse of needing to study."

"Well, okay. Maybe it would do me good to have a little fun," Myra responded somewhat hesitantly.

"Let's go to a place I have heard is really nice, and it's far enough from campus we shouldn't see any of our faculty. Besides, I think they only go to coffee shops, not taverns."

"Oh, a tavern! I, uh, I don't know. I don't think I've ever been to a tavern," Myra replied.

"Well then, it's about time you did. The place I have in mind is downtown and it's called the Blue Devil. It is supposed to be very much like an English or maybe an Irish pub. Come on. I'll drive!" Lurleen grabbed her car keys and slipped on her jacket.

The Blue Devil proved to be everything Lurleen had heard. Inside it looked like an upscale English pub. It had dark wood paneling and a big fireplace which was burning brightly as the two girls entered. "Gosh. This is nice," Myra murmured as they entered. The room was less than half-filled with patrons, but it had a warm and inviting atmosphere. After selecting a booth near the fireplace, the two girls removed their coats and looked over the drink menu. "What should I get?" Myra asked innocently. "I don't drink much," she added, looking over at Lurleen.

"I think I'll order a stout, but it might be a bit too heavy for you. I'd suggest something pretty light, maybe a pilsner on draft."

The waiter walked over and smiled as he asked what they wanted to order. It was obvious he was focusing his attention primarily on Lurleen. "What are you ladies going to have tonight? Is this your first visit to the Blue Devil? I don't think I have seen you before," he said, looking squarely at Lurleen.

"You're right. It's our first visit," Lurleen replied, brushing a lock of hair off her face. "It is so nice in here. My friend will have a pilsner or something really light, and I'll have a stout, both on draft."

The waiter returned promptly with their draft brews. Lurleen took a long drink and sighed contentedly, but Myra ventured only a cautious sip. "Not bad," Myra said with a smile. "It's better than I expected." Two mugs later the two women relaxed and began to talk freely. After a brief pause in the conversation, Myra looked intently at Lurleen and spoke, "Lurleen, you are so lucky. You are beautiful; your body is gorgeous and every man who sees you falls all over himself trying to gain your attention. I think I'd give anything if I ever got one tenth the attention you get. I am pretty much invisible to men. I guess it is no wonder my dad used to call me *church mouse*. I looked mousey and I was always in church. Nothing much has changed since then either.

"Myra, you don't give yourself enough credit. A change in hair style and some more stylish clothes, and you'll have men interested in you. Besides, you should be careful what you wish for. Attention from a man is not always something desirable. For a lot of men, you are just something to conquer, like climbing a mountain."

"What do you mean, Lurleen? Are you telling me you don't enjoy the attention you get from men?"

"If you knew my background and some of my experiences, you'd understand, but I don't want to bore you with the details."

"I would really like to know more about you, Lurleen. We've been roommates for the better part of a year, and about all I know about you is that you are from someplace in Mississippi."

Over the next forty-five minutes, Lurleen gave her roommate an abbreviated personal history. She began by explaining that her mother was German and that she and her father met while he was in the army, stationed in Germany. During his time in Germany her father was assigned to the chaplain's service, so he conducted religious services and became a preacher to the men. He eventually persuaded her mother to come back to the states with him and they married. After his discharge from the army her mother and father moved to Mississippi where her father started a non-denominational church. Over time, the church he started grew quite large. Her mother was always a bit shy and withdrawn blaming her shyness on her poor English. For several years Lurleen literally worshipped her father, thinking he was an honorable man of faith until one day when she was about twelve years old. Her father had left his phone on the kitchen table and Lurleen heard it beep with a text message. She picked it up only to see a curious message from a person named Sharon. Out of curiosity, Lurleen scrolled back through a number of her dad's text messages only to discover he was obviously having an affair with this woman. For several months, Lurleen tried to deny the reality of what she had learned, but eventually she realized that she could see through all her dad's lies. It was almost as if she could read his mind. Finally, she told her mother what she had learned. Her mother made a feeble effort to confront her dad, but he denied the affair and tried to make her mother believe she was just crazy with jealousy. From that time forward, Lurleen's mother became increasingly withdrawn and depressed,

eventually committing suicide shortly after Lurleen graduated from high school.

"My gosh, Lurleen. What a tragic story! I had no idea. I am so sorry. What did you do after your mom died?"

"I knew I couldn't stay with my dad after my mother's death. I couldn't even stand the sight of him, so I lived for a few

months with a high school friend. My mother had established a trust fund for my college education which became mine after her death, and it enabled me to start college at Mississippi State in Starkville. The trust fund covered my expenses for the first year, but I had to find some way to support myself or I would have had to drop out of school. One night I was scanning the internet looking for some kind of part time work when I saw an ad that caught my attention. The ad was for girls to work at a gentleman's club. The pay was good and the hours were in the evening, so I applied."

"Lurleen, I can't believe this. What did you do at the gentleman's club?" Myra was obviously shocked, so she agreed to another draft when Lurleen offered.

I became a stripper, Myra. I was a nude dancer. Very

quickly, I guess I became the feature attraction at the club. I think over time I got used to being naked in front of men. In fact, to be completely honest, I enjoyed it. Along with nightly dancing at the gentleman's club, I got multiple offers to do modeling as well. I did quite a few private modeling sessions for men. It was mostly nude modeling, sometimes it was pretty kinky too. I made good money, but what was really interesting was that I seemed to develop a special talent. I found that I could literally read men's minds. I knew what they thought and what they wanted.

I knew how to tease them and drive them crazy, so I began to use and enjoy the power I had over men. It seemed I could dominate them pretty much any time I wished. I also learned that if they tried to go further than I wanted, I could shut them down too."

"What do you mean shut them down?", Myra asked, an incredulous look on her face.

"If a man came on too strong, I could sorta cloud his mind and confuse him so he seemed to forget what he was doing. The effect was usually temporary, but it lasted long enough for me to leave the scene. So, you see, I can attract virtually any man I want, but can never trust a man. I don't think I can ever love a man because I can never trust him. As a child I thought my father was such a good man until I found out what he had been doing. Ever since then I have become better and better at using my special talent, but I can't say it has brought me any real happiness. If I am attracted to a man, it isn't love, it's just the challenge of the conquest. Can I conquer him? In that way I have become like a man, a true predator." Lurleen ended her story with a somber look, appearing tired and emotionally drained.

"Lurleen, I don't know what to say…except I am sorry." Myra was clearly at a loss for words when the waiter returned to their booth.

"Can I get you ladies another round?"

"No, thank you, I've got to be able to drive. If I had another one, you'd have to put me up for the night," Lurleen responded with a tired smile.

"I'd be glad to arrange it for you if you need a place to stay," the young waiter said in a half-joking manner.

"Thanks, but we'll be on our way." Lurleen looked long and hard at the young waiter, then asked, "What do we owe you?"

"The waiter smiled warmly, "No charge. Since this was your first visit, it is on the house. I...uh, we hope you'll return real soon."

Lurleen thanked their waiter then she and Myra walked slowly to her BMW. As they buckled their seat belts, she turned to Myra and said, "This has been an interesting night. I hope I can drive us back to the apartment without getting arrested or into a wreck. "Fortune smiled on Lurleen and Myra and they drove back to their apartment without incident. Once inside, Lurlene stripped off her clothes and fell into bed; she nearly always slept in the nude. Within minutes she was fast asleep, leaving her roommate in a state of complete shock. During the night Lurleen dreamed. Her dream was about one of her professors, Nathan Richards. Might he be her next conquest?

When Saturday morning arrived, Lurleen awoke with a dull headache and slipped on her oversize Blue Devils sweatshirt. Myra was in the kitchen fixing them both breakfast. "Morning, sleepy head", Myra greeted her roommate with a cheerful look. "How are you feeling?"

"I guess okay, just a little hung over."

"Lurleen, I had one question left over from last night and then I promise I won't discuss the subject with you again, unless you ask me to."

"What do you want to know?"

"Why are you in seminary? I mean… it isn't that you don't be long. You have such serious doubts and suspicion of preachers, and besides with your looks and skills, you could be enormously successful in the business world." Myra seemed apologetic as she asked her question.

"It's a good question, Myra. It's one I have asked myself many times. The honest answer is that I don't really know. Maybe, I am trying to reform myself, trying to see if I am redeemable."

"I see a lot of good in you, Lurleen. God has given you some real blessings."

Lurleen laughed as she replied, "I don't know if God has blessed me or cursed me. Most of the time it feels more like a curse."

"If you'll permit me to give you some advice…I think you should talk to someone who can help you. You are so self-critical, but in other ways so confident, almost too confident. Do you think you could talk to Professor Richards? He's a psychologist and a minister."

After a long pause, Lurleen replied, "I'll think about it."

Chapter Eleven

Raven hair and ruby lips. Sparks fly from her fingertips

-Don Henley of The Eagles

It was Tuesday of spring break, and during the time off from classes Myra and Lurleen went several places together, even making a second visit to the Blue Devil pub. As a result, Myra had decided that draft beer was pretty good after all. Both women had actually grown closer during the past several days. This particular morning Myra had gotten up early, fixed her breakfast, and gone to the nearby convenience store. She was just returning when Lurleen staggered her way into the kitchen still wearing her bathrobe.

"Well, hello, sleepy head," Myra greeted her roommate as she closed the apartment door behind her. "It's almost ten o'clock. Are you feeling okay? You aren't even dressed."

Lurleen pulled her robe together and replied. "Yeah. I 'm okay. I just didn't sleep well last night. I had a lot of dreams…dreams that seemed way too real."

"Maybe it was that dark beer you drink."

"You may be right, but I think it could be more complicated than that."

"What do you mean?"

"There was something I didn't tell you the other night when I told you about my past. I mentioned that my grandparents were from Germany but never came to the states. When I was twelve my grandfather sent me a book for my birthday. It was a beautiful thing with a cover made of some exotic wood from the Black Forest. The problem was much of it was written in old German. It also had some odd-looking lettering, drawings and diagrams, but I couldn't make heads or tails of them. I think my mother could at least understand the German, but she would only say it was somewhat like the Bible. One day when I wasn't looking, she tried to put it in the trash, but I managed to rescue it."

Myra was clearly curious about Lurleen's revelation. "Did you ever find out more about the book?"

"Yes. I kept it hidden from my mom. She clearly was made uncomfortable by the book but never told me any more about it. When I went to college, I took German, and by the second semester I could read enough to figure out some of what the book was about." Lurleen hesitated before continuing her explanation. "Have you ever heard of the

*Grimoire?* "

"I can't say I have. What is it?"

"It is an ancient book of magic. It contains all sorts of spells and incantations. There are still many parts of it I don't understand."

"Why did your grandfather send it to you? Do you have any idea?"

"It took a lot of research and digging, but I came up with some answers, partial answers anyway. I am pretty sure my grandfather was a warlock, a male witch.

"Surely you are joking," Myra interrupted.

"I wish I were, but it is even more complicated than that. I think I too might be a witch." Lurleen blurted out her words and then felt a sudden t desire to take them back. But, like spilled milk, it was too late for that.

"That's crazy. This is the 21$^{st}$ century. There are no witches now, and here never were!" Myra looked and sounded worried, worried about her roommate's sanity.

"Myra, it's true. I really think I could be a witch. I mean I don't ride a broomstick, or boil lizards in a big cauldron, but I may be a witch. I think that is why I have the power over men that I do. I have even played around casting a few spells on men. It seems like my abilities have increased over time, but I feel I have only scratched the surface. If I could read and understand more of the book I told you about and then practiced what I read, I am pretty sure I could enhance the range and power of my abilities. I hope I haven't scared you…you're probably wishing you had a different roommate."

Myra forced a laugh as she responded, "Lurleen, I don't really believe what you are telling me. What makes you so sure you're a witch? Is it that you can seduce and manipulate men? So your grandfather gave you a book of spells, that doesn't make you a witch. Even if it is true, which I doubt, I think it is kinda cool. Just please don't use your magic on me…unless it is to make me irresistible to men!"

Myra, it's more than the book or my ability to read men's thoughts. Let me explain. I guess I was about twelve when one night I was taking a bath and I discovered a reddish mark on my inner thigh. I thought at first it might have been an insect bite because I had never noticed it before, but closer inspection showed it to be a mark, a symbol of some kind. For a long time, I was puzzled by the mark and hoped it would disappear, but it didn't. Then one day I was thumbing through the book my grandfather gave me and I saw the exact same symbol as the one on my leg. It took a while for me to determine what sort of symbol, and when I did, I was shocked. Back during the time of the Salem witch trials women suspected of being a witch were examined for various body marks like an extra breast or a special birth mark. That is when I learned that the mark on my leg was actually the symbol of a witch, and I didn't put it there It just appeared along about the time I had my first period."

Myra was stunned and all she could utter was a weak "Oh, my God." Her fear that her roommate was seriously disturbed increased dramatically, compelling her to suggest that Lurleen really should speak to a therapist.

"If you think I am crazy, let me show you something else." Lurleen walked back into her bedroom and retrieved her copy of the *Grimoire*. Its wooden cover was truly beautiful as she held it up for Myra to see.

This is it. See, I didn't make it up, and I can show you the symbol."

Myra reached out to touch the book but then abruptly withdrew her hand as if shocked. "Oh! I got a funny feeling when I touched the book. It was a tingling sensation like a mild electric shock. Could that mean I am a witch?"

"No, I think it just shows that there is a power in the book. Call it magic or whatever you want, but I think there is a dark kind of power in it." Lurleen then showed Myra the symbol as further proof of her claim to be a witch. Taking a deep breath Lurleen, looked intently at her roommate. "Myra, I know I am asking a lot, but please keep all of this to yourself. Can you do that?"

"I can."

Chapter Twelve

Compassion is not something you have;

It is something you share.

-Shannon Alder

Winter had all but lost its grip on the land, soon to be replaced by the green colors and new life of spring. For some time, Alexis Richards had felt a desire to expand her horizons either through employment or volunteer work. Elizabeth Richards was showing increased verbal and motor skill development, as well an insatiable curiosity so Alexis and Nathan both felt that she could benefit from either pre-K or day care experience. After a rather extensive search, Alexis had found a high-quality day care program only a few miles from their home. Placing Lizzy in a good day care would be beneficial for her development and also permit Alexis to work outside the home. Shortly after spring break ended, she had seen an online ad for a position with The North Carolina Division of Social Services. The opening was for a newly created position within the department for a child placement coordinator. The individual who filled the position would have the responsibility for conducting evaluations and making recommendations regarding foster home placements and adoptions of children. Qualifications for the position were a degree in social work or child development. Alexis' background was in elementary education with a minor in psychology, and even though her education wasn't exactly what was called for, she decided to apply anyway. To her great surprise and excitement, she was hired.

Alexis would have a small office in downtown Durham, but her job required some travel in and around the so-called golden triangle area. It was after six o'clock when she returned home from her first full day on the job. She walked in the door full of excitement but clearly tired from the day's activities. Nathan had already picked up Lizzy from day care and was busily preparing dinner for the family. He greeted her warmly with a hug. "Welcome home! How was your first day?"

"It was really good...all orientation and training. I clearly have a lot to learn about the state's rules and regulations, but I think I am going to like the job. It will give me a chance to feel like I am doing something really worthwhile. I may need to consult you from time to time as I do evaluations of possible foster placements."

"I'll be glad to help any way I can. You have a very good sense of people and their basic nature, so you'll do fine. Sometimes more education just clouds a person's vision. Lexi, I really want you to know how proud I am of you."

Lizzy had been waiting patiently for her mother's attention. Finally, she tugged on Alexis's pants' leg and blurted out, "Look, Mommy! I drew a picture of you and Jake, and our house while I was at my school today." Lizzy looked up at her mom with enthusiasm as she handed several sheets of drawing paper to her mother.

"These are so good, sweetie! I really like the picture you drew of our whole family. I think you must have had a very good day at your school."

"I did! We went on a field trip and saw some farm animals. I wish we could have a goat! If you want me to, I can draw you a picture of a goat."

Alexis laughed with surprise as she responded to Lizzy's comment. "Why a goat, honey? Did you see one today?"

"Yes, and his name was Billy…like in the story about Billy Goat Gruff."

Alexis smiled in reply. "That's one of your dad's favorite story books, isn't it?"

"Yes, I like it too, even though Daddy's book is very old and falling apart."

Clearly it had been a good day for the Richards' family. Nathan's classes went well and he had done a good bit of library research on his list of most evil people. Just as he was preparing to head home, he was notified that the warden at Central Prison in Raleigh had agreed to meeting with him about possibly interviewing the infamous serial killer, Jeremiah Murdoc. After dinner, the family sat in the living room area and shared aspects of their respective days. Only Jake had little to contribute other than an occasional yawn.

After putting Lizzy to bed, Alexis returned to the living room where Nathan had poured two glasses of wine. "I think we should drink a toast to your new position.

"I'll drink to that," she replied, taking a glass from Nathan. "I guess my only concern will be getting Lizzy to and from daycare each day."

"I think we'll be able to manage it. My hours are pretty flexible, and if we got in a real bind, Nancy Bradfield has offered to be a backup." Alexis drained her glass of wine and then hugged Nathan tightly. "I love you so much, and you'll never know how much your support means to me. I think having this job will really be good for me and…good for the whole family, I hope," she said with a smile. "I think I could use another glass of wine. Can I get one for you?"

"Sure, why not? You know, Lexi, I think that doing something for other people makes us better people ourselves. Goodness knows that kids who've been taken from their parents and placed in foster care need a little love and compassion. Maybe God wanted you to have this job."

That night, Nathan and Alexis made love, the first time in over a month. Both slept well. At the time Nathan and Alexis had no way of knowing that a good night's sleep was something that would become rare in the not-too-distant future.

Chapter Thirteen

When you are ignorant of your enemy but know yourself,

your chances of winning or losing are equal

-Sun Tzu

Dr. Richards hung up the phone after scheduling a meeting with the war den at Central Prison where Jeremiah Murdoc was incarcerated. His knowledge of Murdoc was fairly superficial so he decided to learn as much as he could about the man before meeting with the warden. While he was at it, he decided it would be a good idea to learn something about the prison warden too. After a few key strokes, Nathan found a considerable amount of information on Jeremiah Murdoc, mostly from newspaper articles. Murdoc, it seemed, was a complex figure often compared to Dr. Hannibal Lecter, the villain in the movie *Silence of the Lambs*. Like the movie character, Murdoc had been a psychiatrist who apparently was a master of hypnosis and a very cunning interviewer. According to some reports, Murdoc was able to uncover some very deep, personal information from his patients which he would then use to select his victims.

His victims were mostly young women; however, two were older men.

Commentary provided by a psychologist who had evaluated him prior to the trial suggested that Murdoc had some unresolved issues with his father which led to his killing of the two men. It was also theorized that Murdoc had been rejected by a woman he met in college who spurned his affections, and he never got over that rejection.

Nathan found only a small amount of information on the prison warden, Harvel Henderson. Henderson was a career correctional officer who worked his way up from prison guard to assistant warden and then eventually warden. He was put in charge of Central Prison which was where the "criminally insane" were held. The prison had a reputation of being a dangerous and poorly run facility until Henderson took over five years ago. From what Richards could discern, Warden Henderson ran a tight ship. There was a very small amount of information he was able to glean from Facebook and LinkedIn which suggested that Warden Henderson was both politically and religiously very conservative.

On the day of his scheduled meeting with Warden Henderson, the weather was sunny and mild. Nathan Richards arrived early since he was totally unfamiliar with the layout of the prison. Central Prison had a sprawling campus with a curious variety of architectural designs. As he pulled into the main parking area, he was confronted with an oddly triangular-shaped complex of buildings that appeared to be outside the main prison walls which Nathan assumed were for administrative offices.

The unit was a maximum-security prison that housed death row inmates along with the mentally ill and other extremely dangerous offenders. Nathan had done a few evaluations in a prison setting in Ohio and he was familiar with locked wards in a hospital, but nothing had prepared him for what he encountered at Central Prison.

After checking in at the reception desk, Nathan was ushered through security which was far more stringent than any he had encountered in airport security. Once through security he was escorted to the Warden's office. After a brief wait, Warden Henderson emerged from his office to greet Nathan. Henderson was a tall, thin individual with closely cropped hair which looked military. He wore a narrow string tie, white shirt, dark trousers and military style boots. There was nothing in the information Nathan had located to indicate that Henderson was retired military, but he sure looked the part.

"Dr. Richards, I presume," Henderson said, extending his hand in greeting. "I am sorry to keep you waiting. I was on the phone with the governor, and his calls end when he is ready to end them."

"No problem, Warden Henderson. I haven't been waiting long at all. Thank you for seeing me today. I know you must be very busy."

"Come into my office so we can talk. Would you care for a cup of coffee?" Warden Henderson led Richards into his office and motioned to a chair. He in turn sat behind his desk which was covered with papers and folders. Before Nathan could say yes or no to the offer of coffee, the warden poured a cup and handed it to Dr. Richards. "Tell me about the reasons you would like to interview Jeremiah Murdoc."

Before answering, Nathan took a sip of the coffee. It was hot, bitter and very strong, tasting like it had been cooking all morning. "I am doing some research for a book I hope to write. As you know I have a faculty position at Duke. My position is a bit unusual in that I am appointed in Psychology and the Divinity School. My research involves evil and an age-old question about it... Let me explain a bit further. Some theologians believe in Satan, the devil, an arch enemy of God, while others reject that notion and believe that evil is not an entity but just a way to describe behavior which is very harmful in nature. Psychology doesn't really take a position about the existence of an individual called Satan or the devil, it merely focuses on why human beings act in aggressive, hurtful ways. I am trying to ascertain whether some people so completely enmeshed in their evil ways that they can actually evolve or devolve into demonic figures. Does that make sense?"

"That is mighty interesting, Dr. Richards. However, I have never been one to question the good book. If it says there is a devil, then there is a devil. But…I certainly think some people are so dedicated to evil pursuits that they become distinctly different from your garden variety criminal. It's kinda like a mad dog, you know a rabid dog…they are different from a regular dog. A'course we know why they are so crazy, but with people…who knows why. Maybe psychologists like you know.

What do you hope to gain from talking to Dr. Murdoc?" The warden leaned back in his chair and propped his feet on his desk as he looked squarely at Nathan.

"Well, warden, there is only so much I can learn by reading about evil people like Hitler, Charles Manson, or Jeremiah Murdoc. What I would really like to ask Murdoc is how he views his actions. Does he view what he did as evil or does he justify it in some way? Many years ago, the philosopher Socrates wrote that no man knowingly does evil because he finds some way to rationalize it."

Yeah, criminals definitely find a way to justify what they do, even to the point of convincing themselves that what they did really wasn't a crime. I recall a sort of funny example of a fella I knew who was arrested for animal cruelty. He had an old mule that he tied to the back of his pickup, and he pulled the poor animal down the road. He was so convinced that he was just training the beast that he steadfastly claimed he had committed no crime even when confronted with the animal cruelty statute."

"I think that is probably what Socrates had in mind, warden."

After the better part of an hour, Warden Henderson abruptly got up from behind his desk and extended his hand to Nathan. "Well, sir, I have enjoyed talking to you…and I think we can allow you to visit with our good Dr. Murdoc. I don't know how much you'll learn from him or how cooperative he'll be, but if he is agreeable, I'll approve your request. I will let you know what he says.

"Thank you, warden. I appreciate your help and I will be very respectful of Dr. Murdoc's rights."

Warden Henderson laughed as he guided Nathan towards his office door. "Murdoc doesn't have any rights unless I give them to him, so you don't have to worry about him. I'll let you know what the ground rules are." Nathan had already turned to go when Warden Henderson called out, "Dr. Richards, I should warn you that some of the men are very afraid of Murdoc. A few even say he has some sort of special powers, but I personally have never seen that…just thought you ought to know."

As Nathan drove away from the prison, he reflected on his conversation with the warden, and decided it went about as well as it could have. He wondered whether or not Murdoc would agree to being interviewed. From what he had read about serial killers, they enjoyed being the center of attention so maybe that might improve the chances of an interview being granted. The answer to his question came much sooner than he expected. Nathan had hardly walked through the door to his office at the university when his cell phone began to chirp and vibrate. It was the warden's office. Nathan answered quickly, "Hello, this is Dr. Richards."

The voice at the other end of the line was the warden's secretary. "Dr. Richards, this is Betty Knapp, Warden Henderson's secretary at Central Prison." She paused for Nathan's acknowledgement and then continued

"Warden Henderson wanted me to let you know that Jeremiah Murdoc agreed to meeting with you. The Warden will send you some possible dates and times for your initial visit with Murdoc.

"That's great. Tell Warden Henderson thank you. I will look forward to getting those dates from him." As he hung up, Nathan felt a sudden chill which he didn't know if it was from excitement or fear. *Will this be a win for me or a terrible loss?* Nathan thought again about the warden's warning and the character Hannibal Lecter with his frightening powers of mental persuasion. Although he had seen some pretty disturbed individuals in his clinical years, he had never seen anyone like Lecter. He tried unsuccessfully to convince himself that Hannibal Lecter was just a fictional character and that no one had his degree of mind control, but what was the warden warning him about with Murdoc? What special power might he possess? As he sat alone in his office, the word "Svengali" came to mind, so he did a Google search and learned that the term Svengali was the name of a character in a novel written back in the late 1800's. Over time the name has come to mean a person who dominates and controls others with evil intent. Perhaps, he thought, there probably are some Svengali types in the world. Jim Jones or David Koresh might be examples. *Well, if I am to understand truly evil people, I need to meet one in the flesh. There is only so much I can learn from a book.*

## Chapter Fourteen

*I can't get you out of my mind. I think about you all the time*

-Tommy Page

Alexis Richards had only been in her new position as foster care placement coordinator for a little over one month when she did an evaluation of a twelve-year-old boy. The child was a Caucasian lad who had been in and out of six separate foster care homes. In each case the foster parents reported that he was unmanageable, accusing him of theft, animal cruelty, and fire-starting. However, in her assessment, Alexis saw another side of the boy whose name was David Charles. Instead of a budding, antisocial personality, she saw a frightened boy who had been dealt a bad hand from the very start. She felt a deep sense of compassion for him and knew that the writing was on the wall for his future, and that future didn't look good. Try as she might she couldn't get him out of her mind. When she stopped at the day care center to pick up Lizzy she sat in the car for a few minutes before exiting. *I wonder if we could adopt him? How would Lizzy feel about suddenly having an older brother?*

As always, Lizzy was delighted to see her mom. She was literally bubbling over with enthusiasm about her day. "Today, our teacher brought her pet rabbit to school. He was so cute. He was brown and had a pink nose. He was just like Peter Rabbit in my story book at home. Do you think we could have a rabbit?"

"Lizzy, first you wanted to have a goat, now you want a rabbit. I don't think Daddy would approve, and besides, what about Jake? He might not like a goat and he'd probably chase a rabbit." Alexis gave her best argument against adopting a rabbit, but she didn't think Lizzy was about to give up so easily. Trying a distraction tactic, she asked Lizzy a question. "Lizzy, what would you think about having a brother?"

Lizzy looked at her mother with a surprised look on her face. "You mean a baby brother?"

"Maybe or how about an older brother? He could show you lots of things, play games with you, and later on help you with your school work."

That would be okay, I guess, but I'd rather have a rabbit."

Alexis smiled at her daughter and her simple, accepting view of the world. No wonder Jesus loved children so much and saw great value in the simplicity and goodness of a child's view of the world. She wondered where along the way we adults lose that capacity to see the simple goodness of life or the capacity to live so fully in the present moment? Why does life have to become so complicated? Why is it that life can be so unfair to some and so benevolent to others? Once again, in her mind, she saw the sad face of David Charles and felt a lump in her throat. Could she bring up the idea of adopting him to Nathan? It had been an emotionally draining day for Alexis, and she felt a wave of fatigue wash over her as she kissed Elizabeth good night and walked back into the living room. Nathan was watching the evening news with the tv volume turned down so as not to keep Lizzy awake.

He looked up at Alexis as she collapsed onto the sofa next to him. "Hey, hon. You look beat. Rough day?"

Alexis shook her head before responding verbally. "Well, not really…just…emotionally tiring. I guess that's the best way to put it." Alexis was uncertain whether to tell Nathan about her thoughts on adopting David Charles or just sweep the idea under the rug.

"Did something happen at work? If you want to talk about it, I'm all ears."

"I guess I should just tell you. I did an evaluation on a twelve-year-old boy named David Charles. His foster family was sending him back because they said they couldn't manage him, but…that's not the half of it. He has been sent back from foster placements at least five or six different times, and I felt so sorry for him, Nathan."

That is bad. Why have his foster placements not worked out?"

Over the next thirty minutes Alexis gave Nathan as much of the boy's history as she knew about, but she stopped short of telling him about her desire to adopt him.

Nathan shook his head before responding. "Lexi, I guess you know his history is very worrisome. The things you mentioned like stealing, running away, fire-setting, animal cruelty, and bed-wetting all point towards a future diagnosis of an antisocial personality disorder. This kid is likely headed for the penitentiary I know you'd like to rescue him; you've always wanted to save every stray dog or cat, but this is different

You can't save them all. Maybe you can get him more therapy or a better foster placement."

Alexis wanted to respond but kept silent instead. Finally, she spoke as she got up to head for bed. "I know, Nathan. I know. I just can't get this kid out of my mind."

Nathan stood up and hugged Alexis. "You've got a big heart and that is one of the reasons I love you so much. Let's go to bed. You may feel better after a good night's sleep."

Alexis smiled, but deep inside she knew that she would likely not get a good night's sleep and she would not feel better tomorrow. Intellectually, she understood that her husband was right about the boy, but her heart wouldn't give up on him. That night she did sleep and she dreamed a strange and haunting dream. In her dream she saw an old man who resembled Gandalf, the wizard in <u>Lord of The Rings</u>. The old man sought her from out of a crowd and delivered an urgent message, a sort of warning like an amber alert. The message involved a lost boy whose fate rested in her hands. Alexis felt deeply troubled when she awoke from the dream. Nathan was still asleep so she got up quietly and went into the kitchen to fix some coffee. Jake followed silently at her heels. *What did the dream mean? Could it be God nudging me to help some boy or was it just my need to rescue strays?* After Nathan got up and Lizzy was fed and dressed, there were a few moments of quiet before everyone left for the day's activities, and Alexis wanted desperately to talk to Nathan about the dream and her thoughts regarding young David Charles. In

spite of her desire to talk, she kept quiet. After dropping Lizzy off at day care, Alexis' thoughts returned to the dream and her desire to help the boy. *Was he the boy in the dream?*

    Back in her office Alexis pulled David Charles's file searching for anything positive she could use to try to persuade Nathan to at least consider being a foster parent for the boy. To her dismay, she couldn't find much. There was a high degree of consistency among the concerns mentioned by the foster parents. One thing she did notice was that all the foster parents were older, the youngest couple being fifty-one and fifty-three. Of course, she had no way of knowing if age was a contributing factor to the problems experienced by the foster parents. The only thing she thought she could build on that seemed at all positive was her own gut level reaction. She was convinced she had seen something redeemable in the boy. *Will my gut reaction be enough to persuade Nathan to give David a chance?*

Chapter Fifteen

Thou shalt not suffer a witch to live.

-Exodus 22:18

Sometimes in graduate level seminars, class discussion can venture pretty far afield from its initial focus. Nathan Richards was learning this first hand in his course on faith and doubt. The class discussion began with a look at some examples of faith and doubt in the Old Testament, but somehow it morphed into a rather heated debate on several oddities found in the Old Testament and whether or not they had any relevance for life today. Some of the more conservative members of the class were really put on the defensive by the liberal or progressive students. Lurleen Montgomery found herself losing interest in the banter of the class until her daydreaming was suddenly brought to a halt by something her roommate, Myra Napier said. Seemingly out of the blue, Myra brought up the topic of the so-called Witch of Endor found in First Samuel, chapter 28. In those versus King Saul consults the Witch of Endor and asks her to call up the ghost or shade of Samuel from *sheol*, the land of the dead.

Her point in bringing up those verses was to question how anyone could think everything in the Bible was literally true and actually happened, but Lurleen was stunned by her roommate's actions; it seemed like a betrayal of the confidence she had recently placed in Myra.

From the Witch of Endor to the Salem witch trials, the class discussion lurched until Nathan brought the discussion to a halt. "Okay, guys. This has been a spirited and interesting discussion, but we have moved pretty far away from our original considerations," Nathan said as he tried to redirect the group back to the subject he had planned for the day. His efforts were in vain however as the argument about witches continued.

Ivan Osterhouse, the quietest member of the class, suddenly spoke up, his voice full of emotion. "How can anyone take those passages in First Samuel seriously? Does anybody other than maybe a few kooks or weirdos believe in witches? Also, if we consider those verses in Exodus that says witches should be put to death, and the Bible is taken literally, then the Salem witch trials and executions were all justified. I just can't understand people who try to take a literalistic view of the Bible."

After Ivan's comments, the class was silent for a few moments. Lurleen Montgomery made no comments on the subject of witches but inside her emotions were raging. She felt both fear and anger. Her anger was directed mostly at Myra, but her fear seemed more global and less directed at anyone in particular. Acting on impulse, she abruptly got up from her chair and bolted from the classroom. Shortly after her departure, Nathan brought the class session to a close some fifteen minutes early, and Myra Napier hurriedly pursued her roommate. Myra saw Lurleen sitting on a bench outside the Gray Building. "Lurleen, I am so sorry. I didn't mean to upset you. I wasn't going to…"

"You weren't going to what? Tell the class that I'm a witch? How could you do it when I asked you and you promised to keep what I shared with you a secret." Lurleen got up to leave, but Myra caught her by the arm and pulled her back.

"Wait, please! I wasn't thinking about you and I certainly wasn't going to say anything about what you told me. I had just read that section of First Samuel this morning and it was on my mind. It seemed relevant to our discussion so I brought it up, but honestly, I wasn't thinking about you. I really don't believe that you're what you claim to be anyway." Lurleen shook her arm free from Myra and walked away without looking back, her anger at a boil. She went straight to her car and then to her apartment. Almost as if driven by some primitive instinct she went to her bedroom, closed the door and pulled out her prize possession, the *Grimoire*. Not really knowing why, she began flipping through its pages, wishing somehow she could decode more of its contents. After a couple of hours of frustrating attempts to interpret the magic of the Grimoire, Lurleen heard her roommate enter the apartment, so she put the book back in its drawer and took a deep breath in an effort to quell her anger at her roommate.

Myra was standing at the refrigerator door when Lurleen addressed her. She turned and started to speak when Lurleen held up her hand as if to signal stop. "Myra, maybe you didn't intend to reveal my secret this morning, but it seemed more than coincidence to me that you brought up the subject of witches so soon after our conversation."

Myra could tell that Lurleen was still angry and that any attempt to explain would be useless and might even make things worse, so she opted for a simple apology. "I am very sorry, Lurleen, and I will never bring up witches to anyone in the future."

Sensing her roommate's fear and sincerity, Lurleen nodded and Attempted a smile as she responded, "Myra, I accept your apology. Let's just drop it for now."

Myra coughed and took a couple of breaths before she replied. "Uh. Okay. Let's do that."

Chapter Sixteen

I am he as you are he as you are me

and we are all together

-The Beatles

Ever since learning that he would be granted an interview with the serial killer, Jeremiah Murdoc, Nathan Richards had been learning as much as he could about the man. From his extensive background research, he had been able to piece together a fairly coherent picture of Murdoc. Nathan had learned that Murdoc's father was a cruel man who was physically abusive to young eventually Jeremiah and his mother. Murdoc's father murdered Jeremiah's mother in a drunken fit of rage. Murdoc's father was subsequently arrested, convicted and executed by the state of Alabama where the family was living at the time. Since both parents eventually died, Jeremiah was placed in an orphanage, a ward of the state of Alabama. At age eighteen Murdoc ventured out on his own, working as a day laborer. He eventually saved up enough money to start college, but due to his continuing financial difficulties, Murdoc took seven years to complete his undergraduate degree. Because he was intellectually gifted, he did well enough academically to be admitted to medical school at the University of Alabama where he graduated in four years.

Murdoc went on to complete a three-year residency in psychiatry, then took a job at a state mental hospital where he worked for several years. While working as a staff psychiatrist, Murdoc studied hypnosis and became quite expert in its use. After his stint in the state hospital, Murdoc moved to North Carolina and opened a private practice in Chapel Hill. His practice was very successful and included a number of wealthy patients, most of whom were women. According to newspaper accounts Dr. Murdoc kidnapped, tortured, then brutally murdered and dismembered his victims. His two male victims were not his patients, but both were apparently alcoholics whom Murdoc killed with a knife, one in an alley, the other in a parking lot. One of the men was a homeless vagrant and the other was a lawyer who had come out of a downtown tavern in an intoxicated state. Murdoc never explained his motivation for killing the

men. His reasons for having killed the women were bizarre and murky apparently built around his belief that they were all Jezebels that had teased and then rejected men. The prosecution had claimed Murdoc murdered the women as form of revenge for possibly having been rejected by a woman himself.

Finally, the day Richards was scheduled to interview Dr. Jeremiah Murdoc arrived, and Nathan had to admit he was more than a bit anxious. As he parked his car in the prison parking lot, he noticed his palms were very moist. He dried his hands on his pants legs several times before shaking hands with the prison warden. After his brief meeting with the warden Nathan was searched and then escorted by a burly prison guard into the bowels of the prison. On his way to the room where he was to interview Murdoc, Nathan heard the sound of heavy metal gates clanging shut and thought of the sign over the entrance to Hades as described by Dante: *Abandon hope all ye who enter*. The interview room was small but brightly lit. The room contained a metal table which was bolted to the floor and two metal chairs. The room had two doors, one which opened off the main hallway and other which led back to the administrative segregation or solitary confinement area of the prison. The guard opened the interview room for Nathan and gestured to one of the chairs. After a few moments the other door opened and Nathan got his first look at Jeremiah Murdoc. Murdoc was escorted by two guards. His hands and feet were shackled making it difficult for him to walk. Murdoc shuffled over to the table and took the other chair. His guards repositioned his handcuffs locking them to a metal cleat that was welded to the table. The guard who escorted Nathan to the interview room said he would be just outside the door and would wait there until called back in by Richards. The guards that escorted Murdoc left without saying a word.

Dr. Murdoc was smaller and older looking than Nathan had anticipated probably because all of the pictures he had seen of the man were several years old. When Murdoc looked up from the table, he stared deeply into Nathan's eyes, and as he did so, Richards felt a cold chill wash over his body. He struggled to introduce himself to Murdoc, embarrassed by the high pitch of his own voice. He knew it would reveal his fear. Murdoc's expressionless face gradually morphed into a sardonic smile.

Hello, Dr. Richards. I have been eagerly awaiting our little meeting. I get very few visitors anymore. I am so happy to meet you, but I must say you seem a little anxious. Please, let me assure you that you have nothing to fear from me." As he spoke, Murdoc raised his hands enough to draw the chains tight so they would clank and rattle. "You, see…I am quite secure. Now, please tell me what it is you want to learn from me."

"Well, Dr. Murdoc, first let me thank you for agreeing to meet with me. I am sure you have had more than your share of people wanting to interview or evaluate you for one reason or another. I am here to learn from you, not to judge you or condemn you…"

Murdoc interrupted, "That is kind of you, but let's get down to business, shall we? Tell me about yourself. Our dear warden gave me very little information about you other than you are a faculty member at the Divinity School. I love that name…Divinity School… so quaint, so pure…it also reminds me of that candy…you know the one I mean. I got some at the county fair once when I was a boy." Murdoc's smile faded and his cold blue eyes seemed to bore more deeply into the depths of Nathan's mind.

Cautiously, Nathan began his introduction, "My first career was as a psychologist. I worked in the VA hospital system for eight years before I went to seminary which prepared me to become a Methodist minister. I served two churches in Texas before taking a faculty position at Duke. I have a joint appointment in Psychology and with the Divinity School." Nathan paused, hoping to get some sense of Murdoc's reaction, but he saw none and so he continued. "I have had some rather intense encounters with evil, some might say that I faced the devil himself…"

Murdoc's eyes began to glitter and his sardonic smile returned.

"Oh, how very interesting! Tell me about your encounter with the devil. Did he have horns and a tail? Did he carry a pitch fork?"

"None of those things. Frankly he is hard to describe, but he was terrifying, especially his eyes," Nathan felt the sudden coldness and terror he had experienced back at Hell's Gate. He struggled to collect his thoughts before continuing. "I don't know if he was Satan or not, but I don't really want to talk about him."

Murdoc chuckled. "Too bad, I would like to hear more about him, but please continue."

"Well, I am trying to understand what people commonly refer to as evil. As I am sure you know, everyone has their own definition of evil, but what I hope to better understand is how the people who are accused of evil actually see what they do. Do they see it as evil or…"

Murdoc seemed to complete Nathan's statement for him, "Or do they justify it in some way? Dr. Richards, you were obviously going to use Socrates' quotation where he said that no man knowingly does evil, weren't you?" Murdoc's expression revealed his belief in his superior intellect much like that of a parent explaining something to a young, naïve child.

Richards was stunned by Murdoc's words. *How had Murdoc known what I was going to say? Could he read my thoughts?* Nathan continued, "Well, something like that, I guess. You were convicted of several murders and I would very much like to understand how you saw your actions. Did you see them as bad or wrong? I don't want to label what you did. I would just like to see through your eyes as much as possible, Dr. Murdoc."

"Oh, that is nice, but do you really want to see through my eyes? Aren't you afraid of what you might see…or of what it might do to you?"

Murdoc became silent for what seemed to Nathan like several minutes before he spoke again. "Dr. Richards, if you want to see through my eyes, you must first look into my eyes. Focus, then look deeply and blink only when you absolutely have to."

Nathan heard the obvious embedded command in Murdoc's tone of voice, and he began to feel as if Murdoc was attempting to hypnotize him. Because he had some training in hypnosis himself, Nathan felt he was immune to any attempts by others to hypnotize him without his permission. However, he had to admit that staring into Murdoc's eyes was clearly having an unexpected effect. Nathan could almost feel himself being drawn into Murdoc's mind, his inner being, his soul. The interview room appeared to be growing darker and darker!

Murdoc's words seemed to resonate and reverberate in Nathan's unconscious mind almost as if they were his own thoughts. "There is nothing now but darkness, only darkness. It is pointless to resist the darkness. Simply open yourself to a new way of seeing, a new way of understanding. In the darkness there is light. My thoughts are now your thoughts! You are me and I am you!" I am God's instrument, just as you must become His instrument. What God commands, we must do. I am God's instrument, His avenging angel! You also will become one of

God's avenging angels! God does no evil and as God's instrument, I do no evil either. Like me you must learn to see the world's deception for what it is. The truth will set you free. You have so much to learn about what you call evil, and I will instruct you. Evil is not what you think. There are many around you that lie to you. What you have believed about God is false. For so long you have struggled with doubts and uncertainty. Now I can give you the clarity of vision that you

seek." After a brief pause, Murdoc continued, "You surely recall the Book of Job, and in that book please note that Satan does not create evil,

he merely points out to God the evil inclinations and actions of human beings. Satan has always been misunderstood; he is the light-bringer, the morning star, not some vile snake that crawls on its belly."

To Nathan's surprise, Murdoc's words seemed to ring true in spite of the fact that they ran counter to what he had always believed. With a smile, Jeremiah Murdoc continued his teaching, "Satan brought light, the light of knowledge into the darkness of the world. As an instrument of God, you and I have an important role to play in the world. Not everyone has been entrusted to do God's will. I bring light into the darkness, and I also bring God's vengeance. You mistakenly believe that you were called to make followers of Jesus, but what you are really doing is bringing confusion and prejudice into the world. As a true instrument of

God, you must point out the evil actions and intentions of others so that they can be cleansed by God. Do you understand?"

Nathan nodded slowly in response.

"That is very good. Now, I will count to five and then you will open your eyes. You will retain the secrets I have revealed to you in the very deepest levels of your mind, and you will begin to see the light, the light which shines forth from out of the darkness."

Nathan had temporarily lost all sense of time and reality contact until he heard the voice of the burly guard who had been his escort. "Dr. Richards, are you all right? I haven't heard your voice for some time now."

Opening the door, the guard looked briefly at Nathan and then with suspicion at Murdoc. "You have been here over an hour. It is time we took Mr. Murdoc back to his cell."

Slowly Nathan reoriented to his surroundings before he answered. "Oh, yes, I didn't realize we had been here so long. Uh, yeah, I am fine. I was just listening very closely to what Dr. Murdoc was telling me, but you are right. It is time we stopped." Nathan looked at Murdoc, a blank expression on his face, "Thank you Dr. Murdoc. Perhaps we can meet again." The guard summoned Murdoc's guards and then led Nathan from the interview room into the long corridor from which they had come. Nathan signed out on the visitor's log and then walked slowly towards the parking lot. He found it difficult to concentrate or even remember where he had parked. Finally, after wandering aimlessly around the crowded parking lot, he located his car. Once settled in the driver's seat of his faithful old Honda he took a couple of deep breaths and then repeated the Jesus prayer several times. Normal cognitive function returned slowly as Nathan began to drive from the prison parking lot. *What happened back there? I feel like I was drugged.*

*All I seem to remember is that Murdoc and I are instruments of God and that I will begin to see the lies, but what lies? Whose lies?*

Nathan drove back to the university and walked to his office hoping his mind would clear enough that he could record more of the salient details of his interview with the infamous Jeremiah Murdoc; however, the one and only thought that stood out clearly in his mind were the words "instrument of God". *What did that mean?* When he confronted the satanic figure at Hell's Gate in Lubbock, was he acting as an instrument of God? Nathan pulled his battered old Bible from the shelf and began to thumb through its pages; as he did so, a passage in the Book of Acts caught his eye: "But the Lord said to him, go, for he is an instrument of mine to carry my name before the Gentiles and kings and the children of Israel." From somewhere in the dark recesses of his mind, Nathan recalled the words of a hymn which said in effect "make me an instrument of thy peace". *Is that what Murdoc believes? That he is God's instrument who visits God's wrath and vengeance upon sinful individuals? Is that how he brings God's peace?* From his clinical experience with schizophrenics, Nathan understood that such delusional thinking was not uncommon. Psychotics often believed that they were God or Jesus or a prophet and were on some sort of holy mission. Maybe the psychological evaluations of Murdoc were correct when they diagnosed him as schizophrenic or maybe, just maybe what Murdoc said was true! Try as he might, he couldn't explain what had happened during the time he spent with Murdoc. It felt like Murdoc had sucked out all of Nathan's thoughts and somehow replaced them with his beliefs, as if he was pulling up weeds and planting new seeds. Nathan's thoughts and emotions were a whirling jumble, like the "snow" in a Christmas snow globe. Nathan recalled Pilate's question to Jesus in the Gospel of John: "What is truth?" His confused contemplation was interrupted by the sound of his cell phone. It was Alexis calling to see how his interview had gone.

"I guess it went okay, Lexi. He is a strange and rather intimidating guy," Nathan answered in a distracted sounding voice. "I am having a hard time capturing exactly what he told me."

"How long did you spend with Murdoc?" Alexis was feeling mildly concerned because her husband was usually a very good interviewer who was able to recall all the key points from his interviews with people.

"I am not sure. It didn't seem like very long but I believe it was about an hour, maybe a bit longer."

"It's not like you to not remember details of an interview, Nathan…"

"Nothing to be concerned about, Lexi. I just need some time to collect my thoughts and get them down on paper. I'm in my office working on doing that now. I'll be home soon."

## Chapter Seventeen

Workin' on a mystery, goin' wherever it leads.

-Tom Petty

Evan Mitchell, Ph.D. was the Department of Psychology's expert on hypnosis and altered states of consciousness. Nathan had sought him out in hopes of gaining a better understanding of what had transpired during his meeting with Dr. Jeremiah Murdoc. In appearance alone, Evan Mitchell was every bit the stereotype of the analyst. He had a full beard which was turning gray, wore a sportscoat with patches at the elbows; and smoked a pipe whenever it was permitted. As befitting his rank as Full professor, Mitchell had a corner office which was large and lined with books and interesting artifacts he had collected during his extensive travels. Nathan had only interacted with Mitchell briefly during faculty meetings and department socials, so he knew the man mostly by reputation. Nathan did know that Evan Mitchell had studied under some of the biggest names in the field including Milton Erickson and Ernest Rossi.

Mitchell's office door was open when Nathan arrived, so he tapped lightly on the door frame. He was greeted warmly by Dr. Mitchell who rose from behind his desk and shook hands with Nathan. "Dr. Richards, I am so glad you called. I have been wanting to find a time to chat with you ever since you joined our faculty. I am ashamed that I have not already done so. Please have a seat. Can I offer you a soda or some coffee?"

"No, thank you. I should mention that I have read one of your books on hypnotherapy, and it is both a pleasure and an honor to meet with you today. I need to offer an apology of sorts too. I have found that my joint appointment here at Duke has some drawbacks. There are so many people in both my departments that I hardly seem to know any of them very well, and I guess I spend more time in the Divinity School than with Psychology. Please call be Nathan. I have never been much for formal titles, and I never know how people will address me. Some call me doctor, some call me reverend or pastor, and sometimes I have even been called father," Nathan spoke with a smile and a chuckle.

Mitchell smiled an understanding smile as he responded. "Nathan... Good. Please call me Evan. I understand what you mean about joint appointments. My first one out of graduate school was a joint appointment in the medical school and Psychology department at Wisconsin. I thought it would be the best of both worlds, but in reality, I felt like a stranger in both worlds. So, what can I do for you?"

Nathan struggled to find the right words to explain the purpose of his visit even though he had rehearsed them several times. Well, Dr. Mitchell, er...Evan, I don't know exactly how to put it." Nathan commenced to give Evan Mitchell the backstory which led up to his interview with Jeremiah Murdoc. "I guess I am trying to figure out what happened to me during my interview with Murdoc at the prison. I have some training and experience with hypnosis but nothing approaching your level of expertise. I just feel like Murdoc exerted some sort of influence over me, perhaps through hypnosis. I wondered if you think that is possible."

Mitchell had listened intently to the background information Nathan had provided, and he nodded his head and cleared his throat before responding. "Nathan, throughout history there have been many individuals who were thought to be able to exert some degree of mind control over the people they interacted with. I'll be happy to share with you what I know about the subject, but please stop me if I am telling you things you already know."

"Please go ahead. I am very interested."

"Consider the term "Svengali". We use it to refer to someone who is able to control or influence the mind of others. As you may know, Svengali was a character in a novel written by George du Maurier in the late 1800's. In the book, Svengali was a hypnotist who dominated a young Irish girl named Trilby by means of hypnosis. In recent years political figures such as Dick Cheney or Robert McNamara have been described as Svengalis. In fictional accounts the Svengali figure often exerted his mind control by means of hypnosis, but recent research on both rats and humans suggests that hypnosis is not always necessary for such control." Mitchell paused as if to wait for Nathan's response.

"Evan, that is very interesting. Please go on. I have read a little about Svengali but I am not familiar with the research you mentioned." Mitchell continued, "Some mice, that I guess we might call *alpha mice,* seem to dominate the behavior of other mice through a neurological process that has been referred to as synchronization. In humans mirror neurons play a key role in synchronization, empathy and social learning. For example, if we see someone smile, we often smile reflexively, even if we don't know the person or why they were smiling. Conversely, if we witness a child crying in pain, our face and emotional response will often reflect or mirror that same emotion. In therapy, a therapist can tell if there is a high level of rapport in the relationship by making a gesture like scratching an ear to see it the patient will respond similarly."

"Evan, I am somewhat conversant with that research on empathy, but how does that relate to mind control?"

"Well, other research on certain personality disorders,

especially narcissistic and antisocial types seems to indicate that these personalities are often able to control the behavior of others by their strong, confident statements with which the less dominant individual's brain synchronizes rather automatically and unconsciously. This form of influence has nothing to do with people being weak-willed or easily manipulated. Narcissists are not only good at influencing others, but they seem immune to that process themselves because they lack any capacity for empathy, maybe because they lack mirror neurons in the brain."

Hmmm," Nathan responded. "That makes sense and seems to fit Murdoc. He is clearly narcissistic, and he has a manner that reeks of self-confidence and power. Almost everything he says has an embedded command element in it. Even if he just says *good morning*, you almost have to respond in kind."

"And..." Mitchell added, "Murdoc is reputed to be a very skilled hypnotist. So, he has a couple of powerful tools available to him when he wants to influence or dominate another person's thoughts. What do you remember him saying to you?"

"I have really struggled to recall much of anything, even though we were together for more than an hour. Over time I have been able to gradually recall a few shreds of our conversation, however. I remember him saying that he was an *instrument of God*, and if I recall correctly, he said I too am or could be an instrument of God. I think he sees the murders he committed as somehow doing God's will. I also recall him saying something to the effect that if I wanted to see the world as he sees it that I needed to *look into* his eyes. He also spoke about seeing through the lies and discovering the truth. I don't know what he meant by the lies or seeing the light in the darkness. Oh, one other thing…he indicated that he would become my teacher or guide."

Dr. Mitchell nodded and smiled, "It sounds like he probably did hypnotize you using some sort of Ericksonian-type induction. As you know, Milton Erickson was a master at using unexpected and unobtrusive induction techniques that got around people's resistance."

"You mean like the hand shake induction?"

"Exactly…I am wondering about the post hypnotic suggestions he may have implanted in your unconscious? It seems likely that he made some, probably embedded in his statements about you seeing through the lies and learning the truth from him. It sounds as if he expects to see you again."

Yeah, I have wondered about that. I keep having the feeling that he replaced some of my beliefs with his own thoughts, but I can't put my finger on what they might be. I have to admit that there was something frightening about the guy, and I have worked with some pretty disturbed, scary characters over the years."

Mitchell nodded and reached for his pipe. "Darn, I really need to light up this thing. I know I am not supposed to smoke in the building, but would you mind? You won't turn me in?" Mitchell smiled as he opened a window, lit a match and drew several puffs from his pipe. "Much better…I think I am able to reason more effectively when I am smoking my pipe. I guess that is why Sherlock Holmes was a pipe smoker. By the way, didn't you have some sort of frightening encounter with the demonic earlier in your career?"

Nathan laughed and said, "I won't report you, and besides the pipe smoke actually smells good. I have to confess that I too smoked a pipe when I was in graduate school. I guess I thought it made me look more like a psychologist than a mere student. But, in answer to your question…a few years ago I did have an encounter that was truly terrifying. Even now I have trouble talking about it, and it still finds its way into my nightmares."

"Perhaps you can tell me more about it in the future. I am not terribly religious, but I am always interested in occult and unusual experiences. Nathan, I just had an idea. if you'd like, we could do some additional trance work to see if I can help you recall some of the post hypnotic suggestions Murdoc may have left you with. Just a thought…

"Evan, that might be a good idea. I'll check my schedule and get back to you about a time we could meet, and I really appreciate the offer. Also, our discussion today has been most illuminating. Thank you again!"

As Nathan left the Psychology Building and walked toward his office, he felt a sense of inner peace. Maybe, he thought, Mitchell can help me finally figure out what and how Murdoc influenced me. *I will sure feel better if I can solve that mystery.*

Chapter Eighteen

Fair is foul, and foul is fair:
Hover through the fog and filthy air

-William Shakespeare

A dense fog had enveloped the campus when Lurleen Montgomery left the Divinity School Library. Lights which normally illuminated the walkways across the campus all had an aura around them imparting an eerie, dream-like quality to the scene that greeted Lurleen. The evening had been calm and clear when she first entered the library with good intentions of putting in a solid couple of hours of reading and study. However, she quickly tired of trying to read the works of some 16th century Spanish mystic. Instead of reading more about the levels of the soul, Lurleen opened her laptop and began browsing the internet. For reasons not entirely clear to her, she Googled the word *Grimoire*, and one of the references that came up really surprised and interested her. She discovered the witchcraft library collection at Cornell University which contained over 3,000 books and manuscripts on witches, their trials, persecution, and theology. She also learned that over the centuries there have been many *grimoires,* not just one as she had presumed. She made a mental note to get more information on the witchcraft library, then turned off her computer and left the library. To her surprise the fog was so heavy it quickly dampened her hair and clothes as she walked through the gloom and darkness toward her parked car. So caught up in her curiosity about the witchcraft library collection, Lurleen had failed to notice the even darker outline of a person standing in the deep shadow of a large tree beside the walkway. Out of the corner of her eye, she noticed movement as a figure stepped from the darkness onto the walk just behind her. She felt a sudden surge of fear as she turned to confront the individual. "Who are you? What are you doing?" She blurted out with as much authority as she could muster.

The figure on the walk behind her stopped but remained silent. Lurleen wasn't able to discern any distinguishing features of the person, but because of its size and height, she assumed the *it* was a man. In the heavy fog all she could make out was a dark figure who seemed to be wearing a hooded cape.

Grabbing her cell phone from her jacket pocket, Lurleen challenged the figure standing behind her. "I am calling the campus cops!" The figure neither moved nor spoke. Finally able to summon her usual confidence drawn from her occult powers, Lurleen mentally ordered the figure to move away from her.

"Oh, I felt your push! Very impressive indeed," the figure spoke, but did not move. "You needn't worry. I will not harm you. In fact, I have something for you…something which I think you will come to value greatly. While you don't know me personally, I have already conveyed to you a considerable amount of knowledge, and now I have come to add even more to what you have learned."

"I don't know who you are and I don't want anything from you! I am certain that you have never given me knowledge or anything else for that matter. Please leave me alone!" Lurleen took a couple of tentative steps back, as if to resume her walk to her car.

The dark figure closed the distance between them, seemingly without having to move his feet. "Oh, but I have given you much knowledge, Miss Montgomery. I have communicated with you through your dreams and your thoughts and fantasies. Like an infant who is finally ready for solid food, I have something tangible for you. Think of it as the next phase of education as a witch. Are you interested now? To her surprise Lurleen nodded, then reached out reflexively and the stranger dropped something metallic and cold into her waiting palm. Fear gripped her as she realized she had accepted the offer without any thought as to what she was actually going to receive.

The dark figure spoke again, "You now hold a key which can unlock great power…power you already possess but do not know how to control. What I have given you is not entirely free however; there is a price associated with this pendant, but it is very small. I will explain further after you have had a chance to try it out." As he spoke, the fog seemed to thicken around him and then as suddenly and unexpectedly as he appeared, the dark figure vanished. He had become one with the mist and darkness.

Lurleen blinked several times in a vain attempt to clear her vision, but the specter she had encountered was gone, vanished into the thickening fog. *Who or what was that?* Slowly she walked to her car. Once inside, she turned on the BMW's dome light and studied the metallic object the mysterious individual had dropped into her hand. It was a pendant on a thin chain. The pendant looked like a seven-pointed star with a key across its face. The metal it was made of appeared to be gold, and itwas extremely cold to the touch. Lurleen wondered about the message the stranger had delivered…something about it being a key to power, a power which she possessed but didn't know how to wield. *He referred to my powers as a witch? How could he have known that about me? Who was he? What knowledge had he already given me?* As if moved by invisible hands, Lurleen put the chain around her neck and fastened its clasp. Once in place around her neck, she felt a strange sensation, a feeling she couldn't identify. She started her car and drove the short distance to her apartment. Her apartment was dark when she entered, and she remembered that her roommate said she was going home to look in on her mother who had taken ill, apparently with the Corona virus. Lurleen walked to her bedroom and pulled out her copy of the Grimoire. She thumbed through its pages and quickly realized that the wording and diagrams which had previously been unintelligible were now easily understood. It was as if the pendant she wore functioned like a codex, a \Rosetta stone which allowed her to decipher the text of the Grimoire. *I guess this is what that strange man meant. It's like I have finally graduated and am now a full-fledged witch.* Lurleen looked around her bedroom as if searching for an appropriate test of her enhanced powers. She glanced at the tv screen that hung on the wall and thought about turning it on. To her amazement, the screen bloomed to life. A reporter for CNN was talking about a mass shooting which had just occurred in Texas. *I don't know whether I should be thrilled or terrified with what I can apparently do simply by my thoughts.* Outside the fog which had been so thick was now gone, and the crescent moon shone brightly through her bedroom windows. Had she received a gift from the devil? She wondered if it was a gift that had strings attached. Lurleen undressed and strolled into her bathroom intending to take a hot shower and then go to bed. . Lurleen always took pride in her body, but on this night, she was captivated by the sight of the golden pendant she wore around her neck. Stepping into the shower, her thoughts turned to oneof her professors, Nathan Richards. *What would he do if he could see me now?*

    That night Lurleen Montgomery dreamed dreams that were intensely erotic and incredibly real. Her dreams all involved her capacity to dominate others using her charms both physical and occult. During the early morning hours before the first rays of the sun were visible on the eastern horizon, she awoke and got out of bed. The feeling she experienced was like the feeling she had on Christmas morning before her father's betrayal and her mother's death. She would get out of bed while the house was still dark and still to see if Santa Claus had visited her home. This morning she felt that same excitement as she anticipated using her newly discovered power. *I don't know if he was the devil or not, but I definitely value this pendant. I just wonder about the price that may be attached to it.*

Like almost every morning, Alexis Richards got up before her husband to take care of their daughter which gave Nathan a few moments to linger in the quiet darkness of their bedroom. His thoughts at the moment were a carry-over from his dreams, all of which revolved around one of his students…Lurleen Montgomery. Although his dreams about her were exciting, they were also both embarrassing and deeply troubling because he felt himself being inexorably drawn towards her. It was like being in a small boat without oars or a motor and being pushed by the wind and waves ever closer to the rocks.

## Chapter Nineteen

If at first you don't succeed, try, try again.

-Thomas H. Palmer

Whoever said that hope springs eternal in the human breast must have known Alexis Richards. Once she set her mind to something she did not give up easily, and Alexis had her heart and mind set on helping David Charles find a loving forever home. His track record was not encouraging, as her psychologist-theologian husband had pointed out. How often had she heard him say that the best predictor of future behavior is past behavior? Well, she thought that might be generally true but there are always exceptions to every rule. Pulling into her parking space at her office she felt a spark of hope ignite deep in her heart. She had scheduled another interview with David this very morning. She knew she would find a way to help him. Alexis hung up her jacket and filled her mug with coffee when a state vehicle pulled up in front of her office. She watched through the glass office door as the uniformed officer escorted David in her direction. She whispered a silent prayer as the two individuals walked in. "David, I am so glad to see you again." Looking at his escort, she spoke softly, "I'll take it from here, officer. We won't be more than an hour if you want to wait or I can call you when we are finished." The child protective services officer nodded and turn to take a seat in the waiting area. Putting her arm on David's shoulder Alexis nudged him gently towards her office. David Charles was small for his age with brown hair and eyes. His expression was normally downcast and he seldom made eye contact with other people. "David, I wanted to talk to you about some options I am considering for you."

David stopped in the doorway to her office and looked up at her, anger shown in his face. "Why bother? It won't work out. Just leave me at the orphanage, why don't you? I am tired of going to one home only to be sent back."

Alexis continued into her office and gestured to a chair beside her desk. "David, please come on in and sit down. Would you like a coke or something to drink?"

Reluctantly David Charles sat down but refused to look at Alexis. "You don't really know what it is like to feel unwanted. Every time I am sent out, I know it won't work. I used to hope that someday it might work out. It's like I wanted to go to the movies but when I got there, I didn't have enough money for a ticket. After a while I stopped hoping I'd ever get to go in."

Alexis was stunned by David's analogy as it was so close to her dream about the boy wanting to go to the fair. "You are right when you say I don't know what it is like to go through the disappointments you have experienced, but I can understand your reluctance to try another foster placement. David, it isn't always the case that you were rejected. I am not blaming you entirely, but you need to accept the fact that that you have done some things which make it very hard for your foster parents..." going to leave.

"David, sit down and listen to me! I am not your enemy here. If we work together, I think maybe we can find an arrangement that will be good, that will give you a chance to be successful."

Reluctantly David sat down, once again staring at the floor. "Okay, tell me my choices."

For the next 20 minutes Alexis reviewed the three possible foster home placements she had found, but even as she described them a voice in the back of her mind was telling her that none of them would work out. She could tell from his complete absence of interest, that he wasn't really interested or even listening to her. Finally, Alexis closed her placement files and looked long and hard at the twelve-year-old boy who sat in front of her, a sullen expression on his face. Taking a deep breath, Alexis reached out and gently lifted David's chin so he was looking at her. "David...there is one other possibility I want to discuss with you." She thought for a second, she saw the briefest spark of interest in his eyes.

"What is it?" he asked. "I thought you had gone over all of the possibilities in your file. Admit it, I am a hopeless case!"

"It isn't in my placement file. It would be living with me and my family. "David looked stunned. "Are you kidding me? You actually mean you would consider taking me in? I don't believe you!"

"David, it isn't for certain. I would have to discuss it with my husband and make sure he's okay with the idea, but I wanted to see if you were open to the possibility before going any further. I realize that you don't know me very well, so we'd all have to get better acquainted before any final decisions are made. What do you think?"

There was a lengthy silence before David Charles answered Alexis. "I don't know…you don't really know me. All you have is my record and maybe a couple of hours together. Why would you want to bring me into your home?"

"David, I don't know you well, but for some reason I see something good in you, and I am someone who trusts her gut instincts. Do you ever trust your instincts, your intuition?"

"I guess I do. I don't care what you do…go ahead and talk to your husband…I doubt he'll like the idea."

"Okay, David. I will talk to my husband and then I will get back to you." Alexis escorted David back to the waiting
area and the officer led him to the car. Alexis watched as they drove away. Five o'clock couldn't come soon enough for Alexis, but when it did, she hurriedly put on her jacket and locked the office door. The

whole time she drove home she mentally rehearsed her strategy for approaching Nathan. Her emotions were a conflicting mixture. On the one hand she felt excitement and hope, but on the other hand she could feel the warm blanket of pessimism and discouragement. How could she think that she could sell Nathan on the idea of taking David into their home? She could almost predict his exact response to the idea. He would start out being calmly rational, citing all the reasons why it wouldn't work. If she persisted, he would talk about how it would have an adverse effect on Lizzy and then it would be discussion closed. Part of her thought he would probably be correct in what he said, but another part of her had to try. Her inner turmoil reminded her of when she was a little girl and her parents took her to the animal shelter to pick put a puppy. They showed her several attractive and well-behaved young dogs but she felt strangely attracted to one sad-looking, older dog with black hair and a white beard around his mouth. She was adamant and so her parents gave in, and they took the dog home. Her choice proved to be a good one. With love and care her dog, *Blackie* turned out to be a faithful companion for several years before dying of a form of cancer. She fervently hoped her instincts were correct again. After putting Lizzy to bed, Alexis hugged Nathan and held him close as she whispered, "Nathan, let's go into the living room. There is something important I want to talk to you about."

Nathan looked long and hard at his wife before responding. "That sounds serious." He left his arm around her waist and together they walked into their living room and sat down on the sofa. Alexis gave it her best sales pitch, but Nathan's reaction was almost exactly as she had predicted. After the better part of an hour their discussion ended with Nathan saying that he would sleep on the idea but would make no promises.

Lexi hardly slept at all. She awoke before Nathan and got Lizzy out of bed for her breakfast. When Nathan came into the breakfast area to join them, she could tell by the look on his face that his decision was not likely to be positive. Although apprehensive, Alexis couldn't wait to know what Nathan's decision was, but before inquiring, she handed him a cup of coffee in his favorite mug. "Well, have you made a decision?"

"Lexi, I thought about it a lot last night. In fact, it was hard to go to sleep. I know how much you want to give this boy a chance, and you believe we can help him. At the same time, we have a daughter of our own to consider. The boy could be a disruptive influence in our home and maybe a bad influence on Lizzy too."

Disappointment evident in her voice, Alexis responded, "Please, Nathan. Would you agree to meet David? Maybe we could spend a day with hm so you could get to know him? I think if you'd spend a little time with him, you might see some of what I see in him."

To her astonishment, Nathan agreed to the suggestion of taking him on an outing in order to get a better idea of what sort of kid he was and whether they could get along with him. "I am willing to take him somewhere on a Saturday and see how it goes. You might find out what he likes to do. Basketball season is over, but maybe he like to go fishing or hiking."

Thank you, Nathan! I will talk to him and see what he might like to do. I think it should be something that we could interact with him. That would rule out going to a movie or concert. I don't know whether he likes fishing or not but I will find out." Her heart was filled with Joy, and she couldn't wait to talk to David again. Nathan had opened the door a crack, and Alexis was determined that she could open it wide enough to bring David through.

Chapter Twenty

The charm of fishing is that it is the pursuit

of what is elusive but attainable.

-John Buchan

Alexis, after much encouragement and cajoling, found that David Charles had gone fishing once when a group of boys from the ophanage were taken fishing on the coast. He claimed to have enjoyed the activity and even told a story about a large fish he almost caught. As he told the story of hooking the fish, it was perhaps the only time Alexis had seen the lad light up and show some genuine enthusiasm for something. Since he hadn't done any fishing since coming to North Carolina, Nathan talked to a couple of colleagues in the Psychology Department about good places to fish. As a result, he was able to secure permission to fish on a private lake a few miles east of town. As a next step, he bought fishing licenses, some fishing tackle and artificial lures. Alexis made arrangements for a baby sitter to stay with Lizzy and then planned the menu for a gourmet picnic lunch. On a Saturday in mid-April, Nathan, Alexis, and David piled into Nathan's CRV and headed for the lake. After almost an hour of driving, which included a couple of wrong turns, they found the road to the lake. Then they drove several hundred yards down a dirt road, coming at last to a large metal gate. Nathan opened the combination lock on the gate and they drove down to the water's edge. The lake was quite scenic, covering about five acres and was surrounded on most of its shoreline by large trees. The area where they parked the car was open and had a dock which extended out into the lake some 50 to sixty feet. It was a good spot for casting, especially for an inexperienced fisherman. The day was partly cloudy and mild; a gentle breeze created small ripples on the water's surface giving the lake a beautiful sparkling shimmer. David proved to be a true novice fisherman and Nathan was glad he purchased a Zebco spin cast reel for him. He took coaching from Nathan on how to cast and retrieve the lure fairly well, and after about thrifty minutes without a bite Nathan switched David from an artificial lure to a worm and bobber rig. Shortly thereafter, David hooked a nice catfish. The fish put up a good fight and Nathan was afraid it would break the light fishing line, but the fishing gods must have smiled and David was able to land the fish without aid from Nathan or Alexis. Nathan took the catfish off the hook and weighed it. It was almost five pounds. It was always interesting to Nathan what you could use to catch a catfish.

    Alexis had never seen young David look so happy, and her heart was filled with hope and joy. Another hour of fishing and Nathan caught two more small Bass and David caught a nice size bream, and then the threesome took a break for lunch under a large pine tree. The sun ducked behind some clouds darkening the shaded area where they paused for lunch. The wind died down and the birds paused their singing as if they wanted to hear the conversation from the people below.

"David, looks like you are the champ. That catfish you caught was almost five pounds and was the definitely the biggest catch of the day. Alexis got a couple of good pictures of you and your fish which she can print for you. I think you may have a future as a fisherman."

David smiled broadly and popped the top on his Coke can. "Thanks! That was lots of fun! That fish really fought hard." I think that is the first fish I ever caught all by myself."

Alexis handed out the sandwiches and bags of chips, feeling love for Nathan and hope for David. *Maybe this can work out. Thank you, God.* After the last cookie was eaten, Alexis gathered up their trash while Nathan and David put the fishing gear in the car. On the trip back to town David talked more than Alexis had ever heard from him, and his facial expression showed an abundance of youthful joy and enthusiasm. After leaving David at the orphanage, Alexis and Nathan headed home, and Alexis asked the big question of Nathan: "Well, what do you think, Dr. Richards?"

Nathan looked at his wife and smiled. "I think he is a good kid."

"Is that all you can say? Do you think we might consider taking him as a foster?"

"Maybe. We can talk more about it tonight. I did enjoy our time together."

The remainder of the drive home was done in a comfortable silence in which it was obvious that both parties were engaged in their private thoughts about the day and the boy, David Charles. As soon as Nathan turned off the car's ignition, Lizzy and Jake came running from the house to meet them.

Mommy, Daddy, did you catch some fish?" Lizzy was excited and glad to see her parents. Nathan picked her up in his arms and she squealed with delight. "Put me down, Daddy! Put me down!" Nathan lowered Lizzy to the ground and then had to fend off Jake's enthusiastic greeting.

"Come on, everybody. Let's go in the house. "Alexis paid the babysitter and corralled Jake before she showed the pictures from the fishing trip to her daughter. "Lizzy, here are some pictures. Look at the big fish."

"Who caught that fish? Mommy, was it you?" Lizzy looked first at her mother and then at her dad. `Well, neither of us. The boy we took fishing, David. He caught the big fish." Alexis said with a smile; she gestured with her hands to show the size of the fish. "The fish was this big."

"Mommy, is that boy going to be my brother?" Lizzy asked her mother with the openness and innocence that could only come from a child.

Alexis looked at Nathan, a surprised look on her face. "Well, honey…Uh, I don't know. We might have him come over for a visit. Daddy and I will have to talk about it."

After dinner the family watched a recording of Sesame Street and then Alexis put Lizzy to bed and returned to the living room where Nathan and Jake waited. Outside she could hear the wind really pick up, and she could see the flash of lightning through the windows. Thunder rumbled and then Alexis and Nathan heard Lizzy's voice calling from her bedroom, "Mommy, I'm scared!"

Alexis did an about face and returned to her daughter's bedroom to comfort Lizzy. "It's okay, honey. Just a little rain starting outside. Daddy and I will be here to make sure everything is okay. Would you like for Jake to sleep in your room to keep you company?" Lizzy approved of the suggestion, and so Lexi called Jake who trotted into the room. "Jake, stay here with Lizzy." Like a good soldier, Jake plopped down by Lizzy's bed and curled up for a snooze. Jake did not like storms either, but he was always comforted by the presence of one of his family, even if it was the smallest member. Returning to the living area, Alexis almost expected to hear her daughter's voice following the next clap of thunder, but to her surprise Lizzy was quiet. What she did hear was the sound of the rain beating against the living room windows as if it was determined to break in. Had she looked outside she might have seen something move quickly through the yard, something about the size of a large dog or perhaps a wolf.

"Is Lizzy okay?" Nathan asked of his wife as she took a seat on the sofa.

"I think so. I got Jake to stay in her room, and that calmed her down, but we'll see. It is really pouring outside." Alexis turned briefly to look at the window in order to steal a glance at the storm raging outside, and then she spoke in a voice hardly more than a whisper, "What did you think of David?"

"Well, I have to admit things went better than I expected.... maybe there is some hope for the kid. But...remember it was one short visit under circumstances that most any twelve-year-old boy would enjoy. I don't know how much it tells us about how he would adapt to living with us." After a lengthy pause, he added, "I know how much you want it, so I guess you could look into the possibility of taking him on a trial basis. Maybe fostering him...adoption seems premature to even consider right now."

Alexis grabbed her husband around the neck and planted a kiss on his cheek. "Thank you! I will explore the possibility with David. If he is agreeable, and I will get the paperwork started."

"Okay, but make sure he understands that it is a trial run...a time for him to check us out and for us to get a feel for him."

"I will make sure he is on board and understands what we are offering him." Alexis, paused then added, "Maybe it would be good for the three of us to meet in my office and talk about this before we take any additional steps. What do you think?"

"That sounds like a very good idea," Nathan said nodding his head. No sooner had he responded when a crash of thunder rattled the windows and vibrated through the house. Nathan wasn't sure if his uneasiness was due to the storm or the prospect of taking an obviously troubled adolescent boy into their home. "Wow! That was close!" The lightning strike was indeed very close. In the morning Nathan would see just how close the strike actually was. In the morning light, he would discover that one of the large trees in their yard had been hit and split down the middle. That discovery would cause Nathan to wonder if the lightning strike was an omen, a warning of things to come.

Chapter Twenty-one

When the prison doors are opened, the real dragon will fly out.

-Ho Chi Minh

Red dragons have long been referred to by wise men and philosophers as evil creatures, interested only in satisfying their own desires. They were seen as supremely confident in their power, and they delighted in ruin, death, and destruction. Some sages even associated the red dragon with the devil himself. Although not widely publicized, Jerimiah Murdoc, M.D. had a tattoo of a red dragon on his right arm. It was never clear why Murdoc had the tattoo on his arm. Speculation was that it might have been because of the red dragon associated with the movie character Hannibal Lecter or perhaps it was connected to the red dragon described as an enemy of God in the Book of Revelation. Whatever the reason for the tattoo, only the devious mind of Jeremiah Murdoc knew the answer.

There is an old expression about the inmates running the asylum which usually means that incompetents were in charge of an organization. However, in the case of Central Prison, it could be said that really only one inmate ran the asylum. Technically, Central Prison was not an asylum but the penitentiary in North Carolina which housed the "crimi nally insane". One inmate did seem to wield an unusual amount of influence in the facility, and that inmate was none other than Dr. Jeremiah Murdoc. Nathan did not know it but in reality, it wasn't the warden who permitted Nathan Richards to interview Murdoc, it was Murdoc himself. What Nathan Richards had not yet learned was that Murdoc had an uncanny ability to control or at least manipulate the mind of anyone he wished, and Murdoc wanted to see Nathan Richards again. Murdoc made his desire known to one the guards in his area of the prison, a hulking brute of a man named Hector. Hector in turn got the message to the warden who promptly contacted Nathan Richards. Although surprised, Nathan accepted the invitation to meet with Murdoc.

Nathan was in his office when the warden called. After the call, he entered the date and time of the meeting into his iPhone and then called Alexis at her office. Alexis was always good at reading the subtle signs of emotion in Nathan's tone of voice and body language so she questioned him about what she perceived as a certain hesitancy or lack of enthusiasm in his voice. "Nathan, you sound as if you aren't sure you want to meet with Murdoc again. I thought after your initial meeting that you had a lot of unanswered questions."

Well, uh, Lexi, it's not that I don't want to meet Murdoc again, it's…. it's just that I came away from the session feeling very odd."

"Odd? In what way?" Alexis asked.

"I just felt strange and I had very little memory of the details of our conversation. Usually, I remember interview information pretty well. About all I remembered for sure was what he said about being an instrument of God."

"So why don't you just cancel the meeting if you are uncomfortable?"

"In a way I'd like to, but I just feel like I have to meet with him." Simply saying that he felt compelled to meet with Murdoc again was like labeling a fear which had been gnawing at the edges of his consciousness. Although Nathan believed that labeling a fear was usually a good first step in facing it, but in this instance, it didn't feel like a positive step. It felt as if he was being summoned by Murdoc and that he lacked the power or autonomy to exercise his own will.

Two days after receiving Murdoc's invitation to another interview, Nathan found himself making the drive to Central Prison. After signing in, he was met by the Assistant Warden, James Farrier who looked young enough to be one of Nathan's freshmen students. After a brief chat with Farrier who explained that Warden Henderson had been called to the capital and would not be able to meet with him, Nathan was escorted by a guard to the interview room. It was the same small room that he used the first time he met Murdoc, bright, cold, and stark. This time, Murdoc was already in the room waiting. As before, he was handcuffed to the metal table. Once Nathan was seated, the guard who escorted him in exited the room, but the other guard, a huge man remained until dismissed by Murdoc. Nathan was struck by the familiarity with which Murdoc addressed the guard, referring to him as "Hector".

It was Murdoc who spoke first. "Hello, Dr. Richards! It is so good to see you again. Did I tell you at our first meeting that I get very few visitors, and even fewer who are the upstanding scholars and godly men like yourself."

Nathan found it hard to force the words out of his mouth, but finally he replied, "I appreciate your willingness to speak with me again…"

Murdoc spoke again before Nathan could finish, his remark, "I was more than willing to meet with you. In fact, it was I who invited you here. I have thought a great deal about you since our initial meeting, Dr. Richards, and I realized that there was much more I needed to tell you, much you needed to know."

"More that I need to know about you, Murdoc?" Richards was genuinely puzzled.

"Not so much about me, but about you and your situation, Dr.

Richards."

Nathan felt a sense of growing irritation at Murdoc's audacity. "What is it I need to know?"

Murdoc smiled his oily smile before answering. "First of all, you need to know about your wife and her intentions."

Nathan's retort was prompt, "What could you possibly know about my wife or her intentions? You don't even know her name"

"Oh, but you are wrong, Dr. Richards. I may be in prison, but I have my sources, and I do get occasional access to a computer. What I am about to tell you may disturb you, but it is something you need to know. Remember that I am bringing light to your darkness." Murdoc paused briefly before continuing, "Your wife, whose name is Alexis, is bored with you and her relationship with you. She is so bored that she has already taken steps to bring new stimulation into her life which she sees as dull and uninteresting. Does the name David Charles ring a bell?"

Nathan's heart skipped a beat and he felt a cold chill run down his spine, but he remained silent, trying hard to conceal his emotions.

"I thought you'd recognize the name," Murdoc said with a knowing smile. "Your wife wants to bring him into your home under the guise of helping him, but she isn't really interested in helping him. To her, he is like a shiny new toy, something she can play with, clay she can mold as she desires."

Nathan could no longer contain his anger, "You are wrong, Dr. Murdoc. You don't know my wife or what you are talking about! I think this is just another of your delusions!"

"So, calm yourself, please, Dr. Richards! I am only trying to help you. However, there's much more you need to understand. Your wife is doing what she is doing because she is bored, bored with you and her life. You, Dr. Richards, have always been such a straight-arrow sort of guy. You were probably the teacher's pet in school. You know that your life is missing something, and that is why you keep changing jobs, Dr. Richards. What you fail to understand is that your life is missing excitement. Yours is a life without any spice. Unlike me, you are free, but you act more like a prisoner than I. You are a prisoner to your morals, your superego. You may not want to hear what I am telling you, but at the deepest level of your mind, you know what I am telling you is the truth."

Partly to keep his anger under control and partly to avoid any eye contact with Murdoc that would enable him to use hypnosis, Nathan had kept his focus on the table in from of him. After what Murdoc had just said to him, Nathan glanced up at Murdoc and what he saw terrified him. Instead of Murdoc's countenance and sardonic smile, Nathan saw the face of a monster, its teeth bared! *Oh, Dear God!* Nathan wanted to flee from the room as fast as he could, but his legs wouldn't respond. He seemed paralyzed, frozen in his chair. In his panic state, Nathan's vision blurred but then cleared again, and he refocused on Murdoc. When he did, the monster's face was gone, and all he saw was Murdoc's evil smile. Without any comment, Murdoc slowly rolled up the sleeve of the shirt on his right arm revealing the tattoo of a red dragon. As Nathan stared at the tattoo, he felt certain that the wings on the dragon began to move as if the monster were taking flight. Nathan gasped at the sight of the flying dragon and then without any explanation, Murdoc rolled his shirt sleeve back down, concealing the tattoo.

"Dr. Richards, I am sorry to have upset you, but you know the truth can be very unsettling. However, you *will remember* what I have revealed to you. Even though you do not want to believe me, you know that what I have revealed to you is the truth. What is it your good book says about the truth? The truth will set you free."

Nathan did not recall summoning the guards, but they came into the room as though requested. Murdoc was led from the room through one door, and Nathan was escorted out through the other door. Once outside of the prison and seated in his car, Nathan paused for several minutes before starting his old Honda. His mind was reeling and his emotions were on a roller coaster ride. Murdoc's words kept reverberating in his head as did the word "truth". Pilot's question to Jesus had taken on a renewed importance: "What is truth?" Nathan turned the ignition key and his Honda sprang to life, but before he could put the car in drive, he saw something that he could neither believe nor comprehend. There above the prison complex he saw a huge red dragon, just like the tattoo on Murdoc's arm, take flight. He would have sworn he actually saw it and could even hear the sound of its beating wings as it flew away, but then he also saw the tattoo on Murdoc's arm move as if flying. *My God! I am losing my mind! This is like being trapped inside a bad dream.*

Driving out of the prison parking lot it was difficult for Nathan to focus. He had to really concentrate to even recall his scheduled activities for the remainder of the day. *Damn! Which way do I go to get to my office?* His mental fog lifted enough for Nathan to drive from the prison back to the university. When he got back to his office, he checked his schedule on his iPhone and was relieved to see that there were no meetings or appointments scheduled for the afternoon. Because of his interview with

Murdoc at the prison he had given his classes a walk Fear gripped him as Nathan realized he had virtually no memory of what had transpired at Central Prison even though it was less than an hour earlier. All he could remember was the vague image of a red dragon, but he wasn't sure where he had seen it or even if he had. However, there was something else…but what? Suddenly, on an impulse he got up and exited his office. As he headed for the stairs, and he casually greeted a couple of colleagues in the hall. Once in his car he drove off as if on a mission, but a mission to do what or where? Almost as if drawn by a magnet, Nathan pulled into the parking lot of a nearby ABC Liquor Store. He marched inside and selected a bottle of expensive single malt Scotch whiskey, something he hadn't drunk since graduate school. He paid for the Scotch and walked back to his car, his only thoughts were about how much he needed a stiff drink, maybe several stiff drinks. Back in the car, Nathan shoved the bottle e of Scotch under the driver's seat and headed back to his office. Once in his office, Nathan stared out the window at the campus scene below

There was the chapel and the ever-present students walking across the campus. The grass and trees all wore the fresh green of early spring. Flowers bloomed and everything looked serene and tranquil, but that was not how Nathan Richards felt. He was anything but serene and tranquil. In fact, a growing feeling of irritation was emerging from his state of mental confusion. He was feeling increasingly annoyed at his wife Alexis. *Why is she so determined to bring that budding personality disorder into our home? What does she get out of it?* Nathan's brooding was interrupted by a knock on his office door. *Who the hell can that be?* He rose from behind his desk and walked to the door, and opening it he found himself face to face with Lurleen Montgomery. Upon seeing her, his mood changed dramatically, shifting from gloom and negativity to excitement and arousal. *Excitement. That was what he needed!*

## Chapter Twenty-two

You can't start a fire without a spark

-Bruce Springsteen

The sight of Lurleen Montgomery in his office door lit a spark of excitement in Nathan Richards' belly. The spark quickly became a flame which could consume him if allowed to grow. For a moment Nathan felt as awkward as if he were once again thirteen asking the blonde girl in his English class for a date to the prom. "Hello, Miss Montgomery. What can I do for you?" Lurleen smiled as she entered his office, and Nathan closed the door behind her. "Please, have a seat," he said as he gestured toward the empty chair opposite his desk.

"Well, professor Richards…there is something I wanted, needed to talk to you about." Lurleen paused and then looked into Nathan's eyes. With a sheepish but somehow seductive smile she continued, "I didn't know who else to talk to so I came to you. "

Smiling in return, Nathan responded, "Please continue, Miss Montgomery." Waiting for her response he felt excitement growing inside, and then he noticed the gold pendant around her neck. It appeared to be a star, a seven-pointed star and key; he had never seen anything quite like it. It was beautiful and seemed to possess an almost hypnotic quality. Lurleen continued, "I have felt uncertain about something ever since I enrolled here at Duke. I keep asking myself why am I here? Not long ago my roommate asked me that same question, and I couldn't answer her. Most everyone else here seems so sure that they are answering a call, God's call, but me…I don't know. I do know that I enjoy your class, and I feel that I can trust you… that maybe you, of all my faculty could understand my feelings, my doubts."

"I appreciate your trust, and yes, I can certainly understand doubt. Can you tell me about your doubt?"

Lurleen brushed a lock of hair from her face, smiled, and then resumed her story, "I sometimes think I am in seminary for the wrong reason. I'm afraid maybe I am here because I fear that deep down, I am not so pure, maybe even evil." She held up her hand to stop any response from Nathan, and continued, "I have a history I am not so proud of. When I was an undergrad, I had some serious financial problems. The trust fund my mother established for me before she died wasn't enough to get me through college, so I had to find a way to support myself. I took a job as a dancer…an exotic dancer. I performed nude at a gentlemen's club. I became pretty popular and that led to becoming a nude model as well. I quickly found I could make a good deal of money, but what troubled me more than what I was doing was that I enjoyed the work. I loved how men looked at me, wanted me. This is so embarrassing to talk about...maybe it was a mistake to tell you."

Nathan could almost see images of Lurleen doing her strip tease act in his mind, and he found it difficult to respond empathically to what she had just told him. "Well, uh, Miss Montgomery, I suspect most of us have done things in our past that we don't feel so good about, but..."

Before he could finish his comment, Lurleen cut in, "That's the thing! I don't feel bad about what I did. I liked it! I enjoyed it ...probably too much! Feeling that way, what am I doing in seminary? Who am I kidding? Myself? God? I think maybe I should go now." She rose and started to turn for the door, but Nathan put his hand on her shoulder.

"Don't leave, Miss Montgomery...Lurleen. I understand what you are feeling." Lurleen turned back towards Nathan and seemed to draw him to her. Nathan felt the warmth of her body against his and the spark he felt when she appeared at his door had become a four-alarm fire. He wanted her badly and he wanted her now. She looked up at him and they kissed, a long and passionate kiss. Nathan felt the strong desire to begin removing her clothes, but a rational thought forced its way into his awareness. "My office may not be the best place to continue this discussion, Lurleen. There are way too many people in the building."

Lurleen looked up at Nathan and smiled. "You are probably right. We could go to my apartment. My roomie has gone home again to see her mother, so we'll have all the privacy we need. We can go in separate cars. You could just follow me at a distance, and nobody will be the wiser."

Nathan checked his watch. The afternoon was young, and Alexis would not be leaving work until five o'clock, plenty of time.

"Come in she said, I'll give you shelter from the storm," Lurleen whispered as she drew Nathan into the apartment and into her arms. In the background Nathan could hear the nasal sound of Bob Dylan singing those very same words on her stereo. Lurleen's apartment was cool and dark, candles burned in several locations in the kitchen and living area.

The setting was perfect for a continuance of their earlier meeting.

Nathan handed the bottle of Scotch to Lurleen. "I thought this might go nicely with our discussion; it loosens the tongue a bit," he said with a smile. In a more rational state of mind, Nathan might have realized that he was responding in a manner which was totally out of character, and was clearly entering a danger zone.

Lurleen took the Scotch and headed into the kitchen where she took two glasses from a cupboard and handed them to Nathan. "Pour us a couple of glasses, and I will be right back," she said as she retreated to her bedroom. When she returned, all she wore was the gold chain and star pendant.

For the next two hours Nathan knew excitement up close and personal, and he shed his straight-arrow façade. Glancing at his watch he was surprised to see that it was now four thirty. A sudden twinge of anxiety momentarily broke the spell Lurleen had cast upon him, and he realized he needed to start his trip home fairly soon. He donned his clothes, combed his hair, and used some of Lurleen's mouthwash. Lurleen did not bother to put on her clothes. Instead, she asked for his cell phone which she quickly handed back to him.

"Take a few pictures of me so you'll have something to remind you of our little session until we can schedule another."

Nathan smiled as he took back his phone. "Give me your sexiest pose," he said as he aimed the cell phone camera at her. He took several still shots and then even a short video. "This should be enough of a reminder and an incentive to meet soon."

On the drive home, Nathan felt a hint of guilt about his sexual encounter with Lurleen Montgomery which he quickly extinguished. *What Alexis doesn't know won't hurt her and besides I think she hasn't been to tally faithful to me either.* In his mind he was thinking back to a time in Lubbock when Alexis had come home drunk after meeting with someone she said was a faculty member at Tech.

After Nathan left, Lurleen continued to lounge on the sofa feeling proud of her ability to dominate Nathan, bending him totally to her will. She got up from the sofa and strolled leisurely into her bathroom, stopping to admire her figure in the full-length mirror. *The way I look, re Ally didn't need magic to control him.* Lurleen retrieved her cell phone and took several selfies mostly for her own narcissistic pleasure. *Who knows when these might come in handy?*

Nathan's mental state while he drove home was quite different from Lurleen's. While still burning with desire, he also felt slight twinges of guilt as well as self-righteous anger at Alexis. On the car stereo he heard an old tune by the Eagles entitled *Lyin' Eyes*. Although he chuckled at the irony of the song's title and lyrics, he also wondered if his eyes would betray him to Alexis. After all she was damn good at reading his true emotions from facial expression, tone of voice, or body language. He hoped that his feelings of anger and suspicion towards her might effectively mask his guilt. Even if his guilt leaked out, the excitement he had experienced seemed well worth it.

Alexis was just driving in with Lizzy as Nathan pulled into the driveway behind her. Nathan got out of his car and strolled over to

Alexis and waited as she got Lizzy out of her car seat. Alexis turned to greet him with a smile. "Hi, sweetheart."

Nathan responded with a faint smile, "Hi to you too. How was your day?" Looking at Lizzy, he smiled more broadly, "Hi there, princess. How was school?"

After a few moments, the Richards family entered the house, each going their separate ways. Nathan followed Jake into the kitchen to get a glass of water. Alexis turned from preparing dinner to give him a kiss and then pushed back suddenly. "Have you been drinking?" she asked with a surprised look on her face.

"Yeah...I stopped for a drink with one of the psychology faculty to talk about Jeremiah Murdoc. The guy really troubles me for some reason."

"Did it help to talk about it? Did you learn anything helpful?

"I am not sure. I have so little memory of what happened during the interview. Evan Mitchell gave me a few suggestions and even offered to hypnotize me to see if we could uncover anything I might have repressed."

Perhaps sensing the vagueness in his response, Alexis looked hard at her husband. Was this the man she had always loved and trusted or some imposter? "Is that who you had a drink with today? I think you mentioned that before; do you think you'll take him up on his offer?"

Dodging the real thrust of her question, he simply answered, "I might

## Chapter Twenty-three

We don't see things as they are, we see things as we are.

-Anais Nin

Evil doesn't always make its appearance in a grotesque, demonic or terrible form. More often it appears in a subtle, disguised shape. Nathan remembered a book he once read about Adolf Eichmann, one of the architects of the Holocaust. The book, whose author he couldn't recall, entitled his book something like the "Banality of Evil." The author described Eichmann's testimony during his trial as rather flat and unemotional as if he were reporting stock market quotations or a weather forecast. Somehow Eichmann and his Nazi cohorts managed to turn their horrific evil into the foundation of a new kind of righteousness. In the upside-down world they created, Eichmann and his fellow Nazis seemed unaware of creating evil, choosing instead to characterize it as good. Such evil was not limited to members of the Nazi party. Nathan believed the same behaviors flourish today in our churches and political parties to the point they are now commonplace. Every day the news is replete with stories about how political or religious organizations demand full allegiance from their members and then create alternate realities to cloak their dogmatic demands for ideological purity. The sad truth is that most evil is done by people who never made up their minds to actually do evil. Reflecting further on the matter, Nathan realized that human beings have also found a most effective way to legitimize their fear, their hatred, and their evil. They merely project it onto others; in other words, they scapegoat. This psychic mechanism allows people to shed all their guilt and even feel like they are representing or defending the moral high ground. Nathan paused in his research for the book he was attempting to write and wondered if he too was guilty of the very things he was reading and writing about. But like most people who effectively utilize projection, he rationalized that he was not really projecting. After all, he was an experienced psychologist and thus immune to such neurotic strategies.

Nathan's reflection on the nature of evil caused him to wonder if his research efforts were adequate to the task, he had set for himself. Murdoc had proven to be almost too dangerous to interview again and evil seemed to come in so many forms from the banal to the monstrous. How could he possibly hope to make his theory more manageable? It reminded him of the myth of the Gordian Knot. The knot which represents an exceedingly complex problem too difficult for anyone to untie.

According to the story, Alexander the Great solved the problem by taking out his sword and slicing the knot in two. Nathan wondered if he could ever find such a swift and effective solution to his Gordian Knot. Feeling frustrated, Nathan turned off his computer, locked his office door, and walked out onto the campus grounds. It was a quiet afternoon. Fair weather cumulus clouds dotted the sky, and were he not so troubled mentally, he would have found the day to be quite pleasant.

Nathan walked aimlessly past students who strolled by him, their noses buried in their cell phones. For reasons only his unconscious mind knew, he walked up to the main entrance of the Duke Chapel. Without thinking why, he opened the heavy outer door and entered the building. It was cool and somewhat dark inside where the high arched ceiling towered above him. The many beautiful stained-glass windows permitted a rainbow of colors into the quiet sanctuary. At the moment the building was unoccupied, and Nathan walked about halfway down the center aisle toward the altar area eventually taking a seat in one of the pews. The silence of the sanctuary seemed to literally beg for prayer, a prayer for clarity and direction, a prayer for inner peace, but Nathan did not pray. After the better part of an hour, he simply got up and walked slowly back down the aisle towards the door. In times past, Nathan might have spent the hour or so in prayer and meditation, but not this time. He squinted in the bright afternoon sunshine as he exited the chapel, temporarily almost blinded by the light. *What am I doing? Where am I going? He had no answers.* After a few moments, the sunlight did seem to bring a greater awareness of his surroundings, and so Nathan began to walk towards the parking lot where he would find his car and then drive home. After several minutes he located his old Honda CRV and started the drive home. When he got home, Alexis had not yet arrived. She would normally be home in about an hour he thought. Nathan entered the quiet house and was immediately greeted by Jake, his loyal German Shepherd. "Hi, Jake! I am glad to see you, my old buddy. How are you?" After giving Jake a vigorous back rub, Nathan grabbed a beer from the refrigerator and collapsed into his recliner. After several minutes Nathan noticed that the living room had grown several shades darker which struck him as odd since it was not particularly cloudy outside and it was still a few hours until sunset. Nathan glanced at his watch to confirm the time and then looked across the room at an area of increased darkness. What he saw in that darkened area was the outline of what appeared to be a man sitting in in his wife's favorite

chair. Not quite believing his eyes, he blinked several times and cried out, "Who are you? What are you doing here?" Nathan leaped to his feet but the figure in the chair across from him did not move or answer. Nathan's heart was pounding in his chest as he stared at the motionless figure. To his puzzlement, his dog Jake was still lounging at his feet as if he was oblivious to the intruder. *What the hell is going on?* This was one time Nathan wished he had a gun or some sort of weapon in the house, and he felt paralyzed not knowing if he should run or attack his unexpected guest.

Before he could make any move, the dark figure spoke. His tone of voice was unemotional but carried an unmistakable authority. "Please sit down, Dr. Richards! I am not here to cause you any harm."

Nathan sat as if responding to the order of a superior, but he managed to repeat his earlier questions, "Who are you and what do you want?" Focusing intently on the figure in front of him, all Nathan could make out was what seemed to be a man's face but the features were not clear. He was of average height and thin build and dressed entirely in black in what appeared to be a jump suit or jogging outfit. There was something vaguely familiar about the figure.

"My name is of no consequence. As I said before, I am not here to harm you. If that were my intent, you would already be writhing in pain or dead. Actually, I am here to warn you."

"Warn me? Warn me of what?" Nathan stammered in response.

I am here to tell you that your wife has betrayed you yet again. Not only has she been unfaithful, but also, she is about to do something which will bring great pain and suffering to your family, especially your daughter."

"That's insane; Alexis would never do anything to hurt me or our daughter. She loves her..."

The dark figure held up his hand as if to interrupt Nathan. "She is not doing what she is doing in order to intentionally hurt you or your daughter, but her actions will prove quite damaging, I assure you. As you already know she is obsessed with a young boy, and she is determined to bring him into your home. She is thinking only of herself. You will soon see the truth of my words."

"Why should I believe you, and why would you care about our family? I am not even sure you are real, and if you are...I don't trust you." Nathan could feel anger replacing the fear he felt initially. "Go back to hell or wherever it is you came from!"

An icy cold filled the room, and then the shadowy figure rose from the chair as if to walk away, but instead his image simply melted back into the shadows. Nathan scanned the room and confirmed that his mysterious visitor had indeed departed. He glanced down at Jake who was still lying comfortably at his feet, looking back at him. Jake cocked his head as if trying to understand what his master had just said, but he gave no indication of being aware of anyone else having been in the room. Nathan reached down to pat Jake's head. "If you didn't notice our visitor, I wonder if there really was anyone or anything here or just my mind playing tricks on me." Once again, Nathan looked around the living room, but the dark figure was clearly gone. *What was that about? Am I losing it or was that some sort of mirage, a satanic messenger?* Nathan's confusion was interrupted by the sounds of Alexis and Lizzy entering the house. Jake leaped to his feet and ran to greet them.

The evening was uneventful for the most part. Lizzy played with her new doll house while Alexis reviewed some case notes, and Nathan read over the next day's lecture outline. Finally, Alexis got up from the dining table, stuffed the case files into her brief case and announced that she was going to give Lizzy a bath. Nathan nodded but didn't look up from his notes. The silence between them was filled with tension which neither wished to acknowledge. After the 11:00 pm news was over, Alexis headed for the bedroom and Nathan took Jake out to take care of his business. After Alexis turned out the light by her side of the bed, she could tolerate the stony silence no longer.

"Nathan, what's wrong? You haven't spoken two words to me all evening. Are you mad at me for some reason?"

It was several seconds before Nathan responded. "I have just been thinking…wondering about some things."

"Wondering about what things?" Alexis inquired.

"I can't help wondering why you are so determined to foster that boy, David? What do you get out of it?"

"Why are you bringing this up again? I explained my reasons to you several times already. I just see a boy who has never been given a fair chance at happiness, and I think we could give him that chance. I thought you were okay with the plan."

"It's your plan. I know that what you have said, but you aren't being realistic. Surely, you've got to be aware of the risks involved in trying to foster him. You aren't being honest with me or yourself."

"Nathan, I thought we had settled this! Why are you bringing up your concerns again? I have already started the process so that we can foster him, and now you are sounding like you are backing out of the agreement." Alexis was angry now and it showed clearly in her voice.

"Alexis, your anger speaks volumes. I can see you've made up your mind about this. It is something you want, and it has made you blind to the risks involved. There is nothing more I can say at this point."

Silence returned to the Richard's bedroom but neither was able to sleep until well into the early morning hours. The sunrise brought no end to the stony silence between Nathan and Alexis. Even Lizzy was touched by the chill. Instead of her bubbly enthusiasm as she prepared for her school, she was fretful and slow to get ready. Finally, Alexis broke the silence, "Nathan, what do you want me to do? Do you want me to cancel the application to foster David? Have you thought at all about what that will do to him?"

The dark expression on his face said far more than his words when he replied, "Go ahead, you are so determined to have your way, but don't say I didn't warn you."

Warn me? Warn me about what? You act like David will bring some dread disease into our home. I just don't understand what has brought about this sudden change in your feelings."

With an angry look at her husband, Alexis stormed out of the kitchen and went into Lizzy's room to see if she was ready to leave for school.

Chapter Twenty-four

How does it feel, how does it feel?

To be on your own, with no direction home?

-Bob Dylan

When Nathan arrived at his office, he experienced a strong sense of disorientation and unreality. In a word, he felt lost. Nathan Richards had always thought of himself as a realist, a true empiricist. He prided himself on being a goal-oriented problem-solver, but now. Now, he felt like he had entered the twilight zone. He had done something he never thought he'd do, be unfaithful to his wife. He was no longer even sure of the between reality and fantasy. Even his soul felt untethered. His moral compass was broken, and he had no clear direction home. *What the hell is wrong with me?* After a time, the fog of his disorientation cleared enough that he saw the name of Evan Mitchell, one of his colleagues in the Psychology Department, on a scratch pad on his desk. Nathan remembered that Mitchell had offered to use hypnosis as a possible aid in helping Nathan recall more from his meetings with Murdoc. He stared at Mitchell's name and phone number and wondered if perhaps hypnosis might help him sort things out and maybe clear up some of the confusion he was experiencing. Without much further thought he dialed Dr. Mitchell's number, and to his surprise, professor Mitchell answered and offered Nathan an appointment time right after lunch.

Nathan had only been to Professor Mitchell's office one other time, and he remembered it as both large and somehow very welcoming. When he arrived, Mitchell's office door was open and Dr. Mitchell was standing at the window staring out at the campus below. He heard Nathan approach then turned and greeted him with a friendly smile. "Nathan, please come in."

"Evan, thank you for making time to see me on such short notice. I've given your offer of hypnosis a lot of thought and I believe it might be helpful. I don't know if I told you but I saw Dr. Murdoc a second time and was even more confused after that visit."

Mitchell nodded then asked, "What would you like to accomplish in our session?"

"Good question, Evan. I don't know if it is a result of my visits with Murdoc or not but I have had several unusual experiences lately. I guess, I'd just like to sort things out a bit."

"Can you tell me what sort of unusual experiences?"

Nathan gave Mitchell a quick summary but excluded the part about his encounter with Lurleen Montgomery or his mysterious visitor. He described his anger and suspicions regarding Alexis as being "a bit paranoid."

"Okay," Mitchell replied. "I think that gives me some sense of direction. If you're ready, let's get started."

Nathan indicated his readiness, and then Dr. Mitchell suggested that Nathan get comfortable in the leather recliner positioned alongside Mitchell's desk. Feeling slightly self-conscious and maybe a little embarrassed, Nathan settled into the recliner. "I'm ready," Nathan spoke with a smile.

Professor Mitchell moved his chair so that he was seated beside Nathan. "Nathan, I am going to utilize an eye roll, eye closure induction. I imagine you are familiar with it." Nathan nodded, and Mitchell continued. "Please look up at the ceiling and focus on a spot of your choosing. Blink as little as possible. Good. Hold that focus as long as possible. You may notice a desire to close your eyes but keep them open just a bit longer Your eye lids may start to flutter some too." Mitchell waited a few moments and then continued again, "Now, keeping your eyes in the upward position, allow your eye lids to close." Mitchell watched closely as Nathan's eyes closed and he noted the slight fluttering of the eye lids.

Then, he began to deepen the trace. "I am going to count down from ten to one. As you hear the numbers going down you might imagine descending a flight of ten steps. When we reach the count of one, you can find yourself in a very safe, very comfortable place." Dr. Mitchell counted backwards from ten to one. Before continuing he noted that Nathan's breathing had slowed considerably. "Nathan, I want you to see something which looks like a large footlocker in front of you. Once you can see it, signal me by raising a finger on your right hand." After seeing Nathan's right index finger lift ever so slightly, Mitchell instructed Nathan to open the locker and look inside. Mitchell then suggested that each item represented something from Nathan's unconscious mind. In a slow but steady fashion, Dr. Mitchell guided Nathan through the discovery process. At some points Nathan seemed to get stuck and was unable to describe the object he encountered while at other points he seemed to be able to describe what he observed rather easily. The allotted hour flew by quickly and when Mitchell brought Nathan out of the trace, Nathan would have guessed that only a few minutes had elapsed. Dr. Mitchell allowed a few minutes for Nathan to reorient fully and then asked, "Well, how was that for you?"

" Well, uh…it was very interesting. I felt like I was in a pretty deep trance, and I could picture the foot locker clearly. When I opened it,

I found it to be quite full of things, some I could identify, but others...others I couldn't identify at all. Then... there was one item at the bottom of the box that scared me, and I didn't want to touch it."

Mitchell seemed calm but very interested in what Nathan uncovered. "I suspect that the things you couldn't identify were still a bit too deep in your unconscious and you aren't quite ready to identify them. I am most interested in the item which scared you. Can you tell me anything at all about it or your feelings?"

Nathan repositioned the recliner into its full upright position before answering. "It was something very dark, and it seemed somehow alive...like a snake or something alive and dangerous. Maybe a bat or a bird. I don't know what, but it scared the hell out of me!"

Mitchell smiled as he responded, "Interesting choice of words, Nathan." Nathan was clearly puzzled by Dr. Mitchell's comment.

"What do you mean, Evan?"

"I meant your use of the word *hell*."

"Hmmm. Maybe so. I'll have to think about it more." Nathan got up to leave but stopped in the office door and turned back to his colleague. "Evan, I...uh, I remember that during the trance I thought I saw something fly away from the foot locker when I opened it".

"What do you think it might have been, Nathan?"

"I think it was a small bat or bird, no wait…I think it was a dragon, a red dragon. I know I have seen that same thing before, but I'm not sure where?"

Were you frightened by the dragon?"

"Yeah, I think so…maybe more just surprised by it. It reminded me of a painting I once saw of Pandora opening her box of demons. No…wait, I know where I saw the same thing. It was a tattoo on Murdoc's arm!"

"That is likely to be important, Nathan, so give it some more thought. Over all, how do you feel about our session?"

"Evan, I feel pretty good about it. It has given me a great deal to ponder. I believe it will help."

"I hope so. I think we made a good start today. Over the next few days some of the things you looked at may become clearer to you, but don't try to push the river, just let your unconscious thoughts flow into consciousness in their own time and at their own pace. If you'd like, we could meet again next week."

"Thanks, Evan. I'd like that

## Chapter Twenty-five

Thou shall have no other gods before me.

-Exodus 20:3

Spring semester was winding down and Nathan Richards was holding the last class session of his course on faith and doubt before final exams. This session was unstructured in order to give his students an opportunity to raise any questions or issues that were important to them. Because there were no topics to no be covered or parameters for the session, things started slowly until Lurleen Montgomery raised her hand with a question. "Professor Richards, I have been wondering about something for a while now."

"What is that, Miss Montgomery? Fire away."

"Well, we speak of Christianity as a monotheistic religion, right?" She waited for a nod from Nathan and then continued. "When God gave the ten commandments to Moses, the first commandment says *Thou shall have no other gods before me.* The passage says gods, plural, and I think there are other passages in the Bible that also refer to other gods. What are we to make of that? Is it like the Greeks who had a chief god, Zeus, and then a whole host of lesser gods and goddesses?"

Nathan paused and scanned the class before answering. "Good question, and you are correct; there are numerous references to gods, especially in Psalms. This is something many preachers and laity seem to ignore or else treat it as merely stylistic, like the royal we. I don't know if I can give you a solid, definitive answer. The Hebrews did seem to allow for the existence of other gods, but the message of the ten commandments was that God, Yahweh, was the supreme god. Christianity took it further and proclaimed that God is not just the chief god but the only one."

Lurleen's question seemed to open the flood gates and other students began offering their interpretations as well as additional questions. Clearly the class enjoyed the freedom to toss around their ideas and questions, but by the end of the class hour there was no consensus as to the meaning or significance of the use of the plural form of god. Nathan adjourned the class after reminding them of the final exam date and time. Even though the discussion had ended, Nathan continued to ponder its meaning. Though familiar with the many passages that spoke of gods, Nathan realized he too had never settled on the reason for those references. Could it be interpreted as meaning that there was more than one god? Was it support for the idea that there is a Satan as well as good and bad angels and demons? As he reflected further, he realized that anytime this question came up he would mentally shove it back into the closet of his mind and shut the door. With the many Biblical references to gods other than Yahweh, Nathan started to wonder what that could mean for his theory about evil? By the time he reached his office two students from his class were waiting for him outside his door, Myra Napier and Lurleen Montgomery. Somewhat surprised to see the two young women waiting for him, Nathan greeted them and invited them into his office. "Well, ladies, what can I do for you?"

Myra spoke first, "Dr. Richards, I really enjoyed class today, but I am just here to ask you a quick question."

"What is it, Miss Napier?"

"I was just wondering if I could take the final at another time? My parents have rented a VRBO on the coast for a family reunion, and I'd hate to miss part of it."

"I think we can make that happen. You could take it at the time I give my Abnormal Psych class their final." He pointed to the date and time on his desk calendar, "Will that work for you?"

"That would be great! Thank you so much." With a smile, Myra turned to leave, then looked over her shoulder at Lurleen. "I'll see you later, roomie."

Lurleen nodded at her roommate and then turned to Nathan. "You didn't have a solid answer to the question about more than one god. I was wondering if we could discuss it further?" Lurleen knew the answer before he could reply; she was confident that he would accept her invitation. "I'd suggest we make a quick stop at a little microbrewery near here and then visit Al Buehler Trail. Are you familiar with it?"

"I can't say that I am. Where is it?" Nathan had swallowed the bait, hook, line, and sinker.

"It's a lovely wooded trail that runs along the university golf course, and it's complete with heavy woods, a lake, and best of all, it has some nice secluded spots where we can…uh, talk."

Since it was still early afternoon, Nathan knew he had time before he needed to be home. He drove Lurleen to the microbrewery where they picked up two large growlers of draft beer and then continued a sort distance to the parking area for Buehler Trail. Nathan had never visited the trail before. He and Lurleen found the parking area empty, indicating that they would have the trail to themselves. That realization got Nathan's heart pounding. They walked briskly until they reached the edge of the wooded portion of the trail. A variety of trees shaded the path and cooled the air which had warmed considerably since morning. After walking about a quarter of a mile they reached a lake with a wooden foot bridge. They crossed the bridge and came to a bench that was set off some from the trail, making it invisible until one was right in front of it.

"How does this look?" Lurleen asked. "Let's stop here, sip our beer and continue our discussion." Nathan eagerly agreed. The metal bench was hard and dusty but neither Nathan nor his student appeared to mind. They enjoyed the deep, rich flavor of their beer for a time without speaking. Lurleen consumed her beer in record time and then turned to Nathan. She reached over and took his free hand and guided it under her sweatshirt. With a wicked smile she asked, "Do you like this spot? I am finding it quite warm; shall I remove some of my clothes?"

"This is a good spot", he replied, finishing his beer quickly. "I like that, what is someone comes along?"

After a long, impassioned kiss, Lurleen looked up at Nathan, "Perhaps you are right. We'll wait for another time and place." After a moment Lurleen straightened her sweatshirt and then asked, "I was wondering if you liked the pictures you took of me?"

"Yes, yes, I do. I look at them often." Nathan pulled his phone from his pocket and opened the photo file. "See," he said scrolling through the pictures of Lurleen. Before putting his phone away, he noticed the time. "Damn, it's time we start back."

Lurleen made a pouty face and replied, "Ah, do we have to? We were just getting started." As she spoke, she suddenly removed her sweatshirt completely. "Are you sure you want to leave now?"

All Nathan could say at this point was a breathless, "No."

It was after six pm when Nathan finally arrived home. Alexis was clearly disturbed when he walked in. "Where have you been? I called you several times but you never answered. I was getting worried." She waited for his answer but Nathan could tell she was getting angrier by the minute.

Uh, well I stopped off for a beer and talked with Evan about our hypnosis session, and, uh, I guess my phone was still on airport mode after class."

"Nathan, for some reason, I don't believe you. Look me in the eyes and tell me you aren't lying!"

Nathan felt a shudder of fear. He knew Alexis could normally read his facial expressions with uncanny accuracy, better than any lie detector. "Lexi, I am sorry if you don't believe me." He turned and walked away, heading for the bathroom where he could wash his face and use some mouthwash. Once in the solitude of the bathroom, his fear gradually turned to anger. *She has her nerve accusing me of lying when she has been lying about why she wants to foster that kid.* Perhaps, Nathan thought, maybe there really are angels and demons as well as witches and gods of the darkness that like to toy with the lives of mere mortals. The remainder of the evening served as a kind of unofficial cease fire which gave both Alexis and Nathan a chance to calm down. Alexis had already gotten into bed when Nathan came and sat on her side of the bed. "Lexi, I am sorry for the way I acted this evening…for that matter, I am sorry for how I have been acting towards you recently. I don't know what is wrong with me."

Alexis took his hand as she replied, "Nathan, I know something has been eating at you. Do you think it has to do with your interviews with that Murdoc character? What did you and Evan come up with?"

"I am not sure. I'd like to blame Murdoc, but I am responsible for my actions, not him. So far, the hypnosis session hasn't helped me uncover anything very useful except that there is something there, deep down that I am really afraid of."

"But you don't have any idea what it could be?"

"Not really. Sometimes, I feel like it is something in me, but at other times, it feels very alien. I wish I knew Evan better so I would feel free to just open up and talk. Yesterday I almost called Leonard Marshall back in Lubbock. He helped me through some pretty rough times, and I can trust him…plus, he knows a great deal about evil and the occult."

"I think you should call him, maybe even go for a visit. The semester is all but over and you won't be teaching this summer."

"Maybe I will. Thanks for understanding. I don't deserve it.

"Maybe you don't. but I love you…when you love somebody you also learn to forgive."

Chapter Twenty-six

Seasons don't fear the reaper

Nor do the wind, the sun or the rain.

-Blue Oyster Cult

The flight from Raleigh/Durham to Lubbock, Texas included one stop in Dallas and took almost five hours total. The plane to Dallas was only about half-filled which allowed Nathan some quiet time to think and wonder. From his window seat Nathan had seen mostly clear blue sky until the plane crossed over Louisiana. Towering cumulus clouds had sprung up like a mountain range and the tone Nathan heard was a signal that the captain had turned on the seat belt sign. Almost immediately, the Boeing 737 began to pitch and plummet noticeably, eliciting sudden gasps from a few passengers. The turbulence made Nathan wonder if his life was about to experience some real turbulence and very soon. As suddenly as it arrived the unnerving air bumpiness ceased and Nathan's thoughts returned to the question that seemed to haunt him: what was the source of his fear? Was he afraid of Murdoc? Satan or death? Abruptly, as if someone had turned on a light in the darkness of his mind, the thought occurred to Nathan that he was afraid of himself. *What am I afraid of doing or becoming? It doesn't make sense...or does it?* Almost as soon as he entertained the possibility of being afraid of something within himself, Nathan heard the soft sound of the pilot's voice announcing that they had begun their initial descent into Dallas and would be landing soon. After exiting the plane, Nathan's thoughts shifted to the more mundane task of how to get to his next flight that would take him on into Lubbock. His connections were pretty close so he barely got to the gate for his flight to Lubbock when passengers began the boarding process. The flight from Dallas to Lubbock took slightly over an hour. Nathan was met at the airport by Leonard Marshall, Ph.D., a retired psychology professor at Texas Tech. During Nathan's two year stay in Lubbock, he and Dr. Marshall became close friends. Marshall was somewhat of an expert on the occult, and he had in fact, saved Nathan's life when Nathan encountered great evil in both a demonic and human form at a place called Hell's Gate, an allegedly haunted location near the Lubbock City Cemetery. Marshall had warned the police that Nathan would be in danger there and the police were able to intervene in time to prevent Nathan from being shot and killed by one of Arte Mantus' minions. Just as Nathan exited the secure area of the Lubbock airport, he spotted his friend, Leonard Marshall. The two men greeted each other warmly. "Leonard, it's really good to see you. I have missed you. Thank you for agreeing to meet with me on such short notice."

"Nathan, it was no trouble at all. My schedule is never too crowded, especially for you. Do you have any luggage besides your carry-on?" Nathan shook his head and they headed for the exit to the parking area. Lubbock skies were clear and the west Texas sun beat down with great intensity as Leonard and Nathan climbed into Dr. Marshall's silver Impala.

"Damn, Leonard, this town is as hot as I remember, and it's not even officially summer yet."

Marshal smiled and turned the car's A/C to full. "Yeah, some things never change. But you, my friend…you have experienced a lot of change since you left here. I gather from your call and emails that not all of the changes have been good. Am I correct?"

"You got that right, Leonard. There's a lot I need to tell you about. Most of it is stuff I am not comfortable telling anyone else, especially Alexis." It took approximately forty minutes to drive from the airport to Dr. Marshall's home on the south side of town. Nathan had been to Marshall's home only once, but he recognized it immediately as they turned into the driveway. "Leonard, your house and yard look really nice. Do you maintain it yourself?"

Leonard smiled as he replied, "Thanks, I am my own yardman. My wife used to like to work in the yard, and since she died, I have tried to continue her good work. I think she would haunt me if I didn't."

Leonard Marshall's home was a brick ranch style built in the early 1980's. It's cool interior was a welcome escape from the hot Lubbock sun. Leonard showed Nathan the guest bedroom and then ushered him into the kitchen for a cold beer. Both men pulled up a chair at the breakfast table and sipped their beers. Nathan began to update his friend on all that had transpired since Nathan left Lubbock and the church. He started with the relatively safe details of his move and the academic appointment at Duke. Leonard had a number of questions about the demands of Nathan's joint appointment. After about an hour, Nathan got to the hard part, the part he knew he had to divulge. "Leonard, what I need to tell you now is hard for me…I am truly embarrassed by it. Embarrassed and confused, but I need to tell you so you will have a clear picture of the predicament I find myself enmeshed in. Nathan proceeded to tell his friend about his infatuation with Lurleen Montgomery and then about his encounters with Dr. Murdoc at the prison.

Dr. Marshall listened intently, occasionally asking questions for clarify cation. Both men finished their beers and Leonard got two more from the refrigerator. "Well, Nathan that is quite a story, and I must say you are the last person I would have expected to get sexually involved with one of your students, especially one of your seminary students." "You and me both, Leonard! I still can't quite believe it. It's like she has some kind of power over me. It's like a magnet the way I am drawn to her, and it has been that way almost from the beginning of the semester. Looking back, I realize that there were two paths I could take, one was the straight and narrow, the one I have always tried to follow. Then, there was the other path. It looked so inviting, and I guess I thought a little detour wouldn't hurt. What I didn't understand at the time was that path led me into a kind of addiction and I couldn't get off that path. Now,

I wonder if it is too late to get back on the right track. Oh, then there is the serial killer, Murdoc. I feel certain that he has hypnotized me." Nathan laughed an uncomfortable laugh, "I feel like I am incredibly weak-willed the way those two experiences have influenced me."

Leonard smiled as he sipped his beer. "Nathan, weak willed you are not, but I can't help wondering if the two experiences are connected in some way."

"Connected...how do you mean?"

"I mean that it seems like both people had an unusually strong impact on you, and both relationships developed about the same time. Tell me more about your student, Miss Montgomery."

Nathan revealed more about his feelings, his attraction to Lurleen Montgomery. Even as he talked about her, Nathan could feel a certain excitement build within him. "Nathan, do you believe in witches?"

Nathan was caught totally off guard by Leonard's question.

"Uh, I never thought ab

out it before, but I guess not. Why in the world do you ask?"

Dr. Marshall rubbed his chin and cleared his throat before answering. "It's just a hunch. Did you know that North Carolina is apparently home to one of the largest concentrations of witches in the country? There are more covens there than just about anywhere else."

"Leonard, surely you jest! I'll admit she has a bewitching quality but…a witch? I don't think so."

Leonard pressed his inquiry further, "Have you ever seen anything uusual about her appearance…her body? Like a tattoo or birthmark?"

Nathan thought for several moments and then he froze. "Oh, my God, Leonard! Now that you mention it…there was a mark on her thigh. I thought it was a tattoo at first, but it was a birthmark. It looked like a star with five or six points! What could that mean?"

"Well, people have believed in witches since antiquity. Some see them as linked to the devil while still others see them as a distinct species of beings, along with humans, and vampires. Ever read the book <u>Discovery of Witches</u>?"

"I haven't read that book, but if you are right and she is a witch is there anything I can do to break her spells?"

"Good question, Nathan. I'll have to research that one. As to the other fellow…Murdoc, was that his name?"

"That is correct."

"Nathan, you have more expertise with hypnosis than I do, but it seems like the influence he wields is more than post hypnotic suggestion. Did you mention something about a tattoo on his hand or arm?"

"Yes. He had a tattoo of a red dragon on his forearm, like the Hannibal Lecter character in the movie *Silence of The Lambs*. Nathan did not mention that he had seen the dragon appear to fly on at least two occasions. There is one more thing that I should tell you even though it may be unrelated." Nathan proceeded to describe the suspicion and irritability he had been feeling towards his wife, Alexis.

"Nathan, you really have gotten yourself into a big mess of quicksand. Let's catch some dinner, then we can talk more about all this later this evening. Is that okay with you?"

After a quiet dinner at one of Lubbock's many steakhouse restaurants and some excellent red wine, Nathan and Leonard returned to Dr. Marshall's home. Leonard explained that based on what Nathan had told him, it was his suspicion that all three facets of Nathan's dilemma were related and may well indicate dark forces at play. His practical advice was to stay as far away from Lurleen Montgomery and Jeremiah Murdoc as possible. He promised to do some research on methods to counter a witch's hex or spell. As a result of their candid discussion and Marshall's insights, Nathan's level of fear dropped to a more manageable level. Maybe he didn't fear the reaper so much after all… at least for one night anyway. Nathan slept better that night than he had in a long while, which was a good thing since his plane to Dallas and then on to North Carolina left early the next morning.

The return flight to North Carolina seemed to pass in record time. No sooner did Nathan get into his car at the Raleigh-Durham airport than his cell phone buzzed; it was Leonard Marshall. "Hey, Leonard! I just landed in North Carolina. What's up? You sound excited."

"I did a little quick on-line research, and according to some Gaelic legends, witches ultimately derive their power from a pact made centuries ago with the devil. Apparently, their power is passed on from one generation to the next like an inherited trait or characteristic. I also found several possible methods to counteract a witch's spell. I'll email you copies of that information, and I'll do some more reading, but I wanted to get this much to you as soon as possible."

"Thanks, Leonard! You're a real pal. A lifesaver." Nathan's cell phone beeped indicating that he had received Marshall's email message. He glanced at the message but it was too long to read on his phone; it would have to wait until he could read it on his computer and then print it out.

Chapter Twenty-seven

How can you stop the rain from falling down?

How can you stop the sun from shinning?

-The Bee Gees

Nathan entered the last grade for the spring semester into the university's online grading system, and then he sat back from his laptop and looked out his office window. It was a balmy spring day in Durham, and he could see students scurrying across campus, apparently glad the semester was over. Many students would be leaving soon to return to their homes. During the fall and spring semesters student enrollment averages between 15 and 16 thousand, but it drops significantly during the two short summer terms. Nathan would not be teaching during the summer which he thought of as a mixed blessing. It would give him more free time to spend with family, write, and.... get deeper into trouble. Leonard Marshall's advice about staying away from Murdoc and Lurleen

Montgomery kept reverberating in his head, and he knew it was sound advice. But how was he going to resist seeing Lurleen? He might as well try to prevent the sun from rising tomorrow morning.

Almost as if she could hear his very thoughts, Nathan looked up to see her standing in his open doorway looking incredibly beautiful and seductive. "Well, this is an unexpected pleasure, Miss Montgomery. What brings you to my door? I thought you'd be packing up to go home."

"I am not leaving. I am planning to stick around for the summer and wondered if you were going to be teaching or needing any assistance with your research?"

"Please come in and have a seat. I will not be teaching and may be gone on a couple of short trips with the family. My wife will be working full-time so we can't do much traveling. I do plan to continue researching and writing my book, but I hadn't thought of having any help with it.

"Well, I am pretty good at library and online research, and I am available." Lurleen's offer of assistance came with all the force of a hurricane wind. It may have been invisible to an observer, but Nathan felt its impact. Nathan clearly did not miss the command embedded in Lurleen's offer of research help. Realistically, there was, little help she could offer with his book, but he felt powerless to resist. Although he didn't consciously recognize her as casting a spell, he knew he should refuse, but how? All he was able to do was utter a weak and ambiguous reply, "That's kind of you to offer…and uh, I'll certainly keep it in mind.'

Lurleen got up to leave but paused briefly, "I know you will, and I look forward to working with you." She then turned to leave.

It was all Nathan could do to keep from calling her back. He could feel himself being pulled towards her by a force stronger than gravity. As she walked away, he heard her footsteps for a brief moment and then there was only silence. He immediately printed out the information Leonard Marshall had emailed him in on a method to block a witch's hex or spell. What he read made him laugh out loud. The directions called for him to collect small sea shells that had a hole in then. He needed 30-50 such shells which he was to string together so that they could be hung in a window or over a doorway, some place nearby. Apparently, this string of shells was to ward off or prevent a witch's spell from entering

his location, somewhat like garlic or wolf bane was supposed to repel a vampire. Even though he thought the anti-hexing formula sent by Leonard Marshall sounded pretty ridiculous, he remembered that there was a big jar of sea shells he had collected for Lizzy somewhere in the house, probably in her closet. Nathan decided that he would head home and retrieve the shells before Alexis and Lizzy got home. He didn't want to have to explain why he needed them. Nathan promptly drove home and began his search for the sea shells, which he found on a shelf in Lizzy's closet. He took the jar to the garage and poured out some shells to see if any had holes in them. To his surprised he found quite a few that did, so he began to string them up in accordance with the directions Leonard Marshall had emailed him. When he finished, Nathan looked over his work and chuckled to himself. *I don't think this thing will repel anything, but what the heck. I'll give it a try.* As he studied his handiwork Nathan hit upon an idea of how to make the string of shells somewhat portable. He borrowed a metal frame that used to hold a small globe of the Earth. By tying the string of shells to it he could easily move the device wherever he wanted it. He stared at the string of shells and the frame in his car, planning to take it to his office the next day.

After supper Nathan, Alexis, and Lizzy sat down to watch the news, but Lizzy quickly became bored and headed off to her room to play with her doll house. She called Jake to come with her, and he padded dutifully after her. Alexis rather hesitantly brought up the subject of fostering David, and to her surprise Nathan raised no real objections to having him stay with them for a week as a sort of trial run. Their discussion about fostering the lad was interrupted by a weather bulletin. The category one hurricane which had been meandering off the Louisiana coast had suddenly strengthened into a category three storm and had come ashore in eastern Louisiana. The various forecast models were in general agreement that the storm's track would take it in their general direction within 48 hours.

"Nathan, that doesn't look good!" Alexis' facial expression turned suddenly from bright and sunny to dark and worried. "If it comes over our area, I worry about all the big trees near the house. Do you think we'll be okay?"

"I guess so, Lexi. The storm will probably lose much of its punch as it travels over land. Anyway, it's a couple of days off, and we'll know more in the next day or so. We've got other things to focus on in the meantime." Nathan did not elaborate on what those other things might be.

After Alexis got Lizzy to bed, Nathan and Jake walked outside as was their nightly routine. While Jake took care of his business, Nathan scanned the skies. All he saw were clear skies studded

with countless stars. There wasn't the slightest hint of bad weather. Nathan wondered what it was like when he was just a small boy and weather radar was limited in its range, and there were no computer forecast models or satellites feeding data to the Weather Service and TV stations. Still further back, in ancient times, he thought how easy it would have been to blame dramatic changes in weather on the gods.

Despite the calmness of the night, Nathan's dreams were anything but calm or quiet. His dreams were filled with terrifying scenes reminiscent of segments from the *Wizard of Oz* when the wicked witch sent her minions out to capture Dorothy and her companions. Sometimes the witch in his dreams resembled the ugly hag in the Wizard of Oz and at other times she looked like Lurleen Montgomery. Around two am, Nathan awoke in a cold sweat. The house was totally quiet, but Nathan had a hard time returning to sleep. When he did, the nightmares continued, but the theme changed from witches to dragon-like beasts that pursued him with terrifying speed and persistence. When at last the first light of morning crept in through the bedroom window, Nathan was relieved emotionally but exhausted physically. After breakfast he headed to his office at the university eager to set up and test his anti-hexing device. Once in his office Nathan was relieved that nobody had noticed him carrying the string of sea shells into the building. *I wonder where I should place it? Does it really make any difference?* Nathan finally decided to place the stand and string of shells on his desk beside the phone. He decided that if anyone asked about it, he would say it was something his daughter made for him. To his surprise, he was able to focus his thoughts almost entirely on his research which involved gathering data on witches in North Carolina. Consistent with what he had learned from Leonard Marshall, North Carolina had a long history of considerable witch activity. According to what he read, some of history's most powerful witches had once lived in the area around Durham. Interestingly, their number and influence seemed to have diminished soon after slavery was abolished and showed yet another decrease in activity as the tobacco industry began to die out. Nathan wondered if those two evils had in some way empowered witches, and when they were eliminated, the power and activity of area witches also declined. Pushing back from his desk he glanced out the window at the sky which was still mostly clear. His mind too had been mostly clear from any thoughts of Lurlene Montgomery. *Maybe the device I constructed actually works* Nathan chuckled to himself. *Maybe you can stop the rain from falling…at least for a while*

Chapter Twenty-eight

Now in that place there was a

Great Dragon, which the Babylonians revered.

-Bel and The Dragon 1:23

After taking a break from his morning research, Nathan strolled across campus to one of the snack bars that was still open during the break between the spring semester and the first summer term. Sometimes it seemed to him that this was the best time to be on a college campus- when the students were gone. There was really only one of Nathan's students he had any expectation of seeing during the summer and that was, of course, Lurleen Montgomery. As her name crossed his mind, he halfway expected to see her in the snack bar, but she did not appear. After a leisurely meal of a hamburger and fries, Nathan dumped his trash and walked slowly back to his office where he resumed his online research. Perhaps the term research was a bit too lofty for what he was actually doing. It was more like browsing on the internet, sometimes about witches, sometimes about Satan or other demonic figures. For some reason, he began exploring one of the books of the Apocrypha, <u>Bel and the Dragon.</u> Nathan knew from his studies in seminary that this book was considered by some to be a continuation of the Old Testament *Book of Daniel*. From what Nathan read, the story's events took place during the reign of Cyrus the Great and the Jewish captivity in Babylon. According to the storyline the prophet Daniel confronts the false God Bel (Marduk) and exposes him as a priestly fabrication. In addition, Nathan observed that there was an interesting side-note in the book about a dragon which the prophet managed to kill without benefit of a sword. Although Nathan found the material interesting, he wondered why he had chosen to read about a dragon. *What does it mean that I have been thinking about and even dreaming about dragons lately? Does it have something to do with Murdoc?*

While Nathan wondered about his recent preoccupation with witches and dragons, not far away, Jeremiah Murdoc was unusually busy in his cell at Central Prison. Technically, Murdoc was housed in the administrative segregation unit or solitary confinement area of the prison, but his cell was not at all like those of other prisoners. Within the prison itself, he could seemingly demand and receive many privileges not available to other inmates, thus Murdoc's cell was lined with shelves of books and maps built over a small work desk which was covered with papers and assorted folders. In addition, Murdoc had a radio and a small tv set, but most significant of all, he had a laptop computer. Generally, other prisoners had only very limited computer access, for obvious reasons. As Nathan had already discovered from his two visits with Murdoc, the man had an amazing power over the thoughts and behavior of people with whom he came in contact. What was not generally known was that Murdoc's power and influence could extend beyond his immediate physical presence; however, just like most everything else, good or evil, he too had his limits. Satan's power and dominion was limited by God to the

Earth. A vampire's considerable power was limited to the hours of darkness. An arrow shot from an English long bow can travel no more than a third of a mile. A walkie-talkie has a range of a few miles, and even a clear channel radio station has a broadcast range of less than a thousand miles. Unknown to anyone other than Murdoc, he could also project or transmit a life-like image of himself in whatever shape or appearance he wished for about twenty to thirty miles. Within that range his "projected self" could assume a form that had both mass and physical substance

unlike a hologram. Even more frightening, he could also project himself as a large dragon for a much smaller distance, perhaps ten miles. While not quite the same thing, the ability to move objects at some distance is referred to as *psychokinesis*. What Murdoc was able to do was more like the transporter or teleportation device featured in the *Star Trek* movies So, even though Jeremiah Murdoc's physical body was confined by the walls of Central Prison, his actual sphere of influence was considerably greater. On this particular day, Murdoc had been following the Weather Channel's coverage of Tropical Storm Elizabeth closely and with great interest, sensing an opportunity to intervene in the lives of certain people, namely Dr. Nathan Richards, his family, and Miss Lurleen Montgomery. Murdoc was confident that he had already established an initial level of influence with both Richards and Miss Montgomery, but he had plans to expand his malicious control, and the oncoming storm seemed to afford him a unique opportunity to do precisely that. Just as people in Old Testament days believed, Jeremiah Murdoc knew that storms were truly periods of genuine, atmospheric chaos, which is why scholars believe that the storms described in the Bible, especially those at sea, were actually a metaphor for demonic chaos and evil. Meteorologists also knew that tropical storms had been developing much earlier over the past few years, most likely due to climate change or global warming. Murdoc didn't care about such facts, he just saw this early season storm as an opportunity,

and he wanted to strike while the proverbial iron was hot. According to The Weather Channel, what was now tropical storm Elizabeth was moving faster than anticipated and was expected to reach the Raleigh-Durham area tomorrow night, just slightly more than 24 hours away. This same information was made known to Nathan via a warning

statement from the Weather service via his cell phone. Apparently, Alexis got the same notice since she called immediately after he had read

the bulletin. Her voice sounded fraught with worry. "Nathan, I am really worried about the storm. What I just saw on my phone makes it sound like it could be pretty bad. Do you think we should consider evacuating the area?"

Ever the doubting skeptic, Nathan tried to minimize the danger. "I think we'll be okay. Most likely the storm will weaken as it gets closer. It has to travel over some higher elevations before it hits us. Besides, where would we go?"

"I guess maybe you are right. We had thought about starting our visitation period with David this weekend, but I think we should postpone it, don't you?"

"I had kinda forgotten that, but I definitely think we should reschedule it." After he hung up from talking to Alexis, Nathan gathered up his notes and prepared to leave for home when he heard a loud knock on his office door. Before he could even invite his visitor in, the door opened and in burst Lurleen Montgomery. "Dr. Richards, I am glad I found you! I have been trying to get in touch with you. Where have you been?"

"I have been on campus almost all morning. What is so urgent?"

"The storm…it is going to be really bad. I just know it. I can feel it!"

"I was just getting ready to head home so I could make some preparations, but I think we'll be okay...."

Lurleen cut Nathan off, "No! You are wrong! I think there is danger... especially for you and maybe for me too." As she spoke her warning, Lurleen glanced down at the string of shells on his desk. Her facial expression was not unlike that of a person who just discovered a scorpion crawling toward them. "What is that?" she exclaimed.

Nathan chuckled as he responded, "It's just something my daughter made for me. I gather you don't like it."

Trying to hide the intensity of her contempt, Lurleen forced a smile, "Oh, no, uh...I think it is nice. I just wondered what it was.

"Lurleen...Miss Montgomery, we'll all be fine. Unless there is something I can do for you, I really need to be going." As he drove home, Nathan couldn't help wondering about the way Lurleen had responded when she saw the anti-hexing device on his desk. Perhaps there was something to it after all. *Maybe she is a witch and the sea shell contraption Leonard told me how to make actually works.*

While Richards was heading to his house, Lurleen Montgomery stormed back to her apartment, clearly frustrated by what had taken place in Richards' office. For the last day or so, she had tried repeatedly to cast a spell that would compel Nathan to come back to her thus demonstrating her increasing ability to dominate him. However, in spite of her best efforts, she sensed that she had somehow lost much of her power to control his thoughts and inflame his desire for her. Although uncertain why, she did not like the look of the so-called gift from his daughter she observed on his desk. Overhead, skies were beginning to show the first spiral bands of dark clouds portending the oncoming storm.

Chapter Twenty-nine

Red sky at morning, sailors take warning.

-Ancient rhyme

Thursday morning arrived with massive cumulonimbus clouds helping to an unmistakable red tint to the sky. Nathan made note of the sky's color as he walked his dog Jake through the neighborhood. "Well, Jake, it looks like we are in for some nasty weather today…and sooner rather than later." Before their walk was over Nathan felt the wind shift and increase in speed. Because of the closeness of the storm and its counter clockwise rotation, the wind was now coming out of the north-east. Nathan reached down to give Jake a pat on the back as he quoted a line from an old Bob Dylan song, "You don't need a weatherman to know which way the wind blows…and we don't need a weatherman to tell us we need to get on home before we get soaked." Jake and Nathan increased their pace and arrived home just before the first big drops of rain began to fall.

Once inside, Jake and Nathan were greeted by Elizabeth who had been watching for them through the kitchen window. "Daddy, Daddy, you and Jake got home just in time! Mommy said you were going to get wet. Is it going to be a bad storm today?"

"Well, Lizzy, thank you for watching for me and Jake. Yeah, it's going to be stormy today, but we'll be okay."

Alexis turned from putting the breakfast dishes in the dishwasher and smiled broadly at her husband and dog. "My supervisor called a few minutes ago and said that the office will be closed for the day due to the storm. I am really glad that I won't have to drive into town. They just showed the radar on the local news and the storm is a really big and getting very close. It is just a few miles per hour shy of being a category two hurricane."

Feeling more concern than he showed, Nathan tried hard to sound unconcerned, "I guess I was wrong about the storm losing some of its punch, but…we'll be okay. I am sure glad you don't have to go out. If the rain slacks up, I am going to go out and make another pass through the yard and make sure that there is nothing loose that can blow around." Almost as if the weather had responded to Nathan's words, the rain abruptly stopped momentarily, so he headed outside to make a last-minute check of the surrounding yard.

During the afternoon, the wind and rain increased in intensity; thunder boomed periodically causing Jake to pace uneasily through the house. Each member of the Richard's family experienced a sense of growing alarm as the day progressed, perhaps realizing that the night was going to be rough. Nathan picked up his phone to look at the radar and as he did, he got a text from Lurleen. She had just sent him one of the pictures he had taken of her. He felt a sudden surge of panic and deleted the photo as quickly as possible. *Thank goodness Lexi didn't see it!* His fear quickly morphed into arousal as he thought of that time he spent with her in her apartment, and he realized that this was the first time in a few days that he had lusted after her. He wondered if the sea shell charm had to be nearby in order to be protective.

After sending the picture to Nathan, Lurleen felt a wicked sense of satisfaction, hoping that it would either arouse Nathan or perhaps cause problems with his wife if she saw it. Either way, she felt it was like lobbing a terrorist's bomb; it will cause chaos and damage. She went back to her own form of research. Although she didn't know for sure where she learned of it, she had recently become aware of the extensive witchcraft library at Cornell University, and through some online searches and interlibrary loan she had been able to acquaint herself with some valuable information. For one thing she had learned that some of her distant relatives were witches, and that she had, in fact, descended from a long line of powerful witches, some still lived in the Salem area. She also discovered that she had barely begun to tap into her own potential. Competence in the art of witchcraft was like competence playing golf or guitar, it required some guidance and a lot of practice. Lurleen knew she had received no guidance and hence very little practice using her ability. The question had always been where to find a "coach". Once more the material from Cornell was helpful. She learned of a coven in the Durham area where she could probably find someone to mentor her. To her surprise, witches were as modern and tech-savvy as any group. She was able to email the local coven and schedule an appointment, but unfortunately the storm might require a rescheduling of her meeting. Rising from her computer, Lurleen walked into her apartment's kitchen in order to pour herself a glass of wine. She stopped abruptly when she entered the kitchen and uttered a startled scream. In her kitchen stood a man or at least the shape of a man. She was so surprised by the appearance of this stranger in her apartment that she couldn't organize her thoughts enough to use any of her magic on the intruder. For several seconds the man neither moved nor spoke. He appeared to be about six feet tall and was wearing rain gear which included a hood. She couldn't see much of his face as it was partially obscured by the shadow created by the hood. Finally, he spoke. His voice sounded almost like it was computer-generated. "Miss Montgomery, you needn't be afraid. We met once before on the university campus, but you may not remember. I am not here to cause you any harm. In fact, I am here to assist you."

"How did you get in and what makes you think I need your help?"

"Patience, my dear, and don't try to use your witchcraft on me. It simply won't work. I am not here to harm you but to offer my guidance in order to help you further develop your skills as a witch. I know that you found the pendant I gave you to be a valuable key to unlocking centuries old knowledge. Now it is time to receive my tutelage, which you well know you need. With some additional guidance from me, your skills will increase rapidly. Perhaps you recall our earlier visit? I told you then that my assistance comes with a small price. Are you prepared to take the next step in your development?

"I don't know what you mean by guidance, but I do remember when we met. You gave me a pendant and told me more about the *Grimoire*. If you can truly show me how to increase my power as a witch, then I am interested, but what do you get out of it, and what will this cost me?"

"Miss Montgomery, I know more about you than you know about yourself. You are descended from a long line of witches. Your most distant relative was a witch who was murdered in Salem during the witch rials. As a result, some of your other relatives moved to the North Carolina area, but sadly some left the area after the decline of slavery and the tobacco business. You have what it takes to be the most powerful witch your family ever produced. You possess all the necessary ingredients, but you just need to learn to use all of what you have including your gorgeous face and body. I know the source of your power and how you can increase it. All I ask in return for my assistance is that you use your abiity to seduce a man."

"I know what you have just told me already from some digging I did. I don't know for sure how I found the source of that information...did you put that idea in my mind?"

The man merely smiled and nodded.

"Whom shall I seduce and what then?"

"You know the man quite well. His name is Dr. Nathan Richards. I want you to seduce him so that he will do whatever you want. Then, I would like for you to lead him further down the path of temptation in order to ruin his marriage and his reputation. You needn't actually kill him. After your work is finished, I will take it from there. Miss Montgomery, I am certain that his downfall will satisfy a desire you have harbored for quite some time. You will finally gain a sense of revenge for what your father did to you and your mother. Your father may be gone but Ricard's destruction will strike a blow against all the so-called holy men who in reality are nothing but frauds and deceivers. They claim to serve their God but in reality, they only serve themselves.'

"I don't know how you know about my father, but you are right. I hate him for what he did, but I don't really hate Dr. Richards. I actually find him rather attractive, so seducing him shouldn't be too difficult. I have him almost eating out of my hand now, so I can pretty much make him do whatever I want. When you are through with him, can I have him back…to enjoy as my plaything?"

Thunder boomed outside as the mystery man continued with his lies and distortions. "You do not hate Nathan Richards because you don't know his story. Did you know that he molested a woman he was supposedly counseling when he was a pastor of a church in Texas? Of course, nothing was done to punish him because the church swept things under the rug. Were you aware that he abandoned that church when things got difficult? He came here hoping to escape his past."

"I don't know any of the details of his past. All I know is that he was a pastor for a short time before taking the position here at Duke. I won't agree to your proposal if you plan to kill him, but if all you want is to bring him down and discredit him, then we have a deal."

"Excellent. When I am satisfied that Nathan Richards has been brought low then you may have what's left of him if you still want him. He then reached into the pocket of his rain coat and withdrew a small glass object which he handed to her. "Take this glass dragon and keep it close to you at all times. It is the means by which I will communicate with you and guide your thoughts. You might consider it a form of remote instruction. Do you understand?"

Lurleen Montgomery nodded in agreement and then stood silently as the individual she had been talking to seemed to dissolve in front of her.

Before he completely disappeared, she thought she glimpsed a small red tattoo on his forearm that might have been a bird or maybe a dragon. After a few seconds, all that remained of the man were some water droplets on the floor where he had been standing. The water had obviously

dripped off his rain gear. *Jesus, was there really someone here and who exactly was he? How could he come and go like that?* She looked at the glass dragon the stranger had given her and felt a thrill, the thrill of power and dominance. The glass dragon seemed to be emitting a soft red glow of its own. Although she didn't know exactly why, she knew she had made a deal with darkness and hoped she hadn't also sold her own soul in the process. Lightning flashed outside, illuminating the interior of her kitchen for a second in a cold, ghostly white light, and in that momentary flash of light she saw what appeared to be a hideous beast outside her apartment, a beast that reminded her of something out of the Book of Revelation. *Dear God, what have I done?*

While the witch, Lurleen Montgomery, contemplated the domination and likely destruction of Dr. Nathan Richards., he was busy securing lawn furniture and garbage cans at his home. As he ran from the garage to the house an unusually strong gust of wind nearly knocked him down and the rain seemed to be blowing almost sideways, stinging his face. Scrambling in through the door into the kitchen, Nathan stopped and stamped his feet as he exclaimed, "Wow! We are in for a rough night indeed! I think I got everything tied down or put away that might get blown about. "Darkness came to the area earlier than usual because of the heavy clouds and rain. At times the lightning flashes and subsequent thunder were almost constant, and the wind velocity had reached gale force levels already. The lights in the house flickered off and then back on several times as the Richards ate supper and watched the tv news. Severe storm warnings and a tornado watch had been issued for most of North Carolina. The center of the storm was expected to pass very close to the Raleigh-Durham area before curving east towards the coast. It would be a very nasty night indeed.

Chapter Thirty

Never laugh at live dragons, Bilbo you fool.

-J.R.R. Tolkien

The disorganized remnants of the tropical storm passed over the Raleigh-Durham area sometime after midnight, and when it did, the rain stopped briefly. During the lull in the storm Elizabeth Richards came into her parent's room in obvious distress. Between her sobs she cried out, "Mommy, Daddy, there is a monster outside my window! It looks like the dragon in that movie! I'm scared."

Both Nathan and Alexis got out of bed to comfort their daughter. Nathan hugged her close as he laughed, "It's just the storm, baby…nothing to be scared of."

Lizzy was not consoled and his laughter only seemed to fuel her concern. "No. It's not funny! It's a dragon and it was looking in my window. I think it wants to eat me."

Realizing that Lizzy was not to be comforted by mere words or humor, Nathan offered to go into her room in order to banish the monster.

"Lizzy, you and I will go to your room and if the monster is still outside, Jake and I will chase him away. "

Lizzy reluctantly agreed to the plan but still protested meekly. "Okay, daddy, but the monster looks pretty scary." Once in Lizzy's bedroom, Nathan peered out her window. At first glance, he didn't see a dragon or any sort of monster, but he did notice some movement in the yard. It was too dark to determine exactly what he saw, but he knew that there was something in their yard. He wondered if perhaps it might be the wolf that he had seen before that had come back or perhaps just a stray deer passing through the yard.

"Lizzy, Jake and I will go outside and check. I think it might be a deer that has been scared by the storm. You stay in bed with Mommy while I take Jake and we'll go check. Okay?"

Lizzy climbed into bed with Alexis while Nathan slipped on some jeans and a shirt. He put on his boots and grabbed his rain coat and a large flashlight. Summoning the family's German Shepherd, Jake, he went outside. The night was exceptionally dark and the rain had started to fall hard once again. Along with the return of the rain, the wind had picked up as well. Nathan could feel his heart rate increase as he scanned the flashlight's beam around the yard. "Do you see any dragons, Jake?" Nathan said as he tried to inject humor into the situation. Nathan and Jake circled around the garage in order to get a clear view of the back of the house and the window to Lizzy's bedroom. Through the rain, which was now coming down hard, Nathan clearly spotted a large form crouched in some bushes perhaps ten or fifteen yards from the back of the house. Jake obviously saw the same thing and let out a deep growl and then charged towards the dark shape. Nathan tried desperately to call Jake back without success, so he ran hard after him and towards the dark shape. Although the old German Shepherd wasn't as fast as he once was, he reached the intruder well before Nathan and began barking

furiously. Nathan's flashlight illuminated Jake and the reason for his frantic barking, but he could hardly believe what he saw. There before him was a four-legged creature like nothing he had ever observed. Whatever it was, it was about as large as a horse and had an odd, bird-like shape except that it also had a tail and head much like an alligator. The body appeared to be covered in large overlapping scales that looked almost like armor plating. Folded behind and above its back were large leathery wings, while the face of the beast looked like something from a horror movie. The creature had four legs but the two front legs were slightly smaller than the back legs and it seemed to rise up and walk on its back legs alone. Jake's barking was so loud Nathan could hardly determine what sound the creature made, but it seemed to be a loud hiss. In the glare of his flashlight's beam the monster appeared to have a slightly reddish tint. Jake moved quickly in half-circles around the beast frantically barking and snarling. Each time Jake moved the creature would turn its head following his movements, but it did not charge at Jake. Heedless of Nathan's calls to move away, Jake suddenly lunged at the creature, but the beast moved with unexpected swiftness striking the dog with its tail. Jake was hurled backwards with a yelp of pain such as Nathan had never heard a dog make. He rushed towards Jake and so did the beast Nathan's only weapon was the large flashlight which he used to try to club the dragon in the face. He struck the beast on its snout as hard as he could but the blow had little effect. Nathan was sent sprawling to the ground by the force of the monster's charge. Then the dragon stood over him, and Nathan felt certain he was going to die. The beast paused for a moment before seizing Nathan in its jaws, and in that moment, Jake struggled to his feet and made a desperate lunge at the monster, clamping his jaws on one of its front feet. The monster roared and swung its head forcefully to the side, knocking Jake away, but before it could make a fatal strike at either Jake or Nathan, there was a loud blast like that of a small cannon that came from the direction of the house. The startled creature looked in the direction of the sound just as a second blast occurred. Nathan recognized the sound of his grandfather's old 20-gauge shotgun. Apparently, Alexis had gotten the gun, loaded it and fired it in the air hoping to frighten or at least distract the monster. Her strategy must have worked because the dragon took a couple of steps in her direction and then seemed to dematerialize and simply fade into nothingness.

Alexis ran to Nathan and knelt at his side. "Are you okay?"

Stunned but still conscious, Nathan, his face, cut and bleeding, answered, "I guess so. Look at Jake. Is he…is he alive?"

Alexis turned to examine Jake. She knelt at the dog's side and examined his wounds. He was soaking wet from the rain and his own blood, but he appeared to be still breathing. Turning to Nathan she hollered over the sound of the storm, "Nathan, I think he is still alive but hurt pretty bad. We've got to get him inside and try to stop the bleeding. Can you walk on your own?"

Nathan struggled to his feet and together he and Alexis carried their wounded dog into the house. They were met at the door by their daughter who was crying hysterically. "Is Jake dead?" she cried out.

Nathan replied, "No, sweetie, but he is hurt pretty bad. We are going to take care of him now." Alexis dried Jake as best she could with a towel while Nathan got some gauze and peroxide from their medicine cabinet. He cleaned and bandaged Jake's wounds, but the blood continued to seep through the dressing. Jake's breathing was labored but other than the rise and fall of his chest, he didn't move.

Nathan changed the dog's dressing after about thirty minutes and the bleeding finally seemed to slow. Concern was etched deeply on his face as he looked at Alexis. "If the storm slacks up some, I'll drive him to the vet school. They have an emergency room much like a hospital. I don't think we can do enough on our own to save him."

"Do you think you are able to drive? I am so frightened for you and Jake."

"I think I can drive, and you need to stay here with Lizzy. This has been pretty traumatic for her too."

By about three a.m., the rain let up considerably, and the wind died down as well, so Nathan and Alexis loaded Jake into the back of the old Honda and Nathan left for the university veterinary hospital. Upon arrival a couple of second year vet students met Nathan and Jake and they carried him into an examination room where they were joined by one of the staff veterinarians. After a preliminary examination it was determined that Jake's right front leg was broken and he had suffered some internal injuries which required surgery. Nathan was urged to go on home and to call later in the morning to check on Jake's condition. Feeling stunned and deeply troubled Nathan drove back home. The rain was still falling lightly when he reached the house. He reported as best he could what the ER veterinarian had told him about Jake's condition and the treatment plan. Nathan wanted to pray but couldn't seem to find the words. He hoped that God would know what was written on his heart.

Back at Central Prison Jeremiah Murdoc's guards, the ones in his area of the prison, were checking on each inmate. When they arrived at his cell, they looked in on Murdoc, and found him in a trance-like state bleeding from wounds to his right hand and forearm. The prison doctor who sutured Murdoc's wounds thought that they looked like an animal's bite, but Dr. Murdoc was unable to give a coherent explanation. Lacking a realistic explanation, the prison doctor reported that Murdoc had fallen and cut his hand and arm on the desk in his cell. Like Nathan and Jake, Jeremiah Murdoc had a rough night too.

By early afternoon of the next day, the storm had moved out to sea where it spent the last of its fury over the Atlantic. Nathan communicated with the vet school and learned that Jake's surgery had gone well, and his odds of survival had improved. The attending veterinarian wanted to keep Jake there for at least another 24 to 48 hours. This news gave the Richards family a legitimate reason for optimism regarding their beloved dog. With the horrors of the previous night apparently behind him Nathan's thoughts returned to the dragon creature. What exactly was it? Why had it come during the storm? Was it connected somehow to Jeremiah Murdoc? Nathan remembered seeing the dragon tattoo on Murdoc's arm and what he thought he saw rising above the prison after his interview with the man. Had he sent it somehow? Should he have called the police? So many questions and very few answers. It seemed almost like waking up from a nightmare. What was reality and what was a dream?

Alexis confirmed much of Nathan's perceptions of what took place in their backyard the night of the storm. She saw a beast of some kind poised and ready to strike Nathan who was lying on the ground alongside Jake. She wasn't certain what sort of beast she saw but stated confidently that it was like nothing she had ever seen before. During the afternoon while Nathan pondered the significance of the dragon, Alexis turned her thoughts once more to fostering David Charles. That evening she all but begged her husband to agree to set a date to begin the trial period as a step towards eventual adoption of the boy. Initially, Nathan felt it was not a good time to consider fostering or adopting a child in light of the terror of the previous night, but he eventually relented. After some additional discussion, Alexis and Nathan set the following Monday as the date to pick up David and begin the trial period. The actual duration of the trial period was left open, ultimately to be decided by the three participants. Nathan added one qualifier to their agreement. If there were any additional threats on their any of their lives, they would postpone indefinitely the idea of fostering or adopting David. In the meantime, Alexis would begin preparing Lizzy for the possible addition of a new family member.

Chapter Thirty-one

The storms come and go, the waves crash overhead, the big fish eat the little fish, and I keep on paddling.

-George R.R. Martin

Sometimes after a catastrophic event or a significant loss, people often feel like the world should stop turning, but it never does. Nathan Richards felt as though his world had been turned upside down, but he knew he had to keep paddling even if he no longer knew where he was heading. Monday morning after breakfast, Nathan and Alexis took Lizzy to her day care and then went to pick up David Charles from the orphanage. After signing numerous papers, they loaded David's meager belongings into Alexis' car and the three of them headed home, David's new home. Since they would not pick up Lizzy for several hours, it gave Nathan and Alexis some time to get David settled. What had been a quasi-office for Nathan and Alexis was now going to be David's bedroom. They had done very little decorating prior to David's arrival since they wanted to give him a chance to choose the décor, he was comfortable with.

Alexis put David's clothes on hangers in the closet as he watched in silence. "Well, David, what do you think of your room? You and I can go into town and you can pick up some things to put on the wall. Would you like to do that?"

"Yeah, I guess so," David replied softly and with a lack of any real enthusiasm.

"I know you have been through a lot of changes and probably don't know what to think about all this. It takes some time for a new place to really feel like home, your home." Alexis was eager to make David comfortable but she understood that she really couldn't speed up the process. In the back of her mind was the fear that Nathan might seize on David's apathy and lack of enthusiasm as a reason to end the trial period.

From his perspective, Alexis was trying too hard, but Nathan did not intervene or offer any suggestions. He tried to maintain a neutral position about the trial period but he knew that deep down he didn't expect it to work and maybe even hoped it wouldn't. *My life is chaotic enough without adding a troubled preadolescent to the mix.* His self-pity was interrupted by a phone call from the vet school telling him that he could bring Jake home. His mood brightened with that news which he reported to Alexis. "If you and David don't mind, I'll go pick him up."

David made no comment but Alexis replied with enthusiastic approval," Wow. That is really good news. Do you think you'll need any help?"

"No. I am sure I can manage."

Nathan was troubled by Jake's appearance when the technician brought him out. Jake was obviously glad to see his master and wagged his tail enthusiastically, but he looked definitely worse for wear. His right front leg was in a splint type cast and his abdomen had been shaved and was heavily bandaged. To cap it all off, Jake was fitted with an Elizabethan collar to prevent him from licking at any of his wounds. The technician explained Jake's follow-up care and scheduled a return visit in two weeks. Jake walked slowly to the car and then stopped as Nathan opened the CRV's rear hatch. He simply couldn't jump high enough to get into the car.

"Jake, you can't make the jump, can you boy?" Nathan left the car door open and walked back with Jake into the building and asked for some assistance. Two vet students helped Nathan get Jake into the car, but even with the additional help it was obvious that the move caused Jake considerable pain. "We'll get you home boy and then you can take it easy." On the drive home Nathan tried to speak comforting words to his dog as he wondered exactly how much pain the old German Shepherd felt.

Once home, getting Jake out of the car proved to be somewhat easier than getting him in, but Nathan basically had to lift him from the car. Alexis and David came out of the house to meet them. Alexis knelt beside Jake and gently stroked his head and back. Tears bloomed forth from her eyes as she caressed Jake. "You poor thing; let's get you into the house where you can rest." David stood back a few steps from Alexis and Jake, apparently not knowing how to respond.

Alexis looked back at David. "David, this is Jake. As you can see, he has had surgery and doesn't feel too good, but we think he is going to be okay with time."

David responded hesitantly, "I hope he is going to be all right. He looks like a nice dog." As he spoke, David moved closer and patted Jake lightly on the head.

"Let's get him inside", Nathan directed, taking the leash and leading Jake into the house. "Jake, old boy, your bed is ready for you. I hope you can rest with that collar thing around your neck." Once inside Jake walked slowly to his bed which had been moved into the living area, and he plopped down with a sigh. "Let's let him rest. I'll put his water bowl and food bowl close by his bed."

Nathan, Alexis, and David stood silently for a few moments looking down at Jake. Finally, David broke the silence. "What happened to your dog? Did he get hit by a car?"

Alexis and Nathan exchanged glances, neither knowing quite how to respond. Nathan started to answer but Alexis spoke over him. "He went out in the storm the other night and a tree branch fell and hit him." Nathan gave Alexis a startled look but remained quiet. "It was a really terrible storm and we were afraid that a tree might fall on our house too." Glancing at his watch, Nathan offered to go pick Lizzy up at the daycare. "I'll get Lizzy if you two think you can manage Jake."

Alexis answered with hesitation, "Yeah...that, that would be fine. David and I can take care of Jake. Be careful, I understand some roads are blocked due to fallen trees and high water.

"I'll be careful. The road to her daycare was passable this morning so it should be okay now."

"Yeah, of course, you are right. See you soon."

Nathan was thankful for the solitude as he drove to pick up Lizzy. His mind was full of questions that had no answers and his heart was weighed down with fear and doubt." *What is happening to my world? Has everything gone haywire? Did somebody reopen Pandora's box and let out more evil things?* On the way to the daycare Nathan finally saw the full extent of the damage caused by the storm. *That was one hell of a storm.*

Chapter Thirty-two

Rust never sleeps

-Neil Young

On the drive to his office Nathan halfway listened to the car stereo when he suddenly began to pay attention to the lyrics of the song being played by the local oldies station. It was Neal Young and Crazy Horse singing a song from the album *Rust Never Sleeps*. Nathan chuckled as he hummed along with the song *My, My, Hey, Hey*.

Out of the blue and into the black

You pay of this, but they give you that

And once you're gone, you can't come back

When you're out of the blue and into the black.

"Yeah, rust never sleeps and neither does evil. I definitely feel like I have been pushed out of the blue and into the black…I'm just a couple of steps from the real dark," Nathan said to no one in particular. "Am I so far gone that I can't come back?" Nathan pulled into his parking space at the university and prayed a silent prayer before exiting his car. *God, please help me. I feel like I am in the belly of the whale, and I can't get out by myself!* The Gray Building was semi-deserted since the first summer term had yet started. Nathan paused as he approached his office door in order to get his keys from his pocket. Just as he withdrew his key ring, he saw that his office door was ajar. Thinking that perhaps the clean-up crew had forgotten to close it, he pushed the door open and entered his office. A quick scan of the room showed some things were not as he had left them. His anti-hexing device which had been sitting on the desk by his phone had been smashed into a million pieces, and several files had been removed from his file cabinet and left on the floor. Nathan picked up the files and saw that one was from the spring semester, his class on Faith and Doubt. He examined the contents of the file and noticed that the list of students and their final grades was missing along with some of his notes about each student and their performance during the semester. Since no student had failed or done poorly in the class, Nathan could not think of any reason why someone would take the list of grades and observations about each student. Aside from the broken shells and missing notes nothing else seemed to be gone or damaged.

Nathan pulled up a chair at his desk and called the department office where he spoke to the dean's secretary. She reported that no one had mentioned any problems with their office, although she qualified her answer by noting that many faculty were probably still either out of town or just not coming in to their offices. Although he had no clear explanation for what had taken place in his office, it definitely looked like whomever had gotten into his office had a very narrow and specific mission.

What seemed most telling was the destruction of the anti-hexing device that Leonard Marshall had told him how to make. There was no way it could have been knocked off his desk by the cleanup crew. It was destroyed on purpose, and he could only think of one individual who might have wanted to destroy it...Lurleen Montgomery. If she was, in fact, a witch she might have wanted this little string of shells destroyed. Almost as if acting on cue, Nathan's phone rang. *I have a pretty good idea who that is.*

The sultry sound of Lurleen's voice was no surprise, but as soon as he heard her hello, Nathan felt a wave of excitement and arousal. Try as he might, he could not suppress the attraction he felt for her. "Miss Montgomery...what can I do for you?" He could feel his heart beating faster as he waited for her answer.

"I have been thinking about you all morning and I was wondering if you are okay. Did the storm cause any problems for you?"

"Well, as a matter of fact, it did. My dog Jake was injured."

"Oh, I'm sorry to hear that. Are you okay? I'd really like to see you again. It seems like an awfully long time since we were together. I am all alone today...please come by my apartment. I need you!"

Nathan felt himself being pulled by an incredibly powerful force which reminded him of when he was caught in an undertow at Galveston beach. He was in high school at the time and was a reasonably strong swimmer, but he was pulled away from the beach by a strong current, and he feared that he would certainly die. He never knew quite what happened or why, but for some reason he swam parallel to the shore and escaped the current. Once free of its pull, he was able to swim back to land. The pull he felt now seemed even stronger than the undertow and it might be even more deadly. "Okay," he said softly. "I'll be there soon." On the way to her apartment Nathan keep telling himself to stop and turn back, but he drove on. As he pulled into the parking area of her apartment, he saw her BMW and parked next to it. He almost ran to her apartment door. Before his knuckles could rap on her door, it opened and she greeted him with a smile. "Come in", she said, "I'll give you shelter from the storm." Lurleen pulled Nathan to her and he felt the heat of her embrace. Looking into her eyes, Nathan felt as though he had lost the ability to control his movements and even his thoughts. She led him to the sofa in the living area and gently pushed him down. "Make yourself comfortable while I pour us some wine."

Nathan watched her stroll into the kitchen and remove a bottle of wine from the refrigerator which she uncorked. Lurleen was wearing only a very short robe and he could see that she wore nothing under it as she stretched to reach the wine glasses on an upper shelf in one of the kitchen cabinets. Without a word, she walked slowly back to Nathan and handed him a large glass of wine, and as she did, the robe she had been wearing fell to the floor. In a vampire-like fashion, Lurleen descended on Nathan. As he succumbed to her embrace his last thoughts were "And once you're gone, you can't come back. Nathan awoke to the bright morning sun in a disoriented state. He looked around the room, but it was not his bedroom. He turned back the sheet and sat on the edge of the bed trying to figure out where he was and what he was doing there. In the midst of his confusion, a gorgeous woman strolled into the room. She was the most beautiful woman he had ever seen, and she stood before him completely nude. "Lurleen…is that you?"

"Who else would it be my love? Did you enjoy our evening together?"

"What, what time is it? Are we still at your place"?

"It's 10 am, and yes this is my apartment. You spent last night here."

"Oh, my God! I spent the night here?"

"You did, and I turned off your cell phone so we wouldn't be interrupted."

"Oh, I've got to go. My wife will be frantic."

Lurleen pushed Nathan back into the bed and straddled him. "No," she commanded. "I want some more of you."

Nathan's mind seemed to go blank as he felt the warmth of her body on top of him. All he could focus on was the pleasure he felt as she kissed him and then she pinned his arms down. She felt incredibly strong and resistance seemed futile. Nathan felt as if he was sinking, down, down, down as he heard her tell him that he was now her prisoner.

It was late afternoon when Nathan struggled to arouse himself from his slumber. He tried to get out of bed but felt so groggy and unsteady that he sat back down on the edge of the bed. Slowly his vision cleared and he looked around the room. He saw his clothes on the back of a chair. His cell phone was on the dressing table. The bedroom door was partially closed so he couldn't tell if Lurleen was still in the apartment. Slowly and cautiously, he got up from the bed and staggered across the room. As he emerged from the bedroom, he saw Lurleen in the kitchen. He attempted to call to her for help but his voice came out as a garbled croak, "Help…help me please."

"Well, my love. It's good to see you. Here, drink this." Lurleen handed Nathan a goblet which he took but almost dropped. "Let me help you." She took the goblet and raised it to Nathan's lips. "Drink this."

Nathan took a few sips and tried to push the drink away. "It's wine. I've had enough."

"Drink it!" she commanded in a more forceful tone. Nathan emptied the goblet and then she guided him to the sofa in the living area. "You aren't leaving until I tell you to. I am not finished with you, professor. You are now my little slave." Lurleen removed her robe and sat beside Nathan on the sofa. With merely a thought, Lurleen rekindled Nathan's desire for her.

The late afternoon sun slipped behind a wall of dark cumulus clouds as Alexis put her cell phone down on the kitchen table. She had called every number at the university she could think of in a vain effort to locate her husband. Feeling a mixture of fear and anger she whispered softly, "Nathan, where are you?"

Lizzy, sensing her mother's distress watched closely from her spot on the floor where she had been playing quietly with Jake "Mommy, are you okay? Where is daddy?"

"I don't know sweetie, but don't worry. I will find him." Alexis wished she believed her words to her daughter. She picked up the area phone book and searched for the police department number. She punched in the first numbers into her phone when she heard the sounds of a car pulling into the driveway. She dropped the phone and ran to the door. Her heart skipped a beat as she saw Nathan's car come to a halt and the driver's door open. Suppressing her desire to run to meet him, Alexis simply stood in the doorway and watched as Nathan slowly exited from the car and began walking towards her. He looked to her as though he was a man staggering home from an overnight drunk. His clothes were rumpled and wine stained. As he got closer, she could see that his eyes were bleary and his hair had a wind-blown look.

"Nathan, where the hell have you been? I have been worried sick! I was about to call the police and report you as missing."

Nathan stopped and looked at her but did not respond immediately. His eyes seemed to have a blank, unfocused look. After what seemed like an eternity, he spoke but his words were slurred and difficult to understand. "Lexi, I don't really know where I have been...I can't seem to remember."

"You look like you are drunk." Stepping closer she could see wine stains on his shirt and smell the unmistakable sour smell of wine on his breath. Alexis felt her anger grow as she studied the appearance of the man she had always admired and loved. This was not that man. "I think you need to get cleaned up and then we need to talk." She turned to go back into the house and saw that both Lizzy and David had come to the door. Lizzy had tears in her eyes and David looked frightened as if seeing a drunk stagger home had triggered some terrifying memories. The first rain drops began to fall as Alexis ushered Lizzy and David back into the house. Nathan simply stood frozen in his tracks until Jake walked up to him and gently licked his hand.

## Chapter Thirty-three

*Ah, the trust and self-assurance that lead to happiness,*

*they're the very things we kill, I guess*

-Don Henley

A shower and clean clothes did little to help Nathan Richards assemble shattered pieces of his memory for his recent past. All he could remember for certain was going to his office, but the rest was just a jumble, a disorganized collage of sensory input. The only common denominator, if there was one, was the image of his student, Lurleen Montgomery. His inability to give a coherent explanation or time line for his actions during the past 36 hours only served to intensify Alexis' anger and suspicion. Finally, the levee holding back her surging emotions crumbled and she pointed to the door, ordering Nathan to get out. Lacking the ability to think clearly, Nathan trudged to his car and drove to his office on campus. He was relieved that no one was there to see him enter his office where he collapsed into a chair and drifted off to a troubled sleep. It was close to midnight when Nathan was able to regain full consciousness. His improved mental clarity only served to drive home the awful reality of his situation. *Dear God, what have I done?* Outside his office window the night closed in, a rising tide of darkness that threatened to overwhelm and drown him. Nathan contemplated driving to a motel where he might get some badly needed rest, but then he realized that he did not bring his wallet or even his cell phone. *I am really up a creek.* He used his office phone to call Alexis but his call went straight to her voice mail. Every avenue he considered seemed to lead nowhere. He even considered calling Lurleen. Acting impulsively, he left his office and went to his car. Like a wounded homing pigeon, he drove home. When he reached the driveway of his house, he got out and lowered the back seats of his old CRV and climbed in where he promptly fell fast asleep.

The first faint rays of sunlight were just beginning to creep into her bedroom window when Alexis was awakened by her daughter Elizabeth. "Mommy, I had a bad dream. Can I get in bed with you?"

"Sure baby", Alexis said sleepily as she turned back the covers for her daughter. "Come on in." After a few minutes Lizzy was fast asleep so Alexis decided to get up and start breakfast. While she listened to her coffeemaker gurgle and snort, she thought about David. *What a mess we have brought him into. Poor kid.* After pouring herself a cup of coffee, she walked quietly to David's bedroom door where she waited for any sound that might indicate that he was awake. Hearing none, she returned to the kitchen where Jake met her. "Good morning, Jake. Is it just my imagination or are you worried too?" Jake wagged his tail a time or two and then trotted to the door where he stood and whimpered softly. "Do you need to go potty?" Alexis asked as she walked to the door to let Jake out. As soon as she did, he bolted out and ran to the car parked in the drive way. It was Nathan's car. Jake circled the car excitedly and barked loudly. Alexis wasn't sure if the sight of Nathan's car prompted her to feel relieved or angry. She walked to the car and peered in through the window. Nathan was beginning to stir, apparently awakened by Jake's barking. She waited for him to emerge. He had to exit through the back door on the driver's side since there was no way to open the back hatch from the inside.

Before he could summon his response, Alexis greeted him harshly, "I thought I told you to leave!"

Looking like a whipped dog, Nathan responded meekly. "Could we just talk? I left last night without my wallet…"

"Get your wallet and then you should go!"

"Lexi, please…I know how this must look, and I would explain if I could…"

"Okay, I'll cut you that much slack. Let's go inside. Then you can tell me what you mean by saying you'd explain if you could. I want to hear this."

Once inside Alexis began her interrogation of Nathan which promptly brought both David and Lizzy out into the living area. Alexis forced a smile and then guided the two of them into the kitchen. "There are some cinnamon rolls on the counter and milk in the fridge. I need to talk to daddy, uh...Nathan for a few minutes."

"Lexi, I don't think we should hold this discussion with the kids in the kitchen. Could we go outside, maybe take a walk?" Alexis agreed and they both went outside. They walked down the long drive way to the road where they continued to walk and talk. Since Nathan could provide no semblance of an explanation or accounting of his behavior, Alexis was forced to rely on the one thing he did convey, a sense of honesty about his memory gap. He did not seem to her to be lying or covering up something. He really did not appear to know what he had been doing or even where he had been. The only explanation she could come up with was that he was so intoxicated that he had blacked out, and even that he didn't really deny. He just couldn't remember.

Nathan, you know that when a person drinks a lot…too much…they have blackouts. They may continue to function but they can't recall what they were doing."

"Yeah, I know that, but I have never had so much to drink that I passed out or had blackouts. Have you ever known me to do that?"

"No. I have to admit you have never abused alcohol except maybe a time or two when we were in college." Alexis looked deeply into her husband's eyes before she spoke again. Nathan, what is wrong? What is happening to you? You once accused me of being unfaithful, now I can't help but think you are the one being unfaithful."

"I know you never did anything wrong, and I have to admit that one of my students seems to have had some kind of influence over me…kinda like the way Murdoc did after my interview with him."

"Are you attracted to her…that girl with the odd first name? Have you had sex with her?" As she asked, her eyes seemed to bore deeply into her husband's soul.

"Lexi, I have to admit that I've found her strangely attractive, but…I…"

Don't answer! I'm not sure I really want to know right now. I think you need to see a doctor for a thorough evaluation. After that… we are going to need counseling."

"I think you are right. I don't know for sure what is wrong with me, but I do know that I have done a great deal of damage to our relationship and I have caused you a lot of pain."

"Let's go back to the house. We've got to give Lizzy and David some sort of explanation."

The following week Nathan went to the university hospital for a complete medical and neurological evaluation, all of which revealed no underlying pathology. Since the medical evaluation revealed no problem, a psychological evaluation was recommended. Nathan was somewhat embarrassed by the recommendation but reluctantly agreed. The psychologist who conducted the evaluation was not someone Nathan knew which was somewhat of a relief. When that assessment was complete, the psychologist explained that he could not rule out alcohol intoxication as the underlying cause. Neither could he rule out Dissociative Amnesia as a possible explanation. Because of his background and experience Nathan could not fault the diagnoses, but he also knew that they really didn't explain fully his recent behavior. A witch's hex was not a condition listed in the DSM-5. Alexis did reluctantly allow Nathan to move back into the house but their relationship remained cool and distant. Alexis resumed her work, dropping Lizzy off each morning at her daycare. Since Nathan was not teaching during the summer term, he tried to find things to do with David. They went fishing, shot basketball and played video games. Gradually their relationship became somewhat closer, although David maintained a certain emotional distance as if fearing yet another rejection. Nathan made occasional visits to his office but he made scant progress with his research work until one day in mid-August when he received a call from the warden at Central Prison. Dr. Jeremiah Murdoc had requested another interview, which Nathan agreed to only with considerable hesitation.

Chapter Thirty-four

Life is like a mirror. It reflects

back whatever image we present to it.

-Robert Anthony

Although David Charles enjoyed some of the activities he shared with Nathan, he always held back, never allowing himself to get fully invested in the relationship. However, for reasons neither Nathan nor Alexis fully understood, David permitted himself to get a tiny bit closer to Alexis. While it may be true that good paperwork makes for good people work, charts and case files can never tell the whole story of a person, and this was especially true in David's case. His lengthy file at Social Services only contained the superficial high points, never the deep dark valleys of his life where the important details were hidden. Case workers always relied heavily on the adults to provide the details, so it was the foster parents that explained why he was being returned. David was born in rural North Carolina. His father raised tobacco, and his mother held a few jobs as a waitress and cleaning woman for homes and small businesses. His mother and father were both alcoholics who fought frequently. Neither parent finished high school nor attended church with any regularity, and they were suspicious of the government and its representatives. From the time he could walk, David was pretty much left to his own devices. Neighbors would often worry about him as he wandered the streets, dirty and hungry. Some would try to feed him and a few even took him home to his parents. When David was four his mother and father separated. The father promised he would come back for David but he never did. Because of her alcohol dependence and neglect of David, he was taken from his mother and placed in the state's social service system. David learned at an early age that he couldn't trust people, and therefore he began to act as if all people were untrustworthy. His suspicion and aloofness quickly alienated adults who tried be become his foster parents. As he got older his aloofness turned more and more into anger and aggression. He would act out his aggression on animals or sometimes by destroying property. Nathan and especially Alexis tried to show kindness and compassion towards David, but he was keenly aware of the tension in their relationship and naturally assumed that their kindness towards him was nothing but an act, one that would soon be gone. Many was the night he thought of running away, and it was only the remoteness of the Richards' home that prevented him from leaving. It seemed like too far to walk to any place he'd want to go. So, he resolved to stay until a viable opportunity presented itself, and then he'd hit the road. One relationship did flourish, however, and that was David's relationship with Jake. He and Jake became good friends since David took him on many walks and explorations of the woods near the Richards' home. Alexis was keenly aware of how much David cared for Jake, and she thought that was a good step in the right direction.

On a warm summer evening when Nathan was not home and Lizzy was playing quietly in her room, Alexis decided it was a good time to try to talk to David about his feelings toward the family and his place in it. Switching off the tv, Alexis turned to David and smiled warmly. "David, I am wondering if we could we talk?"

Somewhat surprised, David replied, "Uh, yeah…I guess so. What do you want to talk about?"

Well, um, I'd just like to talk about how you feel about being here…being in our family?"

Sensing the possibility of the rejection he fully expected, David responded with great caution. "I like it fine. Have I done something? Is Mr. Nathan unhappy with me?"

"No, no. Nothing like that, David. I…we just want to know how things are going? Are you happy? Is there anything we can do that would make you feel more a part of things?"

"Uh, no…Mrs. Richards. Everything is good." David looked worried until Jake wandered up and put his head on David's knee. Smiling, David volunteered, "I especially like Jake. I never had a dog before. He's my very good friend!"

Alexis smiled in return. "David, you are right. Jake really likes you. He loves the walks you guys take and he can't get enough playing ball. I just hope that maybe someday I can become your friend too."

David made no immediate response to her overture of friendship but instead averted his gaze. After several seconds, he responded with a question that caught Alexis off guard, "Are you and Mr. Nathan going to get a divorce? Is he going away permanently?"

"Gosh, David, why would you ask such a question? No…he's not going to leave. Yes, we are having some problems in our marriage, but all married people do…and our problems have nothing to do with you."

David nodded but made no additional comments, but Alexis wondered if he really believed her. As she got up to check on Lizzy, she thought to herself that what she had told David must be what all parents told their children before the actual breakup occurred. *Maybe we'll be an exception.*

His conversation with Alexis over, David asked if he could take Jake for short walk. Alexis gave a cautious "Okay, but it's dark so don't go far. Take the big flashlight with you and put him on his leash."

"Okay, Mrs. Richards. We won't be gone long." Jake was eager to go for a walk most any time so he almost pulled David's arm out of its socket getting out the door when he heard the word "walk". Once out into the somewhat cooler evening air, David thought briefly of running away with Jake but quickly decided against it. "Jake, I don't think you'd go with me…this really is your home."

## Chapter Thirty-five

Will you walk into my parlour?

Said the spider to the fly"

-Mary Howitt

The morning of his scheduled meeting with Dr. Jeremiah Murdoc at Central Prison found Nathan Richards alone in his office, staring aimlessly out the window. The sky was clear and there was a crispness in the air that hinted of fall, but the beauty of the day did little to calm the growing feeling of dread he was feeling. He glanced at his watch and knew it was time to start his drive to the prison, but his unconscious mind seemed to be warning him against the trip. It was as if part of his mind was shouting "don't go" while another part kept telling him that he must go or his research would suffer. Uttering a barely audible prayer, he rose from his desk and headed for his car. Nathan pulled into the prison parking lot, hoping against hope that he would find the prison on lock down, but such was not the case. He entered the main administration building and walked to the warden's office where he greeted the warden's secretary and was then escorted to the interview room. On this visit, Dr. Murdoc was already in the room waiting for him. The guard left the room immediately and closed the door, leaving Nathan alone with the infamous serial killer

Nathan seated himself and looked across the table at Murdoc. He noted that as usual Murdoc was handcuffed to the metal table, but that fact provided no comfort or assurance. The good doctor looked long and hard at Nathan and then greeted him with a chilling smile. "Good morning, professor Richards. It has been a while since we last talked. Have you been avoiding me? There is so much for us to discuss."

"Hello, Dr. Murdoc. I have been very busy. That's why I haven't been able to meet with you any sooner. "Murdoc smiled a knowing smile, "I know you've been busy. How are things with you and the Mrs.? I hope all is well. You have a new addition to your family, don't you?"

Things are fine at home, but how did you know about David?"

Oh, I have my sources. Is your dog better? That was quite a bad storm we had since our last meeting."

"My dog is fine too. Dr. Murdoc, in your message to me you indicated that you had some information that might help me with my research. If you don't mind, I'd like to get to it." In spite of his best effort to be assertive and take charge of the interview, Nathan felt control slipping away.

"Certainly, Professor Richards. Let's get down to business." Murdoc made eye contact with Nathan before continuing. As usual his penetrating gaze unsettled Richards. "Have you been following my advice from our last visit? Been having a little fun? That student of yours...what a lovely thing. She seems to have you under her spell, does she not?"

"No, no she doesn't, and I don't know what advice you are speaking of, Murdoc."

Dr. Murdoc did not answer but pressed on with his agenda. "Dr. Richards, do you believe in witches? Oh, I supposed not, you being both a scientist and a man of faith." It's like resisting the devil...you can't do it if you don't even admit to his existence. I have it on good authority that witches do, in fact, exist."

"Why are you telling me this, Murdoc?"

"Well, I thought you wanted to learn all you could about evil, and witches...well most people see them as evil. Just think about all the poor souls that people like you, good Christians, burned at the stake or

drowned in the river. You know, I'm not nearly as evil as you think. Just like you I only want to carry out God's will for my life. That student of yours, Miss Montgomery...she is not only very beautiful, but she also possesses some special powers. However, she is just beginning to learn how to use her abilities. I might have given her a few pointers just as I have been trying to educate you, Dr. Richards. I hope you can see that."

Nathan felt himself being caught up in the web of Murdoc's words. The more he struggled to resist his influence, the more entangled in Murdoc's words he became, just like the unfortunate fly who had blundered into the spider's parlor. "Murdoc, I think it is time for me to go."

"No, it's not, Dr. Richards. Listen to me carefully…that dragon you saw during the storm was not your imagination or a hallucination. Miss Montgomery is actually a witch and you…you are powerless to resist her. She owns your very soul, and since I own her…well, I imagine you get it. If you think that God of yours will save you, you are sadly mistaken. He has abandoned you just like he did his own son. I am sure you recall that time in Lubbock when you thought you defeated evil. Let me assure you that you did not; you only tipped the scales for a brief moment. I will restore the proper balance to things. You may not remember all that I have revealed to you today, but you will be deeply troubled by the knowledge I have buried in your mind. Now, you may leave!"

Without uttering a word, two prison guards entered the room from separate doors. One escorted Nathan out while the other did the same with Murdoc. As if in a trance Nathan walked with the guard back to the sign out book where he wrote his name and then existed the building. The bright sunlight was a considerable contrast to the dimly lit prison and Nathan was temporarily blinded by its brilliance. He squinted as he walked to his car, feeling an overwhelming sense of despair and hopelessness.

Not knowing where to go for solace, Nathan drove back to the campus where he parked bis car and walked to the chapel. He entered through its main doors and into the sanctuary. As far as he could tell there was no one else in the building. It was cool and somewhat dark with the only light coming through the large stained-glass windows which lined each side of the sanctuary. Nathan slipped into one of the back pews and began to pray. "Dear God, I am truly lost. Help me! I am trapped and powerless to free myself. I feel like Jonah in the belly of the whale Don't abandon me, Lord. Show me your light. Lead me from this darkness." For the first time in what seemed like a very long time, he felt a sense of inner peace come over him. Taking a deep breath, he started for home, but home was a lot further away than he realized. Nathan's mind wandered as he drove. Was Lurleen Montgomery really a witch who had the power to control him? What did Murdoc mean about restoring the balance to things? Is Murdoc more than a serial killer? Could he have been the demonic presence he had encountered in Lubbock? Thoughts such as these made Nathan wonder if he was losing his grip on reality. He had to admit that Lurleen had a strong hold on him emotionally, but being a witch? Nathan knew that his marriage had been seriously damaged by his actions and he wondered if it could ever be repaired. Thinking back on his experiences in Lubbock and then more recently here in North Carolina, he realized that there were only two viable explanations for these events: either the devil was real and out to destroy him or else his thinking had taken a distinct turn towards paranoia. Just like the line from the old Billy Joel song said, "You may be right, I may be crazy." Instead of continuing home, Nathan changed course and turned onto on Interstate 40 heading west. Nathan drove on as if compelled by some innate instinct, responding to the traffic but little else

until he saw the road sign informing him that he would soon be passing through Ashville. At that point, awareness of his situation and recent actions came crashing into focus. *What am I doing? Where the hell am I going?* In spite of the jolt provided by his sudden awareness that he had driven miles from home, he pressed on. Stopping only for gas, Nathan continued on through Memphis and on towards Dallas. After traveling through Dallas on his relentless journey west Nathan finally realized that he was heading for Lubbock, but why? What unconscious impulse or instinct had motivated him? Was it God or his own unstable mind? When he reached Abilene, he pulled into a gas station and convenience store where he bought a snack and a cold drink. It had been almost twenty hours since he started this unplanned trip, and he felt his body's protest. As he sipped his Diet Coke and munched on salty peanuts, he realized he had to call home and let Lexi know where he was even if he couldn't really explain why he was there. As he looked at his phone, he saw that she had made several attempts to call him but the phone's ringer was turned off. When Alexis answered the phone, he knew instantly that she was extremely upset with him. He tried to make his actions seem reasonable by telling her that he was going to Lubbock to meet with Leonard Marshall. Although that made some sense to her it did not reduce her distress as she argued convincingly that he should have told her of his plan. After he hung up from talking to Alexis, he called Dr. Marshall to say he was coming to see him. Although surprised his friend said he was indeed welcome. Resuming his drive, Nathan couldn't help but feel that perhaps God had directed him to make this trip. Maybe his friend could save him once again.

Chapter Thirty-six

The old that is strong does not wither,

Deep roots are not reached by the frost.

-J. R, R. Tolkien

When Nathan Richards finally arrived at Leonard Marshall's home in Lubbock, he was near total exhaustion, so near that he was beginning to hallucinate. He saw, or thought he saw, a red dragon hovering in the air above the city as he got on Loop 289 which circles the city. His friend, Leonard met him on the driveway where the two men embraced. "Can I help you with your luggage, Nathan?" Leonard asked.

"Uh, I didn't actually bring any," came Nathan's feeble response.

"Traveling light, huh?" Leonard ushered his exhausted guest into the house and offered him something to drink and eat.

Thanks, Leonard, but I am so tired I can't even think straight. Would it be okay if I just crashed and got some sleep?"

"Sure. Come on and I'll show you your bed. You can wear some of my pj's if you like. I think they will almost fit."

Nathan was asleep almost as soon as his head touched the pillow. While he slept, Leonard made a quick trip to Wal Mart and bought Nathan a change of clothes and a tooth brush. It was almost noon the next day when Nathan awoke. After a hearty breakfast and three cups of coffee he was able to think clearly again. He then spent the better part of the next two hours trying to fill Dr. Marshall in on all that had happened since they last spoken, but he zeroed in on the events of the past couple of weeks. Leonard had several questions about the time period when Nathan had apparently gone to Lurleen's apartment and stayed overnight. Unfortunately, Nathan could give few details because he simply couldn't remember. "Leonard, it's just like I tried to tell Alexis…I honestly don't remember. It's like I blacked out. Apparently, I drank some wine but I can't imagine I drank enough to blackout." Nathan revealed as much as he could remember, even telling him things he had not shared with his wife, namely that he had sex with her on at least one occasion.

"Wow. You have had a rough time, my friend. What can you tell me about your last visit with what's his name…Murdoc, Jeremiah Murdoc?" Nathan was able to remember scattered fragments from that meeting so he relayed what information he could to Leonard. Dr. Marshall's countenance revealed deep concentration and concern as he continued asking questions about Lurleen Montgomery and Jeremiah Murdoc. At long last, Marshall offered Nathan some of his impressions.

"Nathan, there is a lot neither of us completely understand about your situation, butI don't think you are insane, and I'd be surprised if alcohol intake explains your memory loss and inability to account for those lost hours. I also think we should take seriously what Murdoc told you…namely that Miss Montgomery may really be a witch. As to your encounter with a red dragon…well, after your experience at Hell's Gate…anything is possible. Murdoc may well be more than just a notorious serial killer."

"Leonard, I just can't seem to put the pieces together. I thought at first that Murdoc might have hypnotized me, but I am increasingly inclined to think there's more to his powers of influence than hypnosis. He knew too much about what was going on in my life for someone locked up in a maximum-security prison. As to Lurleen Montgomery…she is incredibly seductive, but I have a hard time seeing her as a witch."

"Maybe your witch concept is too narrow. Perhaps witchesaren't always ugly and ride broomsticks. Do you remember the tales of brave Odysseus in the *Odyssey?* More specifically, do you remember the part about Circe?"

"Yeah, vaguely. I read it a long time ago. Wasn't she a witch who seduced Odysseus and kept him and his crew on her island for a good while?"

You are right. Circe had the power to change humans into swine, and she kept Odysseus on her island for at least a year. She used not only her magic but also her knowledge of herbs and potions. Even though Odysseus was married and eager to return to his wife in Ithaca, he was seduced into having sex with Circe and their union produced at least two sons. Over the years Circe came to be seen as a veritable archetype of the predatory female. The story of Circe and her dealings with Odysseus have been told and retold by many writers besides Homer, possibly because the story is truly archetypal. Also, consider how many cultures and writers have stories and myths about witches, and many believe that witches ultimately derive their power from Satan. We see references to witches in everything from the Bible to Shakespeare to modern children's' stories. It makes you wonder, doesn't it? Even today, books about witches are found on the bestseller list and they stay there for weeks and weeks. Again, why? Maybe it is because there is a kernel of truth contained in these myths. Is that really so hard to believe?"

"When you put it that way, no, it isn't so hard to believe, but…what about the red dragon and the devil? "When you and I talked on the phone we touched on that subject. Dragons are mentioned in the Bible particularly in reference to Satan. The red dragon specifically has long been associated with evil and Satan. For instance, the legend of St. George slaying the dragon goes back to very ancient, pre-Christian origins. So, the use of dragons as symbols of evil goes back a long way, but even today, think about how popular dragons are in movies and books like *Lord of the Rings* or *How to Train Your Dragon*. There has to be a reason for the popularity and durability of creatures like witches and dragons."

"Okay, Leonard. You win. I see your point, but what should I do about it?"

"First, let me ask you another question. That device to ward off a witch's spell that I told you about…did you make one…and more importantly, did you see any evidence that it worked?"

"Well, actually I did make it, and yes, I did find some indirect evidence that it worked because someone got into my office and smashed it, and I don't think the janitorial staff did it either." If it didn't do something why would someone bother to get into my office and destroy it?

"Nathan, enough talk for now. Let's go into town and buy you a few more clothes and then we'll make plans for my coming back to North Carolina with you. Maybe, just maybe I can be of some assistance to you. And don't even think of saying no because I'd love the challenge and besides what are friends for unless it is to offer help in times like these?"

Their preparations completed, Nathan and Leonard began the long journey to Durham. Leonard planned to stay in a hotel near the campus, but Nathan wasn't sure where he'd stay since he didn't know if Alexis would welcome him home. "I may be staying at a hotel too," he half-jokingly commented. "I guess I'd better call Lexi and see what her thoughts are."

The two men discussed a variety of topics as they traveled, but the one that garnered the most attention was Jeremiah Murdoc. "Leonard, I just can't decide who or what Jeremiah Murdoc is. Is he just a man or something more? Is he a demon or Satan himself?"

"Nathan, I think he may actually be the proof of your theory that when a man devotes himself to a life of pure evil, he may evolve or devolve into something demonic, something more than human. As you explained in your theory, it is the reverse of what happens as a sinner evolves into a saint. Didn't John Wesley talk about sanctifying grace is a process of moving a person towards perfection?"

"You are correct. Wesley took seriously Jesus's call to be perfect as God is perfect. So, are you suggesting that Murdoc is still basically a man who has developed some extra human powers?"

Leonard scratched his head and looked out the car window before replying. "I think that is exactly what I am suggesting. If I remember what you told me about the dragon that appeared during the storm, you said your dog may have inflicted a wound to the dragon's leg and then the dragon seemed to dissolve. Am I correct?"

That is correct and if I could find out whether there was any period of time that Murdoc was unaccounted for during that night…or if he received any sort of wound on bis arm or leg…well, that would be pretty interesting, don't you think?"

Leonard smiled as he replied, "I think you are on to something, but it may be difficult to get such information from the prison. If Murdoc was treated for any sort of injury that would probably be confidential. Is there anyone at the university who might help you get such information if it exists?"

"Maybe…I'll have to think about it," Nathan replied, but in truth, he was doubtful. Prisons are not typically open systems, and wardens can exercise total of what happens within the system.

"Well, give that some thought, but in the meantime, we need to focus on finding a way to protect you from any more hexes." When we get to Durham, I've got my laptop and I'll rent a car so I can do some research in the area. I've got some ideas I want to check out. I think I told you that Durham and North Carolina have a very high concentration of witches or at least people who believe themselves to be witches."

"Leonard, I've got to admit this all begins to sound pretty crazy like a low budget horror movie. Should I wear a silver cross and buy some garlic and wolfbane too?"

Who knows, might be a good idea," Leonard said with a chuckle.

## Chapter Thirty-seven

When the student is ready, the teacher will appear

-Buddha

Two weeks after Lurleen was visited by the mysterious, shadowy personage, she just happened to glance at the glass dragon the visitor had given her. The dragon had been sitting on the window sill in her kitchen ever since his visit, but today it was resting on her kitchen table and seemed to be emitting a pulsating red light. Curious about how it got from the window sill to the kitchen table and why it was emitting light, Lurleen stopped and picked it up. She almost dropped it because it felt icy cold to the touch. She quickly returned the glass dragon to the table, and as she did, she felt an uneasy feeling as if she was being watched.

From the shadows of the apartment's living room a voice called out to her, "Miss Montgomery, are you ready to continue your education? I have come for your final lesson."

"Yes, I suppose I am ready."

"Good. First there are some fundamental truths you need to know and understand." The shadowy figure stepped into the light before continuing, "When this world was created, its creator, whom some would call God, laid down two paths which exist side by side. Each path has many names, but it is ultimately up to the traveler to choose the path he or she will follow. While some might call one path evil, others might refer to it as good. In your theology school, Satan or Lucifer is referred to as the ultimate evil, but is that really an accurate label? Even the name Lucifer comes from a word referring to Venus, the evening star. Lucifer was the light bringer, and what was the light he brought? What is important for you to know is that he brought knowledge, knowledge that in the path many would call darkness, there is power. It is a power that I have learned to harness and you may learn to control as well. Are you listening?"

"Yes, I am listening. Go on."

"Along with the two paths there are powerful forces that govern this world. Gravity would be a simple example. Many of these forces are not understood by the unenlightened, but they exist. These forces, if understood, can be utilized but they cannot be ignored or resisted without serious, inescapable consequences. To do so would be like stepping onto the tracks in front of an onrushing train; the consequences would be devastating while riding within the train would be very useful. The forces of which I speak can be utilized and even redirected but not resisted. Just as

I have learned to do, you may be able to avail yourself of this power through the knowledge brought to us by Lucifer himself."

Looking somewhat bewildered, Lurleen responded, "I hear what you are saying, but I am not sure I fully understand. Can you make what you are saying more specific or give me an example?"

"I will make what I am saying clear to you soon enough, but for now, let me give you an example. In boxing, two individuals pit power against power, force against a counter force until the stronger force dominates the weaker force. In martial arts, force is not met by counter force. An opponent's thrust is not resisted; it is accepted and redirected against the opponent."

"Okay. I follow that example. I guess you are saying that what I need to learn is the martial arts approach. I am eager to learn, but before we go any further, I want to know who you are. I know you aren't normal human being."

"Miss Montgomery, even knowing someone's name gives you a certain power over them. I know your name and that fact alone gives me some power or advantage over you which you do not have because you do not know my name. Perhaps, in time, you will discern my name but for now, I will remain nameless." Unaware of her teacher's name, the lesson continued although in the eyes of a naive observer it would seem as if it was just a case of one individual talking and the other quietly listening. After about an hour, the teacher called a halt to the lesson but assured his student that she had now learned everything she needed to know. He reminded her of their bargain and her commitment, and then he faded from view.

Back in the solitary confinement section of Central Prison, correctional officer Jason Hardwick was making his afternoon rounds when he looked into to Jeremiah Murdoc's cell and saw the prisoner sitting motionless on his bed as if in a trance. He called Murdoc's name several times without getting a response, so, he opened the cell door and stepped into the room.

He shook Murdoc by the shoulder several times and finally Murdoc opened his eyes and looked up at Hardwick and smiled, "Hello, officer. Is something wrong?"

Hardwick responded matter of factly, "I guess not. You looked like maybe you were in a trance or having some kind of seizure."

Not at all, officer. I was just letting my mind wander. It is the only freedom I have, you know."

Chapter Thirty-eight

When you have eliminated the impossible,

whatever remains, however improbable, must be the truth.

-Arthur Conan Doyle

Nathan Richards exhausted all the possibilities he could think of and was still unable to secure a copy of Jeremiah Murdoc's medical records. He had theorized that if medical records from the night of the storm showed that Murdoc had been treated for a wound to his forearm, it would be proof that somehow Murdoc was able to assume an alternate shape and then transport this altered version of himself to another physical location. Nathan knew that holographic images of a person could look quite real and be transmitted to distant sites, but the dragon he encountered was no mere hologram. It had mass, genuine physical substance. The evidence he sought seemed crucial to understanding at least one aspect of the mystery that was Jeremiah Murdoc. As he sat in his office an idea took shape in his mind. Perhaps he could convince Warden Henderson to allow him to interview Murdoc's guards, and he might be able to tease from one of them the information that he needed without having to see Murdoc's confidential medical records. The fates must have smiled on Nathan as he was able to reach Warden Henderson on his first phone call. His sales pitch to the prison warden was that interviewing Murdoc's guards would give him a valuable perspective on Murdoc and thus help him in his quest to understand evil individuals and their thoughts and behavior. Henderson had several questions but eventually agreed. He then transferred Nathan's phone call to his secretary who was instructed to check the duty roster to determine which guard or guards were on duty in Murdoc's cell block on the night of the big storm. After several minutes Nathan got the name of two prison guards, Jason Hardwick and Brent Strom. Nathan then asked the warden's secretary if she could set up a time he could contact the two men either by phone or in person. The warden's secretary sounded a bit annoyed by Nathan's request but agreed and said she would call him back once she had arranged for the contacts. While Nathan Richards labored to set up an interview with Murdoc's prison guards, Leonard Marshall had been doing a search for witch's covens in and around Durham. To his surprise he was able to find several on the internet. One was located on the outskirts of Durham. Its' webpage advertised that it offered workshops on how to perform spells. Marshall was intrigued by one line in the advertisement which stated that "Spells are like knives; they can be used to do good things in the hands of a surgeon or bad things like stabbing someone." The advertisement assured readers that their workshops only taught people how to perform good spells. Dr. Marshall jotted down the coven's web address and phone number as well as the date of the next workshop.

Back at the hotel Nathan and Leonard compared notes and discussed their findings. Both men expressed surprised that witches used the internet just like every other organization or business, and they agreed that attending a workshop could prove to be useful. While they were talking Nathan got a call from the warden's secretary who told him that officer Hardwick would be available for a phone interview when his shift ended in a little over an hour. Nathan could hardly wait to call officer Hardwick. Marshall retired to his room planning to register for the workshop on spell casting while Nathan waited in his hotel room for the appointed time for his call to officer Hardwick.

When four pm arrived, Nathan called the phone number he had been given for officer Hardwick. Hardwick answered on the second ring; his voice sounded wary to Nathan. "Officer Hardwick, this is Dr. Richards. Thank you for agreeing to talk to me. I assume that the warden explained the reason for my call, did he not?"

Yes, sir, he did. What do you want to know?"

"Well, there are many things I would like to ask you about Jeremiah Murdoc, but I don't want to take up too much of your time. I have met in person with Dr. Murdoc on more than one occasion and I have found him to be very interesting, even a bit intimidating. Do you know what I mean?"

"Yeah, I think so. He can definitely get under your skin if you let him. He can also be very persuasive, even scary at times. There is just something about him…I don't know what it is."

"Officer Hardwick, I understand you were on duty the night of the big storm. Is that correct?"

Yes, sir. I was on duty in the administrative segregation area…uh, what you'd probably call solitary confinement."

"Did you look in at any time on Dr. Murdoc or have any contact with him that night?"

I did for sure. I was doing a routine check of each cell in the unit when I looked in on Murdoc. When I did, I found him in his cell in kind of a trance. His forearm was bleeding pretty bad so I called another officer and we escorted him to the infirmary. The doctor was called in and he stitched up Murdoc's arm. According to the doc, Murdoc's wound looked like it was caused by a bite, like a dog's bite maybe. Murdoc apparently told the doctor that he fell and hit his arm on the edge of the little desk in his cell, but I don't think the doctor bought his explanation

"I just have one other question for now. Have you ever known Murdoc to be missing from the prison?"

"Only for specific things like a court appearance, but if you mean like an escape, the answer would be no. Our security measures are very tight. To the best of my knowledge no one has ever escaped from the prison."

Nathan knew that in the past at least two men had escaped from the prison but he made no such retort. Is there anything else about Murdoc that has struck you as odd or unusual?"

"Well, I am not sure what you mean, but the only thing I would say to that is there have been several times I have found him to be sorta unresponsive…like he was in a trance, just out of it. I don't think he has ever been diagnosed with any sort of seizure disorder though." Hardwick paused for a moment as if thinking and then added, "I will say he seems to get a lot of privileges that other men on the unit don't get"

What sort of privileges, officer?"

"Oh, uh, like having a laptop computer. In the prison, computer access is tightly controlled for obvious reasons, but Murdoc has one in his cell."

"Do you think the warden allowed him to have the computer?"

"I guess you'd have to ask the warden, but as far as I know nothing like that could happen without the warden's okay."

"Thank you, officer Hardwick. You have been very helpful. May I contact you again if I have other questions?"

"Yeah...I guess that would be okay."

A couple of days later Nathan called the other guard, officer Brent Strom. Strom was very guarded and gave essentially no information, although he did admit to helping Hardwick get Murdoc to the infirmary. He would not comment on Murdoc's injury saying that Nathan would have to talk to the doctor for that information. After he hung up, Nathan had the distinct impression that Strom had been told to keep his mouth shut, and since the warden had okayed the interview, Nathan could only conclude that Murdoc had warned Strom not to cooperate. In spite of Strom's lack of cooperation, Nathan felt that he had learned enough to draw some basic conclusions, which he shared with Leonard Marshall. "Leonard, I think that somehow Murdoc is able to do a couple of very remarkable things. First, I think he is able to change his form somewhat like supposedly happens in lycanthropy."

"Yes, like Lon Chaney becoming a werewolf, except for real."

"The second thing I think is that he also has the ability to transport an alternate version of himself to another location some distance away. I guess it would be a form of telekinesis except that he is transporting a version of himself instead of a separate object. I know this sounds pretty crazy except it is supported by what officer Hardwick observed and what

I experienced. I think that Murdoc made himself into the dragon and transported this version of himself to my house, but at the same time Murdoc, the man, was still in his cell in some sort of trance. When he came back to himself, he was bleeding from Jake's bite on his arm." Marshall laughed as he replied, "Nathan, it sounds like some sort of science fiction okay, but, as you said, your theory is supported by the facts as we know them. When Murdoc was in the trance state, it apparently took all his mental energy to perform the task of becoming the dragon and attacking you. What Murdoc told the guard may reveal his secret…he said he was letting his mind wander and that was his only freedom. Remember what Spock or was it Sherlock Holmes said about what is left when you eliminate the impossible?"

Yeah, you are left with the truth no matter how improbable. The improbable truth seems to be that Murdoc is still a mortal man, but a man with some pretty amazing powers."

Leonard Marshall got up and stretched, "Nathan, I don't know about you but I have had enough fun for one day. I am going to hit the sack. Remember that tomorrow we are scheduled to attend the workshop on spell casting."

"I remember. Goodnight, Leonard, and thanks for everything. I am going to try to call Alexis before I go to bed." Alexis did not answer Nathan's call.

Chapter Thirty-nine

Love discovers truths about individuals

that others cannot see.

-Soren Kierkegaard

To a twelve-year-old boy, the solution to some of life's most complex problems is all too often seen as being as simple as running away from home. David Charles understood that something was terribly wrong in the relationship between Nathan and Alexis Richards, and he believed that "something" was him. From time to time, he had overheard snatches of their arguments and knew that his name was mentioned. He combined those scraps of information with his past experience in other foster homes and came to the conclusion that Nathan and Alexis were fighting about him. Therefore, he reasoned that the solution was to leave. The only unanswered question in his mind was where to go? For several days he pondered that question until he saw an ad in the paper about a traveling circus that was in Raleigh. Sometime back, he had read a book about a boy who ran away from an unhappy foster home and took a job with the circus. In that story, the boy found his place among the circus performers, thus bypassing the legal system that would send him back to his foster home or to an orphanage, but best of all, he was set free to see the world. Once David had decided to join up with the circus, he began studying area maps and possible modes of transportation since Raleigh was too far to walk. He observed that cutting through the woods behind the Richards' house would be the shortest route to the bus station where he could most likely buy a ticket to Raleigh. A brief search on the internet told him a bus ticket would cost $25. He did not have that much money so he decided to "borrow" enough funds from Alexis' purse to buy a ticket and something to eat. Early the next morning he would put his plan in motion. David slept very little because of the excitement he felt about his pending adventure. Finally, he got out of bed at 4:30 am and slipped into his clothes and shoes. He scribbled a note which he would leave for Alexis. In the note he explained that he knew he was the reason that Dr. Richards had left home, and he stated further that he did not want to ever go back to the orphanage. He lied and claimed that he was going to the home of a distant relative. He closed the note by thanking her for her kindness and reassuring her that he would be okay. He crept quietly from his room, leaving the note on the kitchen table and slipped out the back door of the house headed for the woods. Almost immediately David realized that he should have brought a flashlight, and he cursed himself for his lack of forethought. He decided he would have to make do without a flashlight because going back to the house for a flashlight would likely awaken Alexis or Jake. As soon as he entered the woods, the darkness seemed to grow much deeper, making progress incredibly difficult. What had seemed like a quiet night when he left the house was now filled with unknown and frightening sounds. The cries of night birds were especially chilling, but the hissing screech of a Barn Owl filled him with such terror that he became utterly paralyzed and disoriented. After a few moments and nothing had pounced on him and torn him apart, David began moving again, but now he had lost all sense of direction. He had never ventured very far into the woods behind the Richards' house so he had no idea of the terrain. Branches snagged his clothing and scratched his face and arms. Twice he tripped over unseen obstacles, cutting a gash in his right hand and forearm. He knew his hand was bleeding but he couldn't tell how badly. Hoping the bleeding would stop, David continued on deeper into the woods. What had seemed like such an excellent plan in the daylight now seemed like utter folly. Willing his feet to move he trudged ever so slowly on until he heard the unmistakable sound of movement in the bushes in front of him. He was certain it was caused by an animal and not a small one at that. Perhaps it was just a deer he had startled or…maybe something else…a wolf or a monster. David wanted to run but the darkness and the dense underbrush prevented rapid movement. After taking a few hesitant steps, David thought he heard the sound of moving water like a creek or stream, but in the inky blackness he wasn't sure from which direction the sound came. His next step provided the answer. He stumbled and fell, then rolled down an embankment into a shallow creek. His face and upper body landed in the edge of the creek and the shock of the cold water kept him from feeling the pain that had bloomed in his leg. Then the pain came crashing into his awareness momentarily making it hard to breathe or even think. After a few moments his mind was able to refocus on his situation and he knew he had to get out of the stream. He couldn't get to his feet because of the intense pain in his right leg, so with slow and very painful effort, he pushed his upper body up out of the water onto the muddy bank. There exhaustion overwhelmed him and he lost consciousness. When he regained awareness David could see dim light filtering through the trees, and he knew that he had survived the night. Death had not found him. The pain in his leg reminded him that he was still alive but in a very precarious situation. Summoning all his strength he was able for drag himself a bit further away from the creek which was better but not much. Looking around he saw nothing that told him how far he had traveled or in what direction. He wondered who would possibly find him. At the edge of the creek opposite of where David lay helpless, a lone wolf kept a silent watch.

Alexis was awakened by the sound s of Lizzy playing with Jake, so she crawled sleepily from bed, slipped on her robe and padded into the kitchen. Lizzy and Jake were engaged in a mighty tug of war with one of Jake's toys. Jake always won which Lizzy found to be hilariously funny.

"Jake", she cried between peals of laughter, "You cheat!" Alexis attempted to help Lizzy and the two of them battled Jake to a standstill. Finally, they both let go and Jake shook his toy in triumph. The tug of war over, Alexis walked to David's bedroom to see if he was awake because she needed to get breakfast started. She found his bedroom door ajar and called his name. Hearing no reply Alexis opened the door and stepped into his room. The bedroom was empty.

"Lizzy, have you seen David?" Alexis called to Lizzy.

No mommy, I haven't seen him." Looking at Jake, Lizzy asked their German Shephard the same question, "Jake, have you seen David?" Jake dropped his toy and walked into David's bedroom and sniffed the bed then trotted quickly to the back door. "Look, Mommy, Jake thinks David went outside."

"Lizzy, maybe you are right. Let's see." Alexis hurried to the door and opened it. When she did Jake bolted out and stopped by the driveway and began to sniff the ground. After a few moments of sniffing around Jake ran towards the woods behind the house. Alarmed by her dog's behavior and David's disappearance, Alexis called Jake, "Jake, come!" Somewhat reluctantly Jake returned to Alexis and stood wagging his tail. "Jake, do you know where David went?" Immediately Jake headed back towards to the woods. He would apparently have headed into the woods if Alexis hadn't called him back. Herding Jake and Lizzy into the house, Alexis called her neighbor, Nancy Bradfield. After explaining what she thought had happened, Nancy Bradfield said she would get her husband Robert and they would come over right away.

Some fifteen minutes later Nancy and Robert Bradfield came running over. After a few moments of deliberation, Nancy agreed to stay with Lizzy while Alexis, Robert and Jake started their search for David. Before they left, Nancy spotted the note that David had left for Alexis and called them back to the house. Alexis read the note and began to cry. "Poor kid! We've got to find him! Come on, Jake, show us where David is. Go find David!"

By midafternoon the intrepid trio had yet to find David and were beginning to lose confidence in Jake as their guide. They were just about to turn back and call the police when Jake began barking loudly. He took off running and Alexis and Robert did their best to follow him. Jake made better time and they soon lost sight of him, but they were able to follow his barking. Fighting their way through dense undergrowth, Alexis and Robert came upon Jake. He was barking at what appeared to be a wolf. The wolf turned and ran, enticing Jake to follow it. Alexis and Robert followed Jake's excited barking until they spotted David lying at the edge of a small creek. As they came down the embankment to the stream's edge, Jake was licking David's face and barking excitedly. David was conscious and obviously glad to see them, but his pain quickly dampened his joy. The two adults immediately realized that they could not get David back to the house and to medical help without assistance. Robert told Alexis that she and Jake should stay with David while he went back to the house and called EMS. Only Jake noticed the presence of a wolf watching from the opposite bank of the creek.

By early evening, EMS personnel had gotten David to the hospital where his wounds were treated and his broken leg set, but he remained in the hospital overnight. As she watched him sleep Alexis realized how much she loved David and what a personal sacrifice he had tried to make for her. Nancy Bradfield stayed at the Richards' house with Lizzy and Jake so Alexis could remain at the hospital with David. Reflecting on the events of the day, Alexis kept thinking about the wolf. Was it trying to guide them to David? Around nine o'clock Alexis called Nathan's cell phone to tell him what had happened, but he didn't answer. She left no message.

Chapter Forty

Be fire with fire.

-William Shakespeare

The next morning while Nathan and Leonard consumed their breakfast consisting of sweet rolls and coffee, Nathan received an ominous sounding email from Dean Albritton asking if they could meet this morning about an urgent matter. The message did not go into detail; it simply mentioned that one of Nathan's students had lodged a serious complaint against him. Nathan could feel his heart rate accelerate as he read and reread the dean's email. The message brought back the terrible memory of the time he was accused of inappropriate contact with a member of his congregation in Lubbock. *I can't believe this is happening again.*

Leonard noticed his friend's sudden silence and ashen skin color. "Nathan, is something wrong? You look like you have just seen a ghost."

"In a way, I have. I just got an email from my dean. He wants to meet with me about a complaint lodged by one of my seminary students It feels just like what I went through in Lubbock at my church. "I remember…but you were exonerated then so…

"Yeah. I was exonerated but this time I may really be up a creek."

"Do you think it is …what's her name…Lurleen?"

That would be my guess, Leonard."

"Damn! From what you told me she may really have some proof to back up her claim, and your defense is going to be hard to sell. People aren't too likely to buy the idea of a witch's spell. That would rank right in there with all the Q anon conspiracy stuff."

"You're right. She does have some photos that could be pretty incriminating. Can you go to the workshop while I meet with Dean Albritton?"

Sure. I'll go and see what I can learn. It's probably a long shot that I'll get any really useful information especially since your situation has suddenly become much more urgent."

While Nathan prepared to meet his dean, Leonard Marshall used his phone's GPS to locate the site of the spell casting workshop. The workshop was held in a large older home on the outskirts of town. To Leonard, the place looked like a perfect setting for a scary movie. He parked at the curb about a half block away and walked past several cars already parked in front of the house. He assumed those cars belonged to other attendees at the workshop. *I can't believe how many people are coming to something like this.*

Leonard climbed the front steps of the old house and entered the big front door where he was greeted by an attractive young woman. She signed him in and he explained that Nathan Richards was unable to attend. The greeter handed him some brochures and directed him to an empty chair. Nathan surveyed the room which was obviously the living room of the old house. The furniture had been moved back to accommodate twelve folding chairs which were arranged in a semicircle facing the speaker's table and chair. Eight of the chairs were occupied, all by women who appeared to be in their thirties or early forties. Several of the women turned to look at Leonard as he took his seat, and he surmised from their expressions and shared whispers that he was viewed with considerable suspicion. After several uncomfortable minutes, Leonard saw the woman who greeted him walk out of the room and then return accompanied by an exceptionally attractive woman dressed in a snug-fitting black dress which seemed a perfect match for her raven black

hair. The featured presenter's name caused Leonard to chuckle silently. Her name was Samantha Snow.

Ms. Snow nodded to the hostess and then surveyed the room before speaking. "Good morning, everyone. Some of you I already know since we are members of the same coven." Looking straight at Leonard, she continued, "It is rare that we have a man attend these sessions. Are you a warlock, sir?"

Leonard was taken back by Ms. Snow's question which seemed more like a challenge than a question. "Uh, no. I am not a warlock but I, uh have a friend who I believed has been put under a spell, and I hoped to learn something that might help him break the spell."

Samantha Snow smiled and nodded as she responded, "Well, what you are hoping to learn goes well beyond what I plan to cover today, but if you can stay for a few minutes after the presentation, I may be able to give you some helpful advice for your friend. Leonard gave a sigh of relief as he thanked her. "I appreciate your offer, and I can certainly stay afterwards."

For the next hour Ms. Snow covered the five steps involved in spell-casting, beginning with a cautionary statement that she would only talk about positive or white magic spells. The first step involved the purpose of the spell. She emphasized that the more specific the purpose of the spell the better. The next step involved any special materials that might be needed such as herbs, crystals, or charms. She supplemented this step with a list of websites where people might obtain such material. The third step involved words and symbols that might be used in the spell. She gave several examples, none of which were meaningful to

Leonard. The fourth step involved the timing of the spell. Certain days like Halloween were especially good and sunrise or sunset were seen as powerful times. She mentioned in passing that black magic spells were often more effective at midnight. The final step involved putting it all together. As she talked, Leonard noticed that most of the women in the group took extensive notes, and he thought how nice it would have been if his college students were half as attentive as these would be witches. After the other attendees finally left, Leonard and Samantha exited the living room into a smaller room which served as a parlor. Samantha offered Leonard a small glass of dark red wine which he declined. Leonard explained the nature of Nathan's situation in very general terms while the attractive witch appeared to listen intently, occasionally asking a question for clarification. Her explanation sounded to Leonard like a brief history lesson since she talked about several examples of witches casting similar spells

Leonard was surprised when she began her discussion with the example of Odysseus and Circe. Most of what she explained to him seemed generic and too general to be of much use, so he pumped her with as many specific questions as he could. Her response to one question seemed to strike paydirt. "Ms. Snow, you talked today about the importance of mental concentration, specific words or charms to enhance the effectiveness of the spell, but I am wondering if some witches are born with an innate power to cast spells? Maybe another way of asking might be...are some witches born or inherit their power or spell-casting ability?"

Samantha's expression darkened as she answered, "You ask a very important and sensitive question, Mr. Marshall...or is it Dr. Marshall?"

"Either is fine for now."

"I am certain that some women are born witches. Most of the people, men or women, who come to these workshops just want to feel more powerful or in control, but they aren't really witches. In answer to your question, the answer is yes. Such individuals are like gifted athletes. They have innate talent but in order to fully develop their ability, they usually need some coaching and lots of practice, but given the coaching and practice, they can become incredibly powerful. It is my belief that such individuals are a rare and unique breed, if you will...they are extraordinary human beings."

Is there anything someone can do to counteract their spells by talismans or charms?"

"Perhaps, but if the witch who casts the spell is truly gifted and experienced, countering her spells will prove to be very difficult." Ms. Snow abruptly got up and offered her hand to Leonard. "Mr. or Dr. Marshall, I must be going now. I hope our conversation has been useful."

She handed Leonard what looked like a business card as he turned to leave. "Here is my card. You may contact me by email if you have further questions. Good luck to you and your friend."

Leonard Marshall walked slowly back to his rental car, his mind flooded with questions and troubling possibilities. His scientific side seemed almost overwhelmed by what he had always considered to be superstition, myths, and sheer ignorance. *Could there really be witches, warlocks, and demons? Maybe Nathan's only hope to fight Lurleen's spells is to learn how the game works and then play by a witch's rules.*

## Chapter Forty-one

God, have mercy on me, a sinner.

-Luke 18:13

Nathan paused before entering Dean Albritton's office. He took a deep breath and exhaled slowly in hopes of calming himself just a little, but his effort was largely unsuccessful. He entered the Dean's office suite where he was invited to have a seat. A moment later, Dean Albritton emerged from his office and greeted Nathan, but his greeting seemed stiff and formal. Nathan and Albritton entered the Dean's office and Nathan took a seat while the Dean closed the door.

"Nathan, I really hate having to have this conversation with you, but I have no choice. I hope you understand."

"Dean, I certainly understand your position."

Albritton picked up a manilla folder and pulled out several sheets of paper which he glanced at briefly. "Nathan, I received an email from a female student in your seminar in which she alleges that you took advantage of her sexually. I called her into my office to explain what she meant, and what she told me was pretty shocking. She claimed that you have made a number of sexual overtures towards her, and on one occasion followed her to her apartment, got her drunk and then engaged in sexual acts with her."

"Dean, are you allowed to tell me the name of the student making this accusation?"

Yes. Her name is Lurleen Montgomery. When I asked her if she had any proof to support her claim, she showed me some pictures of her in the altogether, apparently sent to her from your cell phone. I have some copies of those pictures." Albritton held up the printouts for Nathan to see. Note that the emailed pictures appear to have come from your phone." Albritton pointed to the copy of the email which did show the sender as being Nathan Richards. "As if the pictures weren't enough, she said her roommate, Myra Napier, would be willing to say that you have shown an unusual interest in Miss Montgomery." The Dean put the papers back into the file folder which he closed and then looked intently at Nathan. "I'd like to hear your side of the story, Nathan."

"Well, Dean, some of what Miss Montgomery apparently told you I cannot deny, but the real problem is that I cannot explain it either. I admit that she is an attractive young woman, but I have always tried to conduct myself in an ethical, Christian manner. I do not remember taking those pictures of her or sending them to her, even though they seem to have come from my phone."

"Nathan, I'd like to hear your explanation of what happened between you and her or as much as you can give me. In my many years in my position as Dean, I have heard some pretty unusual explanations...and some of them turned out to be true even though they seemed pretty unlikely when I first heard them. So please give it a try."

"Okay. I'll tell you what I know or at least what I think happened between me and Miss Montgomery, but first I have to ask you a question. Do you believe in witches?"

Dean Albritton smiled before answering, "Are you serious?"

"Actually, I am, because there is no point in my trying to explain myself if you are absolutely certain that witches are merely a fantasy or something found only in stories and movies."

"Well, Nathan, I would have to say that there is a lot in this world that I cannot explain or understand. I know that witches are mentioned in the Bible and throughout history. Even today, there are people who claim to be witches or believe that witches are real. At the same time, I'd have to say that I have never personally known or encountered someone I believed to be a witch."

In a voice that was barely audible, Nathan replied, "I guess that is about as open-minded a response as I could hope for. In a nutshell, my explanation for my behavior is that Lurleen Montgomery is a witch and she cast some sort of spell on me."

Dean Albritton's facial expression was one of surprise. "Nathan, do you mean she put a spell on you like Elizabeth Montgomery in that old sixties tv series…what was it called…Bewitched?" The Dean paused and then smiled, "Curious that the actress who played the witch was also named Montgomery."

"I know it must sound pretty lame, but I believe it is true, but I certainly can't prove it. There is more to the story, but I don't want to go into it because it will only convince you that I am truly insane."

Nathan and Dean Albritton continued their discussion for another thirty minutes before Albritton announced his decision, "Nathan, for the time being I am going to take your name off the fall class schedule, and I have no choice but to send this complaint to the disciplinary committee. I have to admit that I think you are telling me the truth as you understand it; however, your explanation would never convince a judge and jury…or for that matter the disciplinary committee. I want you to have no contact with Miss Lurleen Montgomery or Myra Napier. Until this matter is settled, you may continue to use your office and other university resources. Is that understood?"

"Dean, you have been more than fair. I will do as you request."

As he walked from the Dean's office and headed for his car, Nathan felt that he had just received a death sentence. *I am a dead man walking.* Once behind the wheel of his old Honda, Nathan pulled out his cell phone and wondered how the pictures of Lurleen Montgomery could have been sent from his phone to Lurleen unless she did it while he was unconscious. His thoughts were interrupted by a call from Leonard Marshall. "Hello, Leonard. Did you learn anything useful at the workshop?

Dr. Marshall's voice sounded excited, "Maybe so. Let's meet at my hotel room and I'll tell you what I picked up at the workshop."

Nathan saw Leonard's rental car pull into the hotel parking lot just as he was exiting from his car. The two men greeted each other and walked into the building together. Once back in Leonard's room, Nathan asked eagerly, "What did you learn? I hope it is something we can use."

"Well, I didn't get a how-to manual for undoing hexes, but I did get some possibly useful information. After the presentation, Miss Snow, Samantha Snow agreed to talk to me privately. I told her about your situation in general terms and then asked her if some people are born witches. She believes strongly that there are a few individuals, usually women, who are born witches. That is, some have an innate talent that allows them to do some pretty amazing things. Most of the women who come to workshops like the one I attended aren't really witches, just wannabes trying to make themselves feel better or more powerful. I don't think she knew anything about Lurleen but she said these real witches can cast spells that are very hard to counteract."

"Well, that doesn't sound very encouraging, Leonard. I think Lurleen Montgomery is one of those real witches, so is there anything I can do to break her spells? I don't remember if I have already told you, but I should mention that the sea shell contraption did seem to work to some degree. I think that is why she destroyed it."

You hit the nail on the head…I mean we will have to fight fire with fire. Apparently, her magic is real and can't be defeated by conventional practices. We need to understand as much as we can about her spells and then use what magic we can to protect you."

"That sounds good, but do we…do I have the luxury of taking a crash course in witch craft? I mean the Dean has essentially suspended me pending a hearing by the discipline committee. I could be fired and soon. I know it will be all over if Lurleen comes up with any more evidence. That's why I have got to stay off her radar at least until the disciplinary committee reaches its verdict.""

Time is definitely an issue and is not on our side. That Miss Snow did agree to respond to any additional questions we might have, and I think she will be willing to help us, perhaps for a fee."

"Okay. We'll do what we can do. At least the Dean was more open minded about my explanation than I expected. I don't think he bought the idea of me being under a spell, but he did say he thought I was telling him the truth as I understood it. For the immediate future I have to stay as far away from Lurleen Montgomery as I can, and at the same time I have got to try to explain things to my wife. That won't be easy."

Nathan left the hotel and drove to his house. He stopped on the road in front of his house before turning into the long driveway. There in the yard he saw David, Lizzy, and Jake playing ball. The two children took turns throwing the ball which Jake happily retrieved. David was wearing some sort of cast or protective boot on his leg, and when he walked, he did so very carefully. Nathan couldn't see Alexis but assumed she might have been watching the kids from the house. His heart initially swelled with joy at the sight of his family, and then it broke at the thought of what he had apparently lost. With a deep sigh, Nathan drove away, heading back to his motel room. *Dear God, what have I done?* Nathan's painful rumination was broken by the sound of his cell phone.

"Nathan, I just wanted to tell you that Miss Snow has agreed to meet with me, and I am heading for her place. Are you heading to the hotel?"

"I am, Leonard, and I sure hope you learn something we can actually use this time."

"Yeah, me too. Are you okay? You don't sound too good."

I am as good as I can be. I drove by my house but didn't stop. I'll be anxious to hear about your visit. Good luck…and thanks again for all you have done for me.'

"Hey, that's what friends are for. Hang in there, buddy."

Chapter Forty-two

The enemy of my enemy is my friend.

-Ancient proverb

Finally, after several attempts, Leonard Marshall was able to make contact with the witch who led the workshop he attended. Samantha Snow had a small office in a half-empty shopping mall on the north side of Durham. The glass door of her office was frosted and emblazoned with her name and some odd runes that meant nothing to Leonard. He rang the doorbell, waited, and heard her buzz him in. The small waiting area was empty except for a couple of potted plans and a small sofa. From an inner office, Samantha Snow emerged and greeted Leonard with a smile and hand shake. "Dr. Marshall, it is nice to see you…I had a feeling I would hear from you again. How may I be of assistance?"

"Thank you for agreeing to meet with me. The friend whose problem I described for you is really in bad shape and needs to keep his whereabouts a secret from a certain powerful witch. It seems apparent that he can't just lay low…she'll find him and add to his misery. Surely there must be some magic, some spell that can make him disappear or at least hard to find."

"Before we get into that, I have to ask you a question. Do you perhaps know the name of the witch that is persecuting your friend? I fear I may already know her identity."

Well, yes. Her name is Lurleen Montgomery."

Miss. Snow's facial expression revealed the high level of concern she obviously felt. I was afraid of that," she muttered, almost inaudibly. I have met her a coupler of times. She came to one of my workshops almost a year ago, and I have heard rumblings about her from the local coven that she dabbles in black magic. Ms. Montgomery is not someone to trifle with; she is an incredibly powerful witch. In fact, I have never known one as powerful as she. Her magic is certainly enhanced by her beauty. She could probably have most men eating out of her hands without ever having to use magic. How or where did your friend meet her?"

"She was in his class at the university…in the Divinity School of all places."

Miss. Snow chuckled, "That is interesting all right." There is something else about her I think you should know. I suspect she has been tutored by…someone very dark and evil. I don't know who that individual might be, but…. well, I just feel it in my bones. Do you have any ideas?"

"Maybe. I will let my friend know. Now. Can you tell me how my friend can make himself invisible to Miss. Montgomery?"

"Perhaps you are familiar with the old tv series called *Star Trek*?"

"Of course! I grew up with Captain Kirk and the crew of the Enterprise. Why do you ask?"

"In the tv series the Klingon's were able to hide their ships by what they called a cloaking device. Well, I will tell you how your friend may be able accomplish somewhat the same effect; it just won't be quite as effective and the effect is temporary. I guess in a way it is more like camouflage."

"Anything will help. What do I do? How does it work?"

Miss Snow opened a closet and hunted through an assortment of bottles and cannisters on the shelves within. She picked up two small ceramic containers. "This one," she said holding up her right hand, "is a very rare variety of Nightshade. It is also quite toxic as it contains belladonna." In her left hand she held a second container. "This one reduces the potency of the Nightshade.so that a person can safely ingest it. You mix the two together in the ratio I will give you; then your friend will drink the solution. For approximately 24 hours the drug will make it hard for a witch to locate him. He may not be completely invisible, but she will have to concentrate pretty hard to see any evidence of his presence. Unless your Miss Montgomery is in the room with him, she probably won't be able to sense his presence. The drug will tend to scramble his thoughts, maybe even cause hallucinations, but that is what makes it hard for a witch to see him mentally." Samantha measured out a small amount from each container into two small glass bottles which she stoppered. She labeled each bottle and then wrote mixing instructions on a small piece of paper, handing it all to Leonard. "Warn your friend to mix the contents exactly as I have written them and advise him to use it only when absolutely necessary. After he takes it he will probably find it hard to drive or do anything that requires a clear mind."

Leonard drove away feeling hope but also a bit of apprehension. Could he really trust this woman? Was it safe for Nathan to drink a known poison? Then, of course, the really big question would it work, never mind the question any scientist would ask: how does it work?

Back at the hotel Leonard Marshall related to Nathan all that he had learned from Samantha Snow about Lurleen Montgomery. Next, he went into detail about the camouflage method, she had given him.

"Leonard, what she told you certainly confirms my experience with Lurleen and her spell casting ability, but I have to admit taking those herbs makes me very uneasy. Also, if I am to use it judiciously, how do I know when it is appropriate or needed?"

"I don't know the answer to that question, but what I do know is that we need to find a place where you can stay off the grid so to speak at least until the disciplinary committee renders its decision. By the way, that reminds me that I have an uncle who used to have a cabin somewhere close to Ashville. I will try to contact him and see if you might be able to rent it for a few days."

"That would be great, Leonard. Once again, how do I thank you for all you have done and are doing?"

Chapter Forty-two

I can see for miles and miles

-Peter Townshend

Leonard Marshall was able to contact his uncle, Edward Mills, and found that he still owned a cabin in the mountains northeast of Ashville. His uncle said he had rented the cabin through Vocation Rentals by Owner a few times, but not in the past year. According to Mr. Mills, neither he nor any family member had been to the cabin in the past eight or nine months, but he was happy to allow Nathan to use if. All he asked in return was that Nathan or Leonard clean things up and make a note of any needed repairs. He went on to explain that there was no inter net or phone at the cabin but there was electricity and water. TV was by satellite but the service had been discontinued. In other words, the cabin was pretty well isolated

"Leonard, the cabin should be fine, and maybe the isolation will be good. I can pack up a few items and be ready to leave by tomorrow morning at the latest. According to Google Maps, the drive should take just under five hours. I'll go by the house this afternoon and get what I need and leave a note for Alexis. Do you think it might be possible to get internet service anywhere near to cabin?"

"I'll ask Edward. He did say that the cabin sits up pretty high on the side of a mountain, so it is certainly possible."

That afternoon Nathan drove to his house. Alexis was still at work and Lizzy was at her daycare. David, it turned out, had been going to the Boys Club in town and would be coming back with Alexis. That left Jake as the sole occupant of the house. As soon as he pulled in the driveway, Nathan could hear Jake barking inside the house. When Nathan opened the door Jake greeted him with such enthusiasm that Nathan was almost knocked over. "Hello, boy. I am glad you still love me. I missed you, big fella." Jake followed Nathan every step he took inside the house. *There is nothing like a dog's love.*

The next morning Nathan and Leonard traveled in separate cars with Nathan following Leonard. They made good time from Durham to Ashville, but the last leg of the journey between Ashville and the cabin went much slower. The road was winding with numerous hairpin turns and switchbacks. The last mile or so was over a gravel road. After a couple of wrong turns, they pulled up at the cabin. True to Leonard's description, the cabin sat on a wooded lot which afforded ia splendid view of the valley below from its large front deck. The house was a true log cabin with a native stone fireplace. Inside there was a large living area and kitchen. On the back side of the cabin were two bedrooms and a single bath. Leonard located the circuit breaker box and turned on the power. After some searching, he found the water shut off valve and turned on the water. The inside of the house was dusty but not overly so given the its period of disuse. Sounding like a real estate agent, Leonard turned to his friend and asked, "Well, what do you think? Do you still want it?"

"If I had the money and a job, I'd offer to buy it. It's great, and I noticed that we passed a small general store a couple of miles back. I can probably buy whatever food I need there. The kitchen has an oven and microwave, so I think it has everything I'll be needing. Why don't we go there and buy something for dinner and some beer? Maybe you'd like to spend the night here before you head back?"

"Sounds good, let's both go in my rental car." After a dinner of frozen pizza and beer, Nathan settled in for the evening. They sat on the deck and watched the sun go down. In spite of the chill wind, Nathan felt truly peaceful for the first time in what seemed like an awfully long time. As night fell, the air grew cold quickly and a symphony of night noises arose from the surrounding area. After taking the last swallow of his beer Nathan sighed deeply and whispered to his friend, "Leonard, this if so great. It's almost enough to make me forget about witches, marriage problems, and ethics complaints. Let's go inside and build a fire in the fireplace."

"Yeah. It is nice. I can't believe my uncle doesn't use it more. Did you notice that there was internet service down at the general store, and I got at least one bar on the front corner of the deck. Did you get the same?"

"Yeah, I got one or two bars too. That is enough for phone calls and maybe text messages. I really think this place will be as safe and well-hidden as I could hope to find. Combined with

that stuff Miss. Snow gave you; it should be hard for Lurleen to find...at least until the university committee decides my fate."

While Nathan may have found the evening to be peaceful, back in Durham Lurleen Montgomery found it to be anything but peaceful. She had just had another unexpected visit from Jeremiah Murdoc's projected self. He demanded that she do more to totally destroy Nathan Richards. During his visit she was forced to admit that she wasn't certain of his whereabouts or what else she could do to further damage his reputation. Normally, she could focus her thoughts on Nathan and discern his location and even his inner thoughts and feelings rather easily. She knew that her anger towards Murdoc was clouding her ability to focus her mind. *If only I had a crystal ball like the witch in the wizard of Oz that helped locate Dorothy and her companions.* After a glass of Chardonnay, and some deep breathing, Lurleen quieted her mind, allowing her to concentrate on Nathan. *Where are you, my lover? I know you are out there.* Slowly, very slowly her mind began to assemble an image, at first fragmented and cloudy but gradually becoming more detailed. Lurleen deepened her trance-like state in an all-out effort to increase her mental scanning efforts. Finally, as she neared exhaustion, she had a brief but clear image of Nathan. He was sitting and talking to his friend, Leonard Marshall. He was indoors in an unfamiliar setting which looked somewhat like a log cabin.

It was after midnight when Leonard Marshall got up from the recliner, checked the fire, stretched and then announced that he was going to turn in for the night. "Nathan, have you taken any of that nightshade potion? I just happened to think about it." "To be honest, I haven't taken any yet. I suppose I am a bit scared of it. Do you really think it is safe?"

Leonard shook his head slowly before responding, "I'm not sure. If it is toxic and you have a bad reaction, we are a good ways from a hospital. I don't know what to tell you."

"I am inclined to hold off taking it. I don't see how it could work, and I doubt Lurleen has a crystal ball or mental radar that can locate me way out here in the mountains." Sometimes it is true that he who hesitates is lost. Nathan Richards turned out the light by his bedside and darkness flooded the room. The witch, Lurleen Montgomery, had a sudden flash of telepathic awareness. "Nathan, my dear, I believe I have found you! I will visit you soon." She smiled as she undressed for bed.

## Chapter Forty-three

If you are going through hell, keep going.

-Winston Churchill

Alexis checked her cell phone for the umpteenth time before leaving her office to pick up David at the Boys Club. Part of her eanestly hoped she would hear something from her husband and another part wanted to strangle him. *Where had he gone? Was he hurt or even still alive?* The next-door neighbor thought she had seen his car pull into the driveway briefly a couple of days ago, but that was all the information she had about Nathan or his whereabouts. Her world had been turned upside-down in the past few weeks and she felt as if she was wandering through a wasteland without so much as a compass. The sudden and unexplained change in Nathan's behavior had made her life a living hell. If it weren't for her daughter Lizzy and her foster child David, her life wouldn't seem worth the struggle. As she pulled up to the curb in front of the Boy's Club, she spotted David as he emerged from the building. He was talking and laughing with two boys who looked to be about his same age. Seeing the smile on his face brightened her mood for a moment. *I am glad he can find something to smile about.* David waved goodbye to the two boys and turned towards her car.

"Hi, Ms. Alexis," David said with a smile which quickly faded as he saw Alexis's face. "Is something wrong…have you heard from Mr. Nathan?" David seemed to flinch as he asked the second part of his question, perhaps feeling he was out of place asking such a personal question.

"No, no, I haven't, but I am sure he is okay…but, uh, thank you for asking. How was your day? It looks like you have made some friends."

"Yeah, I guess so. We played three on three basketball and they were my team mates.

Alexis backed away from the curb and started to head for Lizzy's daycare center. "David, after we get Lizzy, what do you say to a pizza from Charley's Pizza Shack?"

David's face lit up as he answered, "I think that sounds really good. Their pizza is the best around."

After dinner, Lizzy showed Alexis some of her water color paintings and David went to his room to play with his new video game, the latest version of *Call of Duty*. Alexis pinned two of Lizzy's watercolors to the bulletin board in her bedroom then wandered into the living room area. She turned on the tv to watch the local news more out of habit than any real interest. The local news was never very news worthy, but this evening her attention was captured by a missing person's report. Her heart skipped a beat as the thought that maybe it would be about Nathan flashed through her mind. The momentary flicker of hope was quickly extinguished as the report was about an elderly man with dementia that had wandered away from an area nursing home. She looked again at her cell phone to see if by some chance Nathan had called or texted her, but there was nothing. She dropped her cell phone back onto the sofa with a sigh, and as she did the words from her favorite song from the musical *Les Misérables* echoed through her conscious:

*God on high*

*Hear my prayer*

*In my need you have always been there…*

*Bring him home*

*Bring him home*

Hot tears began to flood her eyes as Alexis kept silently repeating the words, "Bring him home, bring him home." In spite of the anger she felt at what she believed to have been Nathan's betrayal and infidelity, she knew deep down that she still loved him and would forgive him if he would just come home. Somewhere in her past she had heard or read that when a breach of trust occurs in a marriage, that the offender's action should be viewed against that individual's history in the relationship. Was the betrayal a single, isolated even or something that had occurred several times? Obviously, an isolated event could and should be forgiven more readily than a pattern of such betrayals. Almost as if in answer to her to her thoughts and prayer, her cell phone buzzed and danced on the sofa cushion. It was Leonard Marshall. "Leonard, do you know where David is? Is he okay?"

"Alexis, Nathan is safe…I…I can't tell you where he is right now for his safety, but I wanted you to know that I have been with him and he is okay." Leonard paused before continuing…" Alexis, I know you must be very angry at Nathan, but there is so much that you don't know and probably wouldn't believe if I tried to tell you…"

"Try me, Leonard! I need to know. I need to understand. This has been hell for me!"

"Alexis, I can image that it has been awful for you. I don't know how this is going to play out. Nathan may well be fired by the university and there are other dangers yet to be faced, but what I can tell you is that he loves you and desperately wants to see you and Lizzy. More I cannot tell you now…I will do the best I can to give you progress reports. Just try to trust Nathan and pray for his safe return. Now I have to go."

"Leonard, wait, don't hang up!" Her phone went silent as Leonard hung up, and a mixture of hope and confusion swirled through Alexis's thoughts. *What is happening to Nathan? Dear God, help him…and help me to have faith.*

Chapter Forty-four

For in that sleep of death what dreams may come

-William Shakespeare

The day dawned bright and clear. From the cabin's deck Nathan could patches of fog in the valley below. It was so calm and peaceful at the cabin that he had lost track of what day of the week it was, and he could almost forget about the many troubles that waited for him back in Durham. Inside, Leonard Marshall was packing up his clothes as he prepared to begin his long journey back to Lubbock. He swallowed the last sip of his now cold coffee before joining Nathan on the deck. The two Men greeted each other with smiles and nods rather than words as neither wanted to break the stillness that surrounded them. Finally, Leonard patted Nathan on the shoulder and spoke softly, "Well, my friend, I guess I had better be going. I've got a long journey ahead of me. I wish there was more I could do to help, but it seems we are just in a holding pattern for now. If anything changes and you need my assistance, give me a call, and I'll come back as quickly as I can. Have you thought any more about taking that nightshade drug?"

"I think I may go ahead and take it today. I just don't want Lurleen to find me. I think it is worth the risk to stay off her radar at least until the dust settles and I know where I stand with the university and with Alexis. I know I can't hide here forever but a few more days might be good. I will miss you, Leonard, and I can't begin to tell you how much your being here has helped me. I couldn't have made it this far without you. Maybe you could delay your departure for an hour or so just to make sure I don't have a seizure or something when I take that drug."

"No problem. My plane doesn't leave until this evening, so drink up and I'll make sure you don't go into convulsions or something."

Nathan measured out the dark liquid the witch had prepared and swallowed it promptly before his better judgment stopped him. The taste was an odd mixture of bitterness and sweetness that burned as it went down. "Well, that's that. Can you still see me?"

Leonard laughed, "Yeah, buddy. I can still see you. I think it is only supposed to make it hard for a witch to see you. What did it taste like?"

"It wasn't as bad as I expected, and it had a bitter-sweet quality about it, but what I noticed more than anything was that it really burned as it went down."

Leonard waited for about an hour and Nathan reported no ill effects so he began his journey back to west Texas. Nathan went back inside the cabin and settled into the big leather recliner suddenly feeling a great heaviness invade his body. Almost as soon as he pushed the recliner back, sleep overtook him. Consciousness returned slowly as Nathan struggled to focus on his surroundings. He was no longer in the comfortable confines of the log cabin. Wherever he was, it was very dark and he was surrounded by strange night noises. The ground beneath his feet was rocky and uneven. He couldn't be sure, but he seemed to be standing on the edge of a forest. In front of him was a clearing in which he thought he could make out a small fire burning. Someone was speaking but he had trouble understanding the words. Nathan walked slowly in the direction of the fire. As he got closer, he could see that it was a small campfire with several people sitting around it. One individual was standing and seemed to be addressing those seated before him. Not sure of where he was or who the persons around the fire were, Nathan paused and listened intently. Gradually, the speaker's words began to register in his mind. The speaker seemed to be telling a story, a story about a boy on some kind of quest. Eventually Nathan heard a murmur from the people sitting around the fire and then the speaker ended his story and departed. As Nathan watched in utter confusion, the speaker headed directly towards him. Before he could decide what to do, the speaker stood before him. In the darkness it was hard to make out any details. The man appeared to be about Nathan's height. He was dressed in a long robe with a hood. He looked to be quite old with long white hair visible beneath the hood. He held a long-stemmed pipe between his teeth. For several moments neither man spoke or moved. Finally, the old man spoke, "Do you know how the story will end?"

Nathan was totally confused by the questions put to him by the old man. "What story? Were you telling a story? I couldn't hear all of what you were saying."

"You know the story. It is the story of a life. Will it be life or abandonment? Life or death? You must choose." After he spoke the old man turned as if to depart.

Nathan felt a surge of fear and he reached out to grasp the old man's shoulder, "Wait, I don't understand your questions...I don't even know where I am. Please help me. Don't leave me here alone!" Instead of touching the man's shoulder, Nathan grabbed nothing but air, empty space The man faded from his sight, and Nathan was left alone; even the distant camp fire was no longer visible. *Where am I? Is this real or only a drug-induced dream?* He began walking in the direction where he had seen the fire and the small gathering of people. He walked for some time but found no people or even the ashes from a fire. Nathan looked up and saw no stars either, and try as he might he could discern no features of the surrounding landscape anymore, just darkness. It wasn't the total darkness of a deep cave but a darkness that made it difficult to see more than a few feet in front of him. Nathan wasn't sure if the darkness hid all the details of the land around him or that there simply were no details to be seen. The sound of the gravel crunching under his feet was about the only sensory information he had to go on. *Where do I go? What do I do now? Am I dead?* Nathan continued to walk, without direction or purpose. If anything, the darkness became deeper. As he stumbled along the words of Isaiah 9:2 came to mind:

> The people walking in darkness have seen a great light;
>
> On those living in the land of deep darkness
>
> a light has dawned

Nathan muttered to himself, "Where is your light, God? I am certainly, in the land of deep darkness, but I see no light…none at all." As if in response to his words, Nathan saw or thought he saw flashes of light move past him at great speed. Some sped by above him and some alongside him. He looked closer and saw that the flashes of light had shape and form. Although he couldn't be certain, these bright objects that flew past him resembled winged creatures, bats or maybe demons. Then, as suddenly as they appeared, they disappeared and everything returned to complete darkness. *Thanks a lot, God. That was really helpful.*

Nathan continued to trudge forward never knowing if he might run into something or fall off something. It was a frightening, hopeless feeling. Then, out of nowhere he heard a loud noise that sounded for all the world like a rock band tuning up before a concert. The noise was followed by a dazzling light display accompanied by the familiar lyrics of an old Bob Dylan song.

> You're gonna have to serve somebody, yes you are.
>
> Well, it may be the devil or it may be the Lord
>
> But you're gonna have to serve somebody.

Nathan's mind was reeling as he fell to his knees. He remained for several minutes in this prayerful posture, but he uttered no words of prayer, just a soft moan of pain and despair. The bizarre rock concert scene vanished; darkness and silence returned. It seemed to Nathan to be the silence of death.

## Chapter Forty-five

Try as we might to postpone them,

days of reckoning inevitably arrive.

-Brandon Mull

After an unknown period of time Nathan opened his eyes and what he saw took him by surprise. He saw what appeared to be the interior of the cabin in which he had been staying. "I guess I am not dead after all", he muttered to himself. Slowly he pushed himself out of the recliner. Every muscle in his body screamed in protest as he tried to walk. Slowly Nathan made his way into the kitchen in hopes of brewing some strong coffee. As he filled the water reservoir of the Keurig coffee maker, he suddenly felt as if he was not alone, someone was watching him. There in the living area behind him stood Lurleen Montgomery. Her hands on her hips and a knowing smile on her lips.

"Well, well. The lost has been found. I was afraid something terrible had happened to you…I feared maybe you were dead."

"I feel like death warmed over. What are you doing here, Lurleen? How the hell did you find me?"

"You don't seem very glad to see me. It was not easy locating you, and once I did, it was quite a drive to get here. When I couldn't sense your presence in my mind, I started thinking about the reasons why. I knew you might have died or perhaps something had clouded your thoughts. That got me thinking and I realized there was one person in the area who knew how to use herbs in order to make it hard for a witch to use her ability to locate a person by their thoughts. It's a little like locating a cell phone by pinging the tower it has used. When I called Samantha, she told me that your friend, Leonard Marshall had visited her and she gave him a blend of herbs which would cloak a person's thoughts. I guess you know the drug she gave him was pretty toxic."

"I believe the stuff she brewed up is definitely toxic, but you didn't answer my real question…what are you doing here? Haven't you done enough damage?"

"Oh, Dr. Richards, you have hurt my feelings! I thought you found me attractive. Now you say I damaged you. What have I done to you? But in answer to your first question, I am here because I missed you."

Nathan felt his anger rising which seemed to blot out any feelings of sexual arousal that he might have felt. "You ask what damage you did. I'll tell you. You destroyed my marriage, ruined my reputation, caused me to lose my faculty position and probably my faith as well."

"Oh, but you are wrong, Dr. Richards. You pursued me. I never forced you to do anything. Now, did I?"

Nathan knew deep down that the witch's reply did contain at least a kernel of truth which stung. "I admit I found you very attractive, and I guess you didn't force me physically. But I know you are a witch and I am pretty sure you influenced me mentally."

"Oh, I suppose I cast a spell on you. Is that what you are saying?"

"Yes, something like that, a spell, a hex, or whatever you call it."

Lurleen brushed a lock of her dark hair from her forehead and took a couple of steps in Nathan's direction. "Don't you find me attractive anymore? Wouldn't you like to make love to me?"

Nathan felt his sense of self control beginning to slip away. "You know I found you attractive…but…I am finished. You have taken even my soul from of me. Please, let me go. Why are you doing this to me? What have I ever done to you?"

Without a word in response to Nathan's plea, Lurleen simply visualized him responding to her thoughts. "Come hold me, Nathan. Then see if you still want me to leave."

Almost reflexively Nathan found himself drawn to the witch as if by some magnetic force. He knew from past experience he was powerless to resist one of her spells, but in a moment of desperation he experienced a sudden clarity of thought. *Accept and redirect. Accept and redirect.* He would later realize that these thoughts came from some distant training in hypnosis. Nathan knew it wasn't much of a defense, but it was all he had…that and the truth. Lurleen, please stop! Let me speak, please."

Lurleen looked puzzled, but her curiosity was aroused so she effectively cancelled the spell she has cast. "What is it, my dear? Do you want to confess your love for me…your undying affection?"

Sensing the sudden return of volition, Nathan gasped and sucked in a deep breath before speaking again. Looking squarely into the witch's eyes, he began, "Lurleen, when we first met in my class, I found you very attractive. To be honest...I wanted you. But things began to change between us. You changed. Instead of pursuing you, I found myself drawn to you, sometimes against my will. Finally, I think I realized that you probably are a witch and you really can cast spells." Lurleen started to interrupt, but Nathan held up his hand to signal her to stop.

"Wait! Please let me finish. Lurleen, now I am no more than a puppet, a rag doll. You can put me wherever you want and make me do whatever you wish. Where is the fun in that for you? It would be like giving someone a drug that would make them fall in love with you. Outwardly, it would look as if you were being loved, but the truth would be that it wasn't love but the drug that was creating the person's actions. It would be like lying about your golf score or how many fish you caught...you'd know it wasn't true. Besides, haven't you done enough? If you did make a deal with Murdoc, haven't you fulfilled your part of the deal? Lurleen, I believe you came to seminary not to destroy people but to find something. ...to get in touch with the good which still lives within you."

Lurleen felt confusion swirl through her mind. Nathan's words were like the proverbial monkey wrench that had been tossed into the machinery. She didn't know how to respond. None of her spells seemed appropriate. She was temporarily paralyzed by the truth. She took a couple of steps back and looked at Nathan, and he wondered what she saw, what she was thinking. Finally, she spoke. Her voice was soft and without the sarcasm it contained just a few moments earlier. "Nathan…I…I don't know what to say. Maybe there is truth in what you just said. It is no longer fun if I compel you to want me. I can do it but…the fun seems to be gone. There is no longer a challenge. You are right. I did make a deal with Murdoc or whatever his name is, and I guess maybe I have done all he asked."

Nathan started to respond but sensed that Lurleen was still thinking and there was more to come, so he remained silent.

"Nathan, I have to admit that you really never have done any wrong to me. You are not my father, and I am not exacting revenge on him when I debase you." Without another word, the witch, Lurleen, turned slowly and walked towards the cabin door, but instead of leaving she turned back to Nathan and spoke, "Nathan, you may be a psychologist and a minister, but there are dark forces in this world that you neither know nor comprehend. As I came to understand who and what I am, I discovered a power far greater than anything I had ever known. I made a bargain. You might even say I made a bargain with the devil himself. As a result of that deal, my powers as a witch increased dramatically, but there was a price. In return for the powers I gained, I made an agreement to destroy you. Initially I did find you attractive and seducing you was fun, but now I know it has gone too far. I may be a witch but that doesn't mean I am totally evil. I was sent here to finish the job, to utterly and totally destroy you...but I am finding it very hard to do that. Nathan, there is something else, something I need to make very clear to you. What I am about to tell you may be hard for you believe. One night on campus I was confronted by something...I don't know if he was a man, an illusion, or the devil, but I understood that he possessed a great knowledge and power. He revealed some things to me about myself that I had only begun to understand. As a result, my power as a witch grew exponentially, but he wanted something in return for tutoring me. He wanted your destruction or at least your debasement. He seemed to have a grudge against you from something in the past. I guess I got drunk on my new found power as a witch and I agreed as long as he promised not to kill you."

As she explained further, Nathan experienced a growing certainty regarding the identity of Lurleen's mentor. He was convinced that it was Jeremiah Murdoc or perhaps Satan in the guise of Murdoc. It all began to make sense. The pieces of the puzzle had come together at last.

"Lurleen, I believe you, and I am pretty certain of who your mysterious tutor is and why he wanted to destroy me." Nathan explained about his experience in Lubbock and his encounters with Murdoc in the prison. "I think Murdoc is not a normal man. He is something more, something purely evil." Nathan paused before continuing, "What are you going to do? If you came here to finish the job, what were you going to do? What will Murdoc do if he thinks you failed to complete the task?"

"Let me worry about all that. I have decided that I am going to leave you just as I found you. I have proven my power to myself, and you are right. You never did anything to harm me. I think I have done enough damage. In a way, Nathan, I think I may even care for you. That probably sounds pretty hollow coming from me. Maybe I don't really know what love is, but there is something different about my feelings towards you." Lurleen walked over, bent down and kissed Nathan on his forehead, then walked toward the door where she lingered, a look of sadness on her face. Then she was gone.

Nathan sat in stunned silence, starring at the door. Was he correct? Had she made a deal with Murdoc? How had Murdoc known Lurleen and the ways to enhance her ability as a witch? He had no answers to those questions but felt certain that it was Murdoc who was really pulling the strings. His time of silent wondering was interrupted by his cell phone which vibrated nosily on the kitchen table. He was surprised to hear the phone since the cell service in the cabin was spotty at best. Herecognized the number of the caller; it was Dean Albritton. "Hello, Dean. I have been expecting your call."

Dean Albritton's voice sounded business-like and without any obvious emotion as he began. "Nathan, I am afraid I have some bad news. After much deliberation, the ____ has decided ____ you."

"Dean, the phone connection here is very weak. Did you say that I have been terminated?"

"In so many words, yes. Nathan, I really hate that it has come to this. I can't quite believe what has happened, and I am very sorry. I must ask you to clear out your office and turn in your keys and faculty ID card as soon as possible." Emotion crept into the Dean's voice as he ended the conversation, "I will pray for you, Nathan."

"I understand, Dean. I will do as you ask before the week is over. "The Dean's words crushed Nathan's spirits and he felt nothing but despair. For the first time in his life Nathan seriously entertained suicide as an option. He could understand how in ancient Rome falling on one's sword was an honorable response when one had failed miserably at some important mission. Perhaps if he had a sword, he might have been tempted to fall on it, but all he had at the moment was a six pack of beer which he drank in short order and then passed out.

## Chapter Forty-six

Let it happen like it happened once before.

It's a wicked wind and it chills me to the bone

and if you do not believe me come and gaze upon the

Shadow at your door.

-Gordon Lightfoot

After a night of fitful sleep, Nathan awoke with a splitting head and an uneasy feeling in his gut. He struggled into the kitchen and scrambled the two eggs that remained in the refrigerator, toasted the last slice of bread, and used the remaining coffee for his breakfast. He ate slowly without really tasting the food. Only the hot, bitter coffee triggered his taste buds. Nathan felt like a condemned man having his last meal. How could a person enjoy a meal when he faced death? When he finished his meager breakfast, he washed the dishes and put the bed sheets in the washing machine. While the washing machine chugged away, Nathan gathered up his clothes and laptop and stowed them in his car. After replacing the sheets on his bed, he made a quick pass through the cabin to see if he had left anything behind. Then he sent a text message to Leonard Marshall asking him to thank his uncle for the use of the cabin, locked the cabin door and hid the key under the big flower pot on the deck. *I guess I can't hide any longer. It's time to face the music.* A chill wind blew up from the valley below and Nathan shivered as he walked to his car. Nathan started his car and began the drive back to Durham, taking a long last look at the cabin. The vista from the road leading away from the cabin was beautiful in the cold morning light, but Nathan's thoughts were focused on a host of questions that seemed to have no answers. *Where do I go? What will I do? What about my marriage and my family?* When he came to the main highway which would take him back to town, he paused for several seconds then called Alexis's cell phone.

Alexis answered after the first ring. "Nathan...is that you? Where are you? Are you okay?" Her voice sounded infused with genuine concern.

"Lexi, I am okay, I guess." Tears welled up in his eyes as he continued, "I am so sorry for all the pain I have caused. If you will let me, I'd like to come home."

Before he could offer an explanation, Alexis answered in the affirmative, "Yes! Come home! I love you!" Her phone beeped a couple of times and she knew she had lost the connection. She tried several times to call him back but realized there was probably no service where ever Nathan was. As she waited in hopes that he would call her back, her emotions seemed to overflow their banks like a river swollen by flood waters. *Dear God, bring him home.* As if in answer to her silent prayer her phone rang and it was Nathan, and he explained that he would be home in a matter of hours, weather permitting. The sky which had been clear earlier had gradually turned dark as gray clouds gathered and rain threatened. As Nathan reached the city limits of Durham, the rain drops began to plink and plunk on the roof and windshield of his old Honda. Nathan was glad to be out of the mountains as the rain had made the roads slick. The afternoon had become dark enough that the city street lights had come on. The gloom of the day seemed to match the darkness that Nathan felt in his heart. When at last he saw the lights in the windows of his house he felt his mood brighten ever so slightly. *God, it's good to be home!* Nathan parked his car and turned off the engine feeling a deep sense of uncertainty as to the reception he would receive, but before he could exit the vehicle and make a dash for the house, he beheld a sight that he knew he would never forget. Alexis, Elizabeth and Jake burst from the house and headed towards his car. He climbed from his car and raced to meet his family; there in the midst of the drizzle, Nathan Richards felt a joy the likes of which he had never experienced. In that moment he knew God had smiled on him. David Charles, who was still wearing a protective boot on his leg, met the Richards foursome at the door with towels in hand. He too seemed glad to see Nathan. After changing from their wet clothes, Alexis made hot chocolate for everyone except Jake who got one of his favorite treats. Somewhat to Nathan's surprise he was not assaulted with questions about his actions or his whereabouts. Everyone seemed to focus only on the joy of their family's reunification. Later in the evening after he had said his goodnights to Lizzy and David, Nathan walked slowly to his bedroom where he knew it was time to try to explain what had happened to Alexis. He felt a surge of anxiety as he entered their bedroom where Alexis was sitting on the bed gently scratching Jake's neck. Before he could begin, she smiled warmly and spoke, "Nathan, I am glad you are home. I have prayed so hard for this moment!"

"Lexi, there is so much I need to tell you, but the most important thing I can say is please forgive me."

Alexis held out her hand inviting him to sit down beside her. "Nathan, before you go on, there is something I need to say. This whole thing has been a tremendous shock, something I never thought I would have toface. I don't think I have ever felt so much pain and anger, but with a lot of prayer and some long, sleepless nights, I found that in spite of everything, I still love you. I believe that you are a good man. So, I forgive you, and I want to try to understand what happened with you. I also want to know what I can do differently in the future. So, I am ready to listen whenever you are ready to share your thoughts."

For several moments the only sound in their bedroom was that of the rain hitting the windows. Finally, Nathan broke the relative silence with a sigh. "I guess the first thing I should tell you is that I have been fired by the university, so I am now unemployed. I don't blame the university for their action. I am guilty of all that I am accused of, but my greatest sin, my greatest offense was against you and our family. If you want, I will try to explain what happened with me, but I certainly cannot justify my actions, and I want you to know that there was nothing you did wrong."

Alexis wrapped her arms around her husband and whispered, "Maybe that is enough for right now; please just hold me. You can tell me more in the morning." In the silence that followed, Nathan and Alexis could hear only the sound of the rain. It was a peaceful sound.

Chapter Forty-seven

In the shadow of my hurt, forgiveness feels

Like a decision to reward my enemy.

But in the shadow of the cross, forgiveness is

merely a gift from one undeserving soul to another

-Andy Stanley

Alexis woke up before the sun. Her husband lay asleep beside her. Quietly she left the bed and headed to the kitchen to make coffee, and as she did, she heard the quiet click-click of Jake's feet as he followed her. She turned and whispered to heir faithful old German Shepherd, "Jake, be very quiet…no barking." Jake looked up with his big brown eyes as if he heard and understood. The sound of the coffee maker chugging and burping seemed unusually loud in the silent house. When the coffee maker completed its work, Alexis poured two cups of coffee and returned to the bedroom where Nathan was just beginning to stir. "Wake up, sleepy head. I bring you coffee made from beans picked by none other than Juan Valdez."

Nathan sat up in bed, smiled, and rubbed the sleep from his eyes. "Thanks, hon. To what do I deserve this honor?"

"You don't deserve it...I am glad you are home. Do you feel like talking? Lizzy and David are still asleep."

"Yeah. I guess this time is as good as any. Last night, I mentioned that I was fired from my job at the university because of my inappropriate contacts with one of my students. There is a lot more to the story, and I will try to tell you as much as I can remember. Is that okay?"

"Yeah, that sounds okay to me."

Nathan began by giving more of the details of his relationship with Lurleen Montgomery, starting with the first time he saw her picture on his computer where she was listed as one of the graduate students in his class. He readily admitted that there was something about her that grabbed his attention. He explained that she was indeed beautiful but there was something else about her that he couldn't articulate. As he came to know her in class, he saw her as very bright but cynical and rather mysterious. When she showed some interest in him, he admitted that he was both flattered and excited. He went on to divulge that on more than one occasion he had yielded to temptation and had sex with her. He explained that later on, with the help of Leonard Marshall, he became convinced that she was, in fact, a witch who possessed an ability to actually cast spells. He also became convinced that somehow, she was tutored or instructed by Jeremiah Murdoc who in return for his guidance made an agreement with her that she would debase and destroy Nathan.

Alexis listened intently, nodding occasionally but asked no questions until Nathan seemed to end his explanation. "Nathan, I don't think you could make up a story like that, and I believe that you are telling me what you honestly think happened. I know that there was something about that Murdoc fellow that was not normal and then there was the episode with that dragon creature in our yard. I don't know anything about witches, but if Jeremiah Murdoc could do what he apparently did and you could confront whatever you dealt with back in Lubbock, then I guess I can believe in witches. What I still have a hard time with is the fact that you made some advances toward your student even before she started using her witchcraft spells on you. It is going to take some time for me to get over that."

"Lexi, I understand your feelings completely. I don't know when or to what degree Lutleen may have cast her spells on me, but your point is valid. I regret what I did, and I wish somehow I could have a do over, but I can't. I just hope one day you can get past it."

"Just give me some time to work though my feelings. If I can't, we may need to see a marriage counselor. You told me last night that the university fired you. What are you going to do about that? Can you appeal?"

"Lexi, I know everything I told you sounds pretty fantastic, but I swear that to the very best of my knowledge and understanding, it is true. If you'd like, Leonard could back up much of what I have told you. As to the possibility of appealing my termination, I don't think there is any hope of that. I am guilty of severe misconduct, so there really isn't any basis for an appeal."

"Well, I don't need any further proof of what you've just told me, and I am so sorry you were let go by the university. I know how much that position meant to you. I guess we'll just have to make some financial adjustments without your salary, and we could always move back to Texas and get some help from my parents."

"Ugh. Getting help from your parents would be very difficult for me and probably for you too. Let's agree that would be the absolute last resort."

"I agree…and somehow…I believe we'll make it. Are you finished with your coffee?"

After breakfast Nathan headed off to clear out his office and turn in his keys and faculty ID. His mind was flooded with all sorts of memories and painful emotions as he drove to the university. He entered his office building by a side door in hopes that he wouldn't encounter any of his former colleagues. He breathed a sigh of relief when he entered his office and closed the door behind him. Since he had been in his office for less than two full years, he didn't have a lot to remove. He put his diplomas, laptop, books, and some personal items in an empty back pack he had carried with him. He paused at his office door and took a deep breath as if he was once again a kid and was going to try to swim the length of the pool underwater. Instead of traveling though water he hoped that this time he would be traveling through empty halls on the way to his car. After stowing his belongings in his car, Nathan walked back into the building. Once again, he silently thanked God that he had not met up with anyone on the way to Dean Albritton's office. The Dean's secretary was not at her desk so he walked to Dean Albritton's office and tapped on the partially open door. Dean Albritton looked up and motioned for Nathan to enter.

"Good morning, Dean. I have cleared out my office and here are my keys and faculty ID", Nathan said as he offered the items to the Dean.

"Nathan, thank you…could we talk for a moment?

"Sure. I don't have much on my agenda today."

"Nathan...I...I hardly know what I want to say. I saw the evidence presented by your student and I know you didn't deny the accusations, but I feel...well, I feel like there is more to the story. I sense that there is something you are holding back. "Dean Albritton looked at Nathan with a look that conveyed compassion and a desire to understand.

"Dean, I guess in reality there is more to the story, but the explanation is so fantastic that nobody in their right mind would believe it...sometimes I don't know if I believe it. Anyway, it would just sound like a lame excuse, and I don't want to go there. I just want to take my medicine and move on."

"Nathan, I am not a kid and I have heard some pretty wild stories in my career, and some of them...many of them proved to be true. I'm willing to listen if you want to tell me."

Nathan chuckled as he responded, "Dean, I doubt you've heard too many stories that included witches casting spells and men who could transform themselves into dragons."

"Well, you are right about that, but I do recall a quote but not its author. The quote goes something like this: 'The human heart knows things that the eyes don't see and feels things that the mind can't understand'. My heart tells me that you are a good and decent man even though my mind can't understand what you apparently did."

"Thank you, Dean. I appreciate that more than you know, but if you don't mind, I'd like to keep it to myself. Maybe someday when I have a better understanding of this whole situation, I'll try to explain it to you."

"That's okay by me, Nathan. As I told you over the phone...I will continue to pray for you, and you know how to reach me any time you feel the need to do so."

Nathan left the building but instead of going to his car, he walked slowly to the university chapel, not really knowing why He entered the chapel through the main entrance and took a seat in one of the back pews. There were several individuals scattered about the sanctuary praying or meditating. Nathan sat with his eyes closed, not really praying, not really meditating, just sitting. As he sat in the stillness, it occurred to him that his lack of prayer during the past year or two may have been what first opened the door so that evil could enter his life. This sudden insight caused him to open his eyes and stare up at the massive stained-glass windows behind the altar area. Although he had no idea how or why he felt that somehow all would be well. No sooner did that thought cross his mind when someone began to play the organ, and immediately he recognized the hymn: *It is Well with my Soul*. As the final notes of the hymn faded away, Nathan rose quietly and walked from the chapel. Back in his car he sat for a few moments and contemplated the fact that he must bid good bye to what he had thought was his dream appointment, a place he believed to be the pinnacle of his career, a place from which he would one day retire. He had never thought it would be the place where he would be fired, a place of ignominy.

Chapter Forty-eight

You've got to pick up every stitch,

Must be the season of the witch.

-Donovan Leitch

Driving away from the Duke campus, perhaps for the last time, Nathan turned on the car radio and tuned to the local oldies station where he was immediately greeting by a song made popular by Donovan in the 60's. One line of the song caught his attention: "You've got to pick up every stitch...must be the season of the witch". Nathan had heard the song many times but had never given much thought to the lyrics and what they might mean, if anything. He vaguely recalled his mother spending many hours knitting and occasionally she would get upset because she "missed a stitch". He had no idea what one did when they "missed a stitch", but he understood that it was a mistake that had to be corrected right away or the project would contain a fatal flaw that couldn't be fixed later. *Well, I sure can't fix this mistake now. It's too late for that. I guess it really is the season of the witch in my life.* Nathan did not drive directly home; he wandered aimlessly for a time and then realized that he had driven by Lurleen's apartment several times. That realization drew him from his reverie and both alarmed and aroused him. *What am I doing? Is she trying to draw me in again like a fish on a line?* With great effort Nathan made a course correction and headed for home. He looked in his rearview mirror at Lurleen's apartment complex and as he did the wording often found on ancient maps to mark unknown territory came to mind "There be dragons." He chuckled to himself, "There be both dragons and witches, and I've been in the grip of a witch and fought with a dragon!" Nathan had always been a skeptic and to admit to the reality of dragons and witches in the 21$^{st}$ century made him almost doubt his sanity. *If I can't undo what I have done, I wonder if, like Saint George, I can eventually kill a dragon?* There was still much he didn't know about Jeremiah Murdoc and any further direct access to the man would be nearly impossible since he was no longer employed by the university. *Maybe*, it occurred to him, *just maybe the warden doesn't know I have been fired and I can get in one last visit. But what would I do or say?* Nathan contemplated trying to assassinate Murdoc but quickly realized that wouldn't help even if it were possible. He thought back on the time Murdoc, in the form of a dragon, had come to his house. Nathan had gathered enough evidence to tentatively conclude that when Jake bit the dragon, Murdoc ended up with an injury to his arm. Nathan also believed that Murdoc could only transmit or transport himself over a limited distance; he just didn't know the actual range. *I wonder if somehow,*

*I could set a trap and lure Murdoc to the extreme edge of his range and then destroy him there?* This idea seemed plausible but it lacked the essential details. Just before turning into his driveway an idea burst into his consciousness. *Perhaps I could go to the prison one more time and meet with Murdoc where I would try to provoke him into coming after me. I could tell him I was going to reveal his true nature and identity to the world.* When Nathan arrived home, the house was empty except for Jake. Lizzy was at daycare while Alexis was at work and David at the Boy's club. Nathan greeted Jake then set up his laptop computer. He felt silly as he searched the internet for information on how to kill a dragon. He chuckled several times as he read a number of articles. According to what he read, the most common weapon used to kill dragons was a sword. An alternative method involved using a shield or mirror which would reflect the dragon's image back to the creature. He wondered how a mirror could kill such a beast. *Maybe evil can't stand to see itself for what it really is.* His next move was to contact the prison to see if he could schedule a meeting with Murdoc. Much to his surprise, he was able to do so rather easily. His next and hopefully last ever meeting with Murdoc was to be in two days. This gave him very little time to work out the fine details of his plan, details that could mean life or death for himself and possibly his family too. He wondered if it was worth the gamble or should he just focus on picking up the pieces of his shattered life and leave Murdoc and Lurleen alone- if possible. When Alexis and the kids arrived, Nathan waited for a quiet moment and then told Alexis of his plan.

"Oh, Nathan! I don't know! Your plan sounds awfully risky. If you are wrong, Murdoc will almost certainly kill you. Even if your plan works and you kill him, what will be the result? Will it be good or will there be unforeseen consequences?" Alexis made it clear both verbally and nonverbally that she was uncomfortable with the plan. "You really need to think about this before you act!"

"Lexi, I know you are right, but I feel certain that I must do something and soon. I can't undo what I have done but maybe I can put an end to some of the evil that helped to lead me into my sin. Besides, I don't think Murdoc or Satan, or whoever he really is will be content just to humiliate me and get me fired."

"Okay, but what about your former student, the witch? She is still around. What if she decides to cast another spell and lure you back in? You couldn't resist her before, how will you be able to do so now?"

"That's a great question, Lexi, right at this moment I and don't have an answer. I'll just try to take it one step at a time. I know I have to do something; I can't just sit back and hope they'll both go away!"

The morning Nathan was to visit Murdoc in the prison dawned bright and sunny which was in stark contrast to Nathan's dark and gloomy mood. On his way to Central Prison, he reviewed his plan for baiting Murdoc and realized how vague it really was. It was if he was going to enter a lion's cage, jab the big cat with a stick and then run for cover. In truth it wasn't much of a plan. Nathan was pretty sure he could anger Murdoc and that Murdoc would probably come after him, but he wasn't at all sure if he could really destroy Murdoc in whatever shape he appeared. After the guard escorted Nathan to the interview cell, he knew it was too late to turn back. He would just have to jab the beast and then see what happens next. Murdoc looked ever so slightly surprised to see Nathan as he was brought into the room. The guard fastened his hand cuffs to the table and then exited the room.

Murdoc broke the initial silence with a sarcastic greeting, "Well, Dr. Richards, I didn't expect to see you again. I heard that you ran into a little bit of trouble at the university. Shame on you!"

"It's good to see you too, Dr. Murdoc. I just wanted to stop by one more time to tell you that I won't need to schedule another interview and to thank you for your cooperation. I now have all the information I need for my research. Oh…and about my problems at the university…well it may have all come about from a big misunderstanding. I expect to be reinstated soon, but thanks for your concern." Nathan was a little surprised at how easy and provocative his response was. Clearly, he had scored a good hit.

"How fortunate for you, but it must have been pretty embarrassing to be even accused of sexual advances towards one of your students. I am curious what you think you will be able to do with the information you feel like you gained from our visits."

"Yes, the incident at the university was troublesome, but my reputation will soon be cleared, and that is what matters. As to the information I gleaned from our interviews, well…it has helped me better understand one form of evil."

"And what form of evil do you now understand?

Nathan smiled as he replied knowing he had stung Murdoc's ego. "I realized that some very evil individuals respond as they do because of their mental condition. They see the world in a very distorted way. You said it very nicely when you once told me that you were an agent of God, doing God's will. That is classic psychotic thinking, Dr. Murdoc. You of all people should certainly recognize it."

Murdoc's rage was clearly evident in both his facial expression and his rigid body language. Nathan knew he had accomplished step one of his plan, but he was beginning to think he over did it. *I hope Murdoc doesn't kill me before I can even get out of this room!* Nathan buzzed for the guard who entered the room promptly to take him out. As he turned to leave, he looked over his shoulder at Murdoc and issued one last taunt, "Good bye, Dr. Murdoc. It has been very interesting getting to know you."

Just as the guard was closing the door to the interview room, Nathan heard Murdoc's almost whispered reply, "You haven't seen the last of me!"

Before leaving the prison Nathan stopped by Warden Henderson's office to thank him for arranging the interviews and to explain that this would be his last meeting with Jeremiah Murdoc. Henderson's secretary explained that the warden was in a meeting, but she agreed to pass Nathan's message on to him when he got out of his meeting. Nathan sat for several minutes in his car before driving away from the prison, his mind replaying his visit with Murdoc, wondering if he could have handled it better. He felt certain of one thing, Murdoc was angry and would certainly come after him seeking his revenge. Nathan also knew that he had to take steps to protect his family, and he must do it quickly. Although he wasn't sure where the family should go, he felt reasonably sure that it needed to be as far from the prison as possible. He was convinced that Murdoc's ability to transport his image or form was limited. For some reason he felt that his home was probably near the fringe of Murdoc's range, so wherever the family went it needed to be still further out from the prison.

## Chapter Forty-nine

Revenge, the sweetest morsel to the mouth that ever was cooked in hell.

-Walter Scott

After his brief visit with Nathan Richards, Jeremiah Murdoc was boiling over with rage. He wasn't sure whether he was angrier at Lurleen Montgomery for not finishing Nathan Richards off completely or at Richards himself. One thing for sure, he would get them both. After due consideration, Murdoc decided to begin with the witch, Lurleen Montgomery. He felt that he had made her what she was, helping her to develop her full potential as a witch. He had kept his end of their bargain, but she had not. Yes, he would see to her first, and then he would deal with Richards. The small glass dragon he had given her enabled him to determine her location where he would visit her as soon as it was dark.

Lurleen Montgomery no longer had a roommate since Myra Napier had dropped out of school. Being alone didn't bother her, and, in fact, she rather enjoyed the freedom to do as she pleased. When she went into the kitchen to fix her supper, she noticed that the red glass dragon on the counter top glowed bright red for a moment or two. She wondered if it meant that Murdoc was trying to contact her, but after a moment or two she decided it was probably something like a butt call on a cell phone. She picked up one of her text books and strolled into the living area where she had intended to do some reading, but her thoughts wandered instead to Nathan Richards. She missed having him around to seduce and play with, but after her most recent time with him their relationship had changed. Now she almost pitied him. Her thoughts were abruptly interrupted by her awareness that something or someone was in her apartment. She stood up from the sofa and turned towards the kitchen, and there in the shadows stood Jeremiah Murdoc. Suppressing her fear as best she could, she confronted Murdoc, "What do you want?"

Stepping into the living area, Murdoc responded, "We have some unfinished business, Miss Montgomery. You have not kept your end of our bargain, and I am here to find out why.

"What do you mean. I did everything you wanted. Nathan Richards is a ruined man. He has been disgraced and he lost his faculty position. I think his marriage is in shambles also. What more did you expect?"

You exaggerate. He visited me at the prison and did not seem humbled at all. In fact, he told me that he would be reinstated at the university. Clearly, you failed to destroy him. Somehow, he has landed on his feet, and now I am revising the terms of our agreement. I want him dead, and I want you to kill him."

"No. I will not kill him! That was never part of the deal, and I did what you asked. He has lost his job, and I have heard nothing about him being reinstated."

"I know what he told me, and this is non-negotiable. I want him dead, and once you have done that, I will take care of his family as well. If you defy me, I will destroy you too. I made you what you are and I can just as easily destroy you." Before she could mount a counter argument, Murdoc's image dissolved before her eyes

Clearly shaken by Murdoc's sudden appearance and demands, Lurleen found it difficult to sort out her emotions. Part of her was angry and part of her was frightened. She was confident of her own power, but at the same time she knew that Murdoc seemed to possess an even greater knowledge and power. Clearly, she had no experience dealing with an entity like Jeremiah Murdoc. If, as she had learned, witches had ultimately derived their power from the devil, then she was probably over-matched. Her spells would be of no use against him. She really did not want to kill Nathan Richards, but neither did she want to be destroyed by Murdoc. All she could think of was getting in touch with Nathan and talk over their joint dilemma. Rather than attempt to use her mental power to locate him she opted for a more conventional means, the cell phone. To her surprise, he answered after the first ring. "Nathan, I've got to talk to you."

"Lurleen, what do you want? I don't think we have anything to talk about…please don't put one of your spells on me either."

"Nathan, I am not trying to seduce you. Jerimiah Murdoc paid me one of his visits just a few minutes ago. He is demanding I kill you…"

"What? Did he tell you anything else?"

"He said you visited him in the prison and told him you would be reinstated at the university. He seemed to believe that you are on your feet and doing okay. Since he helped me to develop my power as a witch, he said I had not fulfilled my part of the bargain. He said if I didn't kill you, he would destroy me. He also said something about killing your family too. Please meet me outside the university chapel as soon as you can."

"It's getting late but I will meet you there. Give me about thirty minutes."

Nathan explained to Alexis the situation and why he needed to meet with Lurleen. Clearly Alexis had her doubts, but she agreed he probably should meet her. By the time Nathan drove to the campus, parked his car and walked to the chapel, Lurleen was already standing outside the building. Nathan suggested they walk across campus since he no longer had an office and the chapel didn't seem like a good place for them to meet. As they walked, Lurleen gave a more detailed description of her visit with Murdoc. Nathan listened intently, asking a few questions for clarification.

Lurleen stopped and grabbed Nathan by his arm. "Nathan, what are we going to do? I don't want to harm you...any more than I already have, but..."

"Lurleen, I need to tell you what I have done. I have probably precipitated this situation. I met with Murdoc in prison the other day with the goal of goading him into action. I expected him to come after me, and I had no idea he would try to use you to accomplish his purpose. I know my plan is pretty desperate but I see no other way. I am hoping that he can be destroyed."

"What makes you think you can destroy him? That is absurd, Nathan! He is no ordinary man...in fact, I don't think he is human at all."

As briefly as possible Nathan explained his theory about Murdoc, his evil nature, and why he believed that there are some chinks in his armor. Central to his hypothesis was the time Murdoc appeared in the form of a dragon and Jake bit Murdoc's arm or leg.

"Nathan, perhaps you are right, but your plan seems very risky. I think you underestimate him."

"Maybe so, but he is determined to have his revenge, and my only hope is to make him choke on it. Can you stall him in some way? Tell him that I have eluded you? He might decide to take care of me himself and not wait for you to act."

"I can try. I may also be able to cast a protective spell around you. I have never attempted to do something like that, but I am pretty sure I can accomplish it. It might give you some degree of protection."

"Hey, I will take all the help I can get. I need to head on home. As quickly as I can I've got to find a safe place for Lexi, Lizzy, and David. If you learn anything else, call me."

On his drive back home, Nathan thought about his plan and all its limitations. He knew that Las Vegas odds-makers would give his plan a near zero chance of success, but it was all he had. He thought about calling Leonard Marshall, but he decided against it. Leonard had already done so much. Back home, Nathan explained the situation to Alexis and why he felt it was imperative that she take Lizzy and David to a safer location tomorrow. "Lexi, could you visit your friend, Sandra, in Chapel Hill?"

"I guess I could but what could I tell her?"

"I don't know…maybe tell her we discovered a gas line leak at the house and you need to get out for a few days while it is repaired. Tell her I came down with COVID and you need to quarantine for few days. I don't know. Just do it, please." We've got to act fast. I don't know how long before Murdoc comes after me, and I don't want you and the kids to be here when he comes. I am pretty sure Chapel Hill is outside his range."

## Chapter Fifty

When the situation is grim, be the grim reaper.

Andy Reid

Nathan waved goodbye to his wife, daughter, and foster child, David, as Alexis began the drive to her friend's house in Chapel Hill. He looked down at his dog Jake and whispered, "Well, Jake, it's just you and me, boy. I've got a lot to do and probably very little time to do it. Stay close to me as we might have an unwanted visitor at any time." Nathan knew deep down that his situation was truly grim. No, it was worse than that. It was most likely hopeless, but he knew the only rational thing he could do now was to focus on what was within his power to effect. Nathan and Jake walked slowly to the house in order to retrieve his grandfather's old shotgun from the top of his closet. The gun was at least fifty years old. His paternal grandfather had used it to hunt pheasants and quail, scare off or kill small varmints. The gun had been passed down to Nathan's father and then finally to Nathan. Since he had no desire for a gun, he'd kept it only for its sentimental value. Although he was not a hunter, Nathan knew enough to understand that since the gun was only a 20-gauge, it would probably do no more than annoy Murdoc if he came in the form of a dragon. The only way it might be lethal was if he fired it at very close range. Perhaps, he thought, having the gun along with a spear or pitchfork might be his best bet. He had read about how to fashion weapons from common garden tools such as a rake, pitchfork, or hoe, so he could work on doing that which would at least keep his mind occupied. Jake looked apprehensively at Nathan as he got the gun from the closet. "It's okay, boy. This old thing won't hurt you. Come on. let's go to the garage. I've got work to do". Nathan's garage was separate from the house and really quite large. It was made to accommodate two vehicles as well as a workshop area. He seldom used the garage for their vehicles unless bad weather was expected. Leaving the overhead door closed, Nathan and Jake entered by the side door. Once inside he was greeted by a vaguely musty odor. The previous owner had left quite a few tools which Nathan had never used, but now he was glad they were there. Nathan perused the assortment of garden tools hung along one wall. On the workbench were a variety of hand tools, vises, and grinders. *Pretty much everything I might need.* Following the directions he found online, Nathan began reworking a garden hoe into a crude spear. By cutting off the head and then using his shop grinder, he was able to fashion a reasonably sharp point on the tool. After examining his "spear" closely, he decided he could make the point a bit sharper by using a hand file. Placing the spear in a large vise mounted on the work bench, he began filing.

It was early afternoon when Nathan finished preparing his weaponry so he decided to take Jake and go for a walk to the creek which ran through the woods behind his house. Although it was a mostly sunny day, Nathan felt chilled as he and Jake walked deeper into the woods. When he came at last to the small creek, he wondered if this was the spot where they found David. He looked down and patted Jake's head, "Hey, big fella, is this where you helped them find David?" Jake didn't answer but began to sniff in earnest around the creek bank. "I guess we'd better head home. I don't want to get lost." As he and Jake walked slowly back towards the house, he couldn't help but reflect on how ridiculous his plan for combating Murdoc truly was. *I really don't have a snowball's chance of killing him.* When he reached the edge of his back yard, Nathan had the uneasy feeling that he was being watched, but looking all around, he saw nothing other than a few birds flying through the yard. Nathan walked to his garage where he stopped to close its door and then started to walk on to the house when he saw a red BMW pull into his driveway. He knew right away it was Lurleen Montgomery. Jake saw her car too and began to run towards it. Lurleen stopped her car at the far entrance to the long drive way and got out of her car. She looked as enticing as ever to Nathan, but the expression on her face conveyed worry and anxiety.

Jake stopped a few feet from Lurleen where he promptly sat down as if expecting her to give him a treat. She patted him on the head and continued to walk towards Nathan. Jake followed a few feet behind her but never growled or barked. Feeling alarmed, Nathan held up his hand and called out, "Lurleen, what are you doing here?"

"Nathan, I needed to see you so that I could put a protective spell around you. I have to be in close proximity to do so. Will you allow me...I promise that is all I want to do."

"Lurleen, I don't have much faith in any such spell, but I guess I have to admit that you do have a certain...power. I suppose I need all the help I can get, so go ahead."

Lurleen nodded and then gestured toward the house. "Could we go inside? I think it would be a more appropriate environment because I really need to concentrate to make it effective."

Nathan felt uneasy about her request but reluctantly agreed. Lurleen and Nathan entered the house but Jake was left outside to act as a watchdog in case Murdoc showed up unexpectedly. Once inside, Lurleen asked Nathan to have a seat on the sofa. She stood in front of him and placed both hands on his shoulders. "Nathan, I want you to empty your mind as much as possible and be very still. Understand?"

"I guess so. Seems pretty simple. Will it take long? Should I feel anything?"

"It should only take a few minutes, and I don't think you will feel much of anything. Are you ready?"

"Let's do it." Nathan heard Lurleen take a deep breath and then exhale slowly. Next, he heard her voice speaking softly words which sounded vaguely like Latin. Even though he had taken Latin in high school, Nathan could not make any sense of Lurleen's words. After several minutes, she stopped speaking and he felt her increase the pressure on his shoulders. Without warning She uttered one final word in a loud and forceful tone of voice and as she did, Nathan felt a sudden surge of warmth course though his body that felt for all the world like the dye injected into a person before obtaining a CT scan. The spell apparently completed, Lurleen pulled Nathan to his feet and then kissed him on the forehead. "May all the gods protect you!"

Nathan felt light-headed and unsteady on his feet as he attempted to speak. "That, that was unusual…I have to admit. Right at the end, I felt as if something warm surged through my whole body…it was just like when I had to have a CT scan with the contrast dye. I hope your spell works."

"Nathan, I do too. You may not believe me, but I care about you…maybe I even love you, if I am capable of loving someone."

"Lurleen, I'd be lying if I said I felt nothing for you. Whatever I felt, I think it was more than passion or something caused by one of your spells. I…I don't know what I want to say."

"Nathan, I want to do more than cast the protective spell and leave. What if I stayed until Murdoc comes? Together we might have a better chance of destroying him."

"Lurleen, part of me wants you to stay, but the other part says I need to face Murdoc alone. I can't tell you why…I just know I have to do it alone. I think what you have already done really might help. So, I need you to go…before I do something I shouldn't."

Lurleen smiled a sad smile, grasped his hand and held it for a moment as she whispered "Good bye, Nathan Richards."

Nathan watched Lurleen drive away with feelings of both relief and sadness, and he wondered if she really could be of help in his struggle with Murdoc. It certainly seemed as if having a witch on his side was a good thing. Perhaps her protective spell will help in some way that he certainly didn't understand. Maybe it was just a question of believing, a kind of placebo effect. Nathan and Jake walked back to the house where he got a beer from the refrigerator. He twisted off the top of the beer

and began to think: what did he actually know about his enemy? He was pretty sure that Murdoc's physical body was not able to leave the prison but somehow, he was able to project or transport some sort of embodiment or avatar of himself. Nathan recalled something he had studied in seminary. It was part of the Gnostic Christian's view of Jesus. The belief was called Docetism from the Greek word meaning "to seem". Gnostics believed that Jesus did not have a real, corporeal body, but instead had a body that looked and functioned like a human body. In other words, they believed Jesus only seemed to be flesh and blood but in reality, he was a spirit, spiritual energy. Whatever Murdoc's avatar was it undoubtedly involved energy. It took energy to transmit his avatar, and it took energy to maintain it and activate it. Perhaps that was why Murdoc could only transmit his avatar over a limited distance, just like a radio transmitter. It took more energy to send a signal over longer distances. Taking this line of thinking a bit further Nathan reasoned that any resistance, atmospheric or otherwise would possibly weaken the avatar, just as some weather conditions could reduce radio transmissions. *Eureka! I have an idea*

Lurleen Montgomery had barely left Nathan's house when her cell phone buzzed. "Hello, Nathan. Are you calling to invite me back?"

"Not exactly, but I had an idea. It may be crazy but let me tell you what I am thinking and see if you have any suggestions. You cast a proective spell on me, and I am thinking that if it works, maybe it is like a suit of armor. Let me try to explain. In ancient times a suit of armor might protect a knight from an arrow but with the advent of guns and gun power, it couldn't stop a high energy projectile like a bullet."

Okay, I hear you, but I never took physics. What are you suggesting, Dr. Richards?"

"Well, I only had one course in physics myself, but what I am wondering is if you could cast a spell on Murdoc that would require him to use more energy to project himself from his location in prison? Does that make any sense?"

"Actually, it does, and maybe there is something I can do. I might be able to cast a binding spell on him. Binding spells come in different forms and are used for different things. I could cast a spell which would limit his ability to move. In some cases, a powerful binding spell can totally immobilize a person. Now that I think about it, before I even knew that I was a witch I probably cast some sort of binding spell on men who wanted me to go further sexually than I wanted. So, yes, I could do that, and it might help. It may not stop him completely, but it may make it harder for him to do what he does. When I get home, I will work on it and let you know."

"That would be great...please hurry if you possibly can. There isn't much time. I have a feeling that Murdoc may try to pay me a visit as soon as tonight."

Chapter Fifty-one

This heart's a lonely hunter. These hands are frozen fists.

I can't stop thinking about you

-Sting

Chapel Hill was less than an hour's drive from Durham, but for Alexis Richards, it felt like the other side of the moon. She had given her friend, Sandra, a story about their home having a gas leak that was going to take a few days to get repaired. She hated lying but it seemed a lot simpler than the truth, a truth that nobody would believe anyway. She had given a lengthy explanation to David about why it was necessary to make up a story for Sandra, which he seemed to accept. Lizzy was a bit too young to be included in the lie. Although it was generally comfortable at her old friend's house, Alexis' thoughts kept wandering back to Durham and Nathan. What was he doing? Was he alright? She called him several times during the first day apart, but that never really gave her any sense of peace. Between her calls she found herself praying to God to protect him, and she hoped that God was listening. As night approached her anxiety crept higher and higher, to the point that it was hard to make conversation with her host.

After dinner Alexis and Sandra sat on the porch while the kids watched tv or played video games. Finally, Sandra addressed the elephant that had been in the house all day. "Alexis, something is bothering you…you are just not yourself."

Alexis paused for several moments and sighed deeply before responding, "You are right, Sandra…I have a lot on my mind. I am sorry…"

"Hey, no apology needed. Would you like to talk about it? If not, just say so, and I won't bug you anymore."

"Well, I guess I would like to clear the air about some things that are going on in my life. First of all…I lied about why I asked to come here. Our house doesn't have a gas leak. Nathan is in danger and he didn't want me or the kids around until he can resolve the situation."

"Gee, Lexi, that sounds bad. What sort of danger is he in?"

"It's a long story but it involves a man he interviewed in Central Prison for a book he wanted to write on evil. You may recall a serial killer a few years ago named Jeremiah Murdoc?"

"Yeah, I remember something about him. He was a physician, a psychiatrist, I think."

"That's the one. Anyway, Nathan interviewed him several times and discovered that this Murdoc is exceedingly dangerous, and for reasons that aren't entirely clear to me, Murdoc is threatening to kill Nathan."

"But isn't Murdoc still in prison…for life? Has he escaped?"

"Well, that's where the story gets strange. Somehow Murdoc is able to leave the prison for periods of time, but don't ask me how. I don't know. Nathan believes that Murdoc is not an ordinary man, but more than that I don't know or understand. What I do know is that Nathan is in real danger. He thinks he has a plan to defend himself but…"

"Oh, my, Lizzy. That is so scary. Has Nathan called the police?"

"I don't think so. He doesn't believe that the police can or will be able to help him. In truth there is more to the story, but you will think I am crazy if I told you all of it."

"Alexis, I know you aren't crazy, so tell me."

"Do you believe in Satan, the devil? I don't mean as a symbol for evil, but a real being?"

"Uh, I guess so. What do you mean…why do you ask?"

"Well, Nathan thinks this Murdoc is not a normal man, but a purely evil being, like the devil or Satan. I don't really know any more than that, but in my heart, I think he may be right. "Their discussion continued for a while longer until Lizzy came out on the porch and said she wanted her teddy and to go home. Alexis made a vain effort to explain why they would not go home tonight. Lizzy began to cry saying she missed her daddy and was scared. Sandra saved the day by offering ice cream and cookies. After getting the kids to sleep Alexis thanked Sandra and then got ready for bed herself knowing that sleep would be hard to come by. She called Nathan's cell phone one more time, and to her surprise he answered.

"Hi, Lexi. How are you and the kids?"

"We are okay. The real question is how are you? Any sign of Murdoc or the dragon?"

"Not so far, but I am as ready for him as I can be. For some reason, I think he will come for me tonight. I have taken a number of steps that I believe will slow him down and make him more vulnerable. If he comes, I will be pretty busy so don't expect me to answer my phone. I will call you as soon as I can. In the meantime,...in the meantime, just pray for me. Remember I love you!"

Alexis switched her phone off and put it on the night stand as her eyes brimmed with hot tears. *I love you too.*

After her call, Nathan's thoughts kept returning to Alexis and how much he loved her and, sadly, how much he had hurt her. As the minutes slipped by, he had to force his mind back to his present reality, his present danger. *Where is Murdoc? Why hasn't he shown up?* Nathan and Jake made several tours around the yard looking for any signs that might indicate Murdoc's presence, but there was nothing, no sign of the dreaded red dragon. By two o'clock fatigue forced Nathan to retreat to the house where he could at least rest some, but before doing so he decided to make one more pass around the perimeter of the yard. Half way around Jake froze and stared into the woods. "What is it, Jake? Let me shine a light on that area." Nathan directed the flashlight beam to the spot where Jake seemed to looking and there reflected in the light were two red eyes. Nathan's heart skipped a beat and he blinked his eyes several times in an effort to see what was behind the red eyes. Then he saw it. It was the wolf he had seen several times before. Jake did not growl or show any signs of alarm which Nathan thought was unusual. After a few moments the wolf turned and retreated further into the woods. Nathan looked down at Jake, "What do you make of that, Jake? I think that was the same wolf we have seen several times in the past. He just seemed to be checking on us, didn't he? Come on, let's go to the house and get a little rest." Back inside the house, Nathan reclined on the sofa keeping his shotgun close by. Jake curled up on the floor next to him. "Jake, keep your ears open in case I drift off for a moment." The remainder of the night passed without incident, and Nathan awoke with a start as the first light of dawn spilled into the room. Looking around, everything appeared undisturbed and Jake was asleep nearby. Nathan was clearly surprised and puzzled that Murdoc had not made an appearance. He retrieved his cell phone and called Alexis to let her know that he was okay. She was relieved to hear his voice but still apprehensive about her husband's situation.

"What do you think it means?" she asked. "Do you think maybe he won't be coming after you?"

"I wish I thought that was the case, Lexi, but I am pretty sure he will come when he is ready. I just wish I had a better idea of when that might be. I sure didn't get much sleep last night, so I may take a little nap now."

"That sounds like a good idea. I will be thinking about you. Call me if there are any developments."

"Will do. "After a brief nap Nathan got up, fixed some toast and coffee, and then headed out to the garage. He kept thinking about the wolf that he had seen during the night. He couldn't be certain but felt pretty sure it was the same one he had seen in the past. The wolf was never aggressive; it always seemed to be just watching Nathan and the family. When he got to the garage, he pulled up a stool at the work bench and got out his phone in order to do a little research on wolves. What caught his attention were some references to native American tribes in the northwest and their beliefs about wolves. They revered the wolf, seeing it as a spirit being who watched over and protected members of the tribe. The same article pointed to the fact that wolves were social animals and fiercely protective of their pack and offspring. Throughout history, many cultures viewed the wolf as symbolic of God or spiritual beings; however, there were exceptions. Some cultures especially in Europe saw the wolf as a symbol of evil, perhaps even the devil. Somehow, Nathan felt that this wolf meant no harm and was just watching over him and the family.

## Chapter Fifty-two

The waiting is the hardest part.

Yeah, the waiting is the hardest part.

-Tom Petty

By late afternoon the sunny morning sky had given way to a dull gray overcast which only served to increase Nathan's restlessness and feelings of dread. Even Jake seemed jittery and uneasy. Nathan had called Alexis several times and when his phone buzzed, he assumed it was her, but he was surprised to see that the call was from his friend Leonard Marshall.

"Hey, Leonard, good to hear from you. What's up?"

"I was just checking in, buddy. I hadn't heard from you in a while, so I thought I'd call and see how you are doing."

"I am really glad you called. A lot has happened since you headed back to Lubbock. I think you knew that my position at the university was terminated, right?"

"Yes, unfortunately I knew that, and I think that was about the last I heard from you.

For the next twenty minutes Nathan brought his friend up to speed. "I think that brings you up to date. Now, I am just waiting...waiting for Murdoc and the red dragon to show up. I thought sure he'd come last night, but he didn't."

"I think you are right about him wanting to destroy you, but do you think he will do it or will he use the witch?"

"I am pretty sure he will do it himself. If anything, I think Lurleen has had a change of heart. I think maybe she feels sorry for me and even seems to want to help me. She thinks Murdoc is angry at her for refusing to kill me herself, which she says she never agreed to do."

"Do you trust her? I mean she had no trouble seducing you and ruining your career at the university."

"You are right about that, Leonard, but I think she has come to see that I never meant any harm to her, and that I am not like her father. Maybe she has finally seen how evil Murdoc really is.

"I hope you are right. Is there anything I can do to help? I can come there if you need me or think there is something I can do."

"Thanks, my friend, but this is something I must deal with, and I can't put you or anyone else in harm's way. Alexis or I will let you know once it is over and done...hopefully it will be me.

"Okay. Just know I will be thinking about you and I will be ready to head your way at a moment's notice if you need me."

After he ended the call, Nathan felt even more anxious to just "get it over with". He didn't know how much more waiting he could handle. He felt certain that this is what it would feel like to be waiting to undergo an extremely risky surgery. He walked back to the garage and checked on his weaponry. Everything was in readiness. The shotgun was loaded and the spear was still resting where he had left it in the work bench vise. *Damn it, Murdoc, where in hell are you?* Neither Murdoc nor the red dragon made an appearance as afternoon faded slowly into evening. Nathan was beginning to think that he had misjudged Murdoc's reaction. Perhaps he wasn't coming after all. It could be that Leonard was right. Taking the gun with him, he and Jake went back into the house for a quick meal. After rinsing the dishes and putting them into the dishwasher, he looked down at Jake, "Well, big guy, are you ready for some more watch dog duty?" Jake just looked up and wagged his tail. "I'll take that for a yes," Nathan said with a chuckle. "Okay, let's do it."

By nine o'clock, the moon had slipped out from behind the clouds and the only things that had grabbed his attention was a large owl that swooped noiselessly over the yard. Still no sign of Murdoc or his beastly avatar. He was about to give up and return to the house when he noticed considerable noise and motion coming from one of the taller trees behind the garage. It was almost as if a violent wind was shaking just that one tree. He quickly shined the flashlight beam over the tree branches but saw nothing. Nathan was certain that it wasn't his imagination since Jake had heard it too and had run to investigate. *So, now it begins at last!*

Chapter Fifty-three

A lost battle is a battle one thinks

one has lost.

-Jean Paul Sartre

Although he saw nothing in the trees, Nathan felt certain it had to be Murdoc's dragon avatar that had landed there. He could hear Jake barking excitedly as he entered the garage to retrieve his gun and spear. Stepping through the door he caught a glimpse of movement to his left, but before he could turn his head, he felt a searing pain and saw stars, then blackness. When the darkness abated Nathan felt pain and swelling in his head and neck. He tried to move but realized he could not. With considerable effort he forced his body up on his elbows and looked around. He could see that his ankles were bound with plastic flex cuffs. From the pain in his wrists, he knew his hands were bound in a similar fashion. Duct tape had had been wrapped tightly over his mouth so that the only sound he could make was a low mumble. From out of the shadows stepped a figure dressed in black that he immediately recognized...Murdoc! Instantly adrenaline cleared his vision and his mind. Nathan realized that he was completely helpless, and Jake was

outside the garage with the door closed, unable to help him. Murdoc had come in person, not as the dragon, and it seemed to Nathan that the battle was over before it began. He had lost and would surely die.

Murdoc loomed over him with a crooked smile. "Well, Dr. Richards...I told you that I would see you again, but as you can plainly see you are the one who is bound this time and I am free. Yes, I am free to exact my revenge. You may be wondering why I am so determined to have my revenge. You may not realize it but I have known you, at least indirectly, much longer than you know. You and others like you...well, let's just say you have been something of an irritant that must be eliminated. I am sure you remember your little adventure in Lubbock." Murdoc paused as if waiting for a reply. Then he laughed and continued speaking "Oh, yes, the tape makes it hard for you to answer, but

your eyes tell me you recall. I must say I have enjoyed getting to know you better even if you have been a source of some frustration. Some of my opponents have been so weak, no challenge at all...but you, well, at least you made me work a little. You will die soon, but before you do, I want you to know what it is like to suffer. But, take heart, Dr. Richards.

Your suffering will not be totally in vain. You will learn something important before you die. You wanted to learn about what you call evil from me and so you will. You will learn that in this world, evil wins."

Outside Jake's barking increased and he scratched relentlessly on the garage door. The noise seemed to annoy Murdoc but he was enjoying his little lecture too much to stop and silence Jake. He walked over to the work bench where the spear Nathan had fabricated waited in the vise. "Dr. Richards, I recall that you did some research on individuals you considered to be very evil…men like Hitler and Stalin, and you even included Vlade the Impaler. Perhaps you knew about his penchant for impaling his enemies. He was quite good at it. He knew how to make the pain last a good while before his victim died. Sometimes they might last for several hours. We'll find out how long you will last. Of course, a lot depended on the method he used. There was the vertical, bottom to top method and the horizontal method or front to back. I always thought the bottom to top method of impalement was the most interesting as long as you stopped before you got up to the heart." Nathan felt terror like he had never felt before. It was like being trapped in a terrible nightmare and desperately wishing to wake up and find it was just a dream. There was no waking up from this nightmare however. Outside the garage Jake's barking and clawing at the door had reached a truly frantic level such that Murdoc was clearly annoyed. "Damn dog! I've got to shut him up before the neighbors decide to investigate." Murdoc picked up the hunting knife that was lying on the work bench with the obvious intent of stabbing Jake. In a rage Murdoc flung open the door and no sooner did it open than Jake launched his full ninety-pound body at Murdoc. The force of his assault caused Murdoc to stumble backwards where he tripped over Nathan's body lying on the floor. In desperation he grabbed for something to stop his fall but to no avail. Jake continued his attack until Murdoc became impaled on the home-made spear resting in the work bench vise. Murdoc screamed in obvious pain and shock as the point of the spear emerged through the front of his chest cavity. For a few desperate seconds Murdoc struggled to free himself while Jake slumped slowly to the garage floor. In the assault Murdoc had managed to plunge the knife deep into Jake's side. Nathan watched in horror as Jake's blood flowed freely onto the floor. He screamed into the tape gag as Jake ceased all movement. As Jake breathed his last something strange occurred. Murdoc's body began to pixilate and gradually dematerialize. In a matter of moments his body vanished completely, leaving only some of the fabric from the clothes he wore and a dark red stain on the end of the spear. Nathan struggled will all the strength he could muster but he was unable to free himself. Finally, he collapsed as grief overwhelmed him. Jake lay still at his side as Nathan lapsed back into unconsciousness. When his vision cleared again, Nathan realized it was morning and he thought he heard someone calling his name. The garage door opened wide and there in the dim early morning light stood a most beautiful woman. He blinked to clear his vision and saw that it was Lurleen Montgomery.

With a look of surprise and horror she knelt at his side. She unwrapped the tape over his mouth and he was finally able to speak, "Lurleen, is Jake alive? Help me get free. I've got to get him to the vet!"

"Nathan, I am afraid it is too late for Jake. I am sorry. Let me cut off those cuffs. Murdoc must have been here. Where is he now?" As she asked, she gave a wary look at the spear still held firmly in the work bench vise.

Nathan wrapped his arms around his old German Shepherd as soon as she freed his hands. "Oh, Jake, my old buddy. You saved my life but lost yours!" Nathan wept bitterly as he held the cold and lifeless body of his beloved dog.

Finally, Lurleen tried to gently pull Nathan away from Jake as she spoke softly, "Nathan, there is nothing you can do for Jake now, but we need to call the police and an ambulance. You've got a pretty nasty gash on the back of your head."

Some fifteen minutes after her call an ambulance and two police care came roaring up the driveway with sirens blaring. While the paramedic tended to Nathan, the police officers began trying to figure out what had happened in the Richard's garage. After putting a bandage on Nathan's head and checking his vital signs, the paramedic loaded him into the ambulance and whisked him away to the university hospital. Lurleen gently covered Jake's body with an old blanket as she pleaded with the police to take her to the hospital too. On the way there, the police continued to question her. They were clearly confused by what they had seen. At the hospital the attending physician took x-rays and eventually concluded that Nathan had suffered a concussion. He recommended an overnight stay just to make sure there would be no complications. Nathan agreed but asked for his phone so that he could call Alexis and let her know where he was and that he was basically okay. Once settled in his room, the two police officers asked if they could complete their initial investigation. Nathan agreed and told them as much as he could or as much as he thought they would believe. Unknown to Nathan another police team had been summoned to Central prison to investigate what appeared to be a very unusual murder. While on their routine early morning rounds, the guards found Jeremiah Murdoc lying on the floor of his cell dead from an apparent stab wound. The situation was very puzzling to both the guards and the police. Murdoc was dressed all in black which was not any form of prison issue clothing. There was no sign that anyone had forced their way into his cell. His death had been caused by a round puncture wound through the chest, entry through the back. Whatever caused the wound was not present in the cell. Further investigation revealed that no inmates on the unit where Murdoc was housed could have gotten out of their cells, a fact confirmed by a careful review of video camera footage. Authorities were clearly baffled by the apparent murder.

Later in the day, Durham police investigators attempted to put the two events together since they seemed to be connected. Nathan Richards had reported that he was attacked by Jeremiah Murdoc and that it was his dog who ultimately saved him by pushing Murdoc against the spear which Nathan had made. The police even found fabric on the spear tip that matched the clothing Murdoc was wearing when his body was discovered in the prison. As they dug deeper into the case, they found that Lurleen Montgomery had filed a complaint against Nathan Richards which ultimately led to his being fired at the university, oddly enough that same Lurleen Montgomery was the one who found Richards and called for help. Nothing seemed to add up. It was like trying to put together a picture puzzle using pieces from several different puzzles.

## Chapter Fifty-four

*I felt like I had died too,*

*and they just forgot to bury me.*

*-Author unknown*

Gloom hung heavy over the Richards's household as Alexis brought Jake's ashes home in an urn from the vet's office. Nathan sat on the sofa, his head in his hands. David stayed in nis room and tried to read. Lizzy did her best to cheer her father up by bringing him a picture of Jake which she drew with Crayolas. Nathan thanked her and tried to smile but inside his pain only deepened. Alexis set the urn down on the kitchen table then addressed her husband, "Nathan, how is your head? Do you need some Tylenol? Oh, I was wondering…have you called Dr. Marshall in Lubbock? He will want to know you are okay."

"Uh, no. I haven't called him. I'll do so after while."

"I don't want to bug you but I think it would be good to call him and then let's take the kids and get some ice cream or something…anything to get out of the house.

Nathan smiled and got up from the sofa. "Okay, you are right. I'll call him and then we'll do something." Nathan called Leonard Marshall and talked for the next fifteen minutes. After his call ended, he gave a weak smile and then called out, "Who wants ice cream?"

David and Elizabeth both responded enthusiastically, and Lizzy called out, "Let's go the Sweet Charlie's. It is my favorite."

The prospect of ice cream seemed to brighten everyone's mood. There is nothing like ice cream to alleviate a depressed mood. Once at Sweet Charlie's ice cream parlor Lizzy seemed to literally dance with excitement. There were just too many tempting choices. While the rest of the family made their decisions Nathan walked out to the newspaper stand outside on the sidewalk. Such things like newspaper stands had all but disappeared but this one still remained. There was only one paper inside but its headline caught Nathan's attention. He fished out a dollar and fed the machine. Taking out the paper he looked briefly at the headlines then folded the paper in half, put it under his arm, and re turned to the ice cream parlor.

Alexis noticed his brief departure and the paper under his arm and inquired, "Something interesting in the news?"

Nathan nodded, "Maybe. Looks like I made the news. We can read it later. I don't want the kids to see it."

With a look of concern Alexis agreed then asked him what flavor he was getting.

Nathan smiled, "Vanilla. I always get vanilla."

David had already started eating his double dip salted caramel but paused long enough to voice support of Nathan's choice. "I like vanilla too, but this caramel is soooo good!"

The ice cream now consumed, the family started home. Nathan placed the newspaper in the very back of the Honda where it would be pretty much out of the sight of the two children. Once home Nathan took the paper to his bedroom and began reading the story. Sure, enough it was about Murdoc's death and the surrounding mysteries. On page two it mentioned Nathan and what had happened to him and Jake. The story only mentioned that Lurleen Montgomery had found Nathan but did not mention any details about the complaints she had filed against Nathan. The article concluded by stating that police were still investigating Murdoc's mysterious death. After he read the article he told Alexis about it, but she just shrugged her shoulders and replied, "I guess that is pretty much it, isn't it? Maybe the nightmare is finally over. By the way have you thought any more about where you might want to spread Jake's ashes. I put the urn on the mantle for now."

"I haven't decided for sure. I guess part of me is delaying the decision because I just can't accept the fact that he is gone." As he spoke, he wiped away the tears that had begun to leak from the corner of his eyes. "Talk about loyalty and laying down your life for someone you love…"

"Yeah, we could learn a lot from Jake about love and loyalty. He was a great dog, and he saved your life by stopping Murdoc. I know I'll never forget what he did for you and our family."

Nathan hugged his wife, holding her close for several seconds. "Maybe we'll spread his ashes out near the edge of the woods. That was one of his favorite spots and it was near the place where we saw that wolf a few times. I think there was something special about that spot,"

Alexis nodded, "I agree. That seems like an appropriate place all right. Tonight, let's roast hot dogs at the fire ring and then we can all gather to spread the ashes. You were a preacher once so maybe you could say a few words. Okay?"

"I'll try to come up with something, but I don't think I can get through it without crying."

"That's okay. Big boys can cry too. "After the last hot dog was eaten, Alexis brought out Hershey bars and marshmallows. "Who wants smores?"

When nobody could eat another bite, Nathan stood up to make his an announcement. "Everyone, listen up. We are going to have a special ceremony to honor our dear friend Jake. We all loved him and now we will honor him as both a friend and a hero. Then, we will set him free so he can return home to God." He felt the tears start to run down his cheek and he brushed them away with the sleeve of his shirt. "Come on everybody. Mom and I have picked the perfect spot." Nathan led the family to the location he and Alexis had agree upon. Once there, he asked the family to join him in prayer. He took a deep breath and then exhaled slowly before speaking. "Heavenly Father, when you created all the animals of this world, you said that it was good. When you made Jake and gave him to us as a little puppy, it was very good. Jesus once said that 'greater love hath no man than to lay down his life for a friend'. Jake gave his life to protect me. Jake could show no greater love than that. Jake also helped us rescue David in his time of distress. Dear Lord, we will miss Jake so, but now we must return him to you. Dust to dust, ashes to ashes. Amen." Alexis handed Nathan the urn and with tears streaming down his face, he spread Jake's ashes at the foot of a large oak.

With the innocence of a child Lizzy looked up and asked, "Daddy, will Jake go to heaven just like my goldfish Timmy did?"

Nathan smiled warmly, "Yes, sweetie, he certainly will, and Timmy will be there to greet him." Nathan's answer seemed to please Lizzy, and David smiled the knowing smile of an adolescent. The little ceremony completed; Nathan suggested that they all go back inside and watch a good movie. Everyone heartily agreed. When the movie ended about ten o'clock, Alexis tucked Lizzy in bed while Nathan bid David goodnight. After they both returned to the living room, Nathan suggested that the two of them watch the last of the fire burn down and share a glass of wine or two. Outside it was dark but the sky was clear and the full moon lent a good deal of light to the Richard's yard. The quiet time they shared was so wonderfully peaceful Nathan added a couple of logs to the fire to keep it going a while longer. The dry oak logs caught fire quickly sending a stream of sparks high into the night sky. Nathan stoked the fire a few times and as he turned to sit by Alexis he froze, staring out at the woods where they had spread Jakes's ashes. "Oh, my God, Lexi! Look at that. Do you see what I think I see?" Nathan pointed excitedly towards the woods.

Alexis stood and shaded her eyes from the bright fire light and she whispered, "Nathan, I don't believe what I am seeing. It's Jake and the wolf! I am sure of it, but how can it be?"

I don't know Lexi, but we are both seeing it. They are there just watching over us. It's as if they want to check on us and let us know that they are okay too." Nathan and Alexis began to cry but this time their tears were tears of joy, and Nathan knew in his heart that God was real and was incarnate in all of God's creation. "Lexi, I think maybe we can both sleep in peace tonight." Jake and the wolf lingered a moment or two longer then turned and disappeared into the woods. Hand in hand Alexis and Nathan returned to the house. Once in bed Nathan held Alexis close and whispered, "Lexi, I have been thinking about something and what we witnessed tonight has convinced me it is right."

What is it? Tell me," Alexis answered excitedly.

I think we should adopt David if he is agreeable."

"Oh, Nathan. That is a wonderful idea and it means so much coming from you. After what you…we have all been through, I was afraid to ask. I am pretty certain he'll be overjoyed. He and Lizzy have already gotten pretty close. I think he enjoys the role of big brother."

"Okay. We'll ask him in the morning, but before we do, I'd like to spend a little time with him. You have been around him so much more than I have, and I know he cares about you. Instead of taking him to the Boys Club I was thinking I might take him fishing again. That way we can talk. I can see if he has any questions or reservations, and I can also assure him how much I want him to be an official member of our family."

"I think that is a great idea. I love you so much."

"In spite of all that has happened and all my mistakes and you can still say that…"

"I can say it and I mean it!

## Chapter Fifty-five

*If evil takes possession of someone,*

*that person, in turn, may spread evil to*

*everybody around him.*

-Mother Teresa

David Charles was thrilled by the prospect of fishing, so Nathan packed rods and reel, his tackle box and a cooler with sandwiches and drinks in the Honda. He hugged Alexis and Lizzy goodbye and then he and David drove out. The plan was to head to a pair of medium-sized lakes surrounded by camping areas about forty-five minutes east of town. Remembering their earlier fishing expedition, David was excited and full of questions. Traffic was light since it was still early on a Thursday morning, but Nathan had noticed that an old, red Dodge truck had been following them rather closely for several miles. At first, he thought little about it until the truck came uncomfortably close. Since there was very little oncoming traffic, Nathan wondered why the truck didn't pass them

He wanted to swear at the driver of the truck but restrained himself for David's sake. Spotting a wide spot on the shoulder of the road, he looked in his rear-view mirror and then at David. "David, I am going to pull over and let this guy pass me. He has been riding my bumper for a good while." David looked up and nodded. Nathan slowed down and then pulled off the road onto a wide gravel covered area on the side of the road. As he did, he saw that it was an area where several mailboxes were situated. To his dismay and growing anxiety Nathan saw that the truck also pulled off the road behind him. The driver of the old Dodge truck was a white male but that was about all the detail that Nathan could make out. The driver did not exit the truck; he just sat still and waited for Nathan to decide his next move. "That SOB. What the heck does he think he's doing?" Floor-boarding the Honda, Nathan shot back onto the road showering the red pickup with gravel. Back on the road, Nathan accelerated rapidly to 70 then 80 miles per hour. The pick up quickly caught up and resumed its position just off Nathan's rear bumper. Nathan's heart was pounding as he realized the situation had become clearly dangerous. He looked over at David and barked an order, "David, grab my phone and dial 911. See if you can get the police and tell them someone is trying to run us off the road. Tell them we are Old Lake Road about 15 miles east of town. After what seemed like an eternity, David was transferred through to the sheriff's dispatcher who attempted to get a clearer picture of their emergency and approximate location. Rounding a sharp bend in the road, Nathan struggled to maintain control as the Honda's tires squealed in protest. Nathan frantically searched for a side road or turn-off but he saw none. The red pickup made a futile effort to pass Nathan but the attempt made it clear that the driver wanted to run Nathan off the road. Rounding another bend in the road Nathan saw a wooden one-lane bridge about 150 yards ahead and it gave him an idea. Within seconds before reaching the bridge, he slammed on the brakes. His sudden attempt to stop must have confused the driver of the pickup who swerved abruptly to his left in order to avoid a collision.

The driver of the pickup was not totally successful in avoiding Nathan's car; the right edge of his front bumper clipped the edge of Nathan's Honda, causing the truck to spin out of control. Unable to stop the spin the pickup's rear end struck the railing of the wooden bridge which shattered like match sticks. The pickup went airborne and landed with a tremendous crash on the bank of the small creek below. Nathan had been able to stop mere inches before hitting the bridge. Cautiously he exited his car and walked to the bridge. He could see the red pickup resting on its side on the creek bank. The right front tire was still spinning. The driver's side of the truck's cab had been partially crushed by the impact of the truck when it hit the creek bank, and Nathan could see no movement inside the vehicle. David crossed the road and stood beside Nathan.

In the distance they could hear the wail of sirens as a sheriff's car approached. A few moments later a black and white police cruiser stopped behind Nathan's Honda, followed shortly thereafter by a second sheriff's car. The first officer ran to Nathan and David and then seeing they were okay, he peered down into the creek at the wrecked pickup. The second officer joined them and after a few questions, the two deputies edged their way down the embankment to the wreckage. After several minutes, one officer returned to the bridge where Nathan and David were standing and reported that the driver appeared to be dead. He then went to his patrol car and radioed for a wrecker and an ambulance.

While they waited for the wrecker and ambulance the deputies questioned Nathan at some length. There wasn't much he could tell them since he had no idea of the identity of the driver or his possible motivation. It wasn't until later in the evening when Nathan received a call of the sheriff's office telling him that they had found a note in the truck with Nathan's name, address, and phone number on it. The sheriff identified the driver as Paul Chrisman, a name which was totally unfamiliar to Richards. Two days later the local news media reported the event on the six o'clock news. The reporter noted that Chrisman had been released from prison only one week before the episode. What struck Nathan as particularly interesting was the fact that Chrisman had been incarcerated in Central Prison, the same prison where Murdoc had been held.

After watching the news, Nathan turned to Alexis with a look of surprise on his face. "Lexi, do you suppose Murdoc sent Chrisman to kill me?"

"That sure seems like a possibility, but why would he do that since he had planned to do the job himself?"

"Good question…maybe Chrisman was his backup plan in case he was unable to do the job for some reason." Nathan scratched his head and then whispered, "Or maybe he or his spirit sent Chrisman to do the job *after* Murdoc's death. That is a thought that is almost too scary to contemplate."

Oh, my God…you mean a sort of demonic resurrection?"

"Maybe."

"If you are right, could that mean he'll recruit another hit man?"

"I wish I knew. I once read something…I think it was in a Stephen King novel that said *you might beat the devil once but not twice.* I sure hope that isn't true. If it is, then I have put you, Lizzy, and David in real danger."

"Well, we haven't talked to him about adoption, so maybe we could mention that to him when we do."

"I really think we should. After what he witnessed when Chrisman tried to kill us, I think we owe it to him to mention the possible risks."

The next day, Alexis and Nathan sat down with David and told him how much they would like to adopt him into their family. He immediately responded that he had given up hope of ever having a forever family, but that he would love to be part of their family. There were hugs all around, and then Nathan spoke softly, "David, there is something you should know before we make it official. Becoming one of us may put you at some risk."

David's face abruptly looked troubled, "What do you mean?"

"You obviously remember that guy who tried to run us off the road. Well, it is possible that the man from the prison, Jeremiah Murdoc, sent him to kill me, and it is also possible that he might send another hit man to try again. I don't know for sure, but he may have been sent to hurt the rest of my family as well."

David protested, "But isn't that man in the prison dead? How could he send someone else?"

"We don't know that he can or would, but we just thought you should know there is some risk."

David looked near tears as he continued, "I have lived most of my life with risk, risk of abuse, risk of rejection. You and Miss Alexis have been the only people who ever really cared about me, so it is worth the risk. Besides, maybe I can help protect us."

Okay, David, we'll start the process on Monday and make it official as soon as possible."

Chapter Fifty-six

Can the Ethiopian change his skin, or the leopard his spots? Then may ye also do good, that are accustomed to doing evil.

-Jeremiah 13:33

Lurleen Montgomery wandered into The Blue Devil tavern and slipped into a booth near the front door. Since it was early afternoon, the tavern was empty except for the bartender who was cleaning and disinfecting table and bar surfaces. When Lurleen entered, he looked up with an expression of mild surprise on his face, but he greeted her warmly, "What can I get you, Miss?" The bartender walked over to Lurleen and seemed to recognize her. "Oh, you've been here a couple of times, haven't you? I never forget a face…at least not one as pretty as yours."

Ordinarily Lurleen would have enjoyed flirting with a handsome young man, but on this afternoon, she was distracted by a host of troubling thoughts, some expressing fear, others guilt, and still others she couldn't quite identify. She glanced up at the bartender and smiled weakly. "I'd like a dark draft."

"Sixteen or twenty ounces?"

"Might as well make it twenty."

"Coming right up. I'll bring you a fresh bowl of peanuts too."

The bartender brought her drink and the peanuts and paused as if hoping to engage her in conversation, but she showed no interest. Lurleen quaffed her beer with a contented sigh. Before she knew it her glass was empty and she ordered a second. The alcohol began to relax her and still some of the conflicting voices in her mind. The one voice she couldn't quiet spoke loudly of her guilt, guilt about ruining the career and maybe the life of Nathan Richards. She had never really been bothered by guilt over seducing a man, so why now? Did she actually care for Nathan? Had she known that the recent attempt on his life by a hit man apparently sent by Murdoc, she might have experienced even greater fear. Still, she had experienced considerable anxiety caused by her memory of the threats Murdoc had made towards her. After downing the second twenty-ounce draft, she paid the bartender and walked slowly to her car where she sat for several minutes before driving away. *What do I do? Where do I go?* Lurleen left the Blue Devil and headed in the direction of the Duke campus, driving on auto pilot. She parked in a student lot and walked in the direction of the chapel. Although she had no purpose in mind, she somehow felt herself drawn towards the famous campus icon. The campus grounds were bustling with students heading to and from their classes. The iconic Duke chapel was scheduled frequently for many different activities. On this particular afternoon the chapel choir was holding a practice, so Lurleen slipped into one of the unoccupied pews nearest the entrance. She sat quietly, listening to the choir as it ended one hymn and began another. Lurleen did not know the name of the hymn but the opening lines caught her attention.

> *"Will you come and follow me if I but call your name?*
>
> *Will you go where you don't know and never be the same?"*

A verse or two later she heard another line that captured her awareness.

> *"Will you leave yourself behind If I but call your name?"*
>
> *"Will you go where you don't know and never be the same?"*

While she found the hymn to be quite beautiful, she couldn't help wondering why those particular lines had grabbed her attention so forcefully. She wasn't at all sure if she truly believed in God or God's providence. *Why am I here? What is it about those verses?* Troubling questions, but questions without answers. Lurleen continued to sit as the choir practice came to an end, still emersed in her thoughts. Almost as if in a trance she got up from the pew and exited the chapel. Eventually she found her way back to her car, and as she approached it, she noticed a man sitting on the BMW's fender. He was not anyone she knew and he seemed much older than a typical student. His appearance was disheveled and she started to ask the man what he was doing, but before she could utter a sound, he turned and looked her in the eyes.

"Ah, there you are Miss Montgomery. I have a message for you." The man's voice lacked emotion. His facial expression also had a blank, almost lifeless quality to it.

"I don't know you, and why are you sitting on my car waiting for me?

"As I said...I've got a message for you. It's is from your teacher...your mentor. So, listen up, bitch! You reneged on your end of the bargain you made with him...there'll be a penalty for breaking that agreement.

"Lurleen felt a wave of fear which she tried hard to conceal when she replied. "I don't know who you are or whom you represent, and I don't appreciate being threatened! Get off my car before I call for the campus cops or maybe do something worse." The unidentified "messenger" merely stood still leering at her and then took a couple of steps in her direction. Reflexively Lurleen drew on her power as a witch casting a spell which caused the stranger to stumble backwards and then fall on the curb. With a look of genuine surprise, he picked himself up and began a hasty retreat, but he stopped abruptly and glared at Lurleen. Feeling a surge of confidence fueled by her anger, she shouted another warning, "I'd better not see you again or I will do more than give you a gentle push. "As she watched the man retreat across the parking lot and disappear among the parked cars, Lurleen wondered whether she could ever be anything other than what she was, a witch? When she had felt threatened, she automatically drew on her power as a witch. She also began to wonder if she was in real danger even though she believed that Jeremiah Murdoc was dead. Was he still able to reach out to her from beyond the grave or was this individual someone he recruited to scare her before his death? She wished she could talk to Nathan about her situation but doubted that he would agree to meet with her or even talk to her on the phone. She got into her car and locked the door, then finally decided to call Nathan. *What is the worst that he can do besides hang up on me?* Much to her surprise Nathan answered, his voice sounding business-like.

"What do you want, Lurleen?"

"Nathan...uh...I really need to talk to you. Some strange things are happening to me, and they might have some implications for you too."

"What do you mean? What strange things and what could it have anything to do with me?"

"Nathan, I know you have little reason to trust me, but I feel like I am changing in some way, and then just a few minutes ago I had a visitor that I think was sent somehow by Murdoc. I can't help wondering if somehow Murdoc can reach beyond the grave."

Nathan was intrigued by Lurleen's description of the man who threatened her. What she was reporting bore some similarity to his experience with the man named Paul Chrisman. Chrisman was clearly a real man but Nathan was certain he was sent by Murdoc either before his death or possibly even after it, "What did your messenger tell you?"

"He told me that I failed to keep my agreement with Dr. Murdoc and that there would be a severe consequence for that. You know I did make a deal with Murdoc. He agreed to show me how to increase my power as a witch in return for my bringing you down. I never thought I was to do any more than shame or embarrass you, but Murdoc changed the agreement. I told him from the start I would never do more than that. He changed his demand and wanted me to kill you, but I refused."

"Okay. We don't need to get into all that again. Are there other unusual things happening to you?"

"Yes, and I don't know what they mean or what they might involve. It's almost as if God is somehow calling me, reaching out to me."

"Calling you? Calling you to do what?"

"I don't know…maybe to leave witchery behind. I guess I hoped you might help me understand…you know… *discernment*,"

Nathan felt at a loss as to how to respond to Lurleen's plea. It seemed sincere, but he wondered what he could possibly tell her. He had no way of knowing if God was calling her to change her ways, and he sure didn't know what to make of the threat she had just received. The one thing he did feel sure of was that he may not have seen the last of Jeremiah Murdoc or the forces he represented. *Maybe I can't expect to beat the devil twice.* Reluctantly, he agreed to meet with her somewhere on campus, perhaps the chapel. Before he could suggest the university chapel, Lurleen offered it as a possible meeting spot. It seemed to Nathan to be a relatively safe location, and it was one where they had both been drawn recently. Nathan and Lurleen met outside the front entrance to the chapel but decided to take a walk across campus rather than go inside. The late afternoon was unseasonably mild and there were a number of students milling about the grounds, some walking, some tossing Frisbees, and others just sitting and talking. As Nathan took in the scene, he felt pangs of regret and loss as he realized how much he missed being a part of a university. Finally, he broke their silence, "Lurleen, what did you want to talk to me about? You made it sound important.

"Nathan...uh, Dr. Richards...I feel as if I am changing in some ways I can't explain."

"Why, the sudden formality calling me Dr. Richards?"

"Well, I am conflicted in a number of ways, I guess. Recently I have begun feeling real regret about what I did to you."

"It's a little late for that, isn't it?"

"Yes. In addition to regret about how I treated you, I have begun to wonder if I can really change. I know that I am a witch and as such, fundamentally different from other people. I realize I have abilities which I can use to achieve my own personal desires, abilities which can be used to control and even harm others. I am wondering if I can leave all that behind? I guess you could call it a kind of repentance. I don't know if I believe in God or His providence, but I have felt something tugging me in that direction."

I don't know much about witches since you are the only one have ever known. I realize you are different, but I don't know how much you can change. It's kinda the old question about can a leopard change its spots"

"Yeah, and that question presumes an answer…you can't change what you were made to be. I may be biologically different from most people. I may not even be truly human and I probably can't change that aspect of who I am. When that man threatened me, I automatically used my power as a witch to protect myself. I didn't have to think consciously before I acted. So, maybe the only question is can I change my ways…how I think and behave? You are the psychologist, the clergy person. What do you think?

"I would guess you can make some changes, and it appears you have already made some. Even a few weeks ago I don't think you'd be asking me about such matters or apologizing to me. So, maybe change is possible. It might be like learning to love God if you have lived a basically evil life. You can't change all at once, overnight. I once read that if you want to love God, start with simple, small things like loving birds, trees, or dogs and then graduate to people before you try to love God. Did you ever see that old movie called *What About Bob?*"

"Baby steps?"

"Yeah. That's the one. It was a funny movie but the idea of baby steps leading to bigger changes is not a bad strategy."

Nathan and the witch Lurleen Montgomery continued their walk, mostly in silence. Eventually, Nathan broke the silence, "I really must be going, but I am glad we had a chance to talk. I sense that you really are sincere in what you have just told me, and for what it's worth, I forgive you for what you did to me. At the same time, I have to acknowledge my part in what happened. You are a beautiful and charming young woman and you probably didn't need to use your spells to lure me in."

"Thank you, professor. I appreciate that more than you could know."

Chapter Fifty-seven

Sooner or later even the fastest runners

have to stand and fight.

-Stephen King

After their walk both Nathan and Lurleen left with troubling questions, questions about their safety, their future and even their worth as people. In a way, they both wished they could run away from their individual circumstances and have the opportunity for a "do over." Both understood at some deep level that life never gives us "do overs" like the old magic slates we had as kids. If we didn't like what we wrote or drew, we just lifted the page of the magic slate and presto, we got a fresh clean start.

After leaving Nathan, Lurleen walked to her car and started to drive away but instead, she turned off the car's ignition, exited from her BMW, and headed for the Gray Building, the home of the theology department. As if driven by some unseen force, she entered the building and marched straight to the dean's office. She stopped at the secretary's desk and asked to see Dean Albritton, saying it was urgent. The Dean's secretary recognized her immediately and instructed her to have a seat while she spoke to the dean. She returned after a moment and ushered Lurleen into the dean's office.

Dean Albritton greeted her warmly, much to her surprise, and his receptivity encouraged her to "lay her cards on the table. "Over the next half hour Lurleen explained to the dean that she had basically entrapped Nathan and then reported his actions as unwanted sexual advances. When questioned about her abrupt confession, she explained that she had literally compelled Nathan to do what he did but that the dean would never believe her explanation. After she completed her explanation, she asked if it were at possible for Nathan to be reinstated as a faculty in the department.

Dean Albritton sat back in his chair and looked as if he had eaten too big a meal for comfort. "Wow, Miss Montgomery. That is quite a story! I would like to understand how it was that you could compel Dr. Richard's to do what he did. Could you explain? I will try to listen with an open mind."

"In simple terms, Dean…I am a witch. I doubt you believe in such things, but it is true. If you'd like I can demonstrate a little of my skills for you."

Dean Albritton's expression changed abruptly from one of curiosity to apprehension. "What sort of demonstration do you have in mind?"

"Nothing dangerous, I assure you. I just want to show you that I can compel people to do things that I want them to do. Maybe if I do that, you'll believe that I made Dr. Richard's do the things that got him fired." "I guess that would be okay. Please proceed."

Lurleen cast a spell that caused the dean to rise from his chair and go to his bookcase. Once at the bookcase she had him withdraw a large leather-bound Bible and toss it on the floor. The Bible landed with a loud thud which seemed to break the spell. The dean looked down at the Bible which lay on the floor and then at Lurleen. "You did that? Without any conscious thought, I just got up, took the Bible and then dropped it on the floor. Clearly that is something I would not do on my own volition. I am stunned to tell you the truth."

"Do you want another demonstration?"

"No! Please. You have made your point and I am impressed. How long have you known you were a…witch?"

"In reality…for a long time, but only in the last several months have begun to be fully aware of who I am and what I can do."

"I believe you are what you claim to be, but why did you do what you did to Professor Richards? Had he done something to you, something you were angry about or resented?"

"He had done nothing to me. In fact, he was a good teacher, perhaps my best teacher."

"Well, why on earth did you do what you did and then report him?"

"This is the part that is hard to explain." Lurleen reported as best she could about Jeremiah Murdoc and his role as her "mentor". She went on the explain the deal she made with him. To her surprise, the dean did not seem to scoff at or reject her explanation. In fact, he seemed to give it some thoughtful consideration.

"It may surprise you, Miss Montgomery, but I think there could be some truth to what you just told me. I know that Professor Richards had several meetings with Dr. Murdoc in hopes of developing his theory about evil. Then there were those stories in the paper about Murdoc's mysterious death. Miss. Montgomery, I am a man of faith and faith requires that we sometimes believe in things which can't be seen, touched, or proven. As to your request to have Professor Richards reinstated, that isn't up to me alone, but I will bring it to the attention of the disciplinary committee."

Lurleen thanked the dean profusely and then exited his office feeling almost euphoric. *Maybe I can change. Maybe God was with me just now.* On the drive back to her apartment her positive feelings began to fade as she noticed an old Ford Crown Victoria that had apparently been following her for some time. The car looked like a former police car that had seen some hard use. It was still black and white but it was now adorned with several areas of surface rust and assorted dings and dents. In order to be certain that the Crown Vic was indeed following her, Lurleen took several unnecessary turns, sometimes down back streets and alleyways. Sure enough the Crown Vic followed, but if anything it seemed to be getting closer. *I guess my warning to that chump wasn't strong enough.*

Spotting a small city park a block ahead, Lurleen decided to stop the car and get out. She exited from her BMW and waited as the Crown Vic pulled over to the curb about fifteen yards behind her. The man who exited the old Ford appeared to be the same induvial she had encountered on campus. After confirming that it was the same man Lurleen walked slowing into the park. Lurleen saw no other people in the park which appeared to be in a state of general neglect. There was a tennis court with a sagging net and weeds growing though some cracks in its surface. She continued walking past a broken swing set and see saw. At the edge of a dry creek bed she stopped, turned around, and waited, her anger increasing by the moment. The man stopped some ten yards behind her. She studied his appearance carefully. It was definitely the man she had encountered on campus. He was about fifty years of age, ill-shaven, and dressed in clothes that would be considered shabby at best. He did not speak but after standing still for a few moments, he reached into his denim jacket and pulled out a gun. Giving her a grin, he began to attach a silencer to the gun.

The man's intent was clearly obvious so Lurleen cast a binding spell causing the man to be immobilized as if he had suddenly frozen in place. She too a few cautious steps in his direction and called out, "You stupid SOB! I guess you didn't understand my warning. Now I am going to have to make sure you get the message." Channeling every bit of the rage she felt, she cast a spell like nothing she had ever done before. Lurleen raised her right arm and pointed towards the man frozen in front of her. "Bane of dragon's breath, I summon you! Burn fire, burn!" Feeling suddenly exhausted, Lurleen turned and walked towards her parked car. She stopped once and looked back at the man. He was still immobilized but she could see slight whiffs of smoke rising from his clothing, and she could smell the unmistakable odor of burning flesh. By the time she reached her car the man was clearly ablaze. "Burn in hell, you bastard," she uttered as she drove away. *I don't think he'll bother me or anyone else again.*

Safely back in her apartment Lurleen collapsed on her sofa feeling physically spent but emotionally conflicted. It hadn't been that long ago, Lurleen had felt that perhaps she could change and, at the very least, use her witchery for good, but now?! Now, she had used her power to immolate a human being. The man she had destroyed may not have been a good person, and he was clearly intent on doing her harm, but she had destroyed him. She tried to convince herself that she had merely acted in self-defense. *Surely no court would convict me of murder. It was self-defense...wasn't it?* That evening Lurleen watched a tv news report about an unidentified adult male who apparently committed suicide by setting himself on fire in a city park. The mysterious death was still under investigation by police and the Durham fire department. What made the man's death especially mysterious was the fact that a loaded pistol was found near the body, and there was no immediate evidence of any sort of flame accelerant such as gasoline or lighter fluid.

Chapter Fifty-eight

You can't get lost when you are always found.

-Grateful Dead

As with most anything the state does, it takes a lot of paperwork and time, but with an insider's push, Alexis was able to speed up David's adoption process. When the day finally came that David became an official member of the Richards's family, they held a small, informal celebration on the lawn of their home. Alexis' parents, the Richards's neighbors, Leonard Marshall, and Alexis' old friend Sandra McAfee were the invited guests. The celebration resembled a combination of agraduation and birthday party. That evening after the party, David remarked that it was the happiest day of his life. After the trash had been collected and the dishes washed, Nathan, Leonard, and Alexis gathered around the outdoor firepit and enjoyed the quiet, cool evening air. There was no wind and the clear night sky was strewn with stars. Crickets and occasional owl provided the musical accompaniment and fireflies seemed to mirror the stars above. All in all, it seemed like the perfect ending to a

beautiful day enabling Nathan and Alexis to temporarily forget about some of the horrors of their recent past. No sooner did Leonard finish his beer did Nathan dig a fresh bottle from the ice chest. He popped off the cap and started to hand it to his friend, when he froze, staring out into the darkness he remarked, "Oh, my goodness! We have visitors!"

Alexis and Leonard stared into the darkness, looking in the direction Nathan was pointing. Alexis exclaimed, "I can't see anything…oh, wait. Is that Jake and the wolf?"

Nathan nodded as he replied, "It is! It's like they came back to check on us. Maybe they knew we were having a celebration for David."

Finally, Leonard caught sight of the two canines, "Oh, yeah. Now I see them! That's amazing. It looks like they are heading back into the woods. Have you seen them before? I thought you had told me that Jake had died."

Nathan smiled and turned back to his friend, "You're right, Leonard, but we saw him once before just like we saw him tonight with the wolf. I can't explain it but that was Jake we saw, and that was the wolf we saw a number of times in the past."

Ever the proverbial professor, Leonard Marshall laughed and took a long draw from his beer and then explained, "You know that wolves are revered by many cultures, especially the native Americans of the great northwest. They believed that the spirit of the wolf was a symbol, a reminder to all of us that the greatest gifts in life are our relationships with the ones we love. The wolf always makes sure that every member of their family is protected and cared for, so it makes sense that the wolf would show up tonight as you celebrate a new member coming into your pack. I guess there is a kinship between dogs like Jake and the grey wolf."

Alexis hugged Leonard and then looked back to see if the wolf and Jake were still visible. "Leonard, I really feel like there is a lot of truth in what you said about wolves. I think the wolf has been watching over our family almost from the day we moved here, and Jake was our constant protector and a real member of our family. Jake and the wolf helped us rescue David, and there is no question that Jake saved Nathan."

The threesome lapsed into a peaceful silence, each reflecting on the day and what they had just witnessed. Even though Nathan and Leonard were scientists, they understood at some deep level that there are mysteries in life which are clearly beyond scientific, rational explanations. Eventually Alexis broke the silence as she got up and bent down to kiss her husband. "Good night, gentlemen. I am going in to check on the kids and then start getting ready for bed. Leonard, I'll get the sofa made out into a bed for you, and I'll put out an extra blanket too."

Thanks, Alexis. That is very kind of you. "After Alexis went back into the house the two friends sat quietly for a while, then Nathan got up and dug out the two remaining beers from the ice chest. "Here, Leonard. Let's finish these last beers."

Leonard accepted the last beer and then asked the question he had been wanting to ask for some time. "Nathan, what are you going to do now? Have you thought about that? Are you licensed in North Carolina?"

"Leonard, I have thought about that question a lot. I don't have a definite answer, but I know I have to do something. We can't continue to live here on just Lexi's salary alone. I have not pursued getting licensed in North Carolina, but that is something I need to do. Most days I read the want ads but haven't seen too many openings for an unlicensed, recently fired psychologist."

"Hey, it's not that bleak. You shouldn't have any trouble getting licensed, and you have lots of skill and experience. Ever think about going back into clinical work?"

"Yes, but right now I feel like I am damaged goods. Who would hire me if they looked into why I was terminated at Duke? While there weren't any legal charges made against me, it was clearly a major ethical issue."

"Have you decided not to appeal your dismissal from the university?"

"I suppose so. I don't have any basis for a legitimate appeal. I think all it would accomplish would be to open up wounds that haven't really healed yet."

"Maybe you are right. I'll keep my eyes and ears open and let you know if I run across any possibilities."

Their beers finished Nathan and Leonard got up, made sure the fire was out and then headed inside. Nathan undressed and then slipped quietly into bed. From the sound of her breathing Nathan could tell that Alexis was already asleep. Even after several beers, Nathan found sleep to be elusive. His mind kept reliving the past as if he might find some way out of his mistakes. If only he could go back in time armed with his present knowledge. *If only I knew then what I know now!*

Finally sleep overtook him, and Nathan descended into a dreamless slumber. Outside a large grey wolf passed silently through the yard as if checking to see if everything was okay, and everything was okay. One lost child had finally found his home, and Nathan's last thought before falling asleep echoed the words of the hymn he had heard in the Duke chapel.

"Whatever my lot, Thou has

taught me to say it is well, it is well with my soul."

Nathan Richards went to sleep comforted by the belief that somehow all was well, but in reality, all was not well. Some believe that in the eternal struggle between good and evil that good wins, but does it? Evil is not easily defeated. Although for one night Nathan slept well, in the recesses of his unconscious there dwelt a number of unanswered questions. Did Jeremiah Murdoc truly die and was he gone for good or could his evil spirit return? Had Murdoc arranged for one of his lackeys to kill Nathan and his family before his death or had his spirit orchestrated the attempt? There was no way to answer those questions for certain so the door was left ajar allowing anxiety to creep in. Nathan did not know it but Lurleen Montgomery wrestled with the same questions after her experience in the park. Nathan was jarred awake by his alarm clock radio which he did not recall setting the night before. As he rubbed the sleep from his eyes and Alexis stretched reflexively, Nathan heard the lines from an old Rolling Stones song from the 1960's.

"Please allow me to introduce myself

I'm a man of wealth and taste.

I've been around for a long, long year.

Stole many a man's soul and faith."

Was the sudden intrusion of the song and its lyrics merely a coincidence or a message, a warning that evil can come in many forms and guises, and has been around for a long, long time indeed? Alexis frowned as Nathan shut off the alarm, "Did you set that damn thing? It's not even six o'clock yet!"

"No", Nathan replied. "I didn't set it because I knew we didn't have to get up early on Saturday. Maybe Lizzy was playing with the radio and turned it on." Nathan chuckled as he rolled out of bed, "I used to like that song, but now..." *Could Murdoc have stolen my soul and faith?* "I might as well get up. There's no going back to sleep now."

Nathan padded into the kitchen and started the coffee maker. After a few moments, Alexis joined him in the kitchen looking very sleepy and slightly annoyed. Soon Lizzy and David would be wanting breakfast and the morning began to seem almost normal except for one missing ingredient...Jake. Nathan looked down at the mat where they used to keep Jake's food and water bowls. "I sure miss Jake. Do you think we should get another dog for Lizzy and David?"

Alexis smiled a knowing smile as she replied, "You mean get a new dog for you?

"Well, yeah. Me too, but I think the kids would really like a dog. You know how much they liked Jake, especially David. Besides they could lean some responsibility taking care of a dog."

"Okay. After breakfast you could take David and Lizzy to the animal shelter and see if there is a dog you and they might like to adopt."

After breakfast, Nathan loaded David and Lizzy into the car and headed for the Animal Protection Society shelter of Durham. During the drive Lizzy seemed especially excited about the prospect of a new dog. "Daddy, can the new dog sleep in my room? What should we name him?"

"We'll have to see, Lizzy. There may not be a dog we want. We have to get just the right one."

Once in the APS administrative office, Nathan talked with the girl at the front desk about adopting a dog. The girl at the desk, whose name was Nancy Bright, explained that currently their selection of available dogs was lower than usual, but she said with a bright smile, "We have some really nice dogs. Is there a particular breed you are interested in?"

"We had a German Shepherd for many years, and he was a great dog, but we'd certainly consider some other breeds."

As Nancy led Nathan, Lizzy, and David into the dog and puppy area, the dogs began barking excitedly as if they were all shouting, "Take me! Take me!" The dog area consisted of three rows of fairly spacious kennels which reminded Nathan a little of a small-town jail. About half of the kennels were occupied.

As the trio walked down the first aisle Lizzy ran excitedly from one row to the other, which intensified the barking. Nathan walked slowly, studying each dog while David walked ahead with his hands in his pockets until he stopped abruptly and knelt down in from of the last kennel on the row. He looked back at Nathan with abroad smile on his face, "What about this one?"

Nathan quickened his pace and then paused behind David. What he saw caused his heartbeat to quicken and tears to form at the corner of his eyes. He watched in silence as David patted the head of a large dog that appeared to be part Husky and part Shepherd. He guessed that the dog might be six or seven years old and it had been given the name "Jessie". He knelt beside David and reached his hand through the bars. The dog looked deeply into Nathan's eyes and it seemed that a special connection between man and dog had formed. "David, I think you are right! This really seems like the right one. Let's see if Lizzy agrees. Lizzy did agree and Nathan led David and Elizabeth out to the reception desk to report their choice. After completing the paper work and paying the adoption fee, the foursome climbed into Nathan's old CRV and began the journey home, Jessie's new home.

Alexis was waiting at the door when Nathan drove up the driveway. As Nathan opened the back hatch of the CRV, Jessie jumped out and looked around. Alexis hurried to meet the newest member of the family where Jessie greeted her enthusiastically. She smiled at Nathan as Jessie ran to Lizzy and then David. "I think you made a great choice. Does he have a name?"

"Well, the shelter called him Jessie which seems like a pretty good name, don't you think?"

"Sounds good to me.

Over the next several days, Jessie or Jess as the family seemed to prefer, adapted quickly to his new home. He was housebroken and responded to several commands like "sit", "stay", or "shake". Things seemed to be looking up for sure.

## Chapter Fifty-nine

And one day I'll be sleeping, when death knocks on my door, and I'll awake to find that I'm not homesick anymore. I'll be home. Going home, where I belong

-B. J. Thomas

Soon after incinerating the man who threatened her, Lurleen began to feel as if she were surrounded by a sullen darkness which invaded even her waking hours. Her nights seemed especially dark and foreboding. Even inside the chapel on campus she felt as if she were being followed. Was it real or only an apparition created by here increasingly paranoid mind? None of her spells or herbal potions seemed to help. Lurleen knew that here in Durham she was truly alone, a fish out of water. Late one night she picked up her cell phone and started to call Nathan but decided against it. As she set down her phone, she remembered something that Murdoc had once said. He had told her that she was descended from a long of powerful witches. That memory got her to wondering if she might locate one or her distant relatives or a least a coven where she might find support and perhaps some sense of security. A lengthy internet search helped her locate a coven in the Salem, Mass. area that looked promising. She resolved to make some calls in the morning to see if what she had read online was legitimate or just some weirdos. By noon of the following day Lurleen had made several calls to persons listed as part of the coven in Salem and finally spoke to someone who seemed to know of one her distant relatives. For the first time in several days Lurleen's world became brighter and she felt a genuine sense of hope. Maybe she could finally feel like she did have a family and a home. Once she had made the decision to leave Durham and travel of Salem, Lurleen made several other decisions in short order. Her first major move was to drop out of the seminary. Next, she arranged to terminate her lease on the apartment she had been living in. Finally, she decided she needed to let Nathan Richards know of her decision. Rather than call him, she sent him a lengthy text message which began with an apology for the pain she had caused him, followed by an explanation of why and where she was moving. She closed her message by informing Nathan that she had spoken to Dean Albritton taking responsibility for causing the changes in Nathan's behavior that ultimately got him fired. She wanted to tell him that she did, in fact, love him but decided against it. She proof-read her message and then hit send.

A few hours later Nathan noticed that he had received a text from Lurleen Montgomery. He felt his heart rate increase as he opened her message. He read and then reread her message. Not quite sure what he felt. Part of him wanted to breathe a sigh of relief but there was another part of him that felt a twinge of sadness at the thought of her moving so far away. He debated within himself as to whether he should show Alexis the text, finally deciding he would keep Lurleen's message to himself. His revery was interrupted by the sound of barking and children's laughter. Nathan walked outside to find Lizzy and David playing some sort of game with Jessie. Whatever the nature of the game it involved a ball and a lot of running and laughing. Nathan smiled as he watched and he felt that the storm clouds that had seemed to plague him wherever he went were finally clearing. *Maybe the sun will finally shine again.*

    The next day after breakfast Nathan explained to Alexis that he was going to apply for a job, but he refused to answer any of her questions, explaining that he would tell her about it after the interview. Shortly after noon Nathan returned home. Alexis heard his car drive up and went out to greet him. She studied his facial expression as he emerged from the car, hoping to see at least the hint of a smile. What she saw caused her to feel a sense of genuine excitement. "Well," she said, "Are you going to keep it a secret or do I get to hear about your interview?"

"Well, I was afraid I wouldn't get the position. They were concerned I was way over qualified."

"Okay. What is the job?"

"I am a case manager assistant at the local MH/MR facility. Basically, I am a glorified gopher, but I may have an opportunity to work my way up.

"Oh, well…are you okay with that? I mean it seems like a waste of your skills."

"Strange as it may seem, I am happy with it. Salary isn't much but it feels like what I need to be doing right now. We will probably need to do some real belt-tightening financially though."

"It almost sounds like you are doing some sort of penance. Is that what you are doing?"

"Lexi, maybe you are right. I don't know. It just feels like I was drawn to the position, and it kinda seems like I am starting over…like I have gone back home where I belong. Years ago, while I was still in graduate school, I did a practicum at a community mental health center in Ohio. I actually learned a lot there and felt like I was doing something worthwhile."

A few days after starting work at the local community mental health center, Nathan was contacted by Dean Albritton who offered to reinstate him at the Divinity School. The Dean explained that after reviewing the testimony given by Lurleen Montgomery and Leonard Marshall, the disciplinary committee felt there was enough evidence to indicate that Nathan's actions were not entirely voluntary. The Dean did add that the evidence presented was highly unusual but never the less compelling. Nathan was stunned by the offer, so he asked for some time to think it over. That evening he and Alexis engaged in a lengthy and sometimes heated discussion. She urged him to take the offer, but Nathan felt strongly that he needed the change that the MH/MR position offered him. The next day, Nathan declined the offer.

Chapter Sixty

Sin is crouching at the door.

Its desire is contrary to you, but you must rule over it.

-Genesis 4:7

The days and weeks flew by and the Richards family seemed to grow closer together than ever before. In spite of starting in the basement, Nathan quickly moved up the ladder at MH/MR. As the family began decorating the house for Christmas, Nathan announced that he had been promoted to assistant director at the center. After the last ornament had been placed on the Christmas tree, Nathan and Alexis celebrated his promotion with a glass of expensive champagne while Lizzy and David drank fizzy ginger ale. Jessie celebrated with a new chew bone. That night, joy reigned supreme in the Richards's home.

Aided by a couple more glasses of Champagne, Nathan fell asleep almost as soon as his head hit the pillow, but by two a.m. dark thoughts and images found their way into his dreams. In one particularly terrifying dream sequence the red dragon returned and devoured Alexis and Lizzy before confronting Nathan. As he looked into the eyes of the dragon, Nathan knew he was going to die, but before the dragon could close on him, Nathan awoke. Nathan sat up in bed. He was drenched in sweat and his heart was racing, but Alexis slept peacefully at his side. Nathan tried to quiet his thoughts and slow his heart rate but it was then he heard it. It sounded like slow breathing, but the breathing was not his or Alexis'. As he listened intently, the breathing seemed to come from a corner of the bedroom. Nathan tried to convince himself it was just Jessie who sometimes slept in that spot, but clearly it was not Jessie. The sound of the breathing seemed to change location and as it did, Nathan felt certain he detected movement in that corner of the bedroom. Something was there, something was moving. For the second time in his life, Nathan wished he had a gun, something to defend against the dark intruder. Nathan glanced down at Alexis who was still sound asleep. *Am I still dreaming? Is this a nightmare?*

As if in answer to his own questions, Nathan heard a voice, a human voice...Jeremiah Murdoc's unmistakable voice. "Nathan Richards, we meet again. You may have thought that you had seen and heard the last of me, but if you did, you were wrong. You will never be rid of me. I will always be crouching in the shadows...waiting...waiting for my opportunity. That witch was not my only tool. Oh, no...I have many weapons and snares at my disposal. Just as when your Jesus confronted the demoniac and learned that his name was Legion. We really are many!"

Nathan knew the voice was definitely that of Dr. Jeremiah Murdoc and he also knew that Murdoc had quoted Mark 5:9, but what was Murdoc really telling him? Was he saying that evil will always exist and that it came in many shapes and sizes? Was he saying that he will always set snares and traps for Nathan which would eventually lead to his ultimate destruction? Nathan wanted desperately to pray, but somehow the words wouldn't come. *Am I doomed?* Nathan did not sleep for the remainder of the night, and he was clearly relieved when he saw the first traces of sunlight. Reflecting on the awful nightmares, Nathan wondered if his dream was a warning or a threat. He felt like he was about to begin walking across a frozen lake in early spring. *Where is the thin ice?*

Later that morning as he drove to work, Nathan thought of the verse in Genesis about sin crouching at the door. Murdoc in the dream had mentioned something about crouching in the shadows and waiting. Because of his theological background Nathan remembered many discussions and arguments about sin, what it is and isn't. Maybe, he thought, the key part of Genesis 4:7 was the part that says "You must rule over it." *How can I rule over sin? How can I avoid falling into the same traps I fell into before?*

Nathan knew that literature was full of warnings about pride. Greek mythology was replete with examples demonstrating how much the gods disliked pride in humans. Pride, after all, was in the realm of the gods. Nathan also knew that he had been a prideful man as well as vulnerable to the lure of sexuality. *Perhaps Freud was right about the power of sex as a motivating force?* Fortunately for Nathan, his agenda at work was not crowded which gave him some quiet time in his office, time to think. As he looked absent-mindedly at some budget figures, a thought occurred to him. *Perhaps my sins of pride and sexuality, combined to form the key which opened the door allowing evil to enter his life...maybe much the same thing was true for all of us.* Just as the vampire legends all claimed, a vampire couldn't cross the threshold of your room unless invited in. Evil couldn't work its destruction unless invited into the hearts and minds of individual men and women.

Chapter Sixty-one

In the last days, God says I will pour out my spirit

on all people. Your sons and daughters will prophesy, your young men

will see visions, and your old men will dream dreams.

-Acts 2:17

By the year's end, Nathan had been promoted to director of the MH/MR center and Alexis had been elevated to a supervisor's position at Child Protective Services. Nathan agreed to teach one course per semester at the divinity school as an adjunct professor. Shortly after accepting the offer to teach on a part-time basis at the Divinity School, Nathan and Alexis were invited to dinner at Dean Albritton's home. After the dinner, the dean and his wife sat down with Nathan and Alexis and the foursome enjoyed a glass of sherry. It had been a pleasant evening and Nathan decided to share some good news with the dean. "Dean, do you remember when you gave me the idea of researching evil?" Dean Albritton nodded and Nathan continued. "Well, as you know, that led to meeting with Jeremiah Murdoc which was a near disaster, but what I wanted to tell you is that I was able to write a book based on what I learned from all those experiences, and I just found out earlier today that my book will be published."

Dean Albritton smiled as he replied, "Great news! Let's toast to your success! I must order a copy of your book right away. Nathan, I am very eager to know what you concluded about evil. Could you give us a brief summary of your work?"

"Uh, yeah. I'll try." Nathan sipped the last of his sherry, and then replied, "I am inclined to think that evil is not so much an entity or personage but a construct, a way of categorizing behaviors or events. Many years ago, a social psychologist named Stanley Milgram conducted a series of studies on compliance, trying to determine the extent to which people would inflict pain on another person when asked to do so. The results were surprising. A high percentage of people would inflict what they believed to be lethal or near lethal electric shocks when ordered to do so. Phil Zimbardo, another social psychologist, made an interesting comment about Milgram's work when he said that evil occurs in 15-volt increments. Of course, by that he meant that evil occurs, the grows in small steps, gradually building from something minor to something life threatening. The people who carried out the evil in Milgram's studies did not see what they were doing as evil, at least while they were doing it.

They saw themselves as following orders or doing what science required of them. It wasn't until later, after they reflected on their actions, did they begin to see what they had done as wrong or evil. I think even Jeremiah Murdoc viewed his murderous acts as somehow doing God's will. If we do enough bad acts our mind or superego resets itself as to what it regards as wrong or evil. For example, the executioner in a prison who throws a switch and electrocutes another person doesn't see what he is doing as evil. He sees what he is doing as merely administering justice or doing his duty, carrying out the will of the state."

Dean Albritton looked thoughtful and rubbed his chin before responding. "Nathan, does this mean that you reject the idea of the devil or Satan?"

"No, not entirely. It's like my thoughts about God. There is so much I really don't know. There are many mysteries in this life I don't pretend to understand, so I'll just say that at this point in my understanding, I don't find the idea of Satan to be very helpful. In fact, it can often be a way of refusing to take responsibility for our actions. We can just say the devil made me do it.

"Fascinating, Nathan. I am reminded of something Mother Teresa once wrote. She said that we are all capable of good and evil and we are not born bad. Maybe she is right. Maybe Murdoc and people like him weren't born bad. Anyway, I look forward to getting your book."

That evening as Alexis and Nathan drove home, Nathan wondered if his "success" in publishing a book, rising to the position of executive director at MH/MR, and getting an opportunity to teach once again was feeding his pride and opening the door for sin and eventually evil to come back into his life. After parking his car in the driveway, Nathan paused before getting out of the car and put his hand on Alexis' shoulder.

"Lexi, help me harness my pride. If evil is still crouching at my door, I don't want to let my pride be the key that opens the door and lets it in."

Alexis leaned over and kissed her husband. "I promise I will let the air out of your ego anytime it puffs up too much, and if you get to feeling sexy, just look me up. Together, I think we can make your dreams and visions our dreams and visions. I love you!"

Epilogue

The years flew by and Nathan's daughter Elizabeth went on to complete her Ph.D. at the University of Texas in immunology while David became a lawyer who worked as a public defender in the Chapel Hill area. Nathan had recently announced his retirement as executive director of the MH/MR center and his staff had organized a retirement party in celebration. His one remaining task was to give a retirement speech which he dreaded and resolved to make very brief. After the celebratory dinner, he rose to give his speech, tapped his water glass with his knife, and then looked around the room at his wife, daughter, and adopted son. He felt himself choke up as he focused squarely on his old friend Leonard Marshall. "I want to thank all of you for coming. You know, I can't believe how quickly the years have passed. My tenure here at the center has included some of the best years of my life. As some of you know, my career path took some interesting turns, and I needed quite a while to find my way here, which now feels like home. In addition to having a hard time trying to decide what work I would do when I grew up, I have also struggled mightily with my faith, and even gotten lost more than a few times. But, thanks to the love of my wife and my friends, I eventually found my way back. I guess I have learned many things while on my journey, such as how evil grows in a person by small increments or how essential forgiveness is in human relationships. But maybe the most important things I have learned are that what we call sin or evil will always be a part of life, all our lives, and along with that fact, I am now quite sure of one additional thing." Nathan felt a lump in his throat as he continued, "I know that no matter how strong evil appears to be...love is stronger! We may never vanquish evil from this world, but when we love and support one another, in a very real sense, love does win. I think it was John Kennedy who said 'We are not here to curse the darkness, but to light a candle that can guide us through the darkness to a safe and secure future.' So, let's keep lighting candles, people. In that way we can make our world a brighter place. That is my dream."

The End

Made in the USA
Columbia, SC
28 February 2023